The End of Magic

by
Leonora Nattrass

O what can ail thee, knight-at-arms,
Alone and palely loitering?
The sedge has withered from the lake,
 And no birds sing.

John Keats, "La Belle Dame sans Merci. A Ballad." 1819

For Mark, Geoff, and Will

FOREWORD

This would hardly be a twenty-first century tale of Arthur if it didn't take liberties with the characters and events of Arthurian myth. But for all that, and for good or ill, the cardinal events of Arthur's story can never be re-written.

Contents

Arrival   7

Invasion   21

Departure   38

Meetings   57

Woods and Water   74

Dragons   90

Destiny   107

Partings   125

Dreams   144

Awakenings   165

Appearances   181

Secrets   199

Choices   212

Sacrifice   225

Friend and Foe   236

Faith   249

Endings   261

I saw pale kings and princes too,
Pale warriors, death-pale were they all;
They cried – "La Belle Dame sans Merci
                    Thee hath in thrall!"

Arrival

It was all just as Wolf remembered. A stony causeway high above a boiling sea, the scent of grass and mud caught in the horses' shoes as he ran at their heels, and his master in the saddle above him. And then the echoing gatehouse between tall cliffs and the crowded castle yard. A lot of barking and growling from the stable dogs, steamy goodness from the kitchen, and a fog of human smells from the cess pit beyond. And above it all, the long remembered scents of the men, a hubbub of voices and laughter. Words swirled around him as he ran from knight to knight, thrusting his damp nose into their hands and sniffing their boots unnoticed. A warm hand scratched his ears and he remembered that the tall one was always kind. Then there was the young dark-haired one. Wolf gave his hand a lick, but he was listening to the others and hardly noticed.

"Gawain!" a knight just emerging from the stables embraced Wolf's master, his face a mixture of pleasure and worry. "It's good to see your face. Whenever I leave London for this journey I wonder if I shall find all living – and if all will travel safely to meet again! Perhaps I am getting old."

"You worry overmuch Bedivere," Gawain answered, giving his shoulder a mighty slap. "Why should we not travel safely in these times of peace?"

Bedivere himself had only just arrived, it appeared, his travel-stained cloak flung over a dull chain-mail hauberk. Mud caked his boots and his sword still hung at his side. "Are all here?" he asked, as they began the steep climb to the keep. "Even Lancelot and Galahad?"

"Aye, though they both had to leave home more than a month ago," the tall knight Kay answered. "Lancelot complains that the king should keep his stronghold in the middle lands, not remain out here on the edge of the wilderness."

"How unreasonable of Arthur to inconvenience him," said the dark-haired young knight.

"Don't be too hard on him, Mordred. The north was tamed long ago, and he has had hardly a moment's trouble in all these years. If he really consulted his own comfort he would forsake his vows to seek adventure abroad."

The men's voices faded as Wolf lingered behind in the yard to play with the stable dogs and try his luck in the kitchens. But he was tired from the long journey. At length, he snapped half-heartedly at the most persistent of the terriers before trotting after his master up the path to the keep.

He had delayed too long, and the courtyard was empty. He flopped down with a sigh, resting his snout on his foreleg and closing his eyes to wait. He was half-asleep when new voices made him raise his head. The other young knight he remembered, the one with the golden hair, had turned the corner from the chapel and beside him came a priest, trotting to keep up with his long strides. Wolf pulled himself to his feet, stretched, and rambled towards the men, ready to make his greeting. As he reached them, the golden-haired knight sat down on the low wall of the well in the centre of the yard and held out his hand.

"So Wolf, you are here again. That tells me Gawain is returned and we are all here." Wolf licked his face in a friendly way and would have made it a thorough washing, but the priest began speaking and the dog contented himself with settling down and resting his head on the young knight's knee as they talked. The men's words were a comfortable blur, and the young knight's hand was warm on his neck.

"I have been thinking much of you, Galahad, since we spoke together last year. You seemed troubled then, and I have prayed for you many times since. How are you, my son?"

"Oh – the same as always, I suppose. I try to do my duty, but as I told you, I often find myself dissatisfied with my doing of it."

"No one else is dissatisfied, Galahad. You have never done anything to be ashamed of."

"No."

"But I fear you weary of your duties a little, for you were so young when Arthur gave you lordship of your lands. Have you ever thought of marriage?"

"Not really."

"I have been considering your case these many months, and I think a wife could be a helpmeet and a comfort to you, and give you new joy in your work. I might speak to Arthur of it, if you wished me to. How old are you my son?"

"Twenty-five, I think. I was fifteen when the battle for Camelot was won. But father, *you* do not need a wife to share your heavy burdens."

"You are no priest, Galahad."

"And I am the sorrier for it, when I remember how Christ dwelt in poverty with the common people." The young knight frowned and then straightened, his face clearing. "But I would not have you trouble Arthur with my cares. Let us keep this matter between you and me and God, and tell me how fare the souls here, father. I know you have many, high and low, to care for."

"Indeed I try to. Arthur was always distrustful of the new, but even kings need counsel, and he no longer has the Merlin to advise him. At first he saw no need for spiritual guidance at all, but the beauty of the Mass grows upon him and he turns more and more to God."

"All men need some such beauty in their lives I think, and I was lucky to be born to it. It is different for the others, but the queen is steadfast in her faith and that must help the king to see his way. And if the grail comes to Camelot then Arthur's kingdom will be truly one of heaven." He paused, and a number of emotions seemed to cross his face in quick succession. "If it comes."

"Do not fear my son, for it certainly will – each year I grow more sure of that."

Galahad reached out and clasped the priest's hand. "You must say many more prayers for me father."

A clattering from the steps behind them made Wolf start out of his comfortable doze. He ran to lick his master's hand, even as Gawain reached Galahad and clutched him in a vigorous hug.

"Galahad, my boy! Are you ready for the games tomorrow?"

"Ready and eager," Galahad returned, his face brightening. "What say you to a wager on our joust Gawain?"

"Nay, nay, no talk of wagers before the priest! Fie on you Galahad, I took you for a godly youth. And besides, it is for others to make their choice between us – I will back the strength of my own hand as you will yours, I make no doubt."

~

The great hall at Camelot ran the length of the keep and half its width. Tall arched windows looked westwards across the pleasant green garden at its heart. A fire crackled in the hearth to combat the April chill, as the wind slapped and gusted around the walls rattling the casements. A crimson sunset spilled in through the arched windows and bathed the hall in a rosy glow. And beneath a stained-glass window, facing northwards to the sea, sat Arthur, high king of Britain.

Every year since his coronation Arthur had called his knights back to the great round table, to renew the vows he had taught them then. "Let us bring peace," he had said to them on that day. "Let us bring a peace to the land it has never known before. Too long have I watched the people powerless to aid them, while the Merlin has taught me to feel their sorrows as if they were my own. Hard is their lot by any measure, for seasons are fickle and often their crops fail and their animals die. Then their children cry for bread and mothers follow them to the grave with wet eyes and heavy hearts.

"But even when sun and rain are kind, and the crops grow and the children thrive, then troubles still come thick and fast, for the land is rife with witches and wizards. Imps and demons live on every hearth and work their spite until the heart grows sick. And beside such petty troubles, dragons haunt the wild places and monsters lurk in the deep waters. Where they dwell, the people live in fear for their lives, and peace is only a dream.

"So, my knights, let us look to all the parts of the kingdom, and govern it wisely and well. Cast out the fiends that plague our people. Put the woods to sleep once more and send the wraiths back to their barrows till judgement day. Defeat the monsters and banish them far from our lands so that the people may live in peace. For the Merlin has shown me that only without magic can this kingdom find rest."

The knights had promised, and had been as good as their word. Now it was ten years since the land had first known the comfort of the king's peace.

To Kay's eyes Arthur never changed. He always seemed the same young foster brother that Kay had led into a thousand scrapes, and told a thousand secrets, until the day came when Arthur drew the sword from the stone and their lives changed. Even now when their eyes met they shared a secret smile. Then, looking around him at the other faces at the table, Kay could see that they all felt the same. Arthur's gift was to make all men love him.

Mordred sat at Arthur's right hand, Lancelot on his left, leaning towards the queen with a half-mocking smile. Beside Mordred sat Galahad, both young knights listening quietly to the talk of their elders. Kay's eyes turned from Galahad's face to Arthur's and he thought he saw a curious glow about them both, as if they were lit by the same strange inner light.

He looked around from his place at the bottom of the table, and noticed with grim amusement that all the beauty was at the top. Beside him, Gawain's chair creaked under his great weight every time he moved. Food stuck in his beard and drops of ale sparkled in the bristles around his mouth as the firelight played on his red face and on the leather jerkin he wore, polished smooth as a gemstone by constant wear. Wolf slept at his feet, as fierce to look at as his master. Every now and then a choice titbit would fall from Gawain's hand, and each time the dog lifted his head from his great grey paws to shuffle forwards and guzzle up the treat.

"How has life been for you then, Kay my lad?" Gawain looked quizzically at him from under his shaggy eyebrows. "Any excitement since we last met?"

Kay shrugged and shook his head, "Progress, but not what you would call excitement. Traders come daily to our ports, bringing things of use and beauty in exchange for our wheat and barley. The crops seem bigger and better each year. My people thrive. And I take pleasure in it all and guard them as best I can from the occasional wizard selling fake charms and false remedies. Life is peaceful enough."

"Hmph." Gawain eyed him affectionately, "You were always for a quiet life. Is there good hunting to be had in your lands?"

"Good enough. But I warrant you'll have better."

"No doubt of it my boy. Wolf and I would be idle else and as grumpy as two old bears. You must visit me, Kay."

"Perhaps I may," Kay replied, "I grow almost useless at home. I daresay that I could be spared for a few weeks good hunting. But tell me," he continued after a moment, "who is that lady who sits beside Guinevere?" He pointed with his knife to the top of the table, where the queen sat smiling to herself as Lancelot regaled her with some story told with animated gestures. Beside her, speaking to no one, was a small dark-haired girl dressed in a dull green gown which shimmered in the firelight like a pebble in a rock-pool. Her hair was pulled back from her small face. Dark eyebrows frowned above sharp dark eyes, and her lips were set in a decided line. A faint trace of down sketched across her upper lip, which added to the intensity of her face but did not yet detract from its beauty. She would be a fierce old lady, Kay thought, but as yet she was just a passionate maid.

"That is the king's kinswoman, Morgan le Fay," Bedivere replied, from his place beside Gawain. "Have you not seen her before?"

"Morgan le Fay!" Kay shot him a startled glance, "Nay, never. But she is a witch, is she not?"

"She has been a witch," Bedivere replied, licking gravy from his fingers, "But Arthur looks to tame her as he has tamed the rest."

"She looks so young."

"She is only eighteen. But her sorcery began as a child and some say she has lived many ages while her body sleeps peacefully in bed at night. Powerful she has been. Arthur looks to make her good."

Kay pushed away his plate and sat back. "He will succeed, if any can."

"And yet his power came from a wizard too," Gawain said, "even if we have not seen the Merlin for many a long year. Sometimes it makes my poor head ache to make sense of it all."

~

Kay's chamber lay in the tower across the green lawns from the hall. As he stepped from light into darkness he stumbled, half from weariness, half from the wine he had drunk at supper. Behind him he could hear Gawain's hearty laugh peal out. Celebrations were not yet over in the great hall, but they would regret it come the morning and the tournament.

The stars were bright as the clouds scudded swiftly across the sky, and Kay stepped cautiously over to the curtain wall and looked down over the parapet. The sea looked far away and very angry as it boiled around the rocks and beat fruitlessly against the walls.

"Camelot is truly a fortress, is she not?" a voice spoke by his ear, "she withstands all that nature, man or demon can fling at her walls."

Kay turned to greet Mordred with a smile. Youngest of them all, Mordred had long been his favourite. His bright blue eyes watched the world with curiosity, while his slight frame and dark hair gave him an elfin look. Somewhere, Kay realised now, Mordred and Morgan le Fay were kin. Mordred claimed Arthur as an uncle, and in the starlight there was a passing resemblance between all three.

"Camelot may be impervious to wind and water, but I am not," Kay returned. "I was on my way to bed. But it is good to see you again, Mordred. What have you been doing these last months? Has your new falcon flown yet?"

"Only once or twice – the winter winds are too wild to turn her loose. Nay, I have been by the fire, reading mainly."

"You should come to stay with me."

"I should like that, but Arthur takes comfort in my presence here. And even so I have been travelling – if only in my dreams!" Mordred smiled, leaning beside Kay against the parapet, and gazing westwards. "The king bade me read as much as I could about the wild, for it suits my humour to explore the mystery a little and I have brought it all together in a map. I do not know if I shall ever test its worth."

Kay followed Mordred's gaze into the darkness beyond the walls. "Camelot remains the limit of our powers then? We have made no inroads into the west?"

Mordred shook his head. "On our doorstep the people and the ways are wildest of all. Further west the land is kinder, and they say that the people are gentle, but it seems they trade with men from distant lands since all must come to them by water. They would dislike rule from afar I daresay, for the same reason."

"And have you discovered anything of the Land's End?"

"I have, but only a little." Kay heard enthusiasm kindle in Mordred's voice. "How I would love to go there, Kay! There must be so much to discover and to chronicle before we finally drive it from our shores!"

Kay smiled and laid his hand on the young man's shoulder. "You are as ardent as ever, Mordred, and I take pleasure from it. If a history of our time is to be written it will be in your hand. Sleep well, dear friend."

~

The three days of games began with Bedivere and Mordred. They were the first to meet at swordplay on the next morning, but only the squires' excitement lent their fight any glory. The older man's age and experience won handsomely, for Mordred was diffident with a blade, and Lancelot watched with a stern face. Then Kay drew lots with Galahad, and this time battle wisdom went for nothing. Galahad seemed so forgetful of his own safety in the swirling skill of their fight, that the knights murmured with pleasure to see it. Gawain fought like a bear, wrestling as much as wielding his blade, and vanquished everyone but Arthur. At last the king met Lancelot in a hard-fought duel, which only ended when Arthur laughingly conceded defeat, for Lancelot would not be beaten. But everyone knew that Arthur would have won had he consented to use his great sword Excalibur for mere sport.

As they gathered for lunch Kay found himself close to Mordred, who bowed elaborately before him.

"Hail my lord," he said with a grin. "We have both been proved but indifferent swordsmen this morning, but you, at least, only succumbed to Galahad's magic. Arthur tells me that you train your squires yourself, which makes me a little ashamed, for my own lads are sorely neglected I fear."

"I doubt it." Kay answered. "I suppose you spend as much time teaching them to read as I do training mine to fight with sticks. And who can say which will be the better skill in these times of peace?"

"They can all read, it is true. For I can only pass on my own skills, and they do not lie in war."

"You compare your abilities with those of the finest knights the world has ever seen, Mordred. By any common measure your talents are great and if battle came I do not doubt you would prove your worth."

"It is a misfortune to have such perfection before my eyes, however," Mordred said cheerfully, casting a glance towards

Galahad. "I am lucky that my king thinks well of my learning for I fear few others do. None likes to see his own shortcomings held up to so fair a mirror."

Kay could not help but smile, for there was no denying it. Galahad was tall, and his fair hair gleamed in the sunlight as brightly as his armour. Beside him, Mordred was thoroughly eclipsed.

"You have talents that he lacks, Mordred, and Arthur values them, as you well know. Between you and Galahad lies the future of our realm. His heart, your head – and who knows which will be most useful?" His eyes fell to the two plates that Mordred was piling with food as he listened and his face grew serious. "Mordred, I see you wear a lady's favour."

Mordred glanced up at Kay a shade defensively. "I do."

"Is it safe, do you think, to consort with a witch?"

Mordred winced slightly at the word. "Do not call her that, I pray you. She has dabbled in sorcery for so the world once was. But Morgan le Fay is my kin, Kay, and Arthur's too, and living among us she grows softer each day, and cares for our troubles and looks for our well-being."

"But she is still a sorceress. Such powers cannot be undone."

"No, they cannot. But neither can she wield them so long as she remains within the castle walls, for magic will not enter here. So we are safe for the present, Kay, and perhaps we consult our future safety by winning her love. If she ever returns to the wild I hope that she will forbear to harm us."

"I cannot doubt Arthur's wisdom, for it is above mine," Kay answered, but he looked unconvinced. "I daresay the world looks different to you here, on the edge of the darkness. In my own lands sorcery is so remote a thing – perhaps we fear it too much and understand it too little."

"I will not say so, Kay, for of us all you have the best judgement. But I believe that Arthur will keep her close as long as he can, and hope for her salvation. As for me, I would not turn away what little family I own."

Kay bowed his head and watched as Mordred carried the plates away to where Morgan le Fay sat under a tree, slightly apart from the other ladies of the court. Then, having no lady's favour, and therefore no lady's dinner to fetch, he filled his own plate and ate heartily.

~

There was another banquet in the great hall that night and it was almost dawn when Arthur and his queen found themselves alone. They smiled at each other comfortably as they settled into the carved chairs that flanked the fireplace, and warmed their hands at the blaze. For a while they sat in silence, glad of the quiet and solitude. Then Arthur reached over and took Guinevere's hand in his own, his eyes resting with pleasure upon her lovely face. No children had come to coarsen her slender frame, and the long years of peace had kept the lines from her face. She had always been called the fairest woman in the kingdom, and now, a little riper in her loveliness, she was so still.

"Hast taken pleasure in the meeting so far, my lady?"

Guinevere smiled at him and returned the pressure of his fingers. "As much as always. Can you not tell?"

"I saw you watching the swordplay with parted lips like a young maid this morning."

"I cannot watch it with a quiet heart."

"The joust is almost as perilous," the king returned, his eyes creasing into a smile as he watched his wife's thoughtful eyes bent on the fire. "Will you tremble again tomorrow?"

"Perhaps." She looked up at him demurely. "But I shall be too busy planning my own tactics in the falconry to care so much for your sports, my lord."

"What blessed times we live in, where such small matters can grow to such importance!"

"Blessed we are to live in your times, for you are the author of the peace and I am proud of it. But I would not let Galahad hear you deem his joust a small matter."

"I will not, if I value my crown!"

They both laughed then, gazing into the flames, fingers entwined. Arthur's face grew thoughtful.

"Each year that he returns Galahad grows more fair and more noble. Though prophecy seems too close to sorcery for my liking, I believe the thing is indeed set. If anyone is to find the grail, then it will be Galahad. And if he brings the grail to Camelot, as foretold, then it will be our crowning glory – and his. Who better to take my place when the time comes?"

And yet there is Mordred too, who has served you faithfully and is your kin. Do not make him sorrow, my lord, by too marked a preference for Galahad."

"Indeed, you know me too well for that. Mordred has my heart, for he has been a son to me for many years. Mordred or Galahad! I am rich in such a choice."

"And it is early yet to speak of such things," Guinevere added with a blush, her eyes dropping to Arthur's hands where they lay clasped in her own. "We are not yet old. Even yet another heir may come."

Arthur's smile grew more tender as he bent to kiss the fair cheek beside him and then rose stiffly to his feet. "Will you come to bed, my love? For I hear the birds begin to sing and I needs must rest before Galahad knocks me off my horse in the morning."

~

Bad luck seemed to plague the tournament the next day, like a dark cloud just over the horizon. First Guinevere's favourite bird was lost in the falconry contest, flying beyond the castle wall in pursuit of a wild rabbit, never to be seen again. Then one of the stable dogs ran mad through the archery butts, and was killed stone dead by Gawain's arrow. It grieved the great knight deeply though he would not show it.

Worst of all came in the joust, for Galahad's usual skill deserted him. He caught Bedivere's war-horse with his lance twice over, and was disqualified from the contest in disgrace. No one could understand it, and whispered debate ran around the castle green as he led the injured horse away to cool his temper and atone for his wrong by dressing its wounds himself in the stables. No one dared follow except his youngest squire who scampered after him at a respectful distance as the horse clattered down the path to the quay.

After that the pleasure was spoiled. The joust was no less splendid, the horses no less fierce, and the knights hardly less able, but Galahad's sorrow and shame brooded over the field. Still the contest went on. What Gawain lacked in aim he made up for in strength. Like a battering ram he bore down upon his opponents, and dealt them thunderous blows. He knocked Kay off his horse and out of the reckoning with the third lance of their bout. Lancelot and Arthur were so closely matched that it seemed neither could prevail. But on the last charge Arthur broke Lancelot's lance, and the king retired victorious from the lists. Mordred, despite his modesty, did well. He rode well and aimed carefully and did not try to match Gawain's power. Instead he dodged the assault of the bigger man and on his second and third lances took Gawain by surprise to win the bout. Unaccountably he found himself facing his king for the prize.

Galahad returned quietly from the stables while the other knights fought and took a seat beside Guinevere and Morgan le Fay. The girl was leaning forward, chin on hand, absorbed by the contest and hardly noticed his arrival. Guinevere held out her hand and he kissed it before slumping into the seat and watching the proceedings ruefully.

"We thought to see you here, waiting to ride for the victory," Guinevere greeted him, "but luck will play its part. You are not too miserable, I hope, for there is always next year."

Galahad smiled at her. "I will live, my lady. It is a lesson, I daresay, to school me for my pride in my lance. But what galled me most was my stupidity in harming Bedivere's horse. He will soon recover, but I cannot understand how my aim went so awry."

"Are you tired by your long journey? Or have you some old injury that weakened your arm?"

Galahad shook his head. "No, nothing. It was as though, at the moment of impact, my arm was jerked away from me. I cannot explain it. It was though another hand knocked against my own. I daresay it was some stray cramp of the muscle." As he spoke he flexed his arm and twisted it, looking at it with a puzzled air. "But now it seems as well as before." He sighed and turned back to where Arthur and Mordred were lining up for the three lances that would decide the day. "Ah well, it's a mystery and there's no profit in bemoaning it. Let us hope that our king triumphs."

Guinevere smiled quietly and nodded towards Morgan le Fay. "You forget my companion. Mordred wears her favour, do you not recall? I believe our loyalties will be at odds in these seats."

Morgan le Fay turned towards them, and as Galahad met her green eyes flecked with brown he could not suppress a shudder. She smiled at him, and then took Guinevere's hand.

"Indeed I cannot wish either to win. Can we not have it a draw?" She looked back towards the lists and leaned her chin on her hand once more, her eyes narrowing as she bent her gaze on the combatants. Galahad followed her gaze towards the king and his nephew, facing each other from either end of the green, and as he watched he shivered again.

"Indeed, I believe I am not well," he said, "and that may explain my weakness."

Arthur won the joust but only after many lances, for he and Mordred did indeed draw time after time. Mordred had never ridden so well nor bent his mind so clearly on the task, and he took his defeat well when it finally came. To have vanquished every knight but his king was glory indeed, though he doubted that he would have ended in second place if Galahad had shown his talents more truly. His lady Morgan le Fay greeted him with a smile when he came to return her favour.

"You did well," she said.

"Better than I could ever have hoped. Is Galahad still here? I saw him sitting beside my aunt."

"He had to go to his chamber. He is unwell I believe."

"I believe so too. Never did I see such a thing. It was unaccountable. Did he say how it happened?"

"Nay, I think not. But I was hardly listening."

~

Galahad kept to his bed that evening and his fair face was missed at the banquet. Arthur and Mordred were also weary, and Guinevere watched them anxiously from her seat across the table, and only half-listened to the nonsense that Lancelot was speaking in her ear. Her eye swept across the table, and it seemed to her that a strange shadow hung across the feast. She looked again at her husband and her nephew, and she saw a new pallor in their faces. Perhaps it was the food. She shut her eyes for a moment, a vision of sickness sweeping the castle, and all the horror that it would entail for her household. Lancelot's voice grew tender.

"My lady! Are you unwell?"

Guinevere looked at him then, and smiled to see real concern replace the sentiment in his brown face.

"Nay, Lancelot, I am perfectly well, forgive me. But a housewifely thought was discourteous enough to show in my face. At affairs such as this the lady of the house is supposed to pretend that the food reaches the table, and the fires are lit, and her guests are housed, all without her knowledge or connivance."

Lancelot laughed. "And what horrible thought struck you then? Hast forgotten to order the pudding for these hungry knights?"

"Nay, Lancelot. Indeed, to tell you the truth, my thought was more grave. Your son has taken to his bed and my menfolk are pale. I tremble lest the tournament should find itself bereft of half its combatants tomorrow."

Invasion

Long before dawn Kay was woken from a heavy slumber by shouts and footsteps in the courtyard below. Cursing, he swung his legs to the floor and reached for his clothes. As he pulled his shirt over his head and buckled on his sword he caught sight of his face in the mirror above his washstand. He looked grey and drawn, and fiercer than he felt, he thought fleetingly, as he raced from his chamber.

A frightened serving maid ran past him on the stairs and he seized her arm.

"What is happening?" he demanded, "What passes below?"

"Monsters!" she returned and pulled away with a frightened squeal.

"Monsters in Camelot?" he shouted after her, but she was gone. He clattered down the steps and out into the open air. A crowd had gathered down on the jetty and he ran swiftly to join them. He pushed his way to the front and saw a strange shape lying on the cobbles while Gawain's dog stood over it barking.

"What is it?"

"Some kind of merman or other sea dweller," Lancelot replied. "It must have crawled out of the water here where the jetty is lowest."

"Is it to be killed?" Mordred asked.

Kay shot him a startled glance. "Severe punishment for trespass!"

"Trespass and murder." Gawain put in, nodding his head towards a group of dark figures huddled by the stables. "It is one of your number, Kay."

Kay strode across to the knot of figures. Lying face up on the cobbles was his eldest squire. He was seventeen at most, contorted with pain, but not yet quite dead. Something like fronds of seaweed clung to his throat and dug into the flesh, tightening as they dried. The boy choked convulsively with each breath. Kay bent hurriedly and began to tear at the fronds.

"'Tain't no use, master." The lad's best friend laid his hand on Kay's arm. "We tried pulling it off but it won't come."

Kay continued to tear at the fronds, but he could tell that they were tightening with every moment. "Are all the rest safe?" he asked curtly, "No one else is missing?"

The boy shook his head. "We were asleep, Sir Kay. He must have gone outside for a pee. We heard a fight but it was soon finished. That thing got him quick."

"Take the younger lads back indoors will you?" Kay met the boy's courageous gaze with approval. "They are scared and should not witness this nightmare." He turned back to the group around the merman. It was writhing on the stones, its scaly body shining wetly as it looked up at them with fishy eyes. The lank hair that hung from its head looked like the seaweed around the boy's neck.

"The boy is not dead, but will soon be so if this thing does not lift its enchantment from him. Can we speak with it?"

"It will not help you," Lancelot said, "Look at its eyes. It hates us all."

Kay could hear the boy's breath coming in agonised gasps behind him, and for a moment the world swam before his eyes. Gawain's dog was still barking which hurt his head. The knights were tired and still half-drunk from the banquet.

"Killing it may lift the enchantment."

"Or curse us all."

The merman leapt convulsively and began to writhe towards the water. Its long rubbery legs were not made for walking, but were powerful enough to jerk it rapidly across the cobbles.

"Stop it!"

All was confusion for a moment as hands tried in vain to clutch at the slippery figure. Gawain's dog, Wolf, could bear it no longer. He leapt forward with a growl and sank his teeth into the creature's throat. For a moment Kay saw that thick green jelly oozed out at the wound instead of blood. Then the body slipped lifeless over the edge of the jetty, plopped into the dark water and was gone. In the sudden silence that followed, the boy's breathing came slow and laboured.

"Well, that answers the question," Lancelot's voice was hard. "The cur has killed it, and the spell is still unbroken. We cannot help him."

"I fear you are right, Lancelot."

Even in the darkness and horror, the knights felt hope returning, for Arthur was come among them. A faint glow hung about the slight dark figure like a mist as his chain mail shone in the torchlight. He bent over the boy and touched his swollen face. "I fear this magic is beyond our remedy."

"It is not beyond mine," a woman's voice now spoke out of the darkness. Morgan le Fay stood among them though none had heard her footstep. "I can cure the boy."

"Nay, Morgan." Arthur's voice was sorrowful. "I promised the Merlin long ago that I would not suffer sorcery within these walls."

"Sorcery has been done here tonight!"

"And if we fight magic with magic, then magic will prevail."

"You will let the boy die then?" the girl's voice was incredulous.

"Camelot is my keep," Arthur answered, "and I have forsworn magic."

Morgan le Fay laughed and Kay shivered. "You? What then of Excalibur? Is that not a magic sword?"

"Excalibur is strong in my hand," Arthur replied, "Is that magic or skill?"

"And when you fight with another sword? Does your skill remain?"

"I will keep Excalibur as long as I may and be glad of it, as the Merlin bade me, but even so I will not use it lightly." Arthur rose to his feet and looked sorrowfully down at the boy where he lay. "We will tend him as best we can and set a guard among the lads and horses for the rest of the night. I would that this fiend had not crept among us."

"Only give me leave and the boy will live and the sea creatures will die." Morgan le Fay's voice came passionately out of the darkness. "Why be so stubborn? Will you not at least have vengeance?"

"I will have justice if I can," Arthur replied, "But I will also have mastery here. No more Morgan, or there will be harsh words between us."

With an oath the girl turned away into the darkness whence she had come. Then suddenly, and horribly, the boy drew his last breath.

~

A sombre meeting replaced the splendour of the tournament the next morning. The knights were stern as they took their seats at the round table. Its old surface was worn with many elbows, and pock-marked with many a blade jabbed into the timber in a moment of heated debate. Above their heads hung Excalibur, symbol of the king's power, glowing with the same inward light that sometimes seemed to hang about Arthur himself.

"Mordred told me that Camelot was impregnable," Kay said, "but it is not so. Somehow evil entered our gates last night. Was it for the first time?"

"Yes," Mordred sounded anxious. "Sorcery has always clung around us, but it has never entered in before."

"Never unbidden." Gawain spoke curtly. "But evil has been invited in. It is the girl, is it not? Whether by accident or design she has let sorcery loose amongst us. How else but by the presence of a witch might it enter?"

Arthur nodded. "You are right, Gawain. And now I wonder about those strange happenings at the tournament yesterday. Sorcery would explain Galahad's unaccountable weakness in the joust and the waywardness of the animals and birds. Perhaps the murder of that poor lad was but the culmination of her works. But then, what is to be done? Am I simply to banish her into the west along with the rest of her kind?"

"Aye," came the growl from around the room.

"Am I thus to bow to sorcery?" He looked at his knights with mild grey eyes. "I brought Morgan le Fay to Camelot to cure her of magic, to bring her into the light. And if I banish her what then of our kingdom? Will we not seem weak to our enemies' eyes, if we dare not keep my kinswoman among us?"

"You might send her to a convent," Galahad suggested diffidently. "With prayer and the kind counsel of nuns she might in time turn to God. And within its consecrated walls she could neither practice magic nor receive aid from any."

Kay's mouth twisted as he studied Galahad's earnest face. "You will find no surer way to win her hatred, than to confine her in such company."

"Have you a better thought, Kay?" Arthur's eyes met his across the table. "Glad I am of your sense and wisdom. Is there a better way?"

Kay grimaced. "Only a wish that you had never brought her here to bring peril within the walls and to then offer us such perilous aid. Life is so precious and our power so frail against the forces of darkness. And it is a hard fate that I must carry tidings of such sorrow to the boy's mother. "

"Is this the sense of the meeting?" Bedivere rapped his sword hilt on the table adding another dent to its aged surface, "Is Morgan le Fay to be sent to a nunnery till she perish or convert?"

Even as the affirmative grunt came back from the assembled knights Kay met Arthur's gaze with a sardonic smile.

"Of course, none of us has considered how we are to transport her there against her will."

~

Morgan le Fay was pale but calm when she came to the round table to answer for herself. She had not tried to leave the castle, but even so it was only Arthur who sat in his accustomed place at the table. The other knights quietly moved to bar the doorways and windows, standing with arms folded or hands resting on their sword hilts, their faces cool. The girl passed close to Mordred as she entered, but she did not meet his gaze.

"Well, Morgan," Arthur began, his voice gentle as ever, and his hand outstretched. "Strange things have passed since my knights returned to Camelot. Strange things and sad things too, for we have seen murder done."

Morgan le Fay stepped forward to stand close beside him, her hands folded quietly before her and her head bowed. She made no answer.

"We cannot help but think that sorcery has entered our walls, which we believed were proof against magic. And so we thought we should ask your opinion on our plight. Can you help us, child?"

The girl lifted her eyes and looked steadfastly into his face. "Bidden I was to enter Camelot, Arthur. I did not force my way in or gain entry by deception."

"That is so."

"And nor can I help what I am. You sought to give me shelter, knowing I was a witch."

"I have sought out magic then, and bidden it enter," Arthur said ruefully. "So much my knights have already told me. But tell me child, why did you cause so much grief to us all yesterday? Do you hate Camelot so?"

Morgan le Fay tossed her head a little and frowned. "I did not mean to use sorcery, my lord. But it seems that under your roof my wishes find form."

"Go on."

"I meant no harm at the tournament, but what wishes I made came true, as though I wrought spells without effort."

"You wished Mordred to win the joust, I think."

"I wished him to do well. The rest seemed to follow."

"And did you wish harm against Guinevere, that you sent her bird over the wall?"

The girl bit her lip and dropped her eyes. "I meant her no real harm. Only a little less pride in her own beauty and skill."

The knights shifted impatiently where they stood, for none but Morgan le Fay had ever called Guinevere proud.

"And what possible harm could you wish Kay's poor squire? How could he have offended you?"

The girl glanced up sharply and the same tone of contempt that Kay had heard in the darkness of the jetty seemed to enter her voice as she answered.

"I had no part in that mischief. Except to wish that you would let me save the poor lad."

There was silence in the room for a moment. Then Kay spoke thoughtfully, leaning against the great stone windowsill, his arms folded.

"To save the boy through sorcery required that he should suffer from it. Are you sure that you did not wish for magic to be needed?"

"Always." The girl dropped her head and her voice was barely audible. "I always wish for that."

"And do you find Camelot so barren a place without magic, then?" Arthur asked. "Can you not be happy here, living as we do, with reality in place of a dream world?"

"It seems not as reality to me my lord," the girl replied. "Nor do I belong here. As long as you keep me here I cannot help but wish you would end your struggle against magic." She met Arthur's gaze with something like defiance and her voice trembled with passion. "Or call the Merlin back if you must, fight us if you must, but fight us on our own ground! Do you not stifle in this world of common sense that you have created?"

Arthur frowned. "Morgan," he said, reaching out from where he sat as though he wished to save her. "Child!"

"I am no child!" she declared hotly, snatching her hand away from his touch. "Many lifetimes have I lived while you trudge along your weary way, content with but one existence. More, much more, do I know of life than you ever will, king or no!"

"But this dream world you live in is but a nightmare!" Arthur returned. "Can you not see how cruel sorcery is? It has hardly been among us but it has brought death to man and beast!"

"I did not mean that to happen."

"But that is the point, child! Magic is beyond our control – even yours, though you call yourself a witch. Would you not rather command one life, than live many merely as a straw in the wind?"

"I would have you speak no more!" Morgan le Fay replied ardently, her eyes emerald bright as they met Arthur's from under her dark brows. "Arthur, I love you, but I would have you look no more upon me as though I were a thing to pity! And listen no more to the voices of these knights, who call me a murderer for things I did not do!"

Now the knights saw how Morgan le Fay's wishes found form under their roof. They started forward even before she finished speaking, for her words worked upon the king like powerful spells. When she bid him be silent he fell back in his chair, clutching his mouth, contorted with pain. When she bid him look upon her no more, his eyes fluttered and closed. Morgan le Fay stared down at him as though even she were dismayed, then fell onto his breast and took him in her arms just as the knights reached her side.

"Rest Arthur!" she whispered, pressing her face to his. "Rest still now, and sleep, until all is resolved, for something begins it seems that cannot be undone!"

Lancelot's hand closed on her shoulder and dragged her from Arthur's form roughly, his sword raised. Kay started towards Arthur and caught him in his arms as he fell senseless from the chair. Mordred threw himself between Lancelot and the girl, seizing the older knight's sword hand and shaking him fiercely.

"My lord Lancelot!" he cried. "Do nothing rash! If you kill her the spell may never be broken."

Lancelot looked at him blankly for a moment, then grasped the girl's shoulder and sent her slamming against the stone floor to vent his rage. Galahad bent over the king and laid his cool hand on Arthur's forehead, looking at Kay with shock and distress. Wolf howled, and Morgan herself looked up at the assembled knights with a sudden smile of triumph.

"Fools!" she declared. "You are all fools, even Arthur! How else could such a meeting end, if I have magic and you do not!"

"Arthur loves you!" Kay replied. "How can you repay him thus?"

"I tell you again, it is not my will," she declared. "But now that it is done I am glad! For you must wield magic now, or lose your king."

Gawain advanced on the girl his face contorted with rage.

"Undo what you have done!" he bellowed. "Undo your sorcery witch, or I shall have your head!"

The girl looked coolly at his red face and wild eyes and smiled. She raised her arms above her head and for a moment her body shimmered. Then she seemed to vanish before their eyes as her form changed and shrank.

Lancelot lunged for her, but she was a small brown butterfly now and fluttered away from his grasp, out through the narrow window above his head and into the blue sky. He crashed against the wall and then slid to the floor, his head in his hands. Galahad spoke from where he still knelt by the king.

"Where is Guinevere?"

~

At midnight the knights gathered at Arthur's bedside and gazed down at the figure lying motionless as a statue. Only the rise and fall of his chest showed that he still lived. His body was icy cold and, as they watched, a silver filigree spread across his skin like frost. His dark hair became shot through with grey, and his eyelashes lay like goose feathers on his pale cheeks.

"What grieves me most," Bedivere remarked in a hushed tone, "is that we know not if he wakes or sleeps. I fear he is as wakeful as we are, but silenced and becalmed."

Gawain shuddered and turned away. Wolf whined and licked at Arthur's hand where it lay on the coverlet.

"It is dark magic indeed, to lay one so great so low," Mordred whispered. "What is to be done?"

"Nothing." Kay spoke heavily from where he sat in the corner, long legs sprawled out before him. "The queen sleeps outside the chamber door for she is wearied to death, and we can only wait and watch the revenge the witch has wrought, as it turns Arthur into stone."

"Perhaps it was the maid's revenge." Mordred turned away from Kay's eyes to look out of the chamber window into the blackness. "But such malice seems too cruel for her. I thought she loved Arthur. Indeed she said so many times."

"And is he to remain like this?" Bedivere spoke up from his station at the bedside, "Is there no remedy?"

"None that we know, save God's." As Galahad spoke quietly the priest entered, and the knights stood aside to watch as he lit a candle and set it at Arthur's head, took holy water from a flask and sprinkled it over the recumbent figure, and began to murmur the Latin phrases of exorcism.

But even as he began his work the knights shifted and murmured, for where the drops of holy water fell onto Arthur's skin they froze and turned to hailstones. The drops sparkled as they lay scattered on his face and hands like diamonds. For all the priest's incantations the king's form remained motionless. No sound passed his lips. No shudder came to shake him free of his enchantment.

Long into the night the priest went on. At first the knights watched closely, eager to see any change. After a time they took to pacing the room or gazing out of the window into the darkness. Later still they slumped into corners. Gawain sat like a grey rock propped against the wall. Mordred wrapped himself in his cloak and cast himself on the floor, dozing as the hours dragged by, for he too was still ailing from the effects of Morgan's sorcery.

In the very middle of the night Kay left the chamber. Outside sat Guinevere, curled up in a massive oak chair by the door, wrapped in a blanket but not sleeping. As Kay emerged from the room she sat up, a look of hope crossing her pale face. Kay shook his head sorrowfully. "No change, my lady. Rest now while you may."

~

It was first light when the Merlin landed on the windowsill of Arthur's room with a soft flutter of feathers. His steely blue back and pink belly were hard to see at first in the pink and blue light of morning, but as he rapped at the window with his small beak Mordred sprang to his feet to let the bird fly into the room.

He alighted first on the bedpost and regarded Arthur steadfastly with his round yellow eye, tilting his head as all birds must, to examine the still figure under the coverlet. Then he flew to a tall oak chest at the foot of the bed and considered the assembled knights with unblinking eyes. Smallest and shyest of all birds of prey, when the Merlin spoke he spoke softly.

"Well met, knights of the round table."

There was a moment's pause, then all six men sank to one knee and bowed their heads. Wolf whined and fell to his haunches trembling. Unnoticed Guinevere slipped into the room and watched quietly from the doorway, her face flushed with sudden hope. Then, one by one, the knights raised their heads again to gaze on the Merlin with dawning joy. Ten years had passed since they had watched him fly away into the morning sun to be seen no more, and they had forgotten the sober wisdom that shone from his beady eye.

Bedivere laughed suddenly, breaking the reverent silence and the knights rose from their knees with looks of gladness. "And what a comfort to see you here, Merlin! We dared not hope that you lingered close enough to know of our troubles. And yet here you are and the mischief will soon be mended. Where evil sorcery works its harm, who better to overturn it than the greatest wizard and the noblest heart that magic ever made?"

The Merlin looked steadily at Bedivere and then raised a foot as though to silence him. "Bedivere, you were ever flatteringly confident in my powers, but tonight it is misplaced. I am here to help you as best I may, but I cannot lift the enchantment."

The smiles that had begun to spread through the room abruptly vanished and silence descended once more. Arthur's chest rose and fell but no sound of breath escaped him. The Merlin hopped back to the bedpost for another look.

"Indeed, I believe no one could, even the maid herself. In her rage she invoked a dark magic, stronger and fiercer than any wielded in our times. I daresay that powers beyond her took the chance to intervene for their own ends. At any rate the enchantment is fixed."

"But if the enchantment is fixed, what is it?" Kay asked. "What has she done to him? And is there really no help for it?"

"There is help." The Merlin flew to Kay's shoulder and fluttered against his face almost with affection. "But it must come from mortal men through combat and wisdom, not magic. Look!"

Merlin flew to Arthur's pillow. As their eyes followed him they saw a change creep over Arthur's form and they moved closer to watch. Now they could see that the strands of frost that covered him were really chains, as fine and delicate as the chain that bore the crucifix around Guinevere's slender neck. Merlin pointed with his talons and then they saw something else. At his knees, his chest and at eyes, ears and mouth, the chains were joined together by five silver padlocks that bound him into his enchantment.

"What does it mean?" Gawain breathed. As he spoke their sight momentarily blurred, and when they looked again the chains and locks had reverted to the fine filigree of frost.

"Five magic locks bind him," Merlin spoke soberly. "And five magic keys must be found for the locks in order to free him. All must be found before the first key is placed in the first lock. We must succeed utterly or utterly fail."

The men shifted and looked at each other. "You said this was a task for men!"

The Merlin inclined his head. "The keys will not be hard to find. You may wish it was not so, when you see them. They hang on fine silver chains from the necks of the last five dragons in the west.

"Five dragons still dwell in the caves and wilds of the west, the last of their kind. All the rest perished at your hands or fled as magic retreated westwards. But between Camelot and the Land's End the last ones lie, guarding the keys to Arthur's prison, and you must regain them all."

Merlin looked around at the knights' sober faces. Kay looked weary, Gawain perplexed. Bedivere shot a tender look towards Galahad, and Mordred looked all at once like a frightened child. The bird clicked his beak impatiently and his voice lifted. "Why so drear?" he chirped. "This is not all bad news! Many of you have been longing for adventure, for your lives have been too easy for too long, as though you had forgot your vows to Arthur. Now at last is a quest worthy of such gallant knights."

Wolf barked excitedly in response to the bird's tone. He at least was ready for the hunt. "And now at last comes the fulfilment of Arthur's task, even if it comes in a way unlooked for," the Merlin went on, with a kind of gladness in his voice. "Defeat the dragons, and the dark powers that set this enchantment on him will be utterly dismayed. Defeat them, and the king's peace will finally extend to the Land's End and bring comfort to all. A last battle between magic and men this will prove, and why should the knights of the round table be afraid?"

"I do not fear a dragon!" Lancelot's voice came out of the corner where he stood. His voice was harsh, but his face was shining with sudden excitement. "Nor do I fear battle. But what if we fail, despite it all?"

Merlin flew to his shoulder and nuzzled his cheek. "It has been your curse Lancelot, not to be believed or trusted even by those nearest to you. But you are brave enough to speak aloud this hard question. If you fail, Arthur shall go to the barrow of his fathers and the wild magic will return to all your lands as though these last ten years had never been. Events come to a crisis, and one way or another one side will prevail."

"Well, Merlin, I am glad to have you with us, even if you cannot cure our ills," Bedivere said, after a moment's pause. "For who else could have told us what to do in this dark hour? Somehow or other, you always know more than seems possible. But then you are a wizard, and I am always thankful that you make cause with us, for you would be a fearsome foe!"

"Ever have I helped Arthur, and ever shall. But in this task I can only guide you. As you have lived for the last ten years so you must remain, and I must not meddle, for magic must be defeated by the light of reason, not by other magic however good, or the girl's wish will have been granted and all will fall into ruin."

The bird sighed, ruffled his feathers and hopped back to the bedpost.

"Now I must catch myself some breakfast, for like you I have not slept this night. If you will take my advice, eat well and rest yourselves until nightfall. Naught worse will befall Arthur yet, and you may safely leave him to his slumber till then. Tonight we shall lay our plans, and tomorrow we must leave Camelot, for these new adventures will not wait."

~

The knights slept heavily after their long night of watching, and woke to find a feast laid for them once more in the great hall. Guinevere sat in Arthur's seat at the top of the table, for it was she who had laid the banquet after long words with the Merlin that day, and she was grave and composed as though the fears of the night had never been.

After the feast the knights made their way to the round table and took their accustomed places in silence. The Merlin was already there, perched on a pile of books at the centre of the table. As the knights entered he inclined his head and they bowed in return. Mordred carried a scroll under his arm, which he unrolled and placed on the table, holding down the four corners with more books from those piled around the room. It was a map of the west, drawn and annotated in his own careful hand, the fruit of his winter studies.

"How glad I am," he spoke abruptly as he laid the map open, "that my uncle asked me to undertake this task. For otherwise we would have little to guide us beyond the gates of Camelot. Even so, I have gleaned but the barest knowledge of the coast and none to speak of concerning the inland ways."

The Merlin hopped over to examine the map and nodded approvingly as the others watched. "Mordred's map will be of more use to you in this quest than I can be," he said. "I cannot tell you where dragons are to be found, but I do have some knowledge of their likes and dislikes. They favour caves and mountains and wild places for they shun humankind. However they are fierce and fearsome, so people will know where they dwell, and will be able to help you if they wish. You will need to persuade them to do so."

The knights moved to huddle around the map. There was a moment's silence as they studied it, then Lancelot spoke.

"Five keys are to be found, and six knights stand here. We may begin together, but I am eager for battle, so I think it best that we choose separate paths to journey as we go deeper into the west.

When the time comes I will travel alone and go south to these white lands as you name them." Mordred bent to look more closely at his own notes at the spot where Lancelot pointed.

"Aye, I remember this," he said. "Here the land truly is white, they say, for when the fields are turned by the plough the soil is pale and dry. Fine pots and plates are made from it, and the people sell them to traders from the sea. From these white lands, as I named them, you can turn east or west along the southern coast as it seems best to you."

Bedivere and Galahad had been conferring while Mordred spoke. "Galahad and I will travel together." Bedivere said. "Often have we met at my castle in the great city and at Galahad's manor in the East. I would be glad of his strong arm, and he is over young to travel alone."

Galahad laughed and looked sheepishly at the company. "You see his real motive. He thinks me a dreamer and likely to come to grief. Well, I am glad of his care and will accept the offer of his company with a good will."

"We will take our way west along the coast from Camelot," Bedivere decided, pointing to the map. "Here Mordred has read of few settlements, and he writes that the cliffs are high and the seas wild. We may hear rumour of dragons even at our own gates."

Kay spoke next. "I have had a desire to travel to the Land's End since I was a lad. So I will choose a different path, and look for our enemy in the furthest wild."

"Then if you will have me I will come with you," Mordred said, his eye brightening. "Not merely because we have always been friends, Kay, but because I too hanker for the end of the world! And on the way we can explore the inland ways that remain blank on my map. If we head for the Land's End we can travel directly west by inland roads and come to the coast only at the end of our journey. If there are dragons inland we will surely find them on our way and perhaps find another on the shores of the sea at our journey's end."

"Wolf and I hunt happiest alone," Gawain said gruffly. "So though I love you I will take myself west and south to this place that Mordred names here as the Lizard – if dragons are our quarry then that name bodes well. Perhaps I may join some one or other of you for a space as we leave Camelot, but then we shall find our own way."

"None should travel alone," the Merlin spoke at last, now that the knights had chosen their differing paths. "Wolf is company enough for Gawain, but I have chosen a companion for Lancelot." He nodded towards the door and the knights turned to see Guinevere standing there, dressed in a leather jerkin over a chain mail shirt with a bow strung across her back. She looked strange to them in such outlandish clothes and involuntarily the knights murmured a protest.

"I know what you are thinking," the Merlin said. "Your first objection, of course, is that she is a woman, and that women are soft, weakly creatures. But Guinevere and I have spoken together long and closely today, and I deem her fit to accompany you. She loves Arthur and desires to help him, and she will suffer sorely, confined in Camelot waiting for your return. She had practised long and faithfully with a bow as ladies often do – and is she never to test her skill in more than a tournament? Moreover she is brave and gentle, and may offer wiser counsel in a crisis than your hot heads can yield."

The knights still looked doubtful and Kay almost angry. The Merlin seemed to wink at Guinevere and his voice became more confidential. "But you have another objection I know. Long have you feared that Lancelot makes too free with the king's wife. Yes, you may look askance that I say it aloud, but you have all thought so. Lancelot has a charm that few women can resist and you have seen Guinevere colour and smile at his words. Well, as I said this morning, Lancelot's charm is his curse. No one believes him faithful, all doubt his allegiance to Arthur, though you may deny it and I see you shake your heads. Well, well, here is his test. Guinevere shall go with him, she will be brave, Lancelot will be true, and that will be a force as good as magic to wield against these dark powers."

Guinevere stepped into the room and spoke gently to the knights while her eyes rested especially on Lancelot. "Merlin has argued my case, and said things to make me blush, but I do desire to come with you," she said. "For ten long years I have sat at my chamber window watching the sun set over the sea, watching the waves crash on the walls in a storm or lap at the stones on peaceful sunny days. Am I to waste away at the window until I grow old?"

Lancelot stepped forward and took her hand, bowing over it respectfully, as though she were dressed in her usual finery. "My lady, we have sworn to serve you. If you desire this, and Merlin thinks it right, I will protect you with my life. But I have also sworn knightly oaths to protect women from battle – how then am I to lead you into danger?"

The Merlin raised his foot and pointed in the direction of the chapel across the green lawns from the room where they stood. "Tonight Guinevere will fast and pray in the church as you have all done, and tomorrow she will rise from her slumber on its stone floor to find herself a knight as you all did long years since. In Arthur's name I will dub her, and then she will be transformed from your burden into your comrade."

"But what of Camelot and Arthur himself?" Kay asked, as the other knights finally shrugged their assent, whether willingly or because they could see no arguing with the Merlin. "Who is to guard the castle and protect Arthur in his present state?"

"Camelot is safe," the Merlin replied. "You were right to guess that only the presence of Morgan le Fay let magic enter its walls. Arthur may sleep peacefully in our absence so long as she is gone. But I do not think you need take any followers with you on this quest, for mere numbers will not defeat the dragons. So order your best men to sit in your places at the round table and hold the fortress while you are gone, and you may turn your thoughts westwards without fear."

So the knights rose from the table not to return there for many a day. At first light they took their leave of Arthur, and then the small cavalcade clattered down the cobbled path to the causeway, and crossed to the mainland.

And there she lullèd me asleep,
And there I dreamed – Ah! Woe betide! –
The latest dream I ever dreamt
                    On the cold hill side.

Departure

Let us be off then!" cried Lancelot as his horse plunged forwards up the hillside from the causeway. "Let us turn to our right this day, not to our left as we have ever done!" With that he gave his horse its head and it flew away up the grassy track and disappeared from view. The others followed more slowly, but with the same excitement. Long had the way westwards seemed closed to them. It felt strange now to turn on to the forbidden path and find nothing to bar the way.

Kay rode beside Mordred and smiled sidelong at him as they crested the hill. "Of course this is not strange to you, Mordred. You alone are familiar with our road."

"Only on paper." Mordred nodded towards the Merlin who rode on Gawain's wrist like a trained falcon. "There is our real guide. But I had my men copy out the map for each of us, such as it is, and have them safe here to pass on when the time comes."

Gawain was strangely silent as he rode with his dog trotting at the heels of his horse and the Merlin on his wrist. The bird cast him a few quizzical glances, but then tucked his head under his wing and composed himself for sleep. It was not clear whether he really slept, but at last Gawain sighed heavily and broke his silence, rousing the bird from his slumber.

"Have you the gift of foresight, Merlin?"

The Merlin blinked. "Foresight? Well, that depends what you mean Gawain."

"Can you see my future, and the future of this quest, bird?"

The Merlin clicked his beak thoughtfully for a moment. "Of you and your quest? No, Gawain, I cannot see those ends. It is all very well to foresee the doings of wizards and witches, but where mortal men are concerned the picture is more blurred. The acts of men spring from their characters in complicated ways, and then of course luck plays a part when no magic is used to bend events to the will. So no, Gawain, I cannot see into your future."

"Do you seek to deceive me, bird?" Gawain looked fiercely from beneath his shaggy eyebrows. "Is it not common knowledge that some men's fates are known? What of Galahad for instance?"

"Our Galahad was conceived because of a prophecy that the child of Lancelot and Elaine would be a saintly knight and would one day find the holy grail of Christ, long sought by many," the Merlin replied, lifting one foot rather didactically and stretching his talons. "But how are we to say that the youth we know is indeed that child, or that this will be his fate? You may say that he is good and godly, but that may be the result of the prophecy, not the cause. I hold to my view. Men are too complicated for me to predict their ends."

"And what of thine own?"

The bird sighed. "My end is very clear, more's the pity. One way or another I will leave these shores before long. If sorcery defeats you then I must flee the land. And if men prevail and magic is banished then I must be banished too. I shall be sorry to leave these parts, for I was egg and chick on this coast. Never have I travelled over the water like the other birds, but remained here winter and summer. But I daresay there are heaths and cliffs beyond the sea. So the swifts and swallows tell me at any rate."

Gawain cast the bird a glance. "You must be getting old, Merlin, for you speak the feelings of my heart. I used to mock Kay for his quiet pleasures, but now it comes to the point I find that I too am content enough to go hunting the foxes and deer of my own lands and to spend the evenings by the fireside with a pot of good ale. This chasing after dragons seems a hard thing for a man of my years."

The Merlin pecked at his sleeve in a friendly manner. "You speak thus not because you are old but because you do not wish to die with so many pleasures before you. That itself tells me something of your future – and that I need not worry overmuch about you."

~

Guinevere had a lonely ride of it as they turned their faces westwards, riding with the sea to their right. Mordred's map showed a river snaking its way to the coast thirty miles ahead, and they had agreed to remain in company until they reached its banks. There they would part, Bedivere and Galahad riding straight on by the sea while the rest turned inland and followed the river into the unknown.

Since the meeting the day before she had eaten little, prayed much and entered the unfamiliar world of the knights. She had sworn an oath to do good and to protect the weak, and then the Merlin had touched her on each shoulder and she had arisen freed from the constraints of womanhood. No longer need she wear cumbersome dresses that dragged along the floor; no longer need she confine her cares to the running of the castle household. Instead she was free to mount a horse and ride away towards adventure. She half wished she had stayed beside Arthur at Camelot.

Since the meeting at the round table Lancelot had barely given her a word. He seemed to be avoiding her company as they rode and spent most of the time a couple of horse lengths ahead of the rest, wrapped up in his own thoughts. This was strange, but she would not have minded if the others had spared her a kind word. As it was, Kay was grave and distant while Gawain hid his face in his beard and spoke mainly to his dog. She found herself riding behind Bedivere and Galahad and listening to their talk, which ran on God and miracles.

The Merlin landed softly on Guinevere's shoulder and tweaked her ear.

"Our bashful Galahad could out-talk a starling when it comes to his God," he observed, "and that is no mean feat. Methinks I should learn more of this Christianity he is so fond of, for it guides his actions more each day."

Guinevere stroked the Merlin's silky head with her gloved finger, glad of his company. "Do you not understand it?" she answered. "Being so wise a bird and so full of knowledge I supposed that you would know all about it. Or, even for God to have sought you out."

"Well, so far as I know he has not," the Merlin replied in a decided tone. "I daresay I am too heathen a creature for him to bother about. Although when Galahad talks of it I wonder if you have not exchanged one kind of magic for another."

"Indeed, I suppose the Bible speaks of miracles and resurrection," Guinevere conceded, "and of course Galahad thinks long of the grail which is a mystical object. But God is not of this world as magic is. God does not send dragons or spells to trouble us, or curse people with spots or warts as a sorcerer does."

"Though spots and warts can have other causes," the Merlin said dryly, "and many a sorcerer has a fame he does not deserve.

Nevertheless it seems to me that Galahad is somewhat bewitched by this God of yours."

Kay had been listening as he rode behind them and now he pressed his horse forward to ride at their side. "You speak my mind, Merlin," he said. "I wish we could live a little more with nature and a little less with conjurors of any description. If we would only let things take what course they will and take pleasure in things as they be, I believe we should have a happier time of it."

"And is that not just how you do live, Sir Kay?" Guinevere ventured shyly over the Merlin's head, "My lord Arthur has often told me of your kindness and common-sense. I have heard of your wise judgements in disputes among your own people. They love you, I believe, for taking them as they are and helping them to live more happily the lives they have, not filling them with doctrine."

Kay's weather beaten face seemed to redden and he spoke gruffly as he cast her a sidelong look. "Arthur thinks well of all."

"That is not so, and I am sure you know it," Guinevere returned gently. Kay bowed his head and his horse fell back behind hers once more. Guinevere sighed and her eyes blurred a little as she looked down at her reins resting on her horse's neck.

"Do not fear, fair one," the Merlin spoke gently in her ear. "It is not indifference that makes them stiff-necked and stern. When you come to action you will see that they love you and then you will be friends. You must prove yourself, and they must forget to be awkward, and then all will be well."

"If that is so then all may never be well," she whispered in reply. "If I prove myself unworthy then all will be ill."

The Merlin seemed to chuckle in a bird-like way. "Gawain asked me if I could see his future. One thing I know of yours is that it will contain both strength and virtue. And virtue need not lie in arms either. There will be many ways to prove your worth on this quest."

"Indeed," Guinevere replied bleakly, "At least there will be one among us to air the beds and to prepare the food."

~

As the sun rose high in the morning sky the company found themselves steadily descending and soon a small cove came into sight below them. It was long and narrow with a grey sandy beach that led back to a small valley, where a swift stream ran down to the sea. Two or three thatched cottages huddled in the cove and the knights exchanged glances. It was the first sign of life they had met since leaving Camelot.

As they clattered down the hill into the cove they saw that one of the houses was an inn. An ale tankard hung from a signpost at the gate and a dirty sign advertised the inn's wares by the door. At the sound of the horses' hooves and jangling harness a man appeared in the doorway and watched them approach. The Merlin flew back to Gawain's fist at the head of the column and turned to address the others.

"More may be learned by strangers than by enemies," he counselled. "Knights, do you stay silent while you take refreshment and use your ears. Guinevere, you must be the spokesman for the party."

"But what shall I say?"

"Tell them that you are but newly arrived from France, for that will explain your strange dress, and the men's silence will seem natural enough. You need not explain your business – every stranger can keep his own counsel if he wishes."

"From France you say, my lady?" the innkeeper asked as he brought bread and cheese and set a flagon of ale on the table. "When I seen you coming down the hill there, all clad in armour and on such fine horses I thought for a moment you must be from Camelot." He folded his arms and leaned against the wall in a friendly fashion. "But they never come this way, thanks to goodness. They don't bother us and we don't bother them more than we can help it."

"Have you seen Camelot?" Guinevere asked. The man shook his head,

"Nay, never, my 'andsome, and never wish to neither. 'Tis surrounded by great walls hung about with human bones, they say, and they keep a terrible monster within the place."

"Mon Dieu!" Guinevere tried not to smile. "What is the monster for?"

"No one knows, my lady," the man returned darkly, "If they ever do come riding down my hill I daresay I shall find out."

"But we heard that Arthur had banished the wizards from his lands," Guinevere looked puzzled. "Methought he kept no magic creatures."

"Ah, he would say so, wouldn't he?" the man tapped the side of his nose with his finger, "He wants to trick us, now, don't he? Many a witch and wizard has passed through these doors with horrible tales. Children have been taken!" he paused dramatically "Taken and *eaten* in there!"

"Never!" Guinevere exclaimed hotly.

"Ah, I see it upsets you ma'am. Shocking it is I know and hard to credit. But I have seen the bones they cast out on the shore, my lady. A wizard showed me once. Such a small skull it was too – and tiny little finger bones."

Guinevere pushed her plate away, feeling sick.

"They call these parts the dragon's mouth," the man went on, warming to his theme. "We live in the shadow of fear, ma'am. If you carry on this road you'll reach Padstow afore nightfall. There the river Camspell runs to the sea. This side of the Camspell is a dangerous spot but across the river folks feel safer. The witch Demelza has enchanted it, see? The fiends from Camelot cannot pass over it. Thence comes its name."

"Have you ever encountered these fiends?" Guinevere asked him.

"Not in human form ma'am, that's all I'll say." He tapped his nose again. "But in my line of work I see much."

At this Wolf looked up at him so intelligently that the knights were hard put not to laugh.

"We know of this river you speak of," Guinevere said. "If we follow it inland, where will it lead?"

"Onto Bodmin moor, ma'am," the innkeeper replied, "and straight to the keep of Lord Marc, our protector. Would your business be with him now?"

Guinevere looked down at her plate. "Our business is our own," she said, "and I cannot disclose it. Tell me, what if we cross the river Camspell and follow the coast? What will we find there?"

"After Padstow very little, ma'am," the innkeeper shook his head. "It's a wild bleak spot. The waves crash onto the shore day and night for the sea is wild and you can spy no land across it. Some of our fishermen say that there is no land to find beyond it, only endless ocean. Do not pass that way, my lady. Look to Lord Marc – he will give you hospitality and shelter."

"We heard strange rumours at the port," Guinevere hazarded as the man took their plates and turned away. "Tales of dragons I believe. We shall not meet any I hope, here at the dragon's mouth as you call it?"

The man pursed his lips. "The only dragon I know of in these parts lives on the wild coast I told you of beyond the Camspell. But it don't bother us. People do say it has such a hoard of treasure that it dare not leave its cave. Lads go to try and pinch a little now and then, but they never get in. It keeps its nose in the doorway, see? One false move and you're cooked."

"Cooked?"

"Fried, baked, grilled," the man replied. "They breathe fire, my lady, did you not know?"

~

"They fear us more than hate us," Mordred said, when they were mounted once more and riding on their way towards the Camspell. "I wonder what he would have done had we declared ourselves to him?"

"Sworn fealty most likely," Kay replied, "and then run to the nearest wizard for protection."

"Shall we be able to cross the river I wonder?" Guinevere asked, "is it really enchanted against us, do you think?"

"Perhaps," Kay nodded, "but remember my lady, we have defeated all such magic before. Arthur has shown us that all such enchantments yield to reason. We have but to press on without fear and the spell will be broken."

"At any event you may not need to cross," Bedivere said, "It was Galahad and I who chose that road."

"Aye, but should you go on alone if there is a dragon to be found there?" Gawain asked.

"Yes," the Merlin spoke up from his place on Lancelot's sleeve. "Thus were your paths agreed at Camelot. Indeed I have no fear for Bedivere and Galahad against one dragon. I worry more about the rest, who must venture on a meeting with Lord Marc at his manor."

"What do you know of him?" Kay asked. "Is he a danger to us?"

"He is a proud and brooding man," the Merlin replied, "and he has no love for Camelot. He keeps a witch, Demelza, at his court to protect and tend his household. But nevertheless I think you should venture on his hospitality, and in your own guise. He would be a useful ally if it comes to fighting, and in any case you will not be able to pass his door unseen."

The company rode on through the long afternoon past several coves, the sea always on their right. Guinevere had never ridden so far or felt so tired. As the shadows lengthened they were forced to shade their eyes from the brilliant sunlight shining low over the waves. At last the sun dropped lower in the sky, hovering a hand's breadth above the horizon. Pink and gold reflections stretched towards them across the water. Kay had been looking about him for some time and now, as the path descended into a hollow and the cliff edge rose to their right offering some protection from the westerly breeze, he drew rein and stopped. "Here is a place for our camp," he said. "Let us halt while we still have light to see by and make our supper."

All dismounted and set about making camp. Bedrolls were laid on the grassy bank above the path and a fire was kindled in a sheltered spot. The horses were unsaddled and turned loose to crop the short springy turf and to drink from the stream that tumbled through the hollow. Gawain brought water and soon a meat stew was bubbling over the fire and cold hands were warmed at the blazing twigs. Ale and wineskins passed from hand to hand as the light faded and darkness began to loom out of the shadows around them. The fire crackled and spat, illuminating their faces with a flickering glow. Kay stirred the stew and gazed into the flames. Mordred chewed thoughtfully on a hunk of bread while the Merlin, who had disappeared on his own hunting forays throughout the day, took himself off to a stunted tree nearby and settled on a branch for the night.

"I wonder if Arthur dreams," Bedivere said suddenly, as he nursed a mug of ale beside the fire. "It would be a sore trial to suffer nightmares when one cannot wake." A shudder ran through the company and Bedivere shot an apologetic look towards Guinevere. "Pardon me, my lady."

"Nay Bedivere," she replied, "I love Arthur as dearly as any here. You cannot have any dark fear as to his condition that I have not already imagined."

Of all the company Mordred knew Guinevere best, and now he sat down beside her in the darkness and patted her hand. "Most likely he sleeps peacefully," he said encouragingly, "and will wake to our return none the worse for his rest."

Guinevere smiled at her nephew and, as the others moved quietly around the camp, they rested by the fire talking of Camelot and its ways and remembering old times.

"You were not much more than a child when Arthur took the throne."

"I was ten years old," Mordred replied, "too young to understand his victory, but old enough to take great pride in my uncle the king."

"These last years of peace at Camelot must have been especially long to your young eyes, I daresay. What can you remember of the time before Arthur was crowned?"

"I remember endless travelling," Mordred replied. "I remember the tents of our camp and the many men who came to join us. They were a shock to me sometimes, being so young. I thought all knights were like Arthur."

"Indeed they were not!" Guinevere shuddered. "What brutes some of them were, for all that they spoke of God! Sometimes I feared Arthur would perish at their hands even as they professed to follow him."

Mordred nodded. "Yes, even I felt that. I remember practising endlessly with my sword for fear I should be called on to protect him. In the end I fought but once, in the last battle for Camelot and against my uncle's will. I do not believe I struck a material blow."

"If you would help me to practise my bow I would be grateful, if indeed there is any more time for mere practice now that a true fight looms close. I would like to learn a little of the sword too, should I need it." She patted the bundle at her side, "Merlin gave me a blade as befits the knight I am not, but I hardly know how to use it."

"We will be novices together, then, for I study the arts of war less often than I should. Perhaps these warriors around us may lend us some counsel."

"What else do you remember of those times?"

"Oh, the Merlin mainly," Mordred cast a glance towards the withered tree where the bird slept. "To my young eyes he was a wonder. And still is."

"He is a true friend," Kay agreed, as he appeared before them bearing steaming bowls of stew. "And a timely one. He must have been close by for all these years, biding his time until our need was great."

"That is a comforting thought," Mordred said, "somehow all seems safe when he is near."

"And yet it is only grave danger that calls him out," Kay observed. "He is a neighbour we should wish never to see."

"I could never wish that," Mordred replied, before applying himself to his bread and stew.

It was strange to sleep on the scratchy turf after a soft bed. Even Gawain had not slept under the stars for many a long day. But all had thick blankets, which they pulled up to their chins and soon all were pleasantly warm and drowsy. One by one they fell asleep. Guinevere was the first, Mordred was the last. He lay for a long time listening to the others breathing, and gazing out from his warm blankets at the stars which shone brightly in the darkening sky above.

~

Strange dreams came to all the company that night. Bedivere found himself lying in Arthur's place on the bed at Camelot, unable to move or speak. He woke, threshing against his blankets to discover that Galahad had rolled against him, pinning him to the ground. The young knight was an uncomfortable bedfellow for he was restless, turning his head fretfully from side to side and mouthing words of protest that would have puzzled the others had they heard them, for he railed at phantoms with a bitterness that had never entered his waking voice.

Kay roamed the forests of his childhood in his dreams along with his adopted brother Arthur. In the dream Arthur kept calling to him from the trees ahead, but Kay could never catch him up. "Wait for me, Arthur!" he gasped, and woke. For a moment he thought that trees still surrounded him, but then remembered where he was and fell back into slumber.

Guinevere dreamt that she was trapped by grey stone walls on all sides. She felt her way around with mounting fear. Then she looked up and saw the sky far above. Someone was looking down at her. The next moment she herself was the onlooker, and realised that she could see herself trapped at the bottom of the hole. But now she could see that she was dressed in white and lying very still, hands crossed on her breast. The hole was her grave.

As she cried out in her sleep the Merlin flew soundlessly down from his branch. In the darkness he flew three times around the troubled sleepers. One by one they fell silent and still. Their breath came more easily and dreams forsook them.

They woke to a grey dawn with the threat of rain. After yesterday's sunshine the dank air made them shiver as they saddled the horses and collected their belongings. They were subdued as they breakfasted on day-old bread and cheese and drank water from the stream. Guinevere was the only one to wash hands and face in the running water. Already the men looked unshaven and fierce in their worn armour which spoke of many battles.

"Come, Guinevere," Mordred appeared at her side, "Bedivere and Kay are consulting over the map and the Merlin is seeking his own breakfast. Let us test our skill with the bow while we wait."

They balanced small pebbles in a row on the branch of a tree, and took up their stance. Mordred shot first and missed narrowly. Guinevere followed with a shot that flew well wide of the mark. She shook her head angrily and brushed the hair from her eyes. Mordred's second shot was equally wayward. Guinevere cast him a suspicious look, as though she feared that he shot wide on purpose to please her, but his face was red as he retrieved his arrow while Lancelot and Galahad watched without comment. Comforted, Guinevere took her time over the second shot, and was unlucky when the arrow flew neatly between two pebbles. A moment later one of the pebbles fell, dislodged by the shock of the arrow's passing.

Mordred hit a pebble with his next shot and Lancelot murmured approval. Guinevere missed again, but by a narrow margin. As she found her arrow and walked back to her spot she smiled at the watching knights. "Mordred spends little time on the archery range while I spend much," she said. "Yet still he beats me."

"To hit the pebble is a lucky stroke," Lancelot replied. "Few targets would be so small. If the pebble was your enemy's heart then your arrow would still have struck and felled him easily enough."

"Still I will try it once more," she said, "for my pride if naught else." This time the arrow struck the pebble with a satisfying thud and she returned her arrows to their sheath, reassured that not all of the Merlin's praise had been unfounded.

"What of the sword?" Mordred asked Lancelot. "Guinevere has been given a blade but knows not how to use it. Should she be taught something of its use?"

Lancelot shook his head. "Nay, the time remaining to us is too short and the sport too dangerous. Better keep to your bow, my lady, with which you show much skill. If it comes to such close quarters that a blade is needed, you will be best advised to run or to surrender."

Guinevere looked into Lancelot's face as he spoke with such decision. It was a face very different from that which she had known at Camelot, for there he had been only courteous, sentimental and amusing. It suddenly seemed foolhardy to leave the others to journey alone with this man she now found that she hardly knew. But she felt reassured by his words too. If danger came she could trust to Lancelot's skill with the blade.

At last the cavalcade moved off, Lancelot and Galahad riding together some distance ahead of the others their figures straight and tall on their fine horses. Lancelot was silent for a spell, then glanced sideways at his son. Galahad was riding a trifle abstractedly, with a rapt look on his fair face that Lancelot could not read.

"We have barely spoken together since we arrived at Camelot," Lancelot said, breaking the silence and drawing Galahad's blue eyes towards his own. "How goes it with you, my son? It grieves me that we spend so little time together for I hardly know your life."

"There is little enough to know, father," Galahad replied. "Government and prayer, the joust and the sword. Those are my pastimes and some of them my pleasures. I see Bedivere often and he gives me fatherly counsel. All is well with me."

"It was a pity that you were robbed of your joust the other day. But we well know who should have won, had the witch not meddled."

Galahad inclined his head, but did not answer. Lancelot was quiet for a moment then laughed ruefully. "We were indeed blind not to see her hand in Mordred's victories! Never did I think that a knight of the round table could be as he is. His only skill is with the bow, which is but a womanly pastime in my eyes. And his swordplay! I wonder that Arthur does nothing about it."

"Arthur values other things in Mordred," Galahad replied calmly. "New ways demand new talents, father, and Mordred has them. I often wish I had his wits when I am faced with some warring neighbours in my court. My sword and my lance have lain idle these last five years, mere toys for my amusement."

"They shall not be idle now," Lancelot said with energy as he glanced back at the others who had fallen far behind and drew rein to wait for them. "Now knightly acts are called for, and I have no doubt which of us will show their valour best."

As the company met and mingled on the narrow path Mordred found himself riding beside Galahad. They had little enough to say to each other as a rule, for their ways and thoughts ran on widely different paths, but Mordred thought that he saw a new kindness in Galahad's face as they jogged on. He seemed to make a special effort to talk of Mordred's reading over the winter and the map that he had made. Mordred was surprised by some of his questions, and the careful way he listened to the replies. He was almost galled, he realised with a wry smile, that Galahad should prove to have some wit after all. Galahad read his expression and his eyes dropped.

"I daresay that you think me a numbskull, Mordred," he said. "Reading has always come hard to me, and I know that I study less than I should. But when I sit down before a book the letters dance before my eyes, so that I lose sight of their meaning. I suppose I should persist, but then the sunshine beckons and Blade calls me from his stable and I find myself drawn to the outside world once more. But I know that there is much I could learn of my duties if I studied as you do."

Mordred was touched, and kindness entered his own tone as he replied.

"You are the model knight, Galahad, do not blame yourself for not being a scholar. The two seldom go together, as I well know to my own shame. But have you not thought of study as a way to see a little into your own future?"

Galahad turned his eyes enquiringly towards Mordred.

"I only mean that among my reading this winter I came across references to the grail that I thought might interest you. Indeed, I wondered if you had read them already."

"Nay." Galahad shook his head and a little impatience entered his voice. "If the grail prophecy is true, I need not go to seek it. It will find me out soon enough."

"But do you not wish to know more of what may come?" Mordred studied Galahad's fair face with bafflement as he shook his head again.

"The future is in God's hands," he replied, stubbornly. "What will come will come." He nudged his horse forwards as the track broadened and the Camspell came into view before them, and Mordred was left behind. Mordred smiled wryly at Galahad's receding back, then he heard hooves behind him and turned to see Guinevere following.

"Galahad would not be taught by you, Mordred." She was smiling as she drew her palfrey alongside him in Galahad's place.

"It seems not."

"But I will listen, if you wish for a pupil. What did you read of the grail?"

"Oh," Mordred shrugged, and reached up to snap a twig of blackthorn from a bush that grew across the path like a snowy cloud. "Nothing in particular, aunt. But I found many veiled references to the Lord's cup among the books I read last winter, and some of them passing strange."

"Indeed!"

"Nothing I could put my finger on." Mordred's face grew thoughtful. "But it seems to me that the grail frightens men as much as it beguiles them. There is something foreboding and fearful about it, that made me shiver as I read, and made me thankful to be only Mordred."

"In that case I am glad Galahad would not listen."

"I did not wish to frighten him," Mordred replied. "Only to ask what he felt when he thought of his destiny."

"It is natural that the grail should fill us with terror, for it is a thing of the spirit that belongs not in this world," Guinevere said after a moment. "Imagine laying your lips to the same cup our Lord drank from, so long ago! It is awe and homage that makes us tremble, Mordred. Beside it, a dragon is nothing."

Mordred smiled. "And shall I remind you of that tomorrow, when we stand eye to eye with a fire-breathing monster?" Guinevere only laughed and looked away.

The Camspell was close now. In the fields of young wheat that lined the banks peasants were working, pulling weeds by hand. It must be wearisome work, Mordred thought, to be bent double in the wind and rain toiling from daybreak until dusk. The labourers straightened with apprehensive looks as they saw the horsemen approaching.

"Fear not," Galahad called out. "We are but passing through your lands and mean no harm. But we wish to know how best to cross the river – for here it seems wide and fast-flowing. Is there a bridge?"

"Aye," a man replied rather warily. For a moment he seemed reluctant to tell them more, but then he pushed the cap back off his face and wiped his hand across his brow in a more friendly fashion. "Ride but five miles or so along the bank inland and you will come to the crossing place where the river is shallow and narrow enough to ford with the horses. They will not need to swim. You will know the place, as there's a cottage or two and an inn I believe."

"Excellent," Galahad returned cheerfully, and Mordred wondered to see his good humour so quickly restored. "Then a crossing and a breakfast we shall have in one place! Thanks to you, my friend." He offered the man a gold piece and turned to ride away. As he turned the man called after him.

"This be money from Arthur's lands," he said. "Be you from Camelot?"

"Aye," Galahad laughed, and cantered away to join the others who had turned inland at the man's advice. Behind him the peasants gathered, marvelling that such devils should have the look of common men and women.

~

After a hearty meal they left the inn and walked down to the riverbank on foot, leading their horses. They knew that behind them the villagers had gathered to watch their crossing. If they succeeded then their fame would fly before them, proclaiming their power over the witches and wizards of the land. Lancelot glanced down at Guinevere's pale face.

"Fear not, my lady," he said. "This is but a small test to that which will follow. We have always conquered the magic of common witches and wizards when the need has been great. It will be the strong magic of the dragons and the keys that will try our mettle, not this trifle."

"Who then is to cross?" Bedivere asked, "Galahad and I of course, but what of the rest?"

"All should cross," the Merlin advised, "if only because you have an audience ready to be impressed by your power over the witch Demelza. Do you go first, Lancelot, and we shall follow in your footsteps. But mount your horse before you enter."

"Why?" Guinevere asked. "Will that aid the breaking of the spell?"

"Nay," the Merlin replied, "but he shall have wet feet for the rest of the day otherwise."

The knights laughed and Guinevere blushed as she joined in. The hearty peal echoed round the village, seeming to set sorcery at naught, thrilling the villagers as they huddled in their doorways to watch and sending jackdaws flying up from the chimneys in protest. Then Lancelot urged his horse forwards to the water's edge. As the horse's hooves entered the shallow water at the riverbank a shimmer rose from the stream. Tendrils of fog came from nowhere, snaking up around the horse's legs and swiftly enveloping the figure of horse and rider until, as they stepped forward into the river, they quickly vanished from sight. The villagers murmured half in fear and half in anticipation. There was a minute's pause. The Merlin began to preen his feathers looking unconcerned as the seconds went by. Then a voice hailed them from the fog.

"I am across safely enough," Lancelot called, "and in broad daylight once more. All may follow without fear. Any shape that you see is but a phantom and will melt away before it touches you. The only troublesome thing is the fog, but ride quietly and the other bank will soon come into sight."

One by one the others followed. Soon only Kay and Guinevere remained on the near bank. Kay looked at his companion and smiled encouragingly. "Follow me, my lady. Keep your eyes fixed on my horse's tail and attend to nothing else."

With that he stepped forwards into the fog. Guinevere hesitated for a moment, then followed. Immediately she was surrounded by a cold, wet blanket of cloud that blotted out all other sights and deadened all sound. Dimly she could see Kay's horse ahead. Her own mare whinnied in fear and shied as she urged her forwards, afraid of being alone in the eerie greyness. Then, from both left and right, formless shapes began to swoop towards her and for a moment she felt herself transported back into her dream of the night. The grey fog rose like grey stone walls around her and her breath laboured until she felt as though she were indeed in the tomb. Voices echoed in her ears, now loud, now faint. She shut her eyes and swayed in the saddle. When she opened them a moment later there was no sign of Kay ahead. At once fear flooded through her and the world swam in front of her eyes. She was no true knight, whatever the Merlin might say. What strength had she to resist these enchantments? A vision rose before her of wandering in these mists forever, an outcast for failing in her faith. She gasped out a cry for help, but no sound came.

Then all at once she heard jangling harness ahead of her, and a moment later she emerged into daylight. Dazzled she threw her hand up to her eyes, and then slid off her palfrey onto solid earth. Her legs trembled and she clung to the saddle for support. The knights were nearby, talking and laughing, and sharing a drink from the wineskin. No one noticed her wild look and shaking hands save the Merlin, who flew across from his place on Gawain's horse to perch on the pommel of her saddle where he could peer down into her face.

"All is well," he said with brisk kindness. "You see now that fear is but a phantom after all, my lady."

She looked up into his beady eyes and took a shaky breath. Then Kay approached with the wineskin and she drank deeply.

~

They lingered long at the ford, reluctant to part. After a time the villagers returned to their work and the company sat by the stream while their horses grazed. A watery sunshine struggled through the clouds and set the dew sparkling on the grass. Mordred took a copy of his map from the saddlebag and handed it to Bedivere soberly. Galahad sat in a kind of dream, absentmindedly tying and untying the bracers on his wrists. Merlin flew to perch on Mordred's shoulder, the better to speak to Bedivere.

"Do not approach the dragon lightly," he said. "If what the innkeeper said is true then you have both an advantage over the dragon and a weakness. If it will not leave its nest then it can do little to surprise you. On the other hand there will be small room for manoeuvre and you must not forget its fiery breath. If it guards the only entrance you will find it hard to pass."

"I have had the same thoughts," Bedivere nodded.

"Much must be hazarded in this quest," Merlin said, and flew over to peck at Galahad's ear to attract his attention, "do you not agree, Galahad?"

Galahad smiled his slow bright smile and reached up to stroke the bird's wing, "hazards have we never feared, Merlin," he replied, "I am ready to do my part."

Rising to his feet he whistled to his horse. Proudly it came to him across the grass and allowed him to take the reins. He swung lightly into the saddle and bent his head as he adjusted his stirrups. From her seat on the grass Guinevere marvelled at his beauty. He seemed to radiate light from his golden hair and fair face. It was as though all Lancelot's good looks and charm had passed to his son along with the grace of his mother long since dead. But as she looked at him a shadow crossed her face, for she remembered what Mordred had said of the grail. Now she thought that she saw little happiness beneath his smile, and she wondered if the prophecy did indeed hang heavy on his shoulders.

Bedivere mounted his horse more heavily than his young companion had done, and patted the sword that hung from his saddle. Reassured, he looked around at the rest of the company.

"Well, here we part," he said. "Have a care, friends, and here's to a happier meeting at Camelot." He dug his heels into his horse's sides and moved away, riding at an angle to the Camspell back towards the coast. Galahad raised his hand briefly, his blue eyes taking them in with one warm look.

"Will you not go with them Merlin?" Kay asked. The bird cocked its head as he watched them ride away.

"Not yet," he said. "Though I may go to them if counsel is needed by and by." He stretched his wings and looked up at the sky. The sun was already approaching its meridian. "Now we must linger no longer," he said. "It will be a long afternoon's ride to the manor of Lord Marc and we should get there before nightfall. Visitors who arrive after dark are never welcome."

Meetings

When Bedivere and Galahad had disappeared from view across the fields from the ford the others rose to their feet and prepared to ride on. Guinevere cast a last look at the river and shivered before turning her back on it and mounting her grey mare. Wolf rose to his feet, stretching elaborately and yawning, his tongue lolling out between his great white teeth. Merlin flew once more to Gawain's arm and the cavalcade rode off. It felt strange to be suddenly two knights the fewer. Lancelot trotted ahead as before and Kay and Mordred rode abreast behind him, talking of the science of falconry with an earnestness that brooked no interruption. Guinevere found herself riding beside Gawain for the first time. He cast her an inscrutable sidelong glance and then turned back to watch the road ahead between his horse's ears. Guinevere studied him covertly. She decided that it was mainly his beard that made him so forbidding as it shaded his face and hid the expression of his mouth. As she looked, the Merlin whistled to Wolf and the dog looked up with a puzzled air that made Guinevere laugh. It must be hard, she thought, for a doggy mind to comprehend a talking bird.

"How old is Wolf?" she asked. Gawain looked at her guardedly as he answered.

"Five years this midsummer my lady, full grown and strong. It is hard to think that I found him as a weakly pup, abandoned in a barn along with his brothers. His mother had tired of her brood I'll warrant and left them to fend for themselves."

"Indeed? And how many pups were there?"

"Five. Two dogs and three bitches, ma'am. I took one of the dogs as I feared that any animal of mine would have little time for raising a family." Gawain's voice grew warmer as he reached down to fondle the dog's floppy ears. "I did not know then that the poor little creature would grow to be the best of companions."

"You hunt with a passion, I believe, Sir Gawain?"

"I do, ma'am. And Wolf is a fine hunting dog for he fears nothing."

"He is an admirable beast, I envy you such devotion."

"Anyone may have it, ma'am, if they acquire themselves a dog and treat him well."

They fell silent for a space and then the Merlin began to quiz Gawain about his manor and his people. At first Gawain was curt with his answers but the Merlin would not be refused, and soon he was obliged to tell of the state of his farms and villages, the decline of magic over the last ten years and the conflicts he had resolved. Guinevere listened with interest, and thought that she had never heard Gawain speak so much or so well. At last Merlin turned to her and said "you see, my lady, how Arthur's knights have prevailed over these last years. Much was asked of them and they gave it willingly. And now if Gawain takes a little pleasure in the hunt at last, it is only the reward for much labour."

As the afternoon wore on they began to pass more and more cottages along the by-way to Bodmin. They were neat, tidy places with pretty front gardens full of flowers and chickens pecking on the lawns. The folks they saw were well clothed and fat, but they did not smile as the knights rode by. Like the innkeeper the day before and the villagers at the ford, they looked curious but afraid.

"Lord Marc may be a stern man," Kay said, "but his people look well enough. Indeed I would be proud to see such gardens in my own land."

"He is not cruel," the Merlin replied, "except when fear drives him. His faithful tenants are well looked after and live in tolerable comfort. But he is tyrannical and cannot brook insolence. And his witch blights all good things hereabouts. I will say no more of her, for you will soon see her with your own eyes and may judge for yourselves."

Guinevere looked a little bleak at the prospect and Kay gave her an encouraging smile. "Fear not, my lady. After all, you have already defeated one of her spells today." Guinevere smiled back, little comforted. Only she and the Merlin knew how near she had been to failure at the ford.

At last the cottages of Bodmin clustered more closely, and at their centre was a paling with a park within and an iron gate. The company passed through onto a gravel roadway that wound away through the lawns and trees of the park before falling out of sight down a hill ahead. The Merlin took to his wings with something of a clatter and flew ahead to spy out the land. Soon he returned, alighting on Lancelot's helmet.

"The manor lies ahead in a valley, surrounded by trees and water," he said. "Very pretty it looks too, but I fear that the woods and lakes will have a powerful charge of magic about them, so all should beware. I saw none but a few servants about the grounds. No doubt we will meet with a sterner reception when we come in view of the house."

It was not very long before they breasted the hill and began the descent to the house. It was in truth a place of great beauty, nestling in a valley embowered by trees and reflected in the lake before the door. Soon the company was seen, and there was a flurry of activity around the manor as the servants pointed and called to each other and some hastened inside. A few moments of peace and silence followed, then from around the back of the house came half a dozen men mounted on strong cobby horses and dressed in dark leather jerkins. They carried not swords but long pikes, and Kay looked grim.

"These are not courtly men, I fear. If fighting is to be the order of the day I do not like the look of those sticks."

"Nay, sticks can only unhorse us," Gawain replied. "If they swing at you, grasp the stake and wrest it from their hands. Then the odds will soon turn in our favour."

Kay smiled wryly. "Only Gawain can be confident of success in such a venture, but I cannot think of a better plan."

Lancelot rode close to Guinevere. "My lady, these men are ugly, but if fighting comes we shall not all fail. Take yourself back up the hill and wait, and there will be someone left to protect you when battle is done."

"Be not too hasty to look for combat," said the Merlin as the men drew nearer. "Unless my eyes deceive me the staves tremble in their hands."

Comforted by these words the knights nevertheless drew closer together as the men came nearer. Guinevere found herself at the centre of the group, almost jostled by the other horses. Once within hailing distance Kay waved his hand and shouted across to the approaching group.

"Do not fear, we come in peace, and you see that we do not draw our weapons."

"We do not fear," the leading man replied harshly, "it is trespassers who needs must be afraid."

"We are visitors, not trespassers," Mordred volunteered, "travellers in need of shelter as night approaches."

By now the two groups had met and the horses on each side stamped and circled, excited by the unfamiliar animals before them and the tension of the men.

"If you be travellers, whence come you?"

Lancelot looked the leader of the group coolly in the eye. "We left Camelot two days since. Last night we slept by the road, but hearing of your lord and his manor we deemed it courteous to greet him, and indeed we hoped for shelter and a meal if it pleased him."

The leader of the men shifted nervously and beads of sweat stood on his forehead as he eyed the knights' magnificent horses and gleaming armour. "Why not take us to your lord?" the Merlin prompted him suddenly, "he will know what to do with us."

The man flinched slightly to hear the bird speak, but he had seen too much sorcery to be much dismayed. "Come then." He gestured roughly with his pike for the knights to pass through his men's ranks. The knights moved forwards and the Lord Marc's men fell back to either side to let them pass.

Thus they rode down the hill to the manor, with the men and pikes at their backs. Guinevere glanced furtively over her shoulder at them, but their faces were stern and their eyes averted. They clattered over the bridge spanning the lake, which lay so still that their reflections hardly wavered as they passed. At the door to the manor the knights dismounted and turned to face their uncouth escort who wheeled around them balefully.

"Our steeds are tired and thirsty," Gawain said gruffly, "hast a stable boy who may see to their needs?"

One of the men whistled and a pair of thin, pale boys ran from the back of the house. The boys' eyes lit up at the sight of their new charges and they took them away with alacrity.

"There goes our means of escape," Kay muttered ruefully to Mordred, "let us hope we do not need to leave in haste."

There was no time to answer as they were led up the steps and into the hall, stone flagged with a high ceiling and a broad staircase leading to the first floor. Here they were bidden to wait while the leader of the men mounted the stairs and disappeared from view. The Merlin sat on Lancelot's wrist and Wolf crouched at Gawain's feet watching everything that passed with alert brown eyes. The man soon reappeared at the turn of the stair.

"You are bidden to enter," he said gruffly. "But keep your weapons sheathed and offer no insult to the Lord Marc on pain of death."

"We mean him no harm," Lancelot replied, "lead on."

They clattered up the stairs, the jingling of spurs and mail echoing around the stone walls of the stairwell. Kay thought that to those in the room above it would be a daunting din. A moment later they emerged into a large and sunny chamber that ran the full length of the manor with three mullioned windows looking out onto the lake. Rugs covered a dark wooden floor and a fire blazed in a large hearth at the far end of the room. Seated beside it were an old man and an old woman. The man wore a fur-lined cloak and tall leather boots. The old woman wore black and was embroidering on a piece of linen stretched over a large hoop.

The knights advanced on the pair, studying each as they crossed the length of the room. The Merlin pecked at Kay's sleeve and muttered "witch!" in something between a cough and a chirrup. At that Kay studied the woman more closely. He had first taken her for the lord's wife, but now he saw that she was much older. Indeed as they neared the fire he could see that the Lord Marc was not himself so old as he had at first appeared. It was his manner, not his face, which was aged.

The Lord Marc stood up as they halted before him and bowed stiffly. He was a little below middle height and wore a short well-tended beard and hair that fell to his shoulders. His eyes were dark and he did not meet the knights' gaze with anything like frankness. Meanwhile the witch Demelza continued to sew, glancing up shrewdly between each stitch.

"It is a surprise to me to see you here," the Lord Marc said. His tone was flat and a trifle gloomy. Kay remembered the supposedly uncrossable Camspell and smiled inwardly.

"Indeed, we have not made our way into these parts before," he replied courteously. "And beautiful your country is, my lord. We especially admired the neat cottages we passed on the road. They are a credit to your justice and wisdom."

The Lord Marc shifted nervously as though he distrusted compliments, and as Kay introduced his fabled companions his eyes narrowed. When his gaze fell upon Guinevere a look of mingled curiosity and calculation momentarily replaced apprehension on his face, but before he could speak his thoughts the witch cackled to herself loudly.

"And one more there be, though he stays silent. The bird is the Merlin, my lord, as even you may see from his plumage."

"Aye, aye," the Lord Marc replied testily. Then the note of curiosity re-entered his cracked voice. "I miss King Arthur in this illustrious company," he said, his eyes turning from one strange face to the next. "I wonder what circumstance could lead so many of his finest knights, not to mention his wife, into a strange land without him?"

Kay wondered if the pair knew something of Arthur's plight and his eyes flickered to the old woman seeking a look of knowledge or of triumph. But both lord and witch looked back at him with such naked curiosity that he feared them no more on that score.

"We come in friendship," he answered, "as the presence of a lady amongst us shows all too well. Too long has Camelot gazed westwards in ignorance of what lies beyond her walls. We come to melt the coldness between us that has prevailed these last ten years."

"Fine words," the crone addressed her embroidery, "yet the maid is dressed for battle not dancing. I wonder why she travels in the garb of a man?"

"For her own safety and comfort, ma'am," Lancelot put in with a bow. "Not knowing the ways of the west she dresses thus to protect her modesty among unknown men."

The old woman sniffed as though unconvinced and the Lord Marc shot her a look of irritation before seeming to remember his manners. He offered them refreshment, and beds for the night, and summoned servants to lead them to their chambers where they would find their belongings and the means to wash before dinner. The company thanked him in their turn and left him to discuss the mystery of their presence freely with his crone.

Guinevere's room was at the end of the corridor. Its arched window looked down on the woods that grew up to the side of the house. They looked green and inviting and she gazed out for a long time, while the sun set behind the treetops turning the leaves golden before they faded into the purples and greys of dusk. Long she gazed out, half-dreaming at the window, before a shout from one of the knights for more hot water woke her from her reverie and she too remembered to wash and change her grimy clothes. Mindful of the witch's words she dressed in a soft blue and grey gown and dressed her hair before turning to venture out into the corridor in search of her companions. As she turned to the door she could not help but take a last look out of the window. Below her casement on the dusky edge of the wood stood a girl of about fourteen summers. She had just emerged from the trees it seemed, and she held a spray of early campion in her hand. What struck Guinevere though was her expression. She had the saddest face Guinevere had ever seen.

~

The company gathered before dinner in the sunny upstairs chamber where they had met the Lord Marc and his witch that afternoon. Now the evening shadows were lengthening and the room was dark, but it was still cheerfully illuminated by the firelight. Guinevere acknowledged the bows of the knights before turning to extend her hand to the Lord Marc.

"Now we may greet each other in the proper manner," she said, with easy courtesy, "now that my dress befits my station."

The Lord Marc's eyes met hers briefly before he bowed over her hand. Then he turned to Demelza who had appeared at his shoulder. "May I introduce Demelza the wise," he said formally, "who has watched over my house and lands these many years."

Guinevere looked unsuspectingly into the witch's eyes and all at once felt sick and dizzy as though she found herself on the edge of a precipice. The witch's gaze seemed bottomless and black as the sea. She smiled grimly and took Guinevere's hand in a powerful grasp.

"Welcome my lady," she said, "We are glad to have you among us, if only for a short time."

Guinevere smiled back, but fear took her and she trembled. Was the witch cursing her with these honeyed words? She tried to pull her hand away but Demelza's grip only tightened.

"It would be amusing to hear what stories are told of us among your people," the witch said. "Estrangement can lead to many a foolish impression, I imagine."

"We have no false impression of you, ma'am," the Merlin said, as he hopped unexpectedly on to Guinevere's shoulder. His sharp talons dug into her flesh through the thin fabric of her gown and the pain seemed to release her from the old woman's snake-like gaze. Pulling her eyes away Guinevere spoke as one waking from a dream.

"Indeed, ma'am," she said, with more honesty than tact, "your fame had not reached us at Camelot. It was from your own people that we heard your name."

The Merlin half-whistled in a chuckling way. "Aye, so we did. They told us some false tale that you had charmed the river against us. But we soon found it was only a fable."

The old woman sucked her teeth and flashed the Merlin a venomous glance. Afraid to meet that gaze again herself, Guinevere cast her eyes around the room in search of a safer topic. The embroidery hoop that Demelza had been working on their arrival stood neatly in a corner covered with a calico cloth, the silks arranged beside it on a low table. "May I see your work?" she asked.

Demelza hesitated for a moment, then she nodded and gestured Guinevere towards the corner where it lay. Guinevere stepped forward and pulled the cloth away. The Merlin, satisfied that he had broken the witch's spell, now flapped off again to eavesdrop on the conversation between Lancelot and the Lord Marc.

Guinevere felt a tingle in her fingers as she picked up the hoop, then she gasped with pleasure as she looked at the work itself. It was a perfect picture of the manor and its beautiful grounds worked in lustrous greens, blues and browns. The water of the lake almost seemed to sparkle and splash, it looked so lifelike, while the trees grew lush and thick in a springtime array of colours that almost exactly matched what Guinevere had seen from her chamber window. If anything the trees in the embroidery were lusher and greener than in life.

At the edges of the work the picture blurred into browns and greys. Only one corner remained unfinished, that which would show the gravel roadway leading away through the park. But here Guinevere could see that there had once been some stitching that had been unpicked. Needle holes were visible in the fabric and a stray shred of silk showed where the stitches had been.

"This is beautiful," Guinevere exclaimed warmly as she gazed at it. "Indeed, it makes me ashamed of the trifles I have made in my time. You must have put some of your magic into this to make it live and breathe so clearly."

Demelza croaked a sharp laugh as she looked at Guinevere's fair face. "I sew a little of my care into the picture each day," she replied, "if you call that magic. Under my hands, after all, the manor and its people flourish."

"You have been re-working an area here, I see."

"She is never finished," the Lord Marc's voice spoke behind Guinevere making her jump. He had approached silently to look at the picture over her shoulder and she could feel his warm breath on her neck. "Just when I think she is finally happy with the work, she finds some fault and begins anew. Indeed, I believe there is not an inch of it that she has not re-made at one time or another."

"The reward of such pains is clear to see," Guinevere said, reluctantly returning the embroidery to its corner and covering it with the cloth once more. She turned, and her eyes fell upon the young girl she had seen from her chamber window, standing at the Lord Marc's side.

"Allow me to introduce my daughter," the Lord Marc said, "this is the Lady Ruth."

~

Ralph was shutting up the hens for the night when he saw the two knights riding down the hill towards the farm. He had scattered grain on the barn floor to bring the birds in and picked up the last of the eggs before closing the door and driving the heavy iron hook into the latch. As he turned homewards he caught the flash of silver on the knights' helmets reflecting the last of the sunlight on the hill. He stared for a moment, then ran as fast as his legs would carry him towards home.

He was not fast enough. By the time he reached the farmyard the strangers' horses were tied to the old wooden trough and the two large war-horses were drinking deeply. The knights had removed their helmets and stood talking to his sister Charity at the door.

"Here is my brother Ralph," she said as he clattered into the yard. As he looked from one stranger's face to the other he skidded in his wooden shoes on a fresh cowpat and for a moment he wavered, legs and arms windmilling as he fought to stay upright. Then he regained his balance and lurched forwards, eggs flying from his hands. Two smashed on the floor. The younger of the two knights caught the third with deft fingers and laughed.

"Now we have caused damages, Bedivere!" he exclaimed cheerfully. "I hope these were not your supper."

"Nay," Ralph gasped, looking from the knights to his sister and back again. "Charity has made soup I believe."

The young knight laughed again and looked at Charity who blushed. "Now you will fear for your own dinner, I daresay. Fear not, we will not ask to share it, but we would crave permission to sleep in your barn tonight," he gestured towards the hayloft, "we have passed no inn and it threatens rain before morning."

Charity pushed the hair back from her face and wiped her brow with floury hands. "Indeed you're welcome to it – and welcome to dinner too if you wish to share it with such as we."

"That would be handsome indeed, and we will not refuse," Bedivere replied as Galahad handed the girl the egg and winked at Ralph. "But first we must rub down the horses and settle them for the night before darkness falls. They have borne us far. Perhaps your brother will show us the stable."

Ralph had been gawping at the knights as Bedivere spoke, but now he leapt forward. He had never seen such beautiful horses and longed to groom them and to examine their fine trappings.

"Will your parents approve of your hospitality?" Bedivere asked as Ralph led them into the sweet-smelling stable and tethered the horses to the wall. "It is kind indeed to offer supper as well as shelter to strangers."

Ralph did not look up as he answered. "We have no parents living, sire. Charity and I have been farming this land ourselves for near three years."

"Indeed? And how old are you my lad?"

"Twelve sir, and Charity be sixteen."

"You were over young to learn the art of farming then."

"We had been brought up to it sir. 'Tweren't hard to carry on. Only we seem to feel a little tired sometimes."

"Do you have no one to help you?"

Ralph shook his head. "Charity and I have no friends in these parts, my lord."

Galahad had begun to rub down his own horse, now he stopped to look at Ralph and laughed softly. "Now I begin to see that we were lucky to stop here. Perhaps you are strangers here also, of sorts."

Ralph's eyes met his frankly. "And be you strangers sire? Where did you come from if it ain't a liberty to ask?"

"Camelot," Galahad replied, watching to see the lad's expression. Ralph's eyes widened in his broad freckled face, but he turned back to unsaddling Bedivere's horse without comment. Bedivere looked at him searchingly.

"Are we still welcome to share your supper?"

"Aye, and doubly so," Ralph replied fiercely, now a little red in the face. "We are your subjects, sir knights, if you'll have us, for we have long since spurned rule from Lord Marc."

"Indeed? And does he suffer your rebellion?" There was a smile around the corners of Bedivere's mouth in response to the boy's proud tone, but it quickly faded.

"My father and mother were killed by Lord Marc's men for resisting his witch Demelza," Ralph said shortly. "They did not submit to his rule and we will not neither. We have longed to see an army come riding from Camelot for many a year my lord. Glad we are to give you shelter."

Bedivere slapped his shoulder and sent him reeling, out of breath and pink in the face again from his speech. Galahad gave him a thoughtful look and turned back to his horse. "We are proud to accept it," he said. "Now what about some fodder for the horses? Hast oats?"

Ralph fetched water and feed for the animals and ran his hand over their gleaming coats with wonder as they ate. He examined the harness with careful fingers, noting the strength and elegance of the leatherwork and the fine engraving on metal bits and stirrups. Meanwhile Bedivere and Galahad took their saddlebags off to the barn and made themselves beds out of the fragrant hay by wrapping it in their blankets. They washed their faces and hands at the trough in the yard and then Ralph appeared from the stable and beckoned them towards the warmly lit farmhouse kitchen.

Enticing smells wafted out into the yard and the two knights exchanged shame-faced grins. "It seems we have fallen on our feet," Bedivere said. "I pray the others meet with the same luck at the manor of Lord Marc."

"You may pray so," Galahad replied, "but I fear it will not be answered."

They ducked their heads as they entered through the door, blinking in the light of the tallow candles and crackling fire. Charity stood at the range stirring a pot of soup while the smell of baking bread wafted from the oven. She nodded shyly to the men and pointed to the scrubbed table in the middle of the room. "Please sit," she said, and then turned to Ralph, "hast washed thy hands, brother?"

Ralph nodded untruthfully and slipped onto his chair at the table as the knights took their seats opposite him. Galahad's hair glowed like silk in the candlelight and Ralph stared, running his hands through his own tousled mop that was dunked weekly under the yard pump and shaken dry like a dog. Charity ladled thick broth from the pot into four wooden bowls and placed them on the table. Then she opened the range door and took out two large loaves, crusty brown on top and floury on the sides. She brought them to the table and cut them open with a large knife. Steam billowed from their soft creamy centres and Ralph's belly rumbled appreciatively.

The girl sat down and the group fell to with a good will. Little was said for some time as they blew and slurped gingerly on spoonfuls of hot soup, and tore hot chunks of bread to dip in the broth. Warmth and a sense of wellbeing began to steal through them, heightened as raindrops began to patter on the windowpane. Bedivere looked up at the sound and shook his head. "Glad I am that we are not sleeping under the stars tonight, Galahad."

"You may stay here as long as suits your purpose, my lord," Charity said, a little less shyly than before. "Ralph and I will sleep sounder for your presence on the farm."

"Ralph has told us a little of your story," Bedivere replied. "Does the Lord Marc still trouble you?"

"In truth he has not bothered with us since he killed our parents and turned our neighbours against us," Charity answered with a wry smile. "But that is cold comfort, and the memory of those times lingers. We still start at noises in the night."

"What did your parents do to displease him so gravely?"

Charity gazed into the candle flame and absentmindedly crumbled bread into her soup, as she replied with a simple gravity that drew Galahad's eyes to her face. "You must know that we are independent folks," she said. "We live far from the village and close to the sea. If we sat quietly we would hear it even now pounding at the shore. For generations our family has lived here, fearing none but offering none our fealty. We had little to do with the Lord Marc or his household except for paying him our rent on midsummer day each year, for he owns all the lands in these parts. Neither were we much in the habit of consulting sorcerers. My grandmother was wise in the ways of herbs and remedies and my mother doctored us when we were sick. My father likewise tended the animals with medicines, not spells.

"Then five years ago there was a rumour of a man down the coast a way. Folks said he had come ashore on the beach there in some flimsy craft. They said he sailed out of the setting sun one night, with barely a rag to his back. He made a wooden shack above the high-water line there and set about preaching, I think they call it, to all who came near."

"This man," Galahad said, "Did he wear a garment made of sackcloth with a girdle of rope around his middle and leather sandals to his feet?"

"Aye," the girl replied with a look of surprise.

"I have met such men and heard them preach," Galahad said, studying her face, "I daresay he talked to the people of Christ the saviour and God in heaven?"

"I believe he did," the girl said doubtfully, "but we never went to listen. As I told you sir, we keep to our own ways. At any rate, this man stayed in his hut and folks went to hear him, as much for the curiosity as aught else.

"But then the witch Demelza got herself in a passion about it. The holy man had said some hard words pertaining to magic. She flew into a terrible rage, and began to blight the holy man with every spell she could devise. The poor man had spots and sores all over, and his hut was washed away, and the food folks brought him went bad. But he did not leave, and he did not cease his preaching. And after a short while his sores healed and he rebuilt the shack. Then folks said he had a magic as strong as the witch's own. And then at last Demelza herself fell ill and all thought it was the doing of the holy man.

"Then Demelza's wrath was a terror to behold. She tried to turn the people against him, but folks in these parts are tender hearted in the main and they pitied him in his bare hut and his threadbare clothes. So at last Demelza persuaded the Lord Marc to move against him. And it is said he was not loath to do it. Always he fears attack from the east and Camelot, and feared the holy man might sow kindly feelings towards Arthur in the minds of the people. So he summoned all his tenants, including my father, to his manor and told them to arm themselves with spades and pitchforks and march on the saint.

"My father would not do it, sire. He said he had no quarrel with either side, nor no duty neither. Nothing was said that day and the rest marched on the shack on the sand, for none other but my father dared refuse. My father came home and life went on as before. Until all of a sudden misfortunes befell us. Calves died, sheep ran off the cliff and our crops withered. At first we did not mind it and my father's cures worked as before. But then we began to fear sorcery and with that our remedies began to fail. One terrible night our horses woke us, crying with the colic. They thrashed and screamed through the long night and in the morning both were dead."

Charity paused, her eyes wide and dark as she gazed into the candle, remembering. Ralph's lip trembled and he rubbed his eyes with a grimy finger.

"At last she struck her greatest blow against us, for Ralph fell into a fever. Terrible it was, he raved and sweated and cried – he was only eight years old, sir, and my mother's joy. She fell into a fever of fear herself, and my father in turn feared for her mind if Ralph should die. So he set off for the manor of Lord Marc and we never saw him alive again.

"Two days later Lord Marc's men came to the farm with my father's body across the horse's saddle like a bundle of dirty rags. My mother ran out into the yard and tore at the men. A blade flashed out and she died amid the muck of the farmyard."

Charity was silent for a moment and no one spoke. Ralph sniffed audibly into the silence.

"Since that day we have been left be," she said at last. "We cannot pay to replace the dead animals and much of the farm has turned back to heath, but we still have a few chickens, a cow and a handful of sheep and we grow vegetables for our table. The people of the villages and farms around fear to help us and indeed I believe that Demelza has told them that we are cursed. So we are left be and I am grateful for it."

All were silent for a moment as they contemplated the story. The knights had heard many such tales before and were hardly to be surprised by cruelty, but sitting with the boy and girl in the warm farmhouse kitchen they remembered their pledge to Arthur at his coronation and silently renewed their vow.

"We have friends bound for the manor of Lord Marc," Bedivere said at last, leaning back in his chair and sipping ale from the tankard before him on the table. "Your tale makes me wish we had stayed a little longer in their company."

Ralph's eyes lit up, "'Tis an army then, after all, and you are come to free us!"

"Nay!" Galahad laid his hand on Ralph's on the table. Ralph looked down at his strong fingers and the silver ring he bore, engraved with intricate patterns. "Not yet, my son. Not now. Now we come in small numbers on a difficult quest, and we must fear your enemies, not fight them at this hour."

Charity and Ralph were struck by his sombre tone. "What is the quest, my lord?" Charity asked shyly, "Are we permitted to know?"

The knights exchanged a glance and Bedivere nodded. Galahad rumpled his fair hair with a weary look as he answered.

"As you have dealt plainly, so will we. And indeed you come as welcome friends to us now. The truth is that we knights of the round table have ventured into your lands in search of five dragons. We know not where to find them, nor how fierce they will prove, but each bears a chain round its neck and on the chain a key. We are to recover the keys and return with them to Camelot."

Ralph jumped up excitedly. "Witch's breath! I know where one is to be found!"

"You do, my lad?" Bedivere eyed him with astonishment.

"Aye, aye, I saw the key you speak of only yesterday, and wondered where it came from, for the dragon did not bear it before."

"Is this the dragon that hoards its treasure in a cave hard by these parts?"

"Aye!"

"And are you indeed one of the lads we heard about, who goes to steal its treasure but never can succeed?"

Ralph looked a little haughty. "I know not of what others do. I have been there many a time, hoping to snatch some trifle that might buy us a horse for the farm again."

"I know it is too dangerous," Charity said, "but I cannot stop him, and he loves horses so much that it nags his liver that we do not have one now."

"And you saw the key?" Galahad asked, his eyes returning to the boy.

"Aye, only yesterday. I wondered how it had been put there and how the chain did not break, for it was fine and the key small."

Galahad kept no more secrets from them then, but told them all that had passed at Camelot. At first Ralph listened breathlessly, entranced by Galahad's descriptions of the castle and the knights. But as his tale lengthened and turned to the enchantment that had been laid on Arthur, Ralph flushed red and white by turns. At last, as Galahad concluded his tale, Ralph threw himself back in his chair and looked bleakly at the two knights.

"All is lost then," he said flatly. "All these years we have waited for Arthur to come and free us, and now we see that he cannot even save himself. Sorcery has mastery over all, and all hope is ended."

Galahad shook his head. He could see the same disappointment in the girl's eyes though she did not speak. "Nay, that is not so," he said. "I see that in the stories and legends of your land you have made Arthur into something he is not. No one man could defeat all evil single-handedly, not though he wielded the most powerful sword magic could supply. If he could, then Arthur would have been here long since to free you."

"We are but a band of brothers who follow him, and together we make up the round table," Bedivere added. "These last ten years have seen more and more join the work of the table, and in our lands life is good. But all have made it so, all have joined against sorcery and evil powers to share a peaceful life. It is the work of many, not of one man. You offered us fealty, Ralph, when we first met. May we still have it? Will you join the round table and work to destroy evil?"

Ralph stared for a moment as he digested Bedivere's words. It was Charity who replied. "Indeed, I will even if he will not. Are we not to struggle for all good things? But my heart misgives me concerning this dragon. I cannot see how you are to obtain the key."

Ralph rose and came to Galahad's side, and kneeling kissed the knight's silver ring, which he could see now was a symbol of the round table. "I will take you to the dragon," he said, "and you may decide what is best to be done. I will serve you in whatever way seems best to you sire."

Galahad looked at him, noting his tired face and red eyes, and a smile spread across his face. "I would be forever in your debt," he said, "if you would look in on my horse Blade before you go to your bed."

Ralph brightened and stood up with alacrity. "I could sleep in the stable, sire, if it would please you?"

Galahad smiled again. "It would please me well. Sleep in peace Ralph."

Ralph skipped out of the room suddenly light-hearted. Moments later he was snuggled down in the straw of the stable, listening to Blade's soft breathing and sniffing deeply the good, friendly horsy smell that he had missed so long.

The knights stayed in the kitchen until late, toasting their hands at the fire and talking quietly, while Charity sat darning clothes with her hair falling over her face. Galahad's eyes rested long on the maid, though when she looked up he looked away. At last, as the hour grew late, the knights took themselves off to the barn and wrapped themselves in their warm blankets on their pallets of hay. An owl hooted from the woods and Bedivere thought sleepily of the Merlin before falling into slumber.

Woods and Water

When the company woke the next morning in the manor of Lord Marc the Merlin had gone. He had come to Kay early, tapping on his window while it was still dark.

"I shall not leave you for long," the Merlin had said. "But I can feel that Bedivere and Galahad will soon face some test, and I would be with them when it comes. Meanwhile my advice is to watch for discord between the lord and his witch, for I have seen anger in his eyes when he looks at her. Keep a lookout for magic too, for Demelza will not suffer you to stay in her manor without attempting something against you. If you have your wits about you all will be well, so I do not fear overmuch."

"But what of the dragon?" Kay had asked, "Should we loiter here when the beast is somewhere to be found?"

"Patience, Kay," the Merlin replied. "If you leave now you will arouse suspicion in the lord's mind. And if the witch discovers the nature of your quest she can do much to annoy you."

Kay bowed to the Merlin's greater wisdom and watched him fly from the windowsill, circle high into the sky, and disappear into the dawn.

The knights were a little gloomy when they heard of the bird's departure, as they gathered by the lake after breakfast. "Does anyone have an inkling of how to bring the Lord Marc to friendship with us?" Gawain asked testily. Kay shook his head.

"The Merlin said that we should watch for disagreement between Lord Marc and Demelza," he replied. "Or indeed, for my own part, I suppose that we should look for any circumstance that might turn his suspicion of us to tolerance."

Guinevere had been listening with her back to the group, watching the ripples on the lake. There was barely a breath of wind but the water still seemed to live and move. Huge water lily pads covered a part of it, and she could see frog and toad spawn hanging in great chains and lumps from the foliage.

"I have seen something of interest," she said, "that makes me a trifle sorry for his lordship even if it does not seem to offer any chance that he will feel kindly towards us in return. Did you see his daughter Ruth at the banquet last night?"

"I saw her, but do not remember what she looked like, or what she wore," Lancelot replied. "She seemed a dowdy maiden."

Guinevere shook her head. "If she had been pretty no doubt you would have paid more attention. I had seen her earlier, from my window, coming from the woods. Very sad she seemed – too sad for such a young maid. And at dinner she was in truth dowdy as Lancelot calls it – quiet and unhappy. I could see that the Lord Marc watched her with something of sorrow and even despair in his glance. What story there is to tell I do not know, but I felt for both of them and liked him the more for it."

"Her mother is dead I suppose," Kay returned. "And Demelza taken over the running of the household. That would be enough to make the girl gloomy."

"Perhaps," Guinevere said. "But I felt there was more than ordinary sorrow to be told. I would help her if I could – for as you say, she has no woman to turn to."

"Do so," Lancelot said, casting Guinevere a kinder look than he had given her since leaving Camelot. "I remember the Merlin said you would give good counsel, and I see that you alone have noticed anything of interest here. Meanwhile we must exercise the patience we have learned over these last years, and no doubt something will come to help us."

As he spoke the Lord Marc appeared from the door of the manor dressed for the hunt, and a moment later the stable boys appeared leading the company's horses along with the Lord Marc's handsome bay gelding. The horses looked proud and eager despite the rigours of the previous days.

"Come, knights!" the Lord Marc said, with a vain attempt at levity in his gloomy face, "I would be a poor host indeed if I failed to show you the sport of my woods while you stay with me. The day bids fair, and I have ordered a meal to await us on our return. Will you hunt with me this morning? My park is home to many a noble stag."

The knights exchanged a glance and then nodded agreement with something a little closer to real pleasure than the Lord Marc had been able to feign. And indeed, not all of their joy was pretence. Lancelot's eyes gleamed as he looked on his horse ready for the hunt and the Lord Marc's dogs that came yelping around the corner from the stables. Wolf ran to meet them and a certain amount of growling and snapping had to be endured before the dogs became acquainted and ran off towards the wood, looking impatiently back to their masters who still stood by the steps.

Only Guinevere refused, pleading the fatigue of the previous day's journey. Lord Marc urged her to change her mind but she was firm.

"No," she said. "The woods and water here by the house look too inviting for me to resist them on this fine spring morning. Do you go on, and I shall be a better audience for your tales at supper than if I accompanied you for the day."

The Lord Marc gave her a searching look as she spoke but then yielded. "Let me not disturb your pleasures," he said, a little stiffly. "Should you be lonely you will find Demelza in the upper chamber working her embroidery as she does each day."

Guinevere inclined her head politely, but she had no intention of seeking the witch out. Kay looked at her with concern. "Would it please you for one of us to remain with you, my lady?"

Guinevere shook her head. "Nay, Sir Kay, though I thank you. Perhaps the Lady Ruth might show me the grounds, my lord?"

The Lord Marc looked agitated as he answered, and his tone was a little less stiff. "Indeed, my lady, I would be delighted if she would. However, she escapes into the forest every morning and does not return till evening. If you walk in the woods you may meet her."

"She seems troubled, my lord," Guinevere ventured, as boldly as she dared. "Does she suffer some malady or has some sorrow befallen her?"

For a moment the Lord Marc hesitated, then he spoke more freely than before and with more warmth. "I am a widower as you see, my lady. My wife died when Ruth was born, and I have brought her up as best a father may. She was a merry child, and loved by all until this last winter. Then she fell into this sorrow and we cannot lift it from her. It is as though some enchantment has been placed on her, but Demelza swears that no magic save her own may enter our house or grounds. Demelza treats her with every spell she can devise, but Ruth falls deeper into sorrow each day."

Guinevere felt genuinely sorry for the Lord Marc as his shoulders sagged. "I see you love your daughter well," she replied, with the first real warmth she had shown him. Lord Marc raised his eyes to hers with a look of hunger that struck at her heart. The poor man, she thought, has had no love since his daughter fell ill. "I will look for her in the woods," she went on, holding out her hand to him. "Perhaps she may reveal to a stranger thoughts she cannot share with those she loves."

"I pray you will find her, my lady," he returned. "But stray not too far or we may mistake you for a stag."

Guinevere laughed. "I shall listen well for the dogs!"

The knights mounted then, and with a clatter the hunt moved off across the roadway and onto the soft peaty soil of the forest edge. The sound of the horses' hooves changed to a dull thud and they vanished into the wood. Kay looked back and Guinevere raised her hand to him. Wolf came scampering back to nose her hand, then both were gone, Wolf bounding after the others into the trees.

It seemed very quiet after they had left. Guinevere looked around at the park, which suddenly seemed drear and empty. The sun had gone in behind a cloud and the lake looked cold and grey. A breeze blew across the water sending ripples across its surface. Guinevere glanced up at the windows of the manor and saw that Demelza was standing in one of them, watching her. Afraid that the witch would seek her out, Guinevere turned and walked purposefully away into the wood.

It was warmer as soon as she stepped into the shelter of the trees. Sweet smells assailed her from dog-violets which lay half hidden by leaves at the edge of the path. Primroses studded the ground, and late daffodil blooms lay tumbled here and there as though mown by a scythe. Guinevere immediately felt better than she had done out by the lake and set off at a brisk walk. The path lay straight and clear before her, with the horses' hoof prints clear to be seen in the soft earth. She listened for the sound of the men's voices, but they had gone swiftly and were now too far ahead to be heard.

After several minutes the track began to curve gently to the right and ahead was another broad footpath branching away to the left. The hoof prints continued on the first path and, mindful of the Lord Marc's warning, she struck off on the second.

The new track wound through the trees, gradually narrowing and becoming more uneven as tree roots snaked across the path. Guinevere wished then that she had put on her breeches that morning, but it was too late now and she made the best of her light shoes and long gown. Now the path turned to the right, meeting a stream and following along its bank. The gurgle and splash of the stream was a cheerful sound in the silence and solitude of the forest, and she stopped for a while, leaning on a tree stump and watching the water tumble over a small waterfall formed from stones and branches. Out of the corner of her eye she caught the elusive blue flash of a kingfisher, but watch as she might it did not return.

Then Guinevere saw a footprint in the soft mud at the water's edge and bent to look closer. It was the print of a girl's shoe and her heart lifted, in hope that Ruth might after all be near. She scanned the ground more carefully and then saw that there were more prints on the far bank. Ruth had crossed the stream by using the waterfall as a bridge and scrambled up the far bank into denser woodland. On an impulse Guinevere gathered up her skirt and crossed the stream across the same slippery stones. She panted up the bank and saw ahead of her in a clearing the girl, sitting on a mossy stone, deep in reflection.

Guinevere watched for a moment, afraid of startling her, then stepped forward with a cheerful greeting. Ruth looked up and made as if to fly, but then recognised her father's guest and stood at bay, clearly wishing to leave but prevented by her good breeding.

"You will think that I have been tracking you," Guinevere laughed, holding out her hand, "but indeed I have not! I hoped to meet you in the wood but was wandering at my own will until by chance I saw your footprint by the stream."

"Nothing happens by chance here," Ruth returned without a smile. "You saw the print no doubt because you hoped to find me and the forest allowed you to do so."

Guinevere looked around at the trees and gave a mock shiver. "Woods do indeed seem sometimes as though they think and even watch us," she agreed.

"There is no 'seem' here," Ruth said, as soberly as before. "Every morning I wake in the hope that I will escape the forest. But each day it pulls me in and I cannot resist it."

Guinevere's eyes widened and she stepped forward holding out her hand. "My dear, have you told your father of this feeling?"

"Nay." The girl shook her head. "If I try to speak to my father now the words freeze in my mouth. I have been silent before him for many weary months. I am under a heavy enchantment, my lady, and I cannot shake myself free. I am drawn to the woods each day, and each day I wither a little more, and each day the woods grow greener as though they thrive on my sorrow."

Guinevere caught Ruth's hand in hers and pressed it. "These are black thoughts, Lady Ruth!" she said. "If we at Camelot have learned anything it is that magic always withers before a strong will. If you believe yourself enchanted then the sorcerer's power will grow."

"It is not a matter of belief but of fact, my lady, though I can see that you would not easily credit my tale."

"Your father told me of the change that this winter has wrought in you, but he insists that no magic can reach you here."

"Only magic, my lady, that is already within."

"Who do you suspect then? Demelza?"

"Aye, Demelza," Ruth replied. "Ever she has envied my father's love for me. Now she turns it to herself by her seeming efforts to save me from the spells she herself has laid!"

"And does your father not suspect this?"

"I believe he does, if he will only admit it to himself. But Demelza has watched over us for so long that he fears to part with her."

"Come, Ruth! Come with me!" Guinevere said. "Let us quit the wood together and set the witch at naught. I broke one of her spells yesterday and I will defeat another today!"

Ruth allowed herself to be pulled back in the direction of the water. But when they came to the bank, the stream had changed. Now it flowed smooth and deep with no waterfall and no stepping stones. Guinevere stopped, puzzled, at the edge.

We have come down to the bank at a different place," she said, uncertainly. "Was it more to the right or left that we crossed before?"

Ruth did not reply, but pointed silently to the ground. On both sides of the stream their footprints were clearly visible. "We have not gone amiss," the girl said dully, "it is the stream that has altered."

It was far too deep and strong to cross now, so Guinevere led the way leftwards along the bank. Soon a tangle of brambles and young nettles reared before her and she was obliged to lead the way back up the bank away from the water. They followed the stream as best they could, but they could find no way down to the edge again. Indeed the ground began rising and soon there was a steep drop to the water below. The brambles thickened on both sides, tearing at their clothes and scratching their ankles.

After half an hour of such labour Ruth stopped in a welcome clearing and sat down on a stone again. "Let us rest," she said, "and the woods may rearrange themselves a little. Always they allow me home by nightfall, and there is little profit in fruitless searching in the heat of the day."

Guinevere seized Ruth's hand. At first she had doubted Ruth's tale but not now. "Nay, Ruth! We must fight the spell, not give in to it. Let us go on!"

Ruth shrugged and rose wearily to her feet. On they went, for a long time, turning ever leftwards until Guinevere felt they must be walking in ever widening spirals and roaming far from the manor. Now she too felt afraid and drear. The sun was past its height and the afternoon light seemed to be fading early. The trees were so green and the shadows so dim, and the sky above so covered by young leaves that all at once she began to run, even though she knew she should not. Ruth shouted something behind her but Guinevere sped on as though chased by demons. On she fled until her chest was tight and her breath painful. She could hear Ruth running behind her, infected now with the same alarm. Branches slapped her face and roots tripped her feet, then all at once a confusion of sounds and colours assailed her senses. All around her was the baying of hounds and the circling of men and horses. She had run directly from the trees into the group of knights where they had gathered in a clearing. As she fell to her knees gasping a prayer of thanksgiving there was a terrible cry from behind her.

"My daughter!" the Lord Marc cried, his keening sobs suddenly and horribly echoing through the trees. "My daughter!"

Ruth lay senseless among the tangled bushes whence they had run, an arrow through her shoulder. Lancelot stood aghast, his bow in his hand hanging limp at his side. Lord Marc fell to his knees, cradling Ruth's head in his lap and sobbing without restraint. Gawain jumped from his horse and strode over to the injured girl while the dogs yelped and whined in agitation from under the horses' hooves, and Kay and Mordred tended to Guinevere who had fainted at their feet.

"My fault is grave," Lancelot cried. "I have failed in all chivalry to have wounded such a one as she."

"Nay Lancelot," the Lord Marc replied through his tears, his fairness overcoming his grief, "'twas fate or worse that led her into your path in such haste like a bounding stag. I too stood ready to shoot. What troubles me is her flight, and that of your lady Guinevere. How they came to meet, and how they came to fly in such ill-fated haste?"

"We may yet find the answer," Gawain said, "when either lady recovers her senses. Get away Wolf!"

Wolf had crept up to Gawain's elbow and unnoticed begun to lick Ruth's hand. Now he started forward with a gentle growl and began to wash her face with his great wet tongue. Gawain raised his hand to the dog as if to strike him but then forbore. Ruth had opened her eyes and was smiling at Wolf with tear-filled eyes. As he gently licked her cheek she laughed weakly and raised her uninjured hand to his shaggy coat.

~

They carried the Lady Ruth back to the manor on a makeshift litter and put her to bed. Then Gawain came to tend to her shoulder, brushing Demelza aside as she hobbled to the chamber door. The Lord Marc did not intervene and Demelza's lips tightened as she cast the old man a spiteful look. After Gawain had removed the arrow and bound the wound with fresh bandages the witch took his place by the bedside and stared at the assembled faces until they bowed to her indomitable will and left her alone with the maid. Only Wolf refused to quit the chamber.

Guinevere felt uneasy, but unsure what to do or say. As yet she had told nothing of their flight through the wood, and could hardly believe her own fears among the trees now that she stood in the safety of the manor with her friends about her. She opened her mouth to beg the Lord Marc's attention but then stayed silent. Having brought his daughter so close to death she feared to rouse his wrath with an improbable tale.

Instead she went to the upper chamber with the other knights and stood by the fire, resisting their attempts to make her rest. Demelza's embroidery lay abandoned on a chair by the fire, thrown down amid the confused clatter of their return from the forest.

Guinevere studied it idly as she warmed her hands at the blaze, marvelling again that anything so beautiful could be the work of the crone.

But then she noticed something. With an exclamation she picked up the hoop to study the work more closely, for she could see that there were new areas of changes and unpicked stitches in the piece today. The part that showed the gravel road through the park was still half-finished as before, but now there were new bare patches, this time among the vibrant greens and browns of the forest. Guinevere traced the uneven patches where the stitches had been pulled out and some reworked. They made a haphazard line, spiralling senselessly through the embroidered trees, and Guinevere knew with a sudden certainty that it traced exactly the path she and Ruth had trodden through the woods that day in their bewilderment and fear.

She looked up and broke into the knights' hushed discourse behind her.

"Sir Kay!" she said in her soft, clear voice.

"My lady?"

"I have a fancy to walk a little and settle my mind after these troubles. Will you come with me?"

"Gladly, ma'am, if you think you are fit for it."

They descended the stairs to the hall and stepped out on to the stone flagstones before the door. Guinevere pulled her cloak around her with an involuntary shiver and Kay looked at her with concern, but he made no objection as she began to walk up the gravelled roadway through the park, by which they had arrived the previous day.

"You are wise, my lady," he said. "We have all had enough of woods."

She inclined her head without speaking and they walked on in a companionable silence.

"It is a curious thing," Kay said after some time. "But this road does not seem to be as I remember it from yesterday."

"Indeed?" Guinevere's tone was calm, but she said no more. On they walked, up the steady incline from the house until Kay stopped with an oath, staring at the road ahead with a look of disbelief. Guinevere stopped too, looking by turns at Kay's face and then at the view before them. Although they had been walking up the slope directly away from the manor, now, as they breasted the hill, they found themselves looking down the other side to the bridge and the lake and the woods and the manor before them just as they had left it.

"What madness is this?" Kay asked. "Have we mistook our path?"

"Nay," Guinevere said, "come and see." She turned and retraced their steps to the brow of the hill. Sure enough, there behind them was the same prospect. Back or forwards there was no choice but to return to the manor.

"We are bewitched as the Merlin said we should be!" Kay exclaimed, involuntarily clutching his sword. "Bewitched and trapped! We must rouse the others and beset the witch or our quest will end in shame and imprisonment before it has begun." He made to run for the manor but then paused, uncertain which of the two paths to take. Guinevere laid her hand on his sleeve.

"We are enchanted indeed," she said, "but this is not the first time I have been so today. And I believe that I know the manner of the spell and the remedy. I brought you here to test my guess, and I wager that whatever way we turn from this spot we will soon find ourselves at the manor door once more. Let us return there then, as speedily as we may, for if we act wisely we may save others from enchantment as well as ourselves."

As they strode back down the hill to the manor Guinevere told Kay all of her day's adventures. Up the steps and into the hall they went. Kay bounded up the stairs, his sword and spurs jangling, and burst into the upper chamber with Guinevere on his heels. The Lord Marc and Demelza stood before the fire amazed, while the knights wheeled about to stare. Kay strode the length of the room his eye fixed on the witch, and she fell back, beginning to jabber oaths at him as he came.

"See my lord!" she cried, "I told you they meant us harm! Save me my lord! Save me!" her voice rose to a shriek as Kay reached her side and grasped her arm. The Lord Marc started forward, his hand going to his sword, but before he could pull it from its sheath the other knights had drawn their own weapons and stood around the pair in a grim semi-circle, swords glinting an inch or so from their throats.

Kay had no time for the witch, however. Instead he pushed her aside and grasped the hoop of embroidery that still lay abandoned on her chair. At this the witch began to scream, shrill and long, so that

Guinevere covered her ears as she pushed through the knights to reach Kay's side. With one deft motion he threw the thing, hoop and all, into the fire.

For a moment it only smouldered. Demelza threw herself forwards as if to drag it back from the flames, but Kay caught her by the shoulders and held her, spitting and clawing at his face.

"Fool!" the witch screamed at the Lord Marc. "Fool, are you to stand there while all we have wrought turns to smoke and ashes?" But the Lord Marc stood stupefied, his arms hanging at his sides, watching the fabric as it finally caught alight and began to burn, the hoop melting and bending over the hot embers.

And then, all at once, the world went dark and the floor beneath them quivered. All that could be seen in the blackness was the fire and the burning hoop. Guinevere could hear the whinnying of the horses from the stable, and the frightened cries of the servants from the hall below as the building itself seemed to shake and buckle like the melting hoop in the flames. She shut her eyes dismayed at what they had done. In the darkness Demelza slipped from Kay's grasp like water and was gone.

When light returned those in the upper chamber of the manor blinked at each other dazed and trembling. Guinevere had feared that the very fabric of the building would fall as the house in the picture burned, but the manor itself survived. It was when they looked out of the window that they could see what had happened. The Lord Marc grasped the windowsill with whitened knuckles and bent his head.

Lake and woods and park and roadway, all were gone. Instead the manor now stood in the midst of a bleak and featureless heath. All that remained of what had been was a rough sheep track meandering up the hill out of sight towards Bodmin, and a moorland brook running past the door.

The company from Camelot clattered down the stairs and out into the grounds. The trees were gone and they wandered on the short, springy heathland turf in amazement, turning often to reassure themselves that the manor still stood. It seemed unchanged − if a little less mellow, for all the ivy and moss on its old stones was now gone. But though the prospect was bleak there was a freshness in the air that felt more wholesome than what had gone before. It almost made them want to run and shout for joy in the empty landscape. Gawain said it best when he declared to Lancelot, "I did not know that I was imprisoned, but now I feel that we are free at last!"

Then the Lord Marc emerged from the door and descended the steps slowly, looking about him like one dreaming. Lancelot went to his side and took his arm, and the Lord Marc made no objection.

"It was all an enchantment then, sire?" Lancelot asked tentatively as the Lord Marc gazed about him.

"So it seems, Lancelot, so it seems," the old man returned. He looked around him again and began to laugh quietly, even as a tear stole down his cheek. The knights watched without speaking. After a moment he met their wondering eyes, and held out a hand to them.

"It is as though I have returned through time," he said. "Just thus looked the manor the day I came into possession of it as a young man. The trees and the lake were all the work of Demelza, I now see, though I took no heed as it came. I believed that she speeded the growth of the forest by some benign magic but I never dreamt that none of it was real at all."

"Reality can be better than a dream, however beautiful," Kay said, taking his hand and dropping to his knee. "Forgive me if I have broken this dream too rudely."

The Lord Marc looked at him then like one amazed, and seemed at last to realise how the spell had been broken. And as he remembered Kay's hand thrusting the enchanted hoop into the fire, impotent fury lit in his eyes and he snatched away his hand, opening his mouth to speak bitter words.

But at that moment a serving maid appeared behind him on the steps. "My lord!" she cried. "The Lady Ruth is asking for you!"

~

Wolf slept by Ruth's bed from that hour. His was the first face she looked for when she woke, and she fell to slumber with her hand on his neck. Wolf and the Lord Marc spent many an hour at her bedside, and the Lord Marc was wont to joke that he knew not whether to credit the knights or the dog with his daughter's recovery. Ruth was well though. Her shoulder bid fair to heal, and at last all thoughts began to turn to the fulfilment of their quest. There was no sign of the Merlin, but the knights felt little need of his counsel now that magic was defeated at the manor.

When the knights unfolded their true purpose to him, the Lord Marc frowned and rested his chin on his long pale fingers looking thoughtful. "Just such a one as your master have I been, though I could move and speak within my enchantment," he said. "I can find you a dragon, however, no doubt of that. These parts have been terrorised by a beast of that kind for many years. It dwells in a pool, they say, on the moor whence it plunders the surrounding villages." He paused, and a look of doubt crossed his face. "Or at least, so Demelza told me. I never saw the creature with my own eyes, but we have been obliged to send it much coin and countless treasures over the years to blunt its wrath."

The knights said nothing. They sat quietly, and none met the Lord Marc's eyes as he spoke. The old man reflected for a moment and then laughed dryly. "Well, we shall soon see if I have been a fool in all matters. I will rouse the tenants and my own men, and we will march on the beast to see if it exists or not."

It took three days to gather the Lord Marc's people together from the outlying farms, days that Guinevere spent at Ruth's bedside and the knights spent exploring the new landscape around the manor. During that time no sight nor sound was heard of the witch and Ruth grew merrier by the day, feeding Wolf scraps from her plate and teasing Guinevere for tales of the great ladies of the court at Camelot. She studied Guinevere's face, eager to learn the womanly graces that she had never seen, and Guinevere grew to love her as a daughter, both for her present merriment and her previous sorrow. Ruth loved to hear of Guinevere's own childhood, and one day as Guinevere tended her Ruth asked to hear the tale of her first meeting with Arthur.

"I was but your age, Ruth," Guinevere told her, "and like you I was the only child to a great lord. But I had no old witch to trouble me, and my days were as happy as yours used to be and will be again. Yet like all young maids I dreamed a little of my future, of the husband I should have, and the manor, and the children. Someone would come, I knew, for my father was a great man, and many would seek an alliance with him. I hoped it would be someone I could love, but I believed my father would not make me unhappy with a man I hated." As she spoke she stood up to gaze out of the window as if she could see the events of that long distant day unfolding on the heath below.

"Then one day I was flying my merlin on the castle green and the bird flew over the wall and was lost, just as happened the other day at Camelot. I was sorry, for it was a bird I loved and I was afraid of my father's wrath too, for he was a quick-tempered man for all his kindness. So I ran after it out of the gates. I called and called, but there was no sign of it. Far I wandered into the wood, all alone, even though I knew that my wandering would only make my father angrier still. And then suddenly before me I beheld Arthur, trudging along, leading his horse.

I was a little afraid to meet a man in such a lonely place, but I looked again and saw he was a knight. His mail shirt hung over his saddle, for it was a hot day, and he was all alone. I remember thinking how brave he was to go along so defenceless.

We met, I curtsied, and he soon saw that I was a lady and no serving maid. He told me he was coming to my father for aid and counsel. Then he asked me what I was doing alone in the wood and I told him of my missing bird. With that he smiled, and whistled a long quiet note. A moment later a merlin swooped through the trees and landed on his arm.

For a moment I thought that it was my bird, and that Arthur was some kind of wizard, but of course it was our own Merlin, who spoke to me with much courtesy and promised to search out my bird. Off he flew, and I walked with Arthur back towards the castle. And from that moment until this trouble fell on us I was never afraid again, for I felt peace in my heart in Arthur's company and we spoke of many things as though we had known each other always. At the gates the Merlin reappeared with my own bird behind him and we went into the castle to greet my father. Since then I have often wondered whether the Merlin called my bird away from the castle to draw me into the wood to meet my lord."

"And what was Arthur like then?"

"Older than me by ten years, about the age that Galahad is now. If you saw Galahad then you would know a little of Arthur, for they are alike. Both were conceived under an enchantment and a little magic lingers about them still. But where Galahad shines like the sun, Arthur makes me think of the sea. His eyes are grey and still, but like the peaceful ocean there is power beneath."

"Indeed! And did that not scare you?"

Guinevere smiled. "None fears Arthur but the creatures of magic, and even they would love him if he would let them. None meets Arthur but wishes to have his good opinion. I am persuaded that even Morgan le Fay acted out of love, for she could not bear him to reject magic, and her along with it."

"And so you loved him at once?"

"I did, and I felt as though nothing could harm me if he were near. Indeed all feel that, which makes this enchantment upon him so hard to bear."

Ruth was silent for a moment, meditating on the story, as Guinevere began to move quietly about the room tending the flowers that the Lord Marc's hand had laid on the windowsill.

"It is strange that Galahad should resemble Arthur when they are no kin. Is Galahad not like Lancelot at all?"

"Alike in beauty they are, but not in temper. Lancelot is stern in war but merry in his own self, and many a maid has he wooed in fun. Galahad will never do so, nor did Arthur, for both were born to fulfil a prophecy and both know themselves to be made for a higher purpose. Galahad awaits the fated companion for his life's struggles just as the king did."

"And that companion was you!" Ruth gazed on Guinevere's lovely face with admiration as the queen came to sit once more by her bedside. Then a frown appeared between her brows and Guinevere smiled questioningly.

"I cannot believe that any man could be more handsome or more noble than Lancelot."

"You would not say so if you saw his son. Galahad is the handsomest and gentlest of all men. And perhaps you will meet him now that there is peace between our houses."

Ruth sat up eagerly, and then winced, clutching her shoulder. "Oh, how I should love to visit you at Camelot!" she said, clasping her hands. "But yet I would be bashful of Galahad, if I met him. He is too near my own age for comfort. I can admire Lancelot safe in the knowledge that he will never notice me."

Guinevere laughed but a shadow crossed her face as she smoothed the bed cover with gentle hands. Ruth watched her and then spoke more hesitantly, looking curious. "My father says that you are to go with Lancelot on the next stage of the quest, once our own dragon is vanquished."

Guinevere shook her head. "I cannot see beyond this first trial, Ruth. If we do not defeat the dragon on the moor the next stage may never come."

I met a lady in the meads,
Full beautiful – a faery's child,
Her hair was long, her foot was light
And her eyes were wild.

Dragons

Galahad was woken by the sound of a bucket clanking in the yard. The blue dusk of daybreak lay over the farm and the air felt dank and cold. He shivered and pulled his blanket further up to his ears, snuggling down into the soft hay and shutting his eyes. He could not sleep again, though. The clanking of the bucket meant milking time, he realised, as he heard Charity's quiet voice and the soft rhythmic breathing of the cow in the barn next door. Then he heard the clatter of Ralph's wooden clogs across the yard, growing more faint as he passed through the gate into the hens' field whence he had come running helter-skelter the previous evening. Galahad smiled as he remembered the boy's round eyes and furious haste. A pause followed, punctuated only by the sounds of milking, then Ralph's footsteps returned and receded again in the direction of the stable. Now Galahad could see that the daylight was growing. The rectangle of blue in the barn doorway was turning yellow, and he could hear birds beginning to sing in the hedgerow. A pair of swallows suddenly woke in the rafters above him and flew from the barn with a clatter.

He must have dozed for a moment, for the next thing he saw was Ralph's face peering down at him shyly, silhouetted against the growing brightness of the day. He looked relieved to see Galahad wake, but spoke in a hushed whisper for fear of disturbing Bedivere.

"I come for some hay for the horses, sire. Pardon me if I climb about you for a moment."

Galahad nodded and watched as Ralph stuffed hay into netting sacks.

"Once Charity's finished with the cow 'twill be breakfast time," Ralph said as he stepped over Galahad's feet and headed for the door. "Come to the kitchen, sire, if you be hungry."

Galahad lay for a moment longer, then sighed, unwrapped his blanket from his legs, and sat up. Hay stuck to his hair and clothes and he felt grimy, but it would be too much trouble to bathe. He pulled his shirt over his head and boots onto his feet and stood up. Bedivere grumbled in his sleep and Galahad touched his shoulder gently.

"Breakfast time, my lord, if it please you," he said. Bedivere opened one eye to look at him and rolled over with his back to the daylight with a groan. Galahad picked up his jerkin and walked out into the yard in time to see Charity emerge from the cowshed with a brimming pail of milk. They exchanged a nod, then she went into the kitchen and Galahad dipped his face and hands in the trough to clear the sleep from his eyes.

Fully awake at last he looked around at the day. It had been raining hard overnight and now the yard shone as though sluiced clean. The air was clear and the eastern sky was pink and gold.

"Looks like a fine day in prospect," he said to Ralph as the boy emerged from the stable. "But you have been waking for a long while already. Do you rise before dawn every day?"

"Every day until the sun catches up with me, sire," Ralph grinned. "Then in June it wakes me up!"

"It must be grand to be out so early then."

"It is that, for all the birds and animals are waking along with me. But then I cannot stay awake until nightfall, so all works out the same." He stepped from one foot to the other apologetically. "I must needs feed the chickens, sire. I will not be long if you'll wait in the kitchen."

"I will come with you. Then you need not fear I'll eat your share of the breakfast."

They stepped out over the meadow, Galahad taking long strides and looking about him with interest, Ralph running along at his side. A buzzard clattered out from the hedgerow almost under their feet and swooped upwards on its blunt wings, and they exchanged a look and laughed.

"He would be a fine fellow to send into the lists."

"Do you have a falcon, my lord?"

"Nay. That is too sober a pursuit for me. I like to feel my bones rattle a little in my sports after a day's government."

"Government? What is that?"

Galahad laughed. "It is what I do, Ralph. I govern my people as best I can, which means looking after them and resolving their quarrels."

"I wish you governed here."

"Your Lord Marc should do that. Perhaps my friends will teach him."

When they came to the hen house the birds came running towards them eagerly, looking for their early morning corn. Galahad took a handful and scattered it, smiling as a grain fell on his boot and the boldest bird pecked it off. With a swift hand Ralph scooped it up and looked it in the eye. It was a young cockerel, not yet fully grown, and it jabbed its beak at him as he held it by the neck.

"This one'll do for our supper, sire. He's a rare nuisance, for he's too bold, and we have cockerels enough."

Galahad laid a finger on the bird's feathery head. "He pays a high price for his courage then, as all warriors do in the end. Still, it seems good to make peace with a meal before we eat it." Even as he spoke the bird's beak snapped forward and Galahad put his finger to his mouth with an oath. Then he caught Ralph's eye and they laughed.

"Come, show me how you kill him," Galahad said, "for he has lost my sympathy now. And I shall help you pluck him, if you like, for the birds on my table appear roasted and golden with no pains on my part. I believe I owe the world a little labour in return for the good things I get."

They began to walk back down towards the farmhouse, the cockerel hanging from Ralph's hand, and Galahad sniffed the air appreciatively. "A grand day for a dragon hunt maybe," he said as they reached the yard. Then he cast Ralph a sidelong look that Guinevere would hardly have recognised, for it contained mischief as well as friendship. "Now, can you tell that sluggardly companion of mine that he needs must rise, or lose his breakfast?"

Ralph grinned and skipped off to the hayloft to deliver his message. Galahad looked in on the horses and was both touched and amused to see that Ralph had already groomed and fed them and polished their harness. He stroked their noses for a moment before leaving the stable and walking over to the kitchen.

Charity was cutting the remains of last night's loaf into thick slices when he entered, and setting them on the table next to bowls of warm fresh milk. She blushed when she saw him and looked down, wiping her hands awkwardly on her apron.

"Did you sleep well?" she asked.

"Aye, sound and deep," Galahad returned, sitting down at the table. As she turned away he examined her young face and smiled to himself at the wholesomeness of the farm and its inhabitants. She was pleasant to look upon, clean and sweet. Her face was broad like

Ralph's and faintly freckled, but her skin was pale and clear, her brown eyes were ringed with dark lashes and stray curls of her dark hair escaped from her cap.

Bedivere entered then, darkening the doorway for a moment, followed by Ralph. Charity produced butter and cheese for the bread and they broke their fast with zeal.

"This impudent young colt told me to rouse myself or miss my breakfast," Bedivere said with the pretence of a scowl towards Ralph. "He compounded his impudence by telling me that this was a message from you, Galahad."

"Having been rudely awakened from my own slumber by the snorting of a cow, it troubled me to imagine you lying there still fast asleep and snoring near as loud as the beast herself."

"Respect thy elders," Bedivere addressed Ralph who was gawking at Galahad round-eyed. "That is a valuable lesson and not one to be learned this morning from my young companion. Methinks the country air is rubbing away at his courtly manners."

"I believe so," Galahad replied cheerfully. "I must say that I have slept sounder tonight on a pallet of hay than I have for many a moon in my own chamber. I believe the country air agrees with me."

"That may account for your deep slumber – that or the trials of the last days," Bedivere observed. Galahad's merry smile faded abruptly, and he nodded.

"Aye. Well, those trials must be cured and we must do our part. Ralph is to take us to the dragon's lair this morning and we can make our plans thereafter."

"How far is it to the cave?"

"Three hours' march my lord," Ralph said, "that is, by foot. With horses I daresay it would be quicker, but I am not sure if the way is passable on four legs."

"Nay, let us walk," Galahad said, his good spirits banishing his sober look again. "The day bids fair and we have ridden enough over the last days. It will be good to stretch our legs and have time for thought and talk. Let us take some bread and milk with us and enjoy the journey, even if the beast that lies at the end of it is an unwelcome sight." He turned to Charity. "Will you come with us?"

"Nay," she shook her head. "There is much for me to do about the farm."

"In truth? What tasks await you?"

Charity looked a little confused. "Oh – washing clothes and cleaning out the hen house and wringing a cockerel's neck for your supper."

Galahad exchanged a look with Ralph. "Does your sister ever come walking with you?"

"Not often," Ralph admitted. "She lingers close to the farm."

Galahad took her hand and patted it kindly. "Come with us today, Charity. Leave your chores and take some pleasure and exercise. You have had the cares of a mother thrust early upon you, and you deserve some liberty. When we return Ralph and I will sweep the hen house. The cockerel is already hanging in the barn and I promised Ralph I would learn to pluck it, for even a knight must know how to cook his supper. And your clothes will wait till tomorrow, I daresay, without washing."

Charity dropped her eyes and nodded silently, overcome by the unaccustomed kindness, and a tear slid down her cheek as she rose to stack the dirty dishes. Ralph and Galahad walked out into the farmyard and the boy began to chatter freely, his voice receding as they wandered away towards the barn. Even Bedivere was infected by Galahad's enthusiasm and rose to help Charity carry the dirty dishes to the yard pump.

"Galahad is happier than I have seen him for a long while, despite our troubles," he remarked. "He enjoys your brother's young company and the freedom of the quest. We have laboured long and hard in our own lands and I see now that he has missed the pleasures of youth with government thrust so early upon him." He smiled at her. "Like you, Charity, he deserves some playtime."

~

It was pleasant to walk along the cliff path in the bright spring sunshine which turned the sea a deep turquoise blue and the short heathy grass under their feet emerald green. Bedivere strode along easily despite the hauberk of mail that hung to his knees and his sword strapped to his side. He carried his helmet under his arm – all precautions lest the dragon be caught unawares and open to attack.

The others walked ahead, the young folks half-running to keep up with Galahad's long strides. Bedivere thought that he looked like a young colt between them, while the boy and girl watched him with shining eyes and hung on his every word. He too was dressed for battle, but he had left his helmet behind. When Bedivere had reminded him he had only laughed.

"Well, I have forgot it by chance," he said, "and chance shall rule the day no doubt. If it comes to a fight I shall put my neck in fate's noose and fear not the outcome."

Bedivere stared a little as Galahad regaled the young ones with tales of battles, jousts and hunts with unusual freedom. But then the young knight turned the talk to their own doings about the farm. He quizzed Ralph about the plough and the care of the animals, and made Charity explain how she turned the cow's milk into butter and cheese. He listened with such interest that they soon forgot their shyness and told him of their mistakes and mishaps on the farm till at last they all flung themselves onto the grass breathless with laughter.

After a cold lunch of bread and milk they resumed their walk. Now the cliffs began to fall towards the sea and they could see great sand dunes along the coast ahead.

"Here the rocks are weaker," Ralph said, waving an arm to take in the whole prospect, "the sand is soft and plentiful and where the sea pounds against the cliff it has worn away many a cave. The dragon lives here, below our feet, here at the eastern end of the dunes, in a cave under the cliff."

Bedivere and Galahad halted and spoke together in earnest tones. Then they lay down on their bellies and squirmed to the cliff edge, scanning the beach below and looking for a path to descend by. Ralph crawled to join them.

"The path is a little further on," he said. "It winds down the cliff to the beach where the mouth of the cave lies straight before you."

"Is there no other way down?"

"Nay, I have tried many, but all are too steep and too slippery. There is but the one way."

The knights sat up and looked at each other ruefully. "There is no hope from surprise then," Galahad said. "If the dragon watches the path it will see us approach long before we can even catch a glimpse of it."

Bedivere nodded. "Nevertheless we must go down and see its lair, and the beast itself if we can. Some idea may come to us when we see the lie of the land."

They slid and scrambled down the cliff path to the sand. Ralph pointed to the dark mouth of a cave several yards away across the beach. It was low and narrow and Galahad felt cheered – the beast could not be so large if it could fit through such a gap, he thought.

At that moment a cloud of smoke issued suddenly from the mouth of the cave, followed by the largest snout Galahad had ever seen. It filled the opening and he cried out in his amazement. His shout seemed to provoke the dragon as a blue-hot torch of flame erupted from its nostrils and issued for yards across the sands. Even from where they stood they could feel the heat, and they raised their hands to protect their eyes from the glare.

"And you thought to steal this monster's treasure single-handed?" Galahad asked Ralph in disbelief. Ralph did not reply but pointed excitedly towards the beast.

"Look, look!" he cried. "The key!"

The knights looked again, to see that the dragon had somehow snaked its head sideways through the opening and was now regarding them balefully, its head and neck in full daylight. Its scales shone like wet pebbles, tawny brown, red, and black. Its eyes were orange, and it was looking at them with undisguised fury. Around its neck was a silver chain, and the key they sought dangled from it like a tiny jewel.

"It cannot get out," Galahad said. "The cave mouth is too small. It has been trapped by its own treasure, even as it believed itself to be the master. Now it cannot help but guard it, for it has no other choice."

The dragon let out another blast of fire and they heard Charity scream with fright behind them. Galahad spoke to Ralph.

"Go tell your sister that she is safe, for the beast cannot come at us. Then stay there, out of harm's way." Ralph opened his mouth to argue then changed his mind and scampered off.

"It is a hopeless task," Galahad said. "We cannot hope to hurt it, even with arrows, for it will but withdraw into its lair. We cannot tempt it out, and we cannot come near enough to steal the key."

"It must sleep," Bedivere returned. "If we could wait till then, we could creep into the cave and snatch the key. The chain ought to break for it is fine enough."

"Ought to," Galahad objected, "but will not, or it would have already done so. And if we were able to enter the cave, the chance of leaving it again alive, let alone with the key, is a faint one."

Bedivere frowned and scratched his head. "Well, we have found the key at least. We must ponder long, I see, on how to regain it. I hope the others' quest is not so hopeless."

The dragon watched them as they spoke with an unblinking eye, and Galahad suddenly fancied that it was listening to their talk. On an impulse he hailed it.

"Hi! Dragon!"

The beast blinked, and smoke issued from its nostrils.

"We have come to take the key that hangs from your neck!" Galahad cried, stepping a little closer and raising his hand in a gesture of peace. Bedivere stared for a moment, then threw down his helmet in irritation.

"Well, now we have no hope of taking it by surprise," he grumbled. "Not when we tell it all our business."

Galahad paid him no heed but stepped even closer, and the dragon cocked its head to look at him.

"If you understand the speech of men, beast, then listen well. We must take the key, for our lives depend upon it. We shall ponder long on how to take it from you, and we shall have it, by force if needs be."

The dragon seemed to understand that, for it let out a low growl accompanied by a tongue of flame.

"But there need not be bloodshed between us," Galahad continued. "If you will but give us the key we will leave you in peace. And it is, in truth, a small trifle for such a one as you."

The dragon shook its head as best it could, constricted as it was by the cave walls surrounding it, and a fiercer blast of fire shot across the beach towards Galahad.

"Indeed it is, I do not lie!" Galahad cried. "Tell me, is it not true that you have in your cave a heap of treasures, far beyond price?"

The dragon's head swayed a little from side to side as if in agreement.

"And is not the key you bear very small and dull by compare?"

Again the dragon seemed to agree, blowing smoke gently as it looked at Galahad with a calculating gaze. "So will you not give me the key, dragon, to save your beautiful skin from harm?"

The dragon roared then, and the flames shot so far and so fast that they singed the hair on Galahad's head. He fell back in haste, rubbing at his forehead. As he did so, amid the roar of the flames he seemed to hear words sizzling within the din.

"Treasure!" the dragon seemed to be hissing. "Your treasure!"

Then, as suddenly as it had emerged, it withdrew its head into the cave and was gone. A wisp of smoke blew from the cave's mouth and then silence. The conference was over.

The knights waited for a moment, then shrugged at each other and began to walk back towards the children.

"Well, it knows our speech," Bedivere said, after a moment. "And that gives us other choices I daresay. Trickery, deception, something that might tempt it to give up its treasure."

"It will never do that willingly," Galahad returned. "If we learned anything it is that its treasure is its only care."

Bedivere cast him a thoughtful sidelong look. "Trickery, or deception," he resumed, "or, perhaps, *trade*. Would it give us the key in exchange for a greater treasure, think you? Was that its meaning?"

"Maybe. But as we have no such treasure we cannot put it to the test."

~

Ralph and Galahad came to the dinner table together, glowing from the sun and wind and the labour of bedding down the horses before nightfall. Over the meal Ralph told how the dragon's cave was only the first of many that punctuated the cliff for several miles.

"People do say that folks have lived in them betimes," he said, tearing the chicken wing apart in his fingers and sucking the meat from the bones.

"Aye, brother," Charity nodded, wiping her greasy fingers on her apron and buttering herself a thick slice of bread. "A tinker once told me that the holy man betook himself to one of those caves after he was chased from his shack. He said that folks still visit him there, but in deepest secrecy for fear of Demelza."

"The holy man?" Galahad regarded her with his bright blue eyes, "he still lives then?"

"Aye, the people did not kill, only frightened him," Charity replied. After their walk she no longer blushed every time she spoke to him and she dared to raise her eyes to his for a moment. "But he lost all he had – which was not much, I daresay. And his life must now be a cold and comfortless one. The sea only enters the caves at the highest of spring tides, but even so it must be dank and drear."

Galahad laid down his knife and looked at Bedivere. "By your leave, my lord, I will seek him out. Mainly for my own sake, as I always thirst for God's word, but our quest may also gain. Wisdom from any friendly mouth is welcome."

Bedivere nodded. "Do so, Galahad, by all means. Go tomorrow, and take another look at the dragon as you pass. Meanwhile I shall rest here and think upon the problem too, lest your holy man has no advice to give. And speaking of advice, I have a hope, or at least a wish, that the Merlin may seek us out. I would be glad of his counsel."

"The Merlin!" Ralph exclaimed, and his eyes shone. "All my dreams would come true if I could see him!"

Galahad laughed. "Then all your dreams must be homely ones, Ralph, and I daresay they will. My own are a good deal more complicated, more's the pity."

Later that night, wrapped in their blankets amid the hay of the barn, the knights spoke together in soft voices.

"What are your dreams, Galahad, that are so hard of finding?" Bedivere asked into the darkness. "If I may presume on our long friendship to ask you."

Galahad shifted uncomfortably and sighed. "Oh, my lord. Nothing more than a young man's dreams who has spent too much time thinking and not enough doing. Sometimes, as you know, I wish for a hermit's life like the holy man I go to seek. And today I have a new dream, for another kind of retirement. I helped Ralph tonight with his chores and the work felt pleasant to the body. Perhaps I have had too much ease." He was silent for a moment and then added "and it would be pleasant to marry such a one as Charity, and raise a family far from the splendour of the court."

"She is an honest maid," Bedivere agreed. "But such maidens are to be found in higher life also, good-hearted and true. Would you in truth be happy in this poor life if there was no prospect of escape?"

"Nay, by no means." Galahad laughed softly into the darkness. "That is why I called them dreams, Bedivere."

The older knight rolled onto his side, away from Galahad, and shut his eyes. "'Tis cold comfort to blame your youth, my son," he said. "But true nonetheless. A time will come when desire and duty will coincide."

"Aye, I doubt it not," Galahad replied, rolling over and pulling his blanket up to his chin. But he did not sound convinced.

~

It was early the next morning that Galahad found himself swinging along the coast path once more towards the dragon's lair, for he had left the farm at dawn. This morning the sky was greyer and there were raindrops in the breeze from the sea, but Galahad felt happy, and glad to be alone. He could go at his own swift pace, or stop to examine the plants and birds of the cliff edge, or throw himself down on the turf to study the sky, just as he wished. He had had little such solitude or the freedom to go at his own will before. From childhood he had been his father's squire, and he was only fifteen when the battle for Camelot was won. He had fought in that battle bravely and well, and Arthur had knighted him on the battlefield among the slain and wounded as night fell on their victory.

"Strong you are and wise beyond your years," Arthur had told him. "Rise, Sir Galahad, and take your place at the round table. Fear not your youth, for you are as worthy as any to govern our kingdom."

So Galahad had sat in council at the round table and ridden north with his father after the coronation. They had parted on the flat plains of Lincolnshire, Lancelot pressing on to the moors and mountains of the north while Galahad turned aside to take up early the cares of lordship among the fens and dunes of the east. Galahad's realm looked seawards, like Arthur's, but the coast he ruled was a bleak and windy shore, beside a cold grey sea raging along a flat horizon. Here, where he walked this morning, the sea crashed closer to the green fields of the coastal farms, its sapphire waters walled out by the warm grey cliffs. Looking down into the coves and inlets far below him the water shone green and clear over the white sands, and once, stopping to watch a cormorant fishing in a deserted cove, he could see the bird flying underwater, its shadow skimming the seabed. He watched for a long while before walking on.

At length he found the steep path leading down to the dragon's beach once more and he climbed down quickly and quietly, reaching the sand and approaching the lair without alarming the beast. Silence and solitude reigned there this day, and after a moment's pause Galahad began to creep closer to the cave than he had dared to do before. He drew his sword and held it out before him warily, ready to fight or flee at the first sign of the dragon's snout emerging from the cavern.

Closer and closer he crept across the sand towards the dark cave, jagged like a missing tooth in the cliff's smooth side. Closer to the opening he came, stepping over charred driftwood and blasted plants, an uncomfortable reminder of the range and heat of the dragon's fiery breath. Still there was no sign of the beast and now, as he finally reached the aperture in the rocks, he knew why. He could hear a low rumble from within. The dragon was asleep.

Galahad flattened himself against the cliff and thought quickly. Bedivere's plan came back to him at once, as soon as he heard the dragon's snores, and he smiled, clenching his fists as he listened. It would be glorious indeed to return unheralded and unlooked for bearing the key they sought. He could picture Charity's stare and the gruff look of pride on Bedivere's face when he produced it at the supper table. Such a chance for glory could hardly be wasted, whatever his own doubts had been the previous day.

Slowly, slowly he inched around the doorway of the cave and into the velvety darkness within. He paused for a moment, hoping his eyes would become accustomed to the gloom, but the darkness did not lift for the cave was too deep for the sun's rays to enter at all. He would have to feel his way he realised, and hope to make no noise.

On he crept, inching along what seemed to be an endless passageway, keeping his hand on one dank wall to guide him and all the while following the dragon's snores. The corridor of rock gradually widened as he tiptoed forwards, and then all at once he felt warm air on his face. It was a void ahead, large enough it seemed for the dragon's huge body, for as he let go of the wall and stepped into the space beyond the dragon's snores echoed suddenly loud around him, coming from somewhere just ahead. Galahad stopped short to reconsider his hastily formed plan.

His best hope was to creep on, hands outstretched in the darkness, until he touched the monster's body. With luck his fingers would be only as the touch of a fly to its thick scales. Once he knew how the dragon lay he could make a lunge for the key.

It was not a considered plan, and he had only taken a couple of tentative steps forward into the emptiness when disaster struck. Without warning his sword caught on something and brought him up short. Hardly breathing he reached out and felt for the obstruction. It was some kind of heavy chain, suspended from somewhere high above in the vaulted ceiling. It clinked gently against his iron sword and Galahad grimaced into the darkness, experimentally twisting it in his hand. The chain had wound itself around the sword handle. Cautiously he lifted the heavy weight of the chain and began to unwind the sword.

Clang! Sudden and deafening in the confined space of the cave the chain collided with something high above and rang like a great iron bell. Clang, it rang again, as he hastily dropped the chain. Galahad froze as the noise faded. The dragon's snores had stopped. And then in the darkness directly in front of his face a great eye opened, red as fire and luminous as a planet.

Galahad fell back, wrenching his sword free, and turned on his heel to flee. The wall of the cave brought him up short for a moment and he felt frantically with his hands for the way out. Then the welcome cold air of the passageway hit his face and he ran, hands outstretched before him, tripping and sliding on the uneven cave floor in his haste.

The dragon had been deeply asleep or Galahad would not have escaped. He could feel it following, but he reached the entrance before its snapping jaws could catch him. Across the beach he ran helter-skelter and threw himself behind a rock as flame flared behind. The fire licked the rock, singeing his boots. Then the dragon drew breath and Galahad ran on, gaining the path to the cliff as the dragon roared and raged behind him, battering at its prison walls. He fell to his knees safely out of range and looked back at the dragon trapped in the cave. Its red eye rolled in its head as it howled and shot flames towards him across the sands. Then he laughed loud and long, at his own foolishness and his lucky escape. He would have blackened boots instead of a key to show at the supper table.

"Well, you said it was a bad plan," a voice remarked above his head. "I hope this has only confirmed your judgement."

"Merlin!" Galahad only laughed the harder, rolling on to his back to look up at the bird. "Ever you arrive at moments unlooked for. How did you find me?"

The bird cocked its head knowingly from its perch on a strand of bramble, but did not reply. Galahad sat up and examined his boots ruefully, and then inspected his sword, which was none the worse for its mishap in the cave. At length he stood up, and the Merlin flew to his wrist.

"I did not mean to brave the dragon's lair," Galahad explained as he began to pant up the steep slope from the beach. "But when I heard the beast's snores it seemed ungallant not to hazard something. It would have been a glorious end to our quest after all, if I had snatched the key as it slept."

"Naught comes so easily," the Merlin replied, "as you know only too well. But you seem changed since we parted, Galahad."

"Rested and cheered," Galahad replied, "despite the darkness of the hour. Bedivere and I have chanced on good companions and a peace unlooked for."

The Merlin made no comment but preened his feathers thoughtfully for a moment as he sat on the knight's arm. Then he spoke.

"And now you go to visit the saint in the cliff," he said. "That sounds more like the Galahad I know."

Galahad cast him a glance, but did not trouble to ask how the Merlin knew his business. "Is it far?" he asked. "Have you met the saint?"

"No and yes," the Merlin replied. "He lives hard by, and the next path will find him."

"He must know the dragon then?"

"Aye, all too well. But he ought to be glad of any living creature at hand in this wild place."

"And is he?"

The Merlin shrugged and did not answer.

"What like of a man is he?"

"As all such enthusiasts are, Galahad. His conversation runs only on his God and though he seeks converts he cares only for their souls not their bodies."

"You are always harsh on my people, Merlin. We shall quarrel one day I fear, except that I know you do care for their bodies and I thank you for it."

"You are a good man, Galahad." The Merlin pecked his ear affectionately. "And I do not class you among the enthusiasts despite your faith."

"I was born to it, as you know too well, Merlin. A prophecy is a heavy thing to bear, especially from childhood."

"I know it, my son. Your mother cannot be blamed however. Her father believed in prophecy as much as any heathen wizard-worshipper, even though he professed Christianity, and his pride swelled at the thought of having the perfect knight spring from his own blood. Your mother was young and could not resist his will."

"I blame her not, nor my father. But my heart troubles me when I think of the holy grail. I know not whether to wish the time will come for me to seek it, or hope that the prophecy was a lie."

"Prophecies fulfil themselves betimes," the Merlin replied. "You will always be looking for it, whether you will or no."

Soon they reached the cliff path once more and turned westwards.

"How do you think we should defeat this dragon, Merlin?" Galahad asked. "Perhaps now that you are here you could use your magic to aid us. Transform me into a mouse and I could gnaw the chain from the dragon's neck as it slept. Mice are not so clumsy as men."

"Nor so strong," the Merlin replied. "You could never carry the key from the cave."

"Then transform me back to a man as soon as the chain is broken, and I could run for freedom as I did today."

The Merlin shook his feathers irritably. "Magic is not made for our convenience, Galahad. Like all else it observes strict rules that cannot be broken. Transformation is a trick of the eye and the eye is the slave of the sun, as you found out just now in the cave. Once transformed the subject must remain in its borrowed form until the sun sets upon it. Only then can it regain its true shape." The bird cast a severe look at the young knight. "And though I know you jest with me, I hope you remember what I said to you not so many nights ago. To use magic in this quest would bring ruin to us all. It is a battle of men against magic, Galahad. Remember that."

Galahad grinned, though he looked a little chastened all the same. "I take your wisdom like a scolded schoolboy, Merlin, for even Arthur has felt the rough edge of your tongue, I know. Ah well, it seems I must invent my own remedy to defeat this beast then. I have hopes that the holy man will help me. Is this the path?"

They descended to another beach and another cave, very like the one they had just left. There was no one to be seen on the sands and Galahad approached the cavern diffidently, falling to his knees humbly at the entrance. The Merlin flew to a feathery tamarisk branch growing from the cliff above to observe as the knight bowed his head in prayer and drew a cross in the air before rising to his feet and calling out a muted greeting into the darkness of the cave. No one answered and as the breeze blew suddenly cold against his cheek Galahad looked down to see that sand had drifted into the mouth of the cave. No footprints were to be seen on the deep piled sand.

"I believe he is gone!" Galahad said, looking up at the Merlin. "No foot has passed this doorway for some days."

The bird flew down to Galahad's wrist. "Let us enter," he said. "I sense the saint's presence none the less."

Galahad walked forward into a passageway very like the one he had entered earlier on the other beach, and shivered as he remembered the dragon's eye opening in the darkness. Now a glow met his gaze somewhere ahead and a moment later he emerged into a low cavern lit by the dying embers of a small fire. The cave was much as Charity had feared, with very little of comfort and hardly any belongings. Beside the fire a figure huddled in rough sackcloth, its back to the doorway.

"Father!" Galahad stepped forward gently, afraid of startling the monk if he woke him too hastily, and yet also afraid that the saint would not wake at all. "Father! Do you sleep?"

A faint sigh escaped the figure and Galahad came to his side, knelt, and gently pulled the blanket from his shoulders. The monk rolled back at his touch and Galahad could see that he was near to death. Very aged he was, with papery skin that shone transparent in the firelight and crabbed hands that clutched at the air.

"Who comes?" the old man whispered. "Is it my Lord?"

"Not yet." Galahad looked at him compassionately. "But I believe he is not far away. I am Galahad, knight of the round table, and I sought you for counsel and for God's word. But I see now that you are weary and I shall not trouble you. Rather I shall mend your fire and find you water if you wish to drink."

"Galahad!" the old man's eyes opened and he gazed into the young knight's face with a look of wonder. "Thou art Galahad, the grail knight?"

"So they say."

"Then my prayers have been answered, thanks to God and my work is done!" The old man shut his eyes and the shadow of a smile passed across his pale face. "Strange! These heathen fairy tales prove true after all, and perhaps I have not failed." He struggled to sit up, as a violent cough racked his feeble frame, and Galahad supported his shoulders. The old man leant on the young knight's breast, his eyes unnaturally bright as fever shook him. "No one better could I find in this last hour to give my possessions to."

Galahad looked around the bare cave and pitied the monk for his delusion.

"I shall be proud to receive whatever legacy you choose to give me," he replied, "but rest now father while I tend the fire."

"Nay!" the old man clutched his sleeve. "There is no time, for I see Christ smiling at your shoulder ready to lead me home. Look on the shelf, Galahad, when I am gone and take my books. Guard them with your life and they will serve you well."

"Gladly father," Galahad returned, "But be at peace now." He laid his hand on the old man's brow, which shone with a sudden sweat. "Be at peace."

Destiny

Galahad and the Merlin returned to the farm in companionable silence, arriving in the dark and finding their way to the welcoming light of the kitchen and a good meal. Ralph clapped his hands with wonder and delight when the Merlin fluttered through the door after Galahad and tweaked the boy's hair in greeting before alighting on the dresser. The lad could barely believe his eyes and his face glowed pinker and pinker with excitement as he gazed at the bird. When the Merlin spoke Ralph nearly fell off his chair.

"Well, Bedivere," the wizard said. "You nearly lost your young companion today. You had better take better care or you will lose both your king and your friend to the same cause."

At their wondering looks Galahad confessed his escapade in the dragon's cave and showed off his burned boots. Charity exclaimed softly and came around the table, making to kneel and pull them from his feet. Galahad hindered her with a gentle hand to take them off himself, but then she took possession of them and retreated to the fireside with a cloth and a jug of water to rub away at the sooty patches as they talked.

"Foolhardy thou wert," Bedivere chided him gently. "Forsooth, it was thou, Galahad, who counselled against such an attempt."

"I admit it," Galahad said, watching Charity as she frowned over his boots, her hair falling into her eyes as she studied them. "But the temptation was too great, Bedivere. At any rate, I have proved the rashness of the deed. But I have a sadder tale to tell you too."

With that he related his visit to the saint in the cliff and what he had found there, ending with the old man's death in his arms.

"It was providential that you should find him at such a moment," Bedivere remarked, shaking his head and filling his tankard with ale from the jug. "He would have had a lonely death but for your presence."

"Indeed I do not think our presence mattered to him at all. He saw Christ at my shoulder, Bedivere, who beckoned him away. The old man died with a smile of joy on his lips that I shall not easily forget. But we can do something for his body. Tomorrow we should return and bury him with all honour. He also asked me to keep some of his books, which I will find in the daylight and bring away."

"Books!" Charity looked up wide-eyed. "Indeed, I have heard of such things but never saw one. What is a book like?"

"A thing of beauty, maid," Bedivere replied. "Very few there are in the world for they are the work of many years to make. Monks labour at them in their monasteries sometimes for a lifetime. Arthur has the largest collection ever known in these isles."

"They are made from vellum," Galahad tried to explain, "which is something like fine cloth, but easily torn and therefore most delicate. Then the monks write words in the Latin tongue and draw beautiful pictures they call illuminations upon the surface with brightly coloured inks and gold leaf which shines like a polished spoon. Then at last, when all is done, the whole is enclosed by leather boards to protect the pages within. Not many tales deserve such labour, so most books tell the story of our lord."

"I should love to see such a thing," Charity said, returning her attention to Galahad's boots.

"So you shall, tomorrow eve," Galahad replied, "for I guess that the monk's books will be works of this kind since he spoke of them as a kind of treasure. I shall be glad to take them back to my castle to swell my own collection, which is pitifully small. Providence again shows her hand, for they will soon turn to pulp in that damp cave unattended."

"And what of the dragon?" Ralph asked, impatient of these tales of monks and books. "What shall be done about the key?"

Galahad shrugged and tore himself a chunk of bread from the loaf. "We must revert to our other plan, I suppose."

"Which was?" the Merlin prompted. Galahad cast him a doubtful look.

"Indeed, I fear I need hardly tell you, for you seem to know all things by your own magic. Bedivere believes that the beast will trade the key for something better. Or at least that was the burden of its words."

"What were they?"

"It asked for treasure. No more than could be expected of the beast it is."

"Nay," Bedivere spoke thoughtfully. "I remember now it did not ask for treasure only. Its words were 'your treasure'."

"My treasure!" Galahad laughed shortly. "Indeed that is more of a mystery yet for I have none."

"Perhaps it did not mean something necessarily rich and fine," Charity said after a moment. "Perhaps it wants something you value yourself Galahad, however poor. I daresay it has gold and silver enough in its cave. To make its own forfeit worthwhile it may seek a similar sacrifice from you."

The Merlin clicked his beak and looked at the girl admiringly. Then he flew to the back of her chair and leaned down to look into her face in a rather comical manner that made the others smile. Charity did not laugh however, for the Merlin's gaze was a disconcerting thing.

"Now I see that Galahad was right to call his new friends a gain unlooked for," the Merlin said. "You are wise, child."

"She comes of wise parents," Galahad said proudly, and recounted the tale of her parents' lives and worthy deaths. The Merlin watched Charity's face as Galahad spoke and darted a glance towards Ralph every now and then. The bird made no comment as the tale was told, but pulled the girl's hair gently as Galahad fell silent. Charity hid her tears over Galahad's boots. "Well," the Merlin mused after a moment, "as to the dragon I believe the maid is right. What use has the dragon for more gold and more silver? The key is of no value, as you pointed out to the beast yourself. Its value lies in its power to hold the King of Britain in thrall, and that is a mighty one. Something of equal value must be offered in its place."

"Perhaps so, but that is no easier to find than precious jewels," Galahad returned. "What in the Lord's name could we give that would be of equal worth?"

"It said *your* treasure," Bedivere repeated again. "Perhaps it cares less for the power of the thing to be offered but more for your sorrow in giving it."

"I do not relish parting with anything that would give me sorrow enough to warrant the redemption of Arthur." As he spoke Galahad's gaze rested again on Charity and he shivered. The Merlin was watching him and read his thoughts aright.

"Fear not, Galahad," he said. "We will not stoop to human sacrifice. But we must ponder on something to satisfy its thirst for an offering."

Galahad rose to his feet and yawned, before walking across the kitchen in his bare feet to recover his boots from Charity's hand. He bowed as he took them and then turned to tousle Ralph's hair.

"How fare the horses, son?" he asked. "They have had but little exercise since we arrived at your door."

"They have the free run of the meadow, sire," Ralph replied with an earnest look. "But they are mettlesome and a-quiver with the urge to run when I bring them home."

Galahad smiled. "Tomorrow's trip to the monk's cave will be no place for you, Ralph, for burial is a sad affair. Bedivere and I will go early and do what we must, and return as soon as we can for our supper. I fear our horses will have another idle day." He winked at Bedivere. "I do not suppose you would ride them for us, Ralph?"

The boy opened and shut his mouth in silent rapture, which Galahad chose to misinterpret with another mischievous grin. "I know it is an onerous task, but only you can do it, Ralph. Ride as little or as far as you wish and fear not, for they are wise as well as mettlesome and they will not let you fall." His eyes turned to Charity who was smiling at her brother's pleasure. "Indeed I would not fear them even should your sister wish to ride. But I will leave it to your own judgements."

~

Bedivere and Galahad set out on a third journey westwards along the cliff early the next morning. The Merlin came with them, disappearing from time to time to catch his breakfast or to spy out the land ahead. It was almost noon when they came to the monk's cove, and the place looked desolate in the grey bluster of a westerly breeze coming briskly off the sea. They had brought shovels from the farm and began the weary task of digging a burial pit on the cliff top before they descended to the cave. It was hard labour on the thin rocky soil of the cliff and after a time Bedivere paused and mopped his brow, looking out at the grey swell of the sea.

"It is a shame we have no boat," he said, "or we could have taken the body far offshore and left it in God's hands with less labour. But there is hardly a place to launch a vessel along this shore

I see. And indeed we have hardly seen a fishing boat since we came into these parts."

The Merlin perched on his shovel handle to inspect the pit. "If all goes well then Lancelot and Guinevere will see boats a plenty when they come to the southern coast," he remarked, "for there the sea is gentler and there is many a safe harbour along the whole coast. But here the sea is too wild and the cliffs too rugged. The mouth of the Camspell is the nearest port. But labour no more for I believe the grave is deep enough for the poor old creature."

They descended to the cave and carried out the monk's body wrapped in its blanket. Their burden was light for the monk had been but skin and bone. They carried him up to the cliff top and lowered him gently into the grave. Bedivere said a prayer and they paused for a moment, each with his own thoughts. Then Galahad laid his hand on his shovel and looked around him.

"Well," he said, "there is a fine prospect from this place. Here is the whole ocean before us, and as I turn I can see the country spread out for many a mile around. It is no bad spot for a final resting place and I would be glad to know my own was to be as fair."

It was an easier task to fill in the grave and they rested for a while beside it, before descending the steps to the cave again. There was little to find beside the books that the monk had bequeathed to Galahad, and they buried the rest of his belongings in a corner of the cave. Then they emerged into the open air once more and Galahad looked down with interest at his legacy.

There were three books. One, as he expected, was an account of Christ's life with gorgeous illuminations only a little stained by the sea air and damp cave. The next was a slim book of meditations by another saint, each chapter headed by a brightly painted picture. Galahad handled them tenderly as he thought of their authors labouring for so long in the service of the God he also loved. Then he turned his attention to the third volume and frowned as he opened the first page. In this work there were no fine illustrations and no coloured inks. Plain and black it was, the text a little smudged in parts, and it looked older than the rest and more battered as if it had passed through many hands or many trials. Then, as he turned the pages he saw that the text was in an unknown script and that there were maps interspersed between the writing. In the centre fold of the book he came upon a loose page, which fluttered to the sand and almost blew away from his fingers as he snatched it up. Turning it over he saw that it was written in a different hand from the book and formed no part of the original work. He folded it back into the tattered volume and looked up at the others.

"Well," he said. "This is no place for making out our letters. Let us return to the farm where we may decipher the writings at our leisure."

They reached the farm as night fell. Galahad and Bedivere went first to see the horses in their stable, who greeted them joyfully and looked glossy and content in their warm straw strewn stalls. Then they went to the kitchen, to find the Merlin quizzing the children about their day, of which he seemed to know more than was possible. They supped with good cheer and Ralph told them proudly of his success with the horses. He had fallen off, despite Galahad's promise, but he admitted on closer enquiry to have been jumping the wall into the lane when he did so. There was laughter at his expense and he was called upon to show his bruises, but the knights regarded him with admiration nonetheless for the horses were tall and strong and he had done as well as any squire of their own could do.

"Now," said Galahad at last, as Charity cleared the dishes from the table and wiped it clean. "Now for my present from the good old man. Art ready, Charity?"

At that she came and sat beside him, leaning on her elbow with an expectant look. First Galahad opened the volume of the New Testament, and she gasped as the brightly coloured pictures appeared. Neither Charity nor Ralph had ever seen a picture more skilled than the crude scrawls of the tradesmen in the village, of chalk on stone or tar on wood, to advertise their wares. They could hardly believe that the life-like figures exquisitely depicted in the illuminations were not really of flesh and blood. Galahad read haltingly from the text, for it was long since he himself had sat down to a book, but he soon grew in confidence and the children sat open-mouthed as they listened to the fine language. At last he laid the book before them to study the pictures while he turned to the other volumes. As he opened the plainest the loose page fell out again and he looked at it more carefully this time, holding its faded Latin script to the candle flame.

"This is the testament of I, Thomas of Antioch," he began, then looked up at Bedivere frowning. "Antioch? Where is that?"

"I know not, but I believe it is somewhere far distant, if not in the Holy Land itself."

Galahad returned to the paper with a renewed interest, for he began to feel that the very parchment itself had come from a sacred place.

"This is the testament of I, Thomas of Antioch," he repeated, "in the fortieth year of our Lord." Galahad looked up again, clutching the paper with a convulsive grasp. "Do you hear Bedivere! This was writ only seven years after the death of Christ!"

"I hear Galahad, go on."

"Into my possession has come this volume," the text went on. "My namesake Thomas the doubter had it of Peter, Christ's best beloved, and he gave it to me at our meeting in Jerusalem." Galahad paused again, a lump in his throat. Then he went on, dashing a hand across his eyes. "He bade me guard it well for it contains secrets too precious for the eyes of all. I have carried it with me from that hour."

Here the script changed to one yet more spidery and difficult to decipher but after a moment Galahad continued.

"I John of Smyrna take this volume now on the death of Thomas at a fine old age in the year of our Lord 75. Well beloved he was and a saintly man. I shall guard the book well for love of Christ and of Thomas who bade me keep it safe."

A series of differing hands followed and Galahad read them all, as they advanced through the centuries towards the present time and westwards through Rome, Aragon and Aquitaine. As he came to the last he looked up at Bedivere with tears in his eyes. "Is this not a precious thing, Bedivere? See how many have guarded and loved it for so very many centuries, none losing or abandoning it, nor even mislaying this poor scrap of paper wherein lies its history. It is a miracle that the thing has not been lost."

"Yet what is it?" Bedivere asked, leafing through the pages bewitched also by the mystery. "What kind of a book is it to inspire such care and loyalty? All who owned it seem to have lived long and well, and to have died esteemed by their successors. But none explains the mystery it contains and we cannot read the script ourselves."

"Let me see what our old monk has to say," Galahad replied, "for this last entry must be his. Let me see." He tilted the paper to the light and read with emotion.

"'I Thomas of Gascony now take on the precious burden. I have long known of this work and mean to guard it well, and bequeath it in my turn. I am soon to leave for the islands of Britain, and so it continues its westward journey.' There is a break here and then he adds in a feebler hand, 'Here I lie dying on the shores of the great western ocean and the book of the grail can go no further. I pray to God that someone find me, so that I may pass it on, or I will die the last of its keepers and so fail my Heavenly Father."

There was silence around the table as Galahad carefully laid the page aside and turned to the battered volume. He held it in a trembling hand and let it fall open at a page of mysterious text and a well-drawn map. "This is my fate," he said into the silence, his voice strange. "I never really believed it, but it has come at last and in a way I could never have foreseen."

Bedivere laid a hand on his shoulder and leaned forward to examine the page. "Think you that the map leads to the grail?"

"How could it not?"

"Yet why has none used the map to find it before?"

"Oh Bedivere, do you not understand? It is because I am to find it, as the prophecy foretold."

~

For many an hour did Galahad pore over the map and the text, racking his brains to make sense of the strange script. The maps were clear so far as they went, but each showed but a small span of the world, and each could have been as easily a map of Bodmin Moor as of the Holy Land.

"The clue must be in the text," Galahad said, rumpling his hair till it stood up from his head. "The text must tell which land the maps portray, but in this strange script I can hazard no guess at it."

Bedivere sat at his side frowning at the pages helplessly. "I have no notion of how we might solve the riddle," he said. "The book has need of one who can read its language and there is none here who can."

Galahad sat back and groaned. "Yet why should the thing come to me, come across a continent and through many years, seemingly to fulfil my destiny, and then fail me at the last? Is it all mere chance, Bedivere? If so it is a cruel joke to play upon me."

"Mayhap the book bides its time," Bedivere said thoughtfully. "You are over-young to receive it, Galahad, for all the others have been men in their middle years when it fell to their care. Perhaps you are to keep it safe against the time when one will come to aid you in this matter."

Galahad looked at the down at the book before him for a long moment. Then he raised his eyes and smiled at his old friend ruefully.

"You are right, Bedivere, and I am too eager for glory. Why should the book yield up its secrets without a struggle, even if I am in truth the grail knight? And indeed this strange script may be a Moorish one, and therefore is it not possible that I am to take the book eastwards once more when all this trouble is done? In the Holy Land itself I may find someone able to translate the work."

"Depend upon it, that is the answer," Bedivere said, relieved. "Put the book safe among your possessions, Galahad, and fret no more. Let us solve the problem of the dragon and then you may perhaps one day find the way to fulfil your own destined task."

But Galahad was not destined to rest in peace, whatever else awaited him. For the Merlin had been pondering the events of the last days and he had his own view upon them.

"Do you not think it strange, Galahad," he remarked the next day, as Galahad turned the hay in the hayloft for Ralph, raising clouds of dust and making the bird sneeze. "Do you not think it strange that you should find this thing just now, amid all our troubles?"

"I find it strange that my fate should finally find me, Merlin. No man truly wishes his destiny to be fixed."

"How powerful a God is your Lord, Galahad?"

"All powerful, Merlin."

"Bethink you then that he could not find his own cup if he lost it, without your aid?"

Galahad stopped, leaning on his pitchfork, and laughed. "Merlin, thou art too worldly an animal. God does not put his hand down through the clouds to rummage among the sands of the desert. He has left us here to do his will in trouble and difficulty, to struggle with the world in his name."

"It is an inconvenient religion," the bird said beadily, watching him toss hay across the floor. "Yet I think for once luck is with us."

"Indeed, why so?"

"Because I think you should give the book to the dragon, Galahad."

There was a moment of silence as Galahad stared at the bird bewildered. Then he threw down the pitchfork and strode out of the barn without another word.

"Well?" the Merlin demanded, flying after the youth through the gate into the field. "What do you think of my plan? Can you find a better?"

"I hope and trust that I may," Galahad replied, walking swiftly as if he wished to escape the bird. The Merlin flew above his head, however, peering down into the knight's face unabashed.

"Why so? Is it not clear that the book is a treasure sufficient to tempt the beast?"

"Aye."

"Have not your prayers been answered then, Galahad?"

The young knight stopped abruptly and looked up at the bird which now began circling maddeningly around his head.

"Do you not understand?" the words burst from him in a shout and the change in his gentle face would have struck fear into the heart of any human foe. "Or are you mad entirely? This is the holy grail we speak of, not some trinket!"

The bird landed on Galahad's wrist only to be flung back into the air again as Galahad spoke furiously. "This book, which came to my hand but yesterday, leads the way to the grail of our Lord, the cup from which he drank at the last supper, the cup which gives absolute wisdom to all who drink from it in their turn, and which has been lost since the hour of his crucifixion. The book came to me, Merlin, to me who has been fated from my birth to find the grail! And through me it seems that the grail may finally be recovered. Those men, whose words we read last night, have treasured the book for near a thousand years, so that one day it should find my hand and its purpose be fulfilled. And you say I should fail at last, and give it to a dumb beast ruled by base passions, to satisfy its lust for treasure!"

"Aye, I do say so," the Merlin returned, trying and failing to alight on Galahad's wrist again. "There are many years before you to find the grail, Galahad. I begin to fear that you think more of your own fate than that of your king! Is that what you swore at Camelot ten years since?"

Galahad turned and cast the bird a furious glance. "Arthur is but of earth, bird. The grail is of heaven."

"And is Arthur not the best chance of bringing your faith to these shores and nurturing it here? Will you leave Arthur in thrall and Britain to crumble back into chaos while you gallivant across the ocean?"

Galahad stopped short. "I never said so."

"And yet how else are you to succeed, Galahad? Arthur cannot lie enchanted forever. His strength will fail and he will die at last."

"This is not the way." Galahad shook his head, and wiped his eyes with the back of his hand. "It cannot be, Merlin. I cannot cast the grail away."

"Take time to consider, child," the bird replied more gently. "You feared that the sacrifice required would be one you loved. Is it not better to give up ink and paper than a living soul?"

There was no comfortable chatter around the kitchen table that evening. All knew what had passed in the meadow and all waited to see what Galahad would do. The youth himself was pale and stern and looked at the old book no more. The next morning he rose early and threw himself into the work of the farm. Silent and grim he would be for a little while, then filled with wild laughter and mad energy. Ralph watched with a comical mixture of distress and delight as Galahad finished turning the hay in the hayloft in a frenzy of dust, lifted objects that Charity and Ralph had abandoned as too heavy, dug over the vegetable garden, and mended things long broken. But he did it all as one possessed – as a man escaping from himself. By evening the young knight was weary and sorrowful, retreating to his bed early and silent, as soon as he had eaten.

The next day Ralph and Charity grew pale and sad under the shadow of Galahad's affliction, and Bedivere spent many hours talking to the Merlin of his young companion, sitting at the end of the farm track where it met the main road towards Bodmin as they talked. Early that morning the Merlin had seen grim-faced peasants wending their way past the farm bearing billhooks, scythes and spades and he took Bedivere to see the men and to learn what he could. The Lord Marc was mustering his tenants for an assault on the dragon on the moor, the men told Bedivere when he hailed them, for he had made an alliance with the knights from Camelot who had come to kill the beast. None of them knew why, nor did any desire to go, for spring planting and lambing took up their days at this season, but they dared not refuse. Fear and curiosity jostled in their hearts as they thought by turns of the dragon to be faced and the folks from Camelot who were to lead them.

"I must go," the Merlin said to the others as they took their supper in the farm kitchen that night. "If they have joined forces with the Lord Marc as it seems then I daresay that the danger from enchantment is at an end. But I would like to be with them at the battle for counsel if naught else."

"And would you not have us come with you?" Bedivere asked, as he cut a slice of cheese and sandwiched it between two slabs of bread.

"Nay, I would have you wait here until I return, whatever passes." The Merlin glanced towards Galahad and back to Bedivere meaningfully. "There are dragons to be faced here too, both in the caves of the wild and in your own hearts."

Bedivere nodded, following the Merlin's gaze. The youth was not listening and Bedivere knew that his place was at Galahad's side.

~

Bedivere waited and watched through another long day. Galahad left the farm early and returned as light was fading, tired and dispirited by a day wandering the cliffs with no pleasure in the birds or the flowers or the ever-changing sea below, and no solution to his plight.

Bedivere met him at the gate as the sun began to set over the sea. Galahad's shoulders drooped, his fair face looked grim and stern as he approached, and Bedivere's heart ached for the boy suddenly aged by his sorrow.

"The maid is in the fields, fetching the cow," was all he said. "Go to help her, Galahad, and then come in to supper."

Galahad found Charity trudging across the ploughed field towards the meadow, her boots muddy and the hem of her gown grey with dirt. But primroses still blossomed in the hedgerow and harts-tongue ferns grew glossy and green out of the stone field walls, luminous in the golden light of the sunset. As Galahad reached Charity's side he wordlessly took her arm and tucked it under his own to support her steps over the ridges and furrows.

"You are late," Charity said after a moment, glancing shyly up at his face with its new bleak expression. "And you look tired."

"Aye." Galahad frowned and then squeezed her arm, looking down at her artless face with its freckles and earnest brown eyes. "But more in spirit than in body. I am less weary than you I doubt not, for you have been toiling all day for our comfort. We are a heavy load I know. Fear not but we shall pay our board and lodging before we leave you – whenever that shall be." He sighed. "You will think me a wilful burden on you and Ralph when the means of gaining the key seems to lie in my own hands."

"Nay." Charity spoke softly, looking at her boots. "You know that you are a welcome guest. Indeed we will be right sorry when you leave, for we lead a lonely life and it is good to have you here."

They reached the ladder stile into the meadow and Charity gathered up her skirts ready to climb it, but Galahad detained her on the stone steps as he spoke earnestly.

"And do you think me a fool, Charity, for refusing the Merlin's plan?"

Charity sat down and pondered for a moment regarding him quietly from her seat on the top step. Then she dropped her eyes and plucked a daffodil from the wall, pulling it to pieces as she replied. "Not a fool, Galahad. Never could I think that. And yet I mislike it that you would go across the ocean so far away."

Galahad smiled at her then and took her hand, examining her work worn fingers and turning them over to stroke her callused palm. "A knight's life is not like that of other men, Charity. We travel far and face grave dangers. There is no hearth and home we can truly call our own."

Charity did not answer but looked into his face soberly. What she saw there seemed to answer some question of her own, for she threw down the daffodil's petals and turned to climb over the wall into the meadow. Galahad followed. As he leapt down from the stile a last ray of sunshine shone across the field from the sea and lit the back of the girl's neck and her rich brown hair till it glowed like the paintings in the illuminated manuscript the monk had given him. At that moment she turned, unconscious of her radiance. And then Galahad kissed her, taking her arm with his strong young fingers and stooping, his golden hair falling on her upturned face.

His lips were soft and warm, but Charity shivered at his touch and tears started from beneath her closed eyelids. She had loved Galahad from the moment he had appeared at her door, yet she knew that for him this kiss in the meadow was only an impulse. Had he not just told her that his lot was not to be with hers? Sorrow and love showed in her eyes in equal measure as their lips parted and she met Galahad's troubled gaze.

For a moment they were silent and still, faces close together. Then Galahad groaned and cast away from her with a despairing look. "More guilt do I pile on my head with each day that passes," he said. "I seek to do right, Charity, and yet forever I do wrong. Forgive me, maid." With that he strode away into the twilight and Charity brought the cow home alone.

Bedivere was rolled in his blanket in the dim warmth of the hayloft when Galahad returned much later that night. For a moment Bedivere feigned sleep, but then Galahad spoke.

"I have need of counsel, my lord."

Bedivere rolled over and regarded him. Galahad sat on his pallet of hay. His face was hidden by the darkness but the set of his shoulders was weary.

"With all my heart," Bedivere replied. "Speak freely, Galahad, and fear not that I shall judge you harshly."

Galahad sighed and unbuckled his sword laying it tenderly by his bed. Then he pulled off his boots and lay back on the hay. "I am in a sorry state, Bedivere. I know not what I should do and I need your wisdom to guide me. The bird says that I should sacrifice the grail to my king, despite all that he knows of my fate. Tell me what you think, Bedivere, for your counsel is more precious to me. The bird after all is a wizard and moreover he is no man. If you say that I should do as he bids I will do it."

Bedivere grunted unwillingly and was silent so Galahad pressed on. "Tell me then of my own conduct at least. I have been distracted and dissatisfied with my lot for many a day as you well know. And I have taken too much pleasure in the company of Ralph and his sister while Arthur lies in peril at Camelot. I should have been more sober, Bedivere, for my duty is to my king and no joy should I take in aught else."

"There does your duty lie, Galahad, but do not blame yourself for the simple pleasures you have taken here. You are young and none would begrudge you laughter."

"Yet I have done wrong here too Bedivere. In my distraction today I behaved too freely towards the maid and made her sad. I have been so wrapped up in my own troubles that I have failed in my oath of chivalry."

"That is a pity, my son, but fear not for the maid. Many a suitor will she have and many a tear will she shed, but she will find happiness at last."

"Perhaps, Bedivere, but I feel my wrong and wish to right it." He was silent for a moment and then spoke more resolutely, sitting up and leaning towards Bedivere. "Therefore I have resolved to do as you all deem best. In this matter I must believe that you judge more wisely than myself and I shall give the book to the beast if you say I must. Then at least I shall no longer fret. Better a deed badly done than no deed done at all. And my duty to my liege lord will stand fulfilled."

Bedivere sighed again, but Galahad was waiting for his reply and he spoke unwillingly. "How can I guide you, my son? Too well I know the prophecy at your birth, but I do not know if it is to stand fulfilled in this lifetime. Many a promise does a man hold out in his youth, which comes to naught as he grows old. And yet if you are indeed the grail knight then I believe that your destiny will not let you go. Even if you throw away this book now, may your fate not find you yet? I wish that it were my pain, not yours, that were called on to redeem our master, for I love you dearly and would spare you this sorrow. But sorrow brings strength and wisdom and you will be a truer knight for this test."

Galahad bowed his head and was silent for a moment. Then he picked up his sword and held it, hilt-first, towards Bedivere.

"You mean for me to give it up then, I see," he said. "And this I will do, but in return I ask for a pledge from you Bedivere, in place of my king."

Bedivere felt a warning in his heart, but he placed his hand boldly on the sword hilt. "I will promise whatever you wish, Galahad, so long as the oath be a gallant one."

Galahad laughed mirthlessly. "Gallant it is, if not foolhardy. Bedivere, if I give up the book now I must vow to regain it one day or die in the attempt. Promise me that when Arthur is restored to himself, and all at peace once more, the round table will spare me to return here and defeat the beast and bring the book back into the light."

Bedivere looked grieved, for he feared that Galahad sought his own death, but he nodded and grasped the sword more firmly. "I swear, Galahad. None shall prevent you."

Galahad sighed as one released from a long bondage and cast himself upon his bed. "'Tis decided then, and I may sleep in peace."

~

At last the day came that the company set out from the manor with a crowd of peasants armed with farm tools to seek the dragon. Folks began to arrive from early morning and rested quietly on the grass outside the door, used to waiting on their betters. But there was no disguising the changes the visitors from Camelot had wrought at the manor, and the crowd buzzed with excitement and wonder as they looked around. When the Lord Marc clattered into view from the stables mounted on his bay gelding and followed by his men, the people scrambled to their feet and tugged their hair respectfully, bowing before him. He addressed them from horseback, standing in his stirrups to be better seen, as the company from Camelot looked on.

"Demelza the wise has fled," he told the assembled crowd, "and her enchantments here ended. But naught else has altered. I am your liege lord still, and will treat you as I have ever done, no better and no worse. In only one other respect is our lot changed, for I have reached a treaty with these gentlefolk from Camelot – a treaty that will make us only stronger. No longer need my people fear the east!"

The crowd broke into a ragged cheer, but when the Lord Marc frowned they quickly fell silent once more. He spurred his horse forwards and led the cavalcade through the now quiet crowd up the hill towards Bodmin and the moor.

"The Lord Marc may have embraced us," Mordred whispered to Kay, "but he is no less a tyrant than before."

"You speak truth," Kay replied in a low voice, "but I fancy he will find it harder to rule his people harshly without the fear of the witch to aid him."

Guinevere rode among the knights, dressed once more in her mail shirt and leather breeches, and as they rode for more than two hours at the slow walking pace of the crowd she chatted freely with her companions, no longer a stranger in their company. They made their way across the barren heath until at length they came upon a round pool set in a shallow vale amongst the rocks and heather.

Grass grew down to the banks with no bush or tree to be seen, and the pool reflected the sky and clouds like a mirror.

"It is a fair prospect," Guinevere said to Gawain, with whom she rode. "Fair but plain, and I like it. There can be no secrets in such a view."

"No," Gawain shook his head, "but no dragon either, unless he be hidden beneath the water."

Even as he spoke the water rippled and out of it emerged a great head. The crowd gasped and fell back, thrusting their weapons before them in fear. The knights exchanged a look of gladness and pressed their steeds forwards, eager to see their foe, while the Lord Marc remained at the head of his army, watching the beast with a thoughtful face.

It was in truth a terrible sight that the knights beheld as they came to the edge of the pool. The head raised itself higher at their approach, and a part of the creature's neck and shoulder became visible. Around its throat the chain and key were plain to see, and Kay grasped his sword eagerly for a moment. Then, as he looked again, he relaxed his grip and his hand fell to his side.

"Poor thing!" Guinevere exclaimed at his shoulder.

The dragon was old. Older than any living creature ought to be, or perhaps ever has been. Its skin hung from its sides like loose folds of grey cloth, for the colour had long since faded from its scales and now it had become the same muddy hue as the banks of the pool. Scars and sores covered its body that would not heal and its bones stared out, all sharp angles and painful lumps. One wing hung useless at its side, but worst of all its eyes were blind, filmed over with the white membrane of age and disease. Unable to see, it moved its head feebly from side to side, listening to their approach. At the jingling of the horses' harness it made an attempt to lunge forwards, but only fell, almost lifeless, at the water's edge.

Guinevere turned to hide her tears, while the knights looked down at their foe with a mixture of sorrow and disgust.

"This is more of Demelza's cruel magic, I deem," Lancelot said. "She has kept this poor creature alive to frighten the people long past its natural span. Surely nothing but enchantment could keep such an ancient creature from death."

Gawain slipped from his horse and went to kneel by the dragon's head, which lay on the bank of the pool. He laid his hand on its old face and it shuddered as he stroked it gently. "No animal should suffer so," he murmured.

It was thus that the Merlin found them, landing with a flutter of soft wings at Gawain's side and hopping to his shoulder to look down at the dragon's weary face. Gawain barely glanced at the bird.

"This is a sorry sight," he said. "There is no courtly honour to be won against such a foe as this. It may have been a terror once but it is no more."

"Nay," the Merlin agreed, examining the dragon with his head cocked to one side. "But there is honour to be won yet, if only through kindness instead of valour. Much has this beast seen, and yet now it sees no more. But still it feels, and dreams, as all may – even when all hope is gone. I can feel its weary heart labouring in its chest, and hear its clouded thoughts that wander far from this bleak spot where it lies."

The bird was silent for a moment and then all at once he began to chant a harsh melody. It was a dragon's song, such as has never been heard before or since by living men. Cruel and jagged it sounded, like the hide of the beast who made it, but all who listened felt for a moment as though they looked out at the world through dragon's eyes. The open joy of the sky he sang, with the strong wings of the young dragon beneath him soaring high and easy on the rising air. The grim joy of the battle he sang, with the rip of claw and the gouge of teeth and the lick of flame from gaping jaws. The gnawing joy of treasure he sang, lying cold under the wings like precious young, but forever and unchangingly its own. Then the aching joy of death he sang, with the weariness of age falling away and soaring wings once more to bear it away into a golden sunrise.

Gawain drew his hunting knife gently from its sheath as the Merlin at last fell silent. "Sleep in peace friend," he said, stroking the dragon's cheek with a compassionate hand, "or fly to your elders in the sunrise. I release you from this spell." With that he cut its throat.

The dragon barely shuddered as it drew its last breath and its eyes closed peacefully. The Merlin flew to Lancelot's sleeve while Gawain cut the chain from the dragon's neck and put the key carefully in his pocket. Then he turned to the others.

"Well," he said. "Thus ends the first chapter of our quest. Now there are only four dragons in the land. Would they were all as feeble as this one!"

Partings

A feast was held in the great hall that night and even Ruth was there, wrapped in soft blankets like a precious treasure by her father's side. Soft and fond was his look as he gazed at her bright face and listened to the voice that had been silent for so long. The Lord Marc was a tyrant among his people and a man unused to alliance, but he loved his daughter and for her sake looked kindly on their guests.

Guinevere sat at Ruth's other side smiling at her plate as she listened to the girl's chatter. She smiled the more to see Lancelot at last notice the merry girl, now no longer sad and silent. Gawain of all the company was the soberest despite the honour paid to him by his comrades for his deed by the dragon's pool. They could see the chain glinting in his pocket and after the meal was ended he produced the key at their request and it passed from hand to hand. It was fine and delicate, of curious shape and made from a metal none could name. On close inspection the shaft of the key was shaped like a snake, the tail coiling around to form the hoop and the teeth and forked tongue protruding to make up the tiny levers that would turn the lock. Lancelot looked up from it lying in his palm.

"Well, it is a small prize to win from so large a foe, however fallen. Now our thoughts must turn to tomorrow and the days after. What is our plan?"

"To go on as we promised," Kay replied. "Mordred and myself to the Land's End, Gawain hard by to the Lizard, and yourself Lancelot with Guinevere to the south. And indeed we may go on with good cheer knowing that at least one part of our quest is fulfilled."

"I will return to Bedivere and Galahad," the Merlin spoke up from his place on the back of Gawain's chair. "Their quest is also close to its end for Galahad is a true knight and will not fail us. Then they should go back to Camelot, I think, for Arthur may yet need them. But with the Lord Marc's leave I will direct them here on their way, for this new friendship between us should be sealed by all the knights of the round table."

"Let them come," the Lord Marc nodded. "It will be an honour to my house to receive them."

"None knows the outcome of this quest," the Merlin went on. "And all should hold themselves ready for combat, for not every dragon will be as feeble as that which we met today."

All the knights looked sober for a moment, for in the joy of their success that day everything before them had begun to look easy. The bird whistled cheerfully and flew to Ruth's wrist where she stroked his feathers with a gentle finger. "But be of good cheer tonight," he said. "For see what may be won with a stout heart! Not just a key has been found, but a maiden also has been restored to her father by your gallant acts. I believe you will find more wine is in order, to toast the victory of Bodmin and the new alliance between east and west."

More wine and ale came and many toasts were drunk indeed. But the knights of the round table had learned early to bear nobly with little sleep and a sore head. When they met in the upper chamber the next morning they exchanged rueful smiles, but were ready for their day's journey from the manor and the new adventures that lay before them.

"Well, here we meet at the scene of our triumph over the witch," Kay said cheerfully. Gawain grunted.

"Aye, though for my part I would like to know where she betook herself as her enchantments fell. I like not the thought that we may meet her again on our travels."

"She holds no terror for me," Lancelot replied. "She may trouble us a little, but her power is too feeble to undo us entirely."

"Still, trouble is best avoided in all its guises," Kay said. "So let us keep a sharp eye for strange happenings and be on our guard as we travel on."

The others nodded and then by common consent they turned and clattered down the steps out onto the grass before the door. Their horses stood ready, newly shod and with fresh supplies in their saddlebags. The Lord Marc appeared from the house and embraced them all. When he came to Guinevere he bowed low over her hand respectfully and spoke with a warmth no longer feigned. "Come and visit us again, my lady. My daughter will miss your kind counsel and motherly care."

"I will return, Lord Marc, if God spares us. And when Arthur is restored you must come to us at Camelot. My lord will be overjoyed to find an ally so long sought for here in the west."

The Lord Marc bowed again and kissed her hand, even dressed as she was in her travelling garb. Then the comrades mounted their horses and saluted their host for the last time. They turned their horses' heads towards the sheep track to Bodmin that wound up the hill and cantered away from the manor over the soft heathland turf. At the brow of the hill they paused and looked back, down to the manor that now lay in its lonely hollow open to the sky. As they looked, a hand waved from an upper window and they saluted in return. The Lady Ruth was watching them.

"Well, Merlin," Lancelot said to the bird. "You gave wise counsel when you sent us here. My heart misgave me, and I was impatient for valour, but you were right. What do you say now? What wisdom do you have to offer as we part?"

The Merlin blinked like an owl as the company awaited his words. "Be true to one another," he said at last. "And Lancelot, have faith in the Guinevere you see here. Much more of her character is known to you now, so do not waste the knowledge." Lancelot bowed his head, and the Merlin looked around at the rest of the company. "But now it is time to renew your oaths to Arthur," he said. "Be merciful, be gallant, and above all resist magic in all its forms, for it will trick and delude you if it can. Remember that to use magic against magic will bring only defeat. And although I dislike much about your new religion you may learn lessons from it, for if you are willing to sacrifice yourselves, then much will be given in return."

Again his cryptic gaze swept across them. "My heart also misgives me," he said at last. "I fear that we shall not all meet again. But do not be afraid, for I do not necessarily see death ahead. As I told Gawain some days since, men's fates cannot be foretold, for they are free to choose their own paths. Choose wisely then, friends, and you may laugh my forebodings to scorn at Camelot when all is done. I go now to Galahad. Farewell."

Before they could open their mouths to speak the bird was gone, flying swift and low along the hedgerow. The company watched him go then turned to each other with wry smiles.

"Well, such a one is he always," Kay said. "Sudden to appear and sudden to part."

"And such is any quest," Gawain added, "full of dangers both known and unforeseen. I do not fear for myself any longer, but trust to my sword as I have always done." He drew it from its sheath and held it out into the midst of the company. Infected by his mood the other knights drew their own weapons and the blades clashed as they met.

"Here's to a gallant fight and an easy conscience," Kay said. "Remember your oaths, my friends, and return to the round table with only honour and glory to tell."

The knights bowed their heads, then sheathed their swords and clasped hands all round.

"Farewell, brethren," Lancelot said. "Ride swift and return safe for I can ill spare any in this company."

~

It was curious to leave the fellowship and good cheer of the company. Guinevere felt cold and afraid as she followed Lancelot's horse across the lonely moor towards the coast. Lancelot was troubled too, but by the presence of Guinevere not the absence of the others. He was used to riding alone and it felt strange to have a companion, still more a woman. But he remembered the Merlin's words and grudgingly paid her her due, for she had defeated the enchantress of Bodmin and by doing so had led them to the first key. Force of arms alone could not have achieved so much.

They stopped for a cold meal by the road on the top of the moor. A skylark sang above their heads and a group of wild ponies watched them from a neighbouring hilltop. They drank from a cold moorland stream to save their wineskins and let the horses graze for a while as they studied Mordred's map. South of the moor a fertile coastal strip was bisected by a large river. Lancelot looked at Guinevere and grinned rather savagely. "Think you that all rivers are enchanted in this wild land?" he asked. Guinevere looked frankly into his handsome face and smiled in return.

"At least now I shall not fear them if they are," she said. "You will not know it, but I nearly failed at the Camspell. Midstream I feared never to reach land again or see your fair faces more."

"All felt that," Lancelot said, "indeed that was a part of the spell."

"Then why did you not warn me?"

Lancelot shrugged and smiled grimly. "Such is the pride of the knight that he cannot admit his fears. Still, we should have treated you as a page or a squire, for you were young in knighthood then and deserved help."

"Kay was kind," Guinevere replied. "But afterwards I feared the next encounter with magic more than I should. But now such fears are forgotten, if enchantments can be burned on a fire like dry twigs."

Lancelot rose to his feet and proffered a hand to pull her up. "Not all spells are so easily broken, as we know from Arthur's plight," he said. "But we will prevail, Guinevere. Come, this is my plan. Let us follow our noses across the moor while the day bids fair and we can see the country spread out before us. Then when we spy the river we can ride south along its banks to the sea. Mordred has marked a hamlet and a ferry there, so we may stay the night in the village and choose our direction tomorrow. If there is a dragon to be found no doubt we shall hear of it from another talkative innkeeper."

Guinevere nodded, looking at the map as Lancelot spread it out against his horse's flanks. "It is not far to the sea," she said. "We will have an easy journey."

"Then let us use our time to our profit," Lancelot replied. "Here is soft grass and no witnesses. Will you try your swordsmanship for the first time?"

Guinevere looked doubtingly. She had not taken the sword from its sheath since the Merlin gave it to her. "You said I was not to learn."

"Less faith had I then in your prowess Guinevere, I admit it. But the Merlin has always been right in such matters and he gave you the blade."

Guinevere shrugged and laid her hand on the hilt of her sword where it protruded from her saddlebags, but Lancelot shook his head.

"Nay, not yet. A novice you may be, but a lucky stroke may still be enough to kill me."

Guinevere shivered at the thought. "How then?"

"Here, let us find a pair of suitable sticks from this thicket. Then we may fence to no injury."

Lancelot was not quite truthful in this, for Guinevere's hand was sore by the end of the lesson. The force of his blows jarred the rough stick and blistered her palm, and he inflicted sharp raps to her knuckles at her slow attempts to strike him. The harder she tried, the slower she became, and the more easily he dodged and parried only to inflict a blow himself. After half an hour she was panting and her thumbnail was blackening from a painful bruise.

"Enough!" she said at last. "Enough, Lancelot. I am too weary." She threw away her stick and collapsed onto the grass dizzied by her efforts to follow the swift play of the sticks.

"Rest then, my lady," Lancelot replied. He was warm and elated by his own skill and not yet ready to quit the display of his powers. "Rest and watch what may be done with a blade. Imagine yourself at the tournament, observing the swordplay." As he spoke he drew his wide two-edged broadsword from its sheath and, despite its heavy weight, swirled it around through his fingers in a perfect arc. Then, he slashed it from side to side lazily, the sword seeming to hang loose in his fingers as if it hovered in his grasp of its own will.

Next, so quickly that she did not see the blade move, he sliced it across the top of a nearby gorse bush and she flung up her hand against a shower of spines and golden flowers. Their heady scent filled the air as they lay bruised on the heather and she saw that the bush was neatly lopped in two, its upper part cut cleanly from the lower.

"Your sword is sharp," she said feelingly. "At least it is the gorse bush that has lost its head, and not I."

Lancelot looked down at her as he wiped the blade and returned the sword to its sheath. "Few heads are lost in battle my lady," he said, "for a man's neck is sturdier than a branch and well protected. But the sword is indeed sharp as you say, and can inflict a grievous wound."

"To we women at the court such things are hard to imagine. When you return and sit at our table and talk of music or poetry or love it is hard to believe that your hand may have done such injury."

"And yet now you face hazards and perils yourself, Guinevere. Your own hand must be ready to injure and to kill."

Guinevere bowed her head in agreement. "So it must. But I believe my bow will be my best friend. Will you shoot with me a little, now I have caught my breath?"

~

When the Merlin had left them and Lancelot and Guinevere had departed across the moors, Kay and Mordred, Gawain and Wolf were left alone. They looked at each other for a moment, and then laughed.

"Well!" said Kay, swinging out of his saddle to the ground. "So depart the creatures of mystery and romance! And here we remain, mere mortals of no special hue!"

"Speak for thyself, Kay my lad," Gawain returned, as he dismounted. "I have held in a gigantic wind for many a day to spare the blushes of my queen, and that I deem is no mean feat. So do not call me a common mortal." He grunted with satisfaction as he farted loudly and the others laughed.

"Indeed no!" Mordred replied, climbing from his saddle and fishing a copy of the map out of his saddlebag before coming to sit beside the others on the bank of the road. "Never common, barely mortal, Gawain. You are a prodigy of nature."

Gawain growled with mock anger and handed Wolf a morsel from his pocket, which the dog took to a short distance and chewed with an air of satisfaction. Then Gawain looked at the map spread before the others as he took another morsel from his pocket and began to chew it himself.

"There is no difficulty with our path if we continue as we planned at Camelot," Mordred said. "There is a broad highway I believe, running from the spot where we now stand to the Land's End. If Gawain still plans to make his way to the part they name the Lizard we may travel together as far as the small town of Helston before Gawain takes his leave of us and turns southwards."

Kay looked at the map with interest, for he had not studied the parts to which they now planned to go since that morning in Camelot when all roads had been decided. "Indeed," he said now, "it appears that we all of us go to the land's end, for the Lizard too is a far extremity of our world. Two twin ends there are, one facing south, one west. There is something in the idea of an ending very solemn to my mind and I am glad we chose these paths. When we return we alone will know the full extent of the mystery, and have travelled as far as the road leads."

"Either that, or we shall ride far and find little," Gawain replied, unimpressed. "And yet if I were hiding a number of dragons I should think it remiss to leave the furthest wild empty. We will find beasts there I doubt not."

"What like of people shall we meet on our way westwards Mordred?" Kay asked. Mordred shook his head.

"Nay, I know not. Yet I would hazard that we will meet less kindness as we go on. Until now we have travelled only the coast and methinks coastal peoples are as a rule more friendly to strangers and more used to curiosities than those who dwell remote and far from the seaports. Lord Marc is a specimen of that."

"Well, if all of the inland ways be subject to crones such as his Demelza we shall have a rare journey, full of wonders."

They were all silent for a moment, contemplating the last days and those to come. Then Mordred spoke, and his tone was mild.

"Magic is indeed a curious thing,"

Gawain laughed and slapped his leg in a fatherly way. "It is, my boy, it is. That is a good scholarly judgement worthy of you. I could find harder words to call it."

Mordred smiled briefly but pursued his thought. "Aye, but it is indeed strange in its operations. The sorcery we have met with on this journey has depended to some great degree on the blindness or fears of its victims. We were able to cross the Camspell by force of will alone, while I think that the Lady Ruth fell so deep under Demelza's spell because she believed herself enchanted."

"True," Kay replied. "And yet the sorcery around the Lord Marc's manor was real enough and we fell victim ourselves to its power."

"Yet it proved a flimsy power after all," Mordred argued, "for it took but a hand to thrust the tapestry in the fire and the enchantment fell."

"That may be true, but not all magic is of the mind. Dragons I fear will be harder to vanquish. We were lucky to find our first foe so weak, and we will not be so fortunate again."

"And yet Galahad too, we hear, has a battle more of the heart than the body to overcome his beast, if what the Merlin tells us is true."

"Only because he could not come at it by force of arms. If he had been eaten in the dragon's lair we would not have called that a trick of the mind." Kay paused for a moment, lying back on his elbows and regarding his own large feet at the end of his long legs. "And yet you are right in one way, for magic feeds most readily on the fears and weaknesses of men, which it sees and pursues with a clarity cruel and unflinching. Above all, on this quest we must know our own follies, for they will be used against us. And we must use our strengths, even if we knew not until now what they were."

Mordred sighed and threw a pebble at a rock some distance off. It missed. "My strength will be not in arms," he said. "For I have had no occasion to hone my skills as you both have. My understanding is my strength I daresay, though it can be put to bad use as well as good."

"Fear not," Kay said. "We will be together to the very Land's End, Mordred, and we may pool our wits and skill to defeat whatever comes. It is a comfort to me." He looked at Gawain who was watching Wolf sniffing the undergrowth for badgers some distance away. "Art still content to leave us, Gawain? We will ride together most gladly if you wish for company and counsel."

"Nay," Gawain shook his head and heaved his great bulk to his feet. "Wolf is enough company for me, and as talkative a companion as I like."

Mordred and Kay exchanged chastened grins as they stood up and followed Gawain in mounting their horses and turning their heads south westwards once more. "But I have enjoyed your disputations," Gawain added, with a conciliatory look from under his shaggy brows. "It is just that I fear I understand the cawing of the rooks and the bark of the fox more than I grasp your fine distinctions."

"Not much further," Mordred said cheerfully, "and we shall meet the main road. I doubt not but there will be many an inn to rest our bones in come nightfall. And if not, I shall not mind another night on the ground. There is a freedom in making a bed among Gawain's wild creatures that I find I like."

~

It was a lovely ride along the banks of the river to the sea. The stream widened as it neared the ocean and dense green woods grew down to the water's edge. Shallow inlets and creeks branched from the main river, which Lancelot and Guinevere skirted without mishap, and at last they came to the river mouth. Steep cliffs rose to either side and the water itself was wide and deep where it met the sea. Even as they approached they saw a wooden raft punting across the expanse of grey water with a horse and rider aboard.

"There is the ferry," Lancelot pointed it out. "But it seems that we will not need its services today, for I can see the village on this bank. If we can find an inn we shall have had an easy day of it at last."

It was an easy day, for they soon found a tavern among the tumbled cottages that clustered above the jetty in the lee of the cliff. Sheltered from the stiff sea breeze, the village was warm and peaceful as they clattered through the streets. Strangers were common in this deep-water port, it seemed, for none cast them more than a second glance. Indeed, there were two vessels anchored in the mouth of the river that looked of foreign shape.

"Mordred said that the people in these parts traded freely with visitors," Lancelot said, nodding towards the ships.

"Aye, pottery he said was the local art," Guinevere replied. "Perhaps if peace comes I may have some for my table at Camelot."

Lancelot looked at her and his eyes creased in amusement. "A more womanly speech I seldom heard," he said, "and a welcome thought in this dark hour. I will be pleased to see you smiling over a fine banquet when that day comes."

They dismounted outside the inn and gave their horses to the ostler. Then they entered the low building, blinking in the warm darkness within. A woman emerged from the kitchen to offer them beds and refreshment, and soon they sat by a roaring fire that flushed their wind-blown faces to a rosy pink and toasted their legs as they shared a platter of roast fowl and vegetables, dipping bread in the rich gravy and washing all down with strong ale.

"We come to these parts in search of novelty," Lancelot said to the woman as she returned to refill their tankards with the black, smoky brew. "Are there any strange creatures hereabouts that might amuse us?"

The woman gave a short laugh. "That depends how you take your amusement sire," she replied. "Whether you seek to be the hunter or the hunted. There are fine deer in the woods that may provide you with good sport for your bow and arrow if that is your pleasure, for we owe no lord allegiance here and the land is free to all."

"Indeed?" Lancelot feigned a degree of interest. "That may suit us well. And yet you puzzle me with the hint that we may yet be the quarry. What kinds of fearsome beasts have you in these parts? Wolves or bears?"

The woman shrugged, and took a swig out of the jug with which she had just replenished their own tankards. "There is a great lizard they say, in the wood."

"Is there indeed? That sounds like a beast to be shunned. Where is it, that we may seek to avoid it?"

"I know not," the woman replied. "But my man will know if you seek him out."

"Where will we find him?"

"Out in the brewhouse beyond the stables."

After they had swallowed the last of their ale and wiped the plates clean with their bread, they left the inn and walked around the back in search of the brewhouse. Guinevere's mare whinnied to them across the yard, for she was still fresh from their easy day's journey and well supplied with oats and hay. Guinevere crossed over to stroke her nose while Lancelot walked on to a low barn next to the stables where clouds of steam were billowing out of the doorway.

He ducked through the door and stood for a moment, his eyes growing used to the cloudy gloom within. A man stood, stirring a great vessel over a roaring fire, while a young lad fed the blaze with sticks, hopping around in what seemed an inferno. The sweet smell of malt made Lancelot wrinkle his nose as he stepped nearer, over sacks of grain left tumbled on the dirt floor. The man noticed him then and threw down the great stick he was stirring with, striding over to meet him halfway.

"Greetings friend!" he said, holding out a hand and meeting Lancelot's gaze frankly. After the suspicious looks of the Lord Marc's tenants Lancelot found himself liking this independent village which owned no master. "How can I help you? Or have you come to inspect your tipple in the making?"

"Nay." Lancelot replied. "Though I have tasted it at your table and it is a fortifying brew."

"It is that. We are famed for some miles round, you will find, though I think you are a stranger to these parts?"

"I am. We are but travelling through, and sought a bed for the night and a good meal. I sought you out because your wife was telling us some tale of lizards or dragons or some such monster nearby. I do not relish an encounter with such a beast, so looked to know its whereabouts so that we might avoid it."

The man wiped his sweating brow with an old rag and turned to shout to the boy to keep the fire hot.

"Pardon, sire," he said, turning back to Lancelot. "You have found us at the most ticklish point, for the heat must not lessen for a good two hours and 'tis tiresome labour for the boy to feed the flames. Aye, I can direct you well enough. Keep from the woods on the other side of the water, that's all you need to know, for it prowls all along that bank. When we cross the river we stay close to the seashore and hurry as best we may until the woods lie far behind."

"What manner of a beast is it, exactly?"

"It is a brute, that's certain. Not much taller than a man, but its teeth are sharp as knives and slime drips from its jaws at the sight of flesh. A vile green is its colour, which makes it hard to spy among the trees and bushes until too late. Many a man or boy has returned one arm or leg the poorer from its grasp."

Lancelot thought he was glad that Guinevere had lingered by the stables and missed this news.

"Well," he said, with mock-merriment. "We shall do our best to keep our limbs about us. And I shall leave you to your labours."

"You shall," the man agreed cheerfully. "The stars will be high before the lad and I are finished for the night. Sleep well, sire, and a safe journey onwards."

Lancelot left the barn and saw Guinevere still standing by the horses, talking gently to them and feeding them scraps that she had brought from the table. He took her arm as he reached her side.

"Come," he said. "Shall we enjoy the night air for a while longer? My head is full of that fellow's brew, both its taste and smell."

"Gladly," Guinevere replied. "Let us find the water for I have missed it these last days on the moor."

As Lancelot led her down towards the water's edge beyond the inn through a maze of streets darkness was falling and Guinevere looked with interest into the hovels they passed. A small girl squatted on an earth floor in one cottage playing with an assortment of pebbles as her mother stoked the hearth. An old man slumbered in the doorway of the next, his head resting on a gnarled old palm.

"The people seem contented in this place," Guinevere remarked as she studied them. "Perhaps these souls have less need of us than those by the Camspell."

"They are of a cheerful disposition," Lancelot replied, "but they dwell alongside fear nonetheless." He told her some of what the innkeeper had said. "So we may do them a service after all."

"And has none attempted to defeat the beast, did he say?"

"He did not say. The beast's main strength lies in its secrecy among the trees and the surprise it may inflict."

"More than surprise, I fear." Guinevere was silent for a moment. "Well, the Merlin warned us that the next beast might not be so feeble."

"He did, though we never expected weakness in any such foe. We will have use of our weapons at last, Guinevere, that is some comfort. Too much there has been of trickery and illusion thus far in this quest. I would take an honest fight in preference, however arduous, for it is in arms that my strength lies."

"Indeed, I believe this will be your battle," Guinevere agreed. "And I shall be but a bystander I fear, and use my bow as best I may."

"You have already done well," Lancelot replied. "There is no shame in letting one skilled in warfare take the brunt of the battle."

"I have long felt that I would fear no skirmish if you were by my side," Guinevere replied. "Come what may tomorrow, I will sleep peacefully tonight."

The water lapped against the jetty in the darkness, the waves reflecting the silvery sheen of starlight as Lancelot looked down at Guinevere. He had always believed her the loveliest woman he had ever seen, and he thought so now, as he regarded her earnest expression and dark eyes as she watched the water. Not all of the other knights' suspicions against him were unfounded, and the moment was favourable to love as he knew from long experience. But then he remembered the Merlin's words at Camelot even as he examined her fair face, and he vowed silently to remain true to his king as the bird had promised that he would.

"Come, let us away to our beds," he said, with a new conviction in his voice. "Let tomorrow come as soon as may be. I fear no evil."

~

An early morning mist lay over the farm, lingering in the hollows and softening the outlines of the old house and its barns, as the Merlin flew silently along the hedgerow and into the yard. He alighted on the gatepost and listened attentively. From the dairy he could hear milk spurting rhythmically into a pail, while from the hen house came the clucking of the fowl as they ran through the opening door and into the day. No other sounds were to be heard, so the Merlin spread his wings and flew to the hens' field where he found Ralph filling their water trough from a bucket and scattering grain while the chickens pecked around his feet. His face was grimy and his hair tangled and wild, for he had not yet paid his daily visit to the water pump in the yard. But his grubby face shone a welcome as the bird reached him and perched on the hen house roof.

"Well met," said the bird, "and a good morning to you, if it is one."

Ralph looked around at the mist and shivered. "'Tis a raw morning, Merlin, but I believe we shall have sunshine by noon."

"I think you are right," the Merlin replied, "for flying high the air is clear and the sun will soon burn this haze away."

Ralph scattered the last of the grain and picked up his empty bucket to walk back to the yard. The Merlin flew to the bucket and perched on the rim rather precariously as it swung to and fro.

"What news is there?" the bird asked. "Has anything interesting happened?"

"Aye, much. Galahad has been right grieved since you left, Merlin. Fair wracked he was and wandered for one day and worked like a demon for another. But at last he decided to do your bidding."

"Did he? And what happened?"

"Yesterday morning we all went back to the dragon's cave. Galahad was sad as we went, though Bedivere consoled him and told him what a fine knight he was. Yet still he was silent and sorrowful, which grieved Charity, so we were a gloomy party."

"I can imagine all of that. What happened when you reached the dragon's cove?"

"We went down to the beach as before. The dragon was awake, for we could hear it grumbling to itself inside the cave. Then Galahad went close to the cave mouth so that Charity cried out with fear, and I was afraid too. But the knights were as calm as a summer's day. Galahad shouted into the cave, something like 'Beast! I have brought you my treasure!' The dragon's snout popped out straight away, and we all jumped out of our skins except for Galahad who never flinched. The dragon must have heard what he said though, for it did not fry him, which it could have done being so close. It looked at Galahad and Galahad looked back.

"Then Galahad started to talk and we could see that the beast understood his speech. He talked for a good while, but too low for us to hear it all. I think he was telling the monster who he was, and all about the prophecy at his birth. Then I heard him tell the beast about the monk and at last he got out the book and showed it to the beast.

"He was pale, sir, pale as milk, and I heard tears in his voice as he told the dragon of the grail. Then he stopped speaking and stood back to see what the beast would do.

"The dragon was looking at him, Merlin, weighing him up and deciding whether to make the bargain I thought. But at last he leaned down his great jaw, sir, and snapped that chain about his neck as gently as a finch takes a seed. Galahad shouts at the beast to throw the key, for he trusts it not and will go no nearer. The beast gives him a look and then obeys, but he throws it nearer to his own hand than to Galahad's. And as Galahad runs forward to pick it up the dragon shoots out a tongue as long as a barn door and snatches the book out of Galahad's hand and into his own mouth.

"Well, we all cried out at that, for we feared the beast would swallow it whole, but then we saw it holding the thing between its teeth, careful like, and back it went into the cave."

They had stopped at the yard gate, Ralph leaning his elbows on the top bar and the Merlin perching on the post. Ralph sighed and wiped his nose with the back of his hand.

"I don't rightly understand it all," he said. "What the grail truly is, and such like. But I seen how it made Galahad right sad to lose the book that showed the way. He came back quiet and grieving and ate no supper. But I heard him and Bedivere talking as I went to bed and he sounded more cheerful on account of Bedivere's oath."

"Indeed, and what oath was that?"

The boy shrugged. "I did not hear it all, for I am no sneak. But I believe Bedivere had promised Galahad that the king will let him return to us and fight the dragon for the book one day." He picked up the bucket and opened the gate. "And that will be a rare day for us, sir, whatever the danger, for we will grieve to see them leave us today."

The Merlin clicked his beak thoughtfully. "They leave today?"

"Aye, at least I guess they will, now that you are here. They wait on your return before they leave for Camelot."

"And are you sure of this oath Ralph, and of Galahad's intention to return?"

"I am." The boy looked at the Merlin proudly. "But I daresay he may change his mind when he finds himself back among the fine folks of Camelot with all the jousting and all."

"Nay." The Merlin fluttered his feathers as though he felt a chill. "A knight's oath is sacred, Ralph. He will indeed return, and if he does so he will die, devoured by the beast's fiery breath. Listen boy." The Merlin hopped onto Ralph's shoulder and peered into his face sternly. "Do me this service. Tell no one that I am returned for a little while. I shall be back by noon and you may greet me as one newly come. Will you do this for the love of Galahad?"

"Aye." Ralph looked at the bird wide-eyed.

"And keep him at the farm."

~

It was nearly noon when the Merlin flew back into the farmyard, and the sun was shining weakly as Ralph had predicted. Galahad was shelling dried beans outside the kitchen door, sitting on the milking stool with his long legs folded under him awkwardly. Still, he looked at peace, his golden head bare to the sky and bereft of his mail, dressed only in breeches and a leather jerkin. Bedivere slumped against the house wall on a bench, his chin on his chest and his eyes closed.

"Hail, valiant ones!" the Merlin called out as he landed beside Bedivere who woke with a start. "You have prevailed I see and fulfilled your part of the quest."

Bedivere grunted and rubbed his eyes. "Thou knowest too much as ever Merlin. I should like to know where you glean your knowledge. But yes, the key is ours. What passed at Bodmin? Did the others succeed?"

"They did, Bedivere, though their beast was less fearsome than your own. They feasted after their victory, and then left the manor of the Lord Marc yesterday for new adventures. All have dispersed as we agreed at Camelot and I shall go to them when new trials come near."

"We waited here as you asked, bird." Bedivere said. "Or we should have left this morning, for we are eager to take our treasure back to Arthur and anxious for his safety with none to guard him."

"I think you are right, though your men have done well thus far and there is no hurry to return, for every key must be found before the spell can be broken. But if you begin your journey homewards now mishaps may be avoided, and the key will be safer within the castle walls."

"It is as safe in my pocket, bird. Bedivere is a strong wall against intruders."

"I know it," the bird agreed, "but follow your feelings and return to your king. However I have promised the Lord Marc a visit in your name and I think you should stay there for a night or two on your way. He will be a useful ally. And he has a pretty daughter who may help to reconcile Galahad to courtly life once more."

Galahad looked up from his bowl of beans and shook his head. "Do not speak to me of such matters, bird. You lack all judgement of the heart."

"Indeed, your human hearts are a mystery to me," the bird replied cheerfully, "and I bear you no ill will for the rebuke."

Galahad put the bowl aside and stretched out his legs before standing up and looking at the sun.

"When do you think we should leave?" he asked.

"As soon as you can," the bird replied. "You may reach the Lord Marc's door by nightfall if you leave at once."

Galahad looked towards Bedivere, and his face paled a little. The older knight saw his look and took pity on him. "Tomorrow will be soon enough," he said, "for it is late to reach Bodmin today. Let us gather our belongings and our thoughts, and take pleasure in our last night under this roof. Then we will away at dawn."

Galahad nodded, but the Merlin fluttered his wings a little anxiously. "Indeed I tell you that the journey will be an easy one, even if you linger for an hour over your leave taking. It would be better to be gone."

"Is there some trouble you are keeping from us?" Bedivere asked, eyeing the Merlin narrowly. "For otherwise this haste seems vain."

"No new trouble, Bedivere," the bird answered, "but should you not put your king before your ease?"

Bedivere's face reddened and the bird flew up suddenly to the porch roof out of reach. "You speak out of turn, bird! When has any questioned my loyalty?"

"Never, Bedivere," the Merlin replied. "But I would have you hasten nonetheless."

"And I would linger one night more," Galahad said, a little shame-faced, "if you think it right, Bedivere. You spoke of the mystery of the heart, bird, and you will perhaps think me foolish, but I would take my leave of all here."

"Gladly, if you choose to stay against my advice," the bird agreed, fluttering back to the knight's wrist and pecking his sleeve peaceably, "they have been good friends to you both."

"Nay, I meant not the young folk," Galahad returned. "If you will spare me I must return to the dragon's lair and bid farewell to my legacy for a little while. In some strange way it is a comfort to me that the book is safely guarded and that I will always know where to find it."

The bird shook his feathers and looked cross. "Nay, Galahad, nay! How many times must you tread that wearisome path along the cliff only to find sorrow at the end of it?"

"Indeed, the path is a pleasure, for something new and beautiful is always to be seen along the way. And I will not lack company for I believe that Ralph and Charity will come with me."

"And can you not rest safe in the knowledge that the book is in the dragon's grasp without returning ever to the spot?" asked the bird in a vexed tone.

"No, I cannot. Not today. For many days will come when I must be far from here and must trust to that knowledge. I cannot rest, Merlin, knowing that I am to leave tomorrow."

"It will be dark before you return."

"But the sky is clear, and starlight will guide us home. What troubles you so, Merlin, that you cast so many objections in my way? Fear not, I will not fight the beast today. See, I do not even wear armour."

"If you must go, then so should we all," the Merlin said heavily. But to himself he added, "and the misgivings of my heart will be proved true at last."

I set her on my pacing steed,
And nothing else saw all day long,
For sidelong would she bend, and sing
                    A faery's song.

Dreams

Kay and Mordred, Gawain and Wolf had a peaceful journey that first day. They saw few villages, few people, and no glimpse of the sea for they were far from the shore, riding through the inland ways of the west. Inns they did pass, but they were ramshackle places and Mordred declared that he preferred the hard ground to the lice that were sure to inhabit the sheets of their beds. So after a brief halt at one inn to feed the horses, they found a sheltered back lane and camped on the verge, contenting themselves with a supper of bread and wine. Kay lit a fire and Wolf lay with his head in Gawain's lap, dreaming a little, twitching his long legs and whiskery snout in his sleep. Mordred sat a little apart, his back against a tree and his eyes closed. Kay squatted beside the fire and began to polish his sword with a clean cloth, examining the blade for blemishes or rust. Those he found he rubbed away with strong and patient fingers.

Mordred opened his eyes and watched him, and then moved closer to warm his hands at the blaze while he sipped his wine, cupping the mug in his palm. "Many years have you tended your sword I warrant, Kay."

"More years than bear remembrance," Kay returned. "But lately it has been a habit more than a dire need. Until this enchantment fell upon Arthur judgement has been my weapon for many a year. And just as skilful must he be, Mordred, who wields justice as he who wields a blade, and just as carefully must he tend his judgement to prevent its edge being dulled by age, or ease, or indolence."

"And have you not missed the fray?"

"Never!" Kay looked towards Gawain sheepishly, but the burly knight was nodding over his supper and took no heed of their talk. "I have never sought battle, for life is too precious. I did my part in all our wars, but I was glad when they ended."

"Not like Lancelot."

"Nay!" Kay laughed shortly. "Lancelot is a strutting peacock, and his pride is his valour and his skill, which he must display."

"But he is no fool for all that."

"Indeed not. He has always been first amongst the knights of the round table. From the moment that Arthur met him his place was assured."

"He has spent much time with the king over these many years. Often has he visited us at Camelot."

"He has." Kay was silent for a space. "And much time has he spent with the queen also."

Mordred flushed. "Yet no one has ever spoken evil of my aunt, for she is gracious and loyal to her lord."

Kay looked up and smiled at Mordred's earnestness. "Indeed, you speak truth, Mordred. You love the queen, do you not?"

"Of course. She has been more than a mother to me, Kay, ever since I could talk. I have always felt like a fraud at the round table, for I am no knight, but she above all others has led me on to study and to use my head in the king's service. All who know her love her, for she is fair and kind and altogether good."

"She is all those things, and you should know it more than most, for you have lived under her roof your whole life. But forgive me if I say that for even longer, since Guinevere came to wed Arthur as a young maid who barely knew her husband, Lancelot has seemed a danger to the king's peace. The queen loves and reveres Arthur and I can find no fault with her. But there is too much beauty between Guinevere and Lancelot. It has something of sorcery about it, and it has ever seemed to threaten our brotherhood."

"Yet the Merlin has sent them away together on this quest. He must see more."

"Who knows what the bird sees! That too is full of wizardry and mischief. The Merlin is our friend, Mordred, but he does not judge as we do. None of the creatures of magic can – how should they? It is the very danger I fear that the Merlin relishes. Their passion and beauty is a magic to wield against our enemy as he said himself. But the bird cares not for the consequences."

Later it seemed to Mordred that he woke in the dark hours before dawn to find Morgan le Fay sitting by the fireside, now sunk to a pile of embers. She wore her favourite dull green dress, which glistened in the glow of the fire, and she seemed to him as lovely as Guinevere, though dark where the queen was fair. Her hair swung across her face and her eyes were like emeralds, gleaming in the firelight. Mordred gazed in wonder as she smiled roguishly.

"Is there danger in this beauty, Mordred?" she asked, echoing Kay's words before they slept. "Do you fear me?"

"No!" Mordred reached for her, but she was gone, standing beyond the fire, her face lit with a dull red light.

"That is well, for there is no danger in beauty, Mordred, without knowledge. Is that not so?"

Mordred frowned. "Yes – no – I know not what you mean."

"Danger comes from within, not without, as I think you do know. Is there danger within you, Mordred?"

He shook his head. "I hope not, Morgan. There is knowledge in me, but that need not be danger."

She laughed and again her hair swung across her face. "But secrets may be. Did you tell Arthur of the books I showed you?"

"He must know what lies in his own library."

"Then you did not tell him!" Now there was triumph in her tone. "Do you remember what you read, child?"

"I am no child!"

"Oh, but you are, Mordred!" she mocked him, even as his eyes fell on the sheen of her skin, smooth and warm, and he reached for her again. "You are ever the dutiful child! Will you always be so?"

"Do not tease me, Morgan," he answered. "You used to mock those who thought me weak."

"Show me your strength then!" She smiled and her teeth flashed white against her skin like a gypsy. "Do you want me, Mordred?"

"I do!"

"Then make me come to you!" There she stood on the far side of the fire, but he could not move and he knew then that he was dreaming. "Call me, Mordred!"

"Come, Morgan, come!" he said hoarsely, his hand outstretched. "You know that I love you!"

She laughed, and there was contempt in it. "Can Mordred the wise do no better than that? 'Come, Morgan,'" she whined in mockery. "''Morgan, I love thee!' Do you not know words more powerful than that?"

He was angry then, and the words she spoke of came into his mind unbidden. Of a sudden he remembered a book in his uncle's library which Morgan had shown him. It was an old tale of a dragon guarding a princess in a tower, and only words from the old language could summon her to the hero's arms. Now they rose to his lips hot and fervent. *"Dos omma!"* He heard himself speaking, but the words sounded strange in his ears as though it was still the hero from the story who spoke, not himself. "Come to me! *Dos omma, Morgan le Fay!"* The fire blazed for a moment and then all at once she was beside him, as he had bid her, warm and soft. He flushed with pleasure as he wound his fingers in her dark hair and laid his lips against her neck. "This is your strength, Mordred," she whispered. "Do not fear the wits that nature gave you!" She took hold of his face in both her hands and for a moment her lips touched his, hot and sweet. His head swam. "Be ready," she whispered, "for there will soon be one who needs you, and only your wits will save her."

Then she was gone, and Mordred lay suddenly wide-awake in the silence, staring into the embers of the fire and aching after empty space.

~

They left the farm together, the young ones merry in Galahad's company now that his sorrow had passed away. Bedivere and the Merlin followed behind, Bedivere musing on their previous walks along the same path and all that had transpired since they had left Camelot, and the Merlin wrapped in his own thoughts. Charity looked a little pale, Bedivere thought, at the prospect of their leaving, and Galahad held her hand as they walked along the rough path with tender care.

As soon as they reached the cliff top above the dragon's beach they could see that something had happened, for the ground rose and fell under their feet, torn and gouged. Galahad cast the others an agitated look, then he plunged down the steep path slithering and sliding down to the cove with the rest behind him. On the sand he stopped and put his hands to his head, bewildered.

The cave had been ripped apart, great chunks of rock thrown down around its mouth as though a mighty sea had battered and eroded it away in the course of a single night. The narrow passageway to the inner chamber was gone, and the dragon's hidden lair laid open to view. The dragon itself was nowhere to be seen, though great claw tracks led across the firm sand to the sea, the dragging marks from its tail showing behind. To the sea they led, and then vanished. The beast had swum from the shore.

Bedivere and the children ran towards the cave, pausing in the entrance to make sure that all was really safe. Then they stepped inside with cries of wonder, for the dragon had left all his treasure behind. A great pile of precious things lay jumbled on the rocky floor of the cave, gold and silver and jewels all heaped together and bearing the impression of the beast's body, for it had lain on them like a great jagged nest.

"See!" Ralph cried towards Galahad where he still stood at the water's edge. "See Galahad! It is a king's ransom!" He held up a pewter goblet to the light and traced a finger along its simple decorative lines. "I shall have a horse after all!"

Galahad was barely listening. He was staring out at the blank horizon and scanning the cliffs at either side of the cove. But there was nothing to be seen. If the dragon was still nearby it was submerged beneath the vast ocean or hidden in some cove invisible from the shore.

Then Galahad turned and sprinted towards the cave. He fell to his knees beside the great pile of treasures and began to rummage through them feverishly, throwing precious objects aside in his search. Almost at once he stopped again, for the task was too great and the heap of objects too vast. He rose to his feet and began to scan the cave floor and its innermost shelves and ledges. The Merlin flew into the cave and settled on the top of the treasure pile, watching him calmly, until at length Galahad fell to his haunches again and looked at the bird.

"Well, Merlin? Hast any wisdom to impart this time?"

"No wisdom, Galahad, but I can tell you what has passed here, and where the beast and the book have gone."

"Indeed!" Galahad stared at him, confounded. "Is this your usual magic or something more?"

"My knowledge is always something more than it seems," the bird returned unperturbed by Galahad's tone. "But I have been here only this morning and saw the beast leave the cave."

"You saw it? How came that good fortune?"

"It was not fortune." At last the bird looked a little abashed. "I may conceal some things from you, Galahad, but I will not tell a lie. It was I that set the dragon free."

For a moment there was silence. Then Galahad smote the ground so violently with his fist that blood ran from his knuckles. "Bird, what are you, that you thwart me at every turn? You have stolen this thing from me twice over and I would know your purpose."

"I am your friend, Galahad, your friend only."

Galahad murmured something disbelieving, turning his head away as though he did not trust his own temper if he looked at the bird. The Merlin spoke in a gentler tone.

"Do you think I do not know how much you desire to find this book again? Do you think I do not know how much your thoughts run on the grail? Indeed, you may have seemed at peace when I returned to the farm today, but I knew that was not so. I knew that Bedivere's oath filled your thoughts and that your stay at Camelot would have been but a short one, had the book remained here."

"How do you know of my oath?" Bedivere demanded. He too was regarding the bird with hostile eyes.

"It matters not how I knew. But once the knowledge came to me I foresaw that time was short for Galahad. He would return with all speed to fight the beast and regain the book. And do you think he would have succeeded?"

There was silence. "How could he succeed? With all the strength and goodness he possesses he could not defeat such a beast in such a stronghold, when the beast was bound about with sorcery and he had none. Galahad would return and he would die. So I flew here this morning and I let the beast go and saw it take the book with it. For now it too is consumed by the thought of the grail, and it left its treasures behind without a backward glance."

"And do you think I shall let it go unfollowed?"

"I know not. For I hoped you would return to Camelot without knowledge of my deed. By the time you returned here the beast would be long gone and the trail cold. Now I do not know what you will do, for as I have said too often, men's paths are hidden from me."

Galahad gazed out of the cave mouth at the grey sea, biting on his injured fist thoughtfully. Bedivere gave a grumbling sigh and began to pick aimlessly through the treasures flung about on the sand. Ralph and Charity hugged their knees, sitting together in the shadow, watching Galahad's face. At length he stirred and looked at them, and then he smiled, suddenly at peace again.

"Is fate not a curious thing?" he said, and held out his hands to them. "Who knows what the Merlin thinks, or how much or how little he understands of men and their hearts. But now I see that knowingly or by chance, the Merlin has advanced my fate. For he is right. The book could not remain in this cave, for though it was safe it was utterly beyond the reach of man while the dragon lived. Perhaps it would have given me more time to serve Arthur, and perhaps to seek my own happiness, for the quest for the grail would have been beyond me. I might even have died at the beast's hands as the bird fears. But now the quest is set in motion. My destiny is upon me and the prophecy is fulfilled. For what else can I do now, except follow my fate and pursue the dragon? Indeed, as I think of it I can see that all that has happened has led to this moment, even the giving of the book to the beast."

They were all silent, shivering in the dank air from a chill of the heart as well as the body. Galahad went to Charity, taking her hand and pulling Ralph close to his side. "So it seems that I will leave you for longer than I hoped," he said. "For I know not where my path leads or how long my feet will walk upon it. Tomorrow I must find a boat in Padstow, and a crew willing to undertake a perilous journey." He glanced at the piles of treasures around them and laughed grimly. "At least I shall not lack a reward to tempt them to my service."

The Merlin hopped to his shoulder then, and the young knight stroked his feathers. "Forgive me bird," he said. "I know you are no devil, for all that you mock my God."

"And I have never meant to harm you, Galahad," the bird replied, "for you are worthy above all other men save Arthur. I must confess to you that I wish the grail would stay unfound, but I do not suppose you will heed me."

"I fear I must heed my fate, for it will not let me rest."

"And yet you are still young, and you might put your king above your God for many more years if you tried." Galahad only shook his head, and the bird sighed. "But listen, I will not hinder you, for I see it is vain. If you will take the aid of a wizard I might even do you some good. Do you see any treasures here that mean something to you?"

Galahad turned with surprise to examine the heap of precious things more closely than he had done before. He shook his head as he surveyed the piles of treasure, but then he laughed and reached out his hand to grasp a sword that hung from a chain beside the entrance to the cave.

"Tell me Merlin – is this the article I tangled myself with so sorely when I crept in here before?"

"It is. Your own sword wrapped itself around the chain and in the darkness you could not loosen one from the other. And look above, for there you will see what woke the dragon."

Galahad grasped the chain and pulled as he looked up. Once again came that sonorous ringing that had sounded so loud in the confines of the dark cave.

"What is it?"

"The shield of the knight who bore the sword. Can you free them?"

With some hazard Galahad retrieved the shield from its place in the roof of the cave and unwound the sword from the chain. The weapons were old and heavy, and the shield bore a red cross on the front.

"This armour and this sword belonged once to a knight of great renown," the Merlin said soberly. "Indeed I met him once, many years ago, when I travelled with Arthur and Kay. He was not an amiable man, but in those days no dragon could stand before him and the wrath of his God. Now it seems that he met his end in this cave, and perhaps his bones moulder among these treasures. Well then, Galahad, I bid you take these weapons which have served your God against dragons before. If you meet the beast again use them, for they have been in his keeping too, and to use the dragon's own weapons against him will bring you great power."

Galahad threw down his own sword among the treasure trove and buckled on the new one. He took the shield in his hand, grimacing under its weight, but he could feel its solid strength and he knew the bird spoke the truth. Then he turned to Bedivere and grasped his arm with a look of respect and affection. "Our first quest is indeed at an end, Bedivere, and you have the key. So I shall not hold myself a traitor to my king if I go now on a new one. Go home, good friend, and rest until the others return. All will be well."

~

When Lancelot and Guinevere left the inn that same morning bright sunlight reflected off their mail shirts and the fine harness of the horses. They clattered through the streets down to the jetty, followed by the good-natured stares of the villagers and groups of children who ran behind the horses laughing and shouting.

"I like this place," Guinevere said, scattering a handful of gold into the dusty roadway behind her for the children to scrabble up with nimble fingers. "If the west is to be free one day I will return for my pots, and for the pleasant manners of the people."

"We will need to come with caution and good will," Lancelot replied, shortening his rein as the horses' hooves rattled onto the wooden jetty. "For they will welcome us less warmly if they think us a threat to their independence and the free use of their woods that they have enjoyed so long."

"Arthur does not seek dominion for its own sake," Guinevere said. "He looks to bring good, not take it away."

"Well, if we can rid them of this lizard in the forest we will have begun the work."

As Lancelot spoke they could see the large ferry raft approaching across the river mouth, rowed by several strong men. The cumbersome vessel came slowly, smaller and lighter craft giving way to its ponderous progress. At last it collided gently with the jetty and ropes were thrown across and lashed to the timber corner posts. Lancelot and Guinevere slipped from their saddles and urged their horses forward onto the deck. The animals went at last, trembling a little and sweating as their hooves left the solid safety of the jetty and stepped onto the swaying raft. Guinevere stroked her mare's neck comfortingly as the ferry moved out into the sparkling expanse of water. There were no other passengers, and the crew was taciturn as they rowed the unwieldy vessel through the water. Lancelot too was silent, his eyes fixed on the green woods that grew down to the waterline on the opposite bank, the leaves a tapestry of colours in their spring freshness. After a moment he turned to Guinevere.

"I do not think the woods of Bodmin were so green, for all their magic."

"It is the climate I believe," she returned. "We have descended many yards from the height of the moor to this spot, and there is a new warmth in the air I have not felt before."

"You are not deceived, ma'am," the ferryman nodded from his place beside her, though his eyes never left the river. "We are fortunately placed here, in an elbow of land you might say, and facing the sun. We reckon to harvest our beans a full month before folks inland."

Lancelot smiled and winked at Guinevere. "Well, that decides it, for the beans will not lie nor profess any local attachment without cause. And now you mention it I believe I do feel a good deal warmer than at any time since we left Camelot, even here in the midst of the water where the breezes blow from the sea."

His tone was cheerful, but Guinevere could see his eyes turn ever to the woods ahead and she shivered suddenly as if to belie his words. It had been one thing to ride against a dragon in the company of many knights and with Lord Marc's small army. Now she did feel afraid, even with Lancelot beside her.

They reached the far bank after many minutes, long enough for the horses to quieten and begin to nibble at the straw strewn over the wooden planks of the deck. At the far shore a handful of cottages clustered beneath a steep cliff. A couple of fishermen sat on a rough bench outside the nearest. Lancelot and Guinevere could see the eaves of the wood lowering a quarter of a mile distant inland along the riverbank.

They paid the ferryman and led the horses off the raft which tied up to the bank, the crew sitting down in the sunshine glad of the rest, and ready for a chat with the watching fishermen while they waited for their next passengers. Under the pretence of adjusting the mare's girth Lancelot spoke quietly to Guinevere.

"I would make a course for the forest without so many eyes upon us, for we know not if all folks here are as friendly as we think, nor whether any have dealings with wizards. A dragon will be fearsome enough without sorcery. Let us ride up the hill as though we purpose to travel along the coast like other men. We can turn back towards the woods when we are out of sight."

"As you wish," Guinevere replied, "though I like not the look of the hill for it is over-steep. I will walk to save the mare's legs."

Accordingly they set off up the road which grew steeper as it cut its way up the tall cliff. A fine prospect of the sea gradually unfolded before them and they could see the coastline curving away to both north and south as the ferryman had said.

It was a hard climb and they spoke little and breathed hard, for Lancelot also slipped down from his saddle halfway up the slope. The horses for their part stepped out eagerly, glad to be on dry land once more. As they crested the hill they saw the land stretching away before them laid to pasture and fields of grain on both sides, and more or less level as far as the eye could see, for the cliffs remained lofty for many a mile ahead. Lancelot remounted and stood up in his stirrups to look behind him.

"Well, we are safely out of sight of the villages and the river, whatever else may be watching," he said. "Let us turn to our left and make our way across these fields and meadows back to the wood."

Guinevere turned her horse's head to follow him as he left the safety of the coast road into the green fields. They skirted around the edges, mindful of the tender shoots of the farmer's crops. A hare bounded away in front of them, crashing into the hedgerow. A buzzard clattered out of an old tree stump and flapped lazily in pursuit.

"I feel as though I walked through a dream," Guinevere said, "for all is so beautiful and yet so laden with menace."

"Do not waste your strength in fears yet," Lancelot returned. "In the fields we are safe I believe. It will be only when we gain the woods that we shall need to be on our guard."

They said no more as they approached ever nearer to the margin of the woods. Guinevere prayed, her lips moving silently, and thought of Arthur lying at Camelot to strengthen her resolve. Lancelot grew taut and ready as a bowstring as the trees grew nearer. Long had he wished for danger and adventure and now they were upon him. He was hardly conscious of Guinevere at his side as the pulse beat in his head. Battle was near, and he must trust to his own strength in arms to save her if the need came.

To their heightened senses the forest seemed dark and foreboding as the horses stepped into its shadow, following a narrow track that presently broadened so that they could ride abreast, eyes turned ever towards the dense undergrowth on either side. But both their fears and their readiness soon seemed wasted, for they rode deep into the forest without seeing or hearing anything of the beast they sought. Lancelot's heart slowed, and even Guinevere's fears began to subside as they rode on and on and the sun rose higher in the sky towards noon. The trees became sparser, and dappled sunlight found its way through the branches so that flowers grew in the occasional clearings and birds fluted from all sides.

"Well!" she said at last, with a short laugh. "It is trying to the nerves and the heart to strain the eyes and ears for so long to no purpose! I half hope that the dragon knows who comes to seek him and cowers away from us like a hunted beast. Do you think the fame of Lancelot can have penetrated even here?"

"It may have done," Lancelot replied, with neither modesty nor pride. Then, on an impulse he stood in his stirrups "Hi! Beast!" he shouted, so that his voice echoed and re-echoed amid the muffled silence of the trees, "come forth if you be not afraid! For I am Lancelot, greatest of all the knights of the round table! Will you meet me in combat or skulk forever in the bushes like the lizard you are?"

Lancelot sat down, his voice hoarse, and the echo of his words faded away. Guinevere had involuntarily covered her ears and quailed, expecting the monster to come bursting out of the undergrowth in answer to his call. Now she slowly lowered her hands with a shaky breath and turned her head to listen. No sound came in answer. Nothing moved in the bushes save a thrush that flew out under the horses' hooves and skulked along the path ahead before finding a way back into the tangled branches of the undergrowth.

For a moment all was still as they listened, then they looked at each other and Lancelot gave a shame-faced grin. Guinevere shook her head at him and laughed with relief.

"Verily, verily, Lancelot, are you not the same youth I met so many years since, so impetuous and so foolhardy?"

"I am, Guinevere, in all essentials," he replied, leaning over to take her hand and kiss it with brash gallantry. Then he sobered, and sighed. "Aye, that I am! Older and no wiser I fear."

Guinevere retrieved her hand, and smiled to herself as they began to move slowly along the woodland track once more. Since Lancelot's outburst the woods had returned to their wonted peace and silence, apart from the occasional rustle in the undergrowth that told of a bird or a rabbit fleeing before them.

"I remember well when we first met," she said. "I believe I thought that Arthur's knights were a myth before I wedded him. But there you all were at the ceremony. A handsome company!" She was silent for a moment, and the only sound was the thud of the horses' hooves on the dirt track. "Indeed, we were all handsome, young and artless. But it is many, many years since then."

Lancelot looked across at her slender figure, sitting gracefully astride her mare, her hair loosely plaited to keep it from her face, falling down her back like a river of gold, and he smiled. "The years have not robbed you yet of youth or vigour, Guinevere. Indeed, you are as fair here in this wood as you were on your wedding day."

Guinevere cast him a derisive look. "It is well that we keep no likeness of ourselves from those days. I believe you would see a difference if you could now but see me as I was then."

"Years give as well as take away. I do not believe you would have chosen this road in those days."

Guinevere nodded. "Indeed, you speak the truth. Youth is prey to fears, and the girl looks for a nest. Yet when I had found my own and sat at the window at Camelot, watching the seasons change as my life went on unaltered in its habits, I came to believe that I could see my life stretching before me even to death." She shivered. "It was a fearsome thing, Lancelot, and you will not believe me when I say that I feel less real terror here in this wood with all its menace. The future is now a mystery once more and my life the richer for it." She paused again and then added in an altered tone. "Indeed, I do not rejoice that this should come through Arthur's danger, but so it is and it cannot be helped."

"Much may come from events unwished for." Lancelot replied. "I too was chained by the regular train into which my life had fallen. What capricious creatures we are, Guinevere, that we cannot make ourselves safe without forging cages to dwell in, which only make us repine for the danger we have lost!"

"Sometimes I wonder if our quest to pacify the land and purge it of magic will not make all folks feel likewise," Guinevere said. "And yet how can we suffer witches like Demelza to wreak their cruelties unchecked? And indeed, how can I speak ill of the path which has guided Arthur's steps since we were wed?" She hung her head again and her lip trembled suddenly.

"You must not reproach yourself," Lancelot urged, his voice kind. "Always you have been faithful to Arthur, faithful against all temptation. You have nothing to be ashamed of."

His tone made Guinevere raise her head and look at him. "And do you reproach yourself Lancelot?"

"Hourly, and yet never." His tone was grim.

"You have little to repine for. You are the bravest and strongest and noblest of Arthur's knights and ever have been. Where others are faithful and do their duty, you blaze out in glory. What can you have to regret?"

Even as she spoke, Guinevere knew his answer and wished that she had not asked him. Lancelot looked sidelong at her and put his hand to his heart in a courtly bow.

"You of all people must know, Guinevere. And had I not a fine son to show for my faithlessness and unruly desires I should be more ashamed than I am. Indeed, Galahad is Arthur's noblest knight, not I."

"He is a jewel," Guinevere agreed, glad to turn the conversation. But then, somehow, riding as they were deeper into the forest and further from the haunts of men, Guinevere felt all at once an overmastering longing to know at last if the rumours of many years were true. Words unbidden rose to her lips and she added "he is the very image of his mother."

Lancelot cast her a startled look as she trod this dangerous ground, never before canvassed between them, and then he laughed bitterly.

"Aye! And what irony it is that he should, when I so clearly saw you in my arms that fateful night!"

"But you were bewildered with a potion they say," Guinevere spoke questioningly, looking at her hand as she stroked the mare's mane.

"Bewildered I surely was, but that did not lessen the betrayal of my king. I met temptation, Guinevere, and unlike you I could not resist it."

Guinevere was silent, and her face was stern, but inwardly her heart glowed. Always rumours had pursued them, always folks had whispered that Lancelot loved her and that he had begotten Galahad under an enchantment that lent Elaine her own appearance in his eyes. And now she found that it was all true and she rejoiced, for while she would never betray Arthur she could not help but glory in Lancelot's love.

There was a conscious silence between them for a space, for Lancelot had never before told his passion in earnest and Guinevere had never owned any knowledge of his heart. But out of their momentary embarrassment came a deeper understanding and mutual warmth. All those troubles had happened so long ago after all, and their own friendship had endured for so many years. Lancelot's words only drew them closer in fellowship and they turned their eyes back to scan the woods around them with braver spirits.

"Do you hear anything?" Lancelot asked after a while, his voice returned to its normal tone, yet perhaps kindlier than before.

"No, nothing," Guinevere returned. But even as she spoke a twig snapped loudly at their backs and Lancelot wheeled his horse around, his hand going to his sword. Guinevere's mare whinnied in fear and reared on her hindquarters before the reins slipped from Guinevere's fingers and the mare bolted, crashing through the undergrowth in wild career with Guinevere clinging to her mane.

~

Lancelot found her lying on the ground close to the river bank, fallen into a swoon and with a streak of mud across her forehead where it had hit the ground. Her horse stood at a distance and as Lancelot approached the mare snorted with fear, showing the whites of her eyes and baring her teeth in a nervous grimace. For the moment, though, Lancelot had eyes only for the rider, whom he approached fearfully, kneeling beside her on the loose litter of the forest floor and lifting her into his arms as he tried to revive her. The mare approached a little closer across the clearing and snorted again. Lancelot shook Guinevere gently and called her name, and after a moment she sighed and opened her eyes to look around her, bewildered.

"My lady!" Lancelot urged her gently, "Guinevere! Have you any hurt?"

Guinevere shifted in his arms and gave a cry of pain. "Aye!" she said weakly. "Dreadful pains in my hands and feet, and an ache from lying so awkwardly here on the ground." She struggled to a sitting position and hung her head, feeling her own limbs gingerly and running a hand around her neck to check that all was well. Then she looked up at Lancelot and smiled faintly. "But indeed I am in one piece and all as it should be. How dazed I feel, and how strange!"

"What happened? Did the mare throw you?"

"Aye, for I am a feeble horsewoman after all, it seems. She charged into the bushes and I lost my seat."

"You did not see the beast?"

"No! Did you?"

"No. Something moved in the woods behind us and startled the horses. But I flew after you too quickly to see what it was. I feared that if I lost you in this wilderness I should never find you more."

Guinevere said little, and Lancelot regarded her with compassion as she stretched experimentally and then struggled to rise. Swiftly he went to help her and she stood unsteadily on her feet, leaning on his arm as he called to the mare. No nearer would the horse come however and Guinevere seemed to rally as she looked at her.

"Poor thing! She has received a fright greater than my own, I fear. I wonder if she saw something we did not? Do not press her, Lancelot. She mistrusts me, it seems, for my part in her fright. You lead her for a while and I shall walk. Indeed, it will do me good to find my feet."

They both walked, Lancelot leading the horses and Guinevere gaining strength and purpose with every step. They found their way back through the broken branches and shattered undergrowth of the mare's flight to the path they had been following and stood quietly for a moment listening. Nothing stirred but the horses, who stamped and breathed heavily, still restless and ready for flight. Lancelot shook his head.

"I fear that the monster lurks nearby, for the horses sense danger and I too feel a sense of dread about me. But we can do nothing but wait till it reveal itself to us. How fare you, my lady?"

"Better," Guinevere admitted, "yet tense and nervous like the animals. How hard it is to wait and watch and do nothing!" She was silent for a moment and then Lancelot began to walk on in the direction they had been going before the mare's flight, deeper and yet deeper into the woodland. Guinevere's voice came from behind him with a tone of plaint almost childlike and he paused to let her take his arm. "How will you defeat the beast, Lancelot? If we can only wait for it to reveal itself, how can you triumph? Will it not be upon us before we are aware?"

"It may," Lancelot said grimly, "and such a surprise it has sprung many times. But I am hopeful, Guinevere. Never has Lancelot been defeated in a test of arms, and my arm has always been quick to answer many an unseen blow. But we must be as watchful as we can, for while I fear no ambush I do not court one either."

"I am ever listening," Guinevere said. "But I fear we must rest soon, Lancelot, and perhaps take some refreshment, for I am weary and not myself. When we find a spot that seems safe let us pause a little."

The sun was now well past its height and Lancelot looked at her with renewed concern for they had eaten nothing since leaving the inn. "Indeed, I am a thoughtless brute myself!" he said, "for I have given you neither rest, food nor drink for many an hour. And indeed I too am weary from much watching. Let us tarry a while and rest the horses and ourselves."

So when they came to a sunny clearing with a glimpse of the river through the trees they made their way to the water's edge and rested with their backs against the broad trunk of an old pine, leaning out over the quiet reaches of the river. It was a beautiful place, where ancient woods grew down thickly to the water's edge. Herons perched in the branches of meadow trees on the opposite bank and gulls wheeled noiselessly over the water up and down stream.

"Here we are as safe as anywhere," Lancelot said, "for the beast can come at us but from one side, and we can flee to the water if it appears and make for the open fields on the opposite shore."

"Think you that it cannot swim?"

"I know not. I know little of dragons."

Guinevere sighed with sudden contentment and leaned her head back against the tree trunk, closing her eyes. "Here I could sleep, Lancelot! How peaceful it seems!"

Lancelot looked at her, and saw that her skin was almost translucent, and dark shadows circled beneath her eyes where the sunlight played over her face. "Indeed, you are not well!" he said with renewed concern. Guinevere opened her eyes and rolled her head towards him with a ghost of a smile.

"Do not fret, Lancelot. I am well enough. I will not destroy our hopes through womanly weakness. Give me something to eat and drink and I shall be better."

Lancelot left her reluctantly to rummage through the saddlebags for the provisions they had brought from the inn. He laughed as he found that the landlady had tucked a bottle of the inn's strong beer in among his possessions and he showed it to Guinevere who smiled and wrinkled her nose. They sat down to a plain repast of bread and butter and water from the river. Guinevere wished for meat to give her strength but there was none.

"What shall we do if the sun sets on our search and we have not found the beast?" she asked, when they were finished and sat quietly looking at the river.

"That I do not know. I mislike the notion of a night in the woods, and I think we shall need to retrace our steps soon if the beast remains hidden, in order to reach the fields once more before dark. I had counted on the dragon revealing itself to us. If it does not we must make a different plan." He sighed and glanced behind him at the thick undergrowth. "And yet the day is young and I will not tempt fate by deeming our search already vain." He rose to his feet and proffered her his hand as he had done on the moor the previous day, but now there was no flirtation in the act. She took it and stood up with a grunt of pain.

"I would walk still," she said, "for I trust not the mare's temper in this place and would avoid another fall if I could. Ride if you wish to, Lancelot, and I shall walk beside you."

But Lancelot would not ride while his lady walked, so they continued on foot for some while, Lancelot keeping an anxious eye on the sun as well as the surrounding trees. Guinevere appeared to listen too, but Lancelot thought her faint and distant, and he watched her equally anxiously. After some time she groaned and began to fumble at her leather jerkin with awkward fingers. "Indeed, I am hot!" she said, and as Lancelot looked at her he saw that her face glowed feverishly and her skin was flushed. "I am too hot to bear this weight about me!" She found the straps that held the jerkin cinched about her waist and released them, pulling it over her head and throwing it across the mare's back to reveal her mail shirt which now hung loose to her knees. Lancelot said naught but stopped the horses and offered to lift her into the saddle. The mare broke away nervously and Guinevere pushed away his hand. "Nay, fear not Lancelot. I will be well. But the fall has left me a little light-headed and heavy of foot. Let me take off this mail shirt also and I shall walk easier for the loss of the burden."

"I like that not, my lady," replied Lancelot, "for you will be unprotected should the beast strike. Your mail will guard you if I cannot."

"Yet I cannot bear its weight and confinement," Guinevere returned, "and I fear that I will never have the strength to leave this place for weariness with it on me. Let me take it off and in return I will mount your horse, for he seems calmer than the mare. Then if the beast comes I shall be carried to safety no doubt, whether I will it or no."

Lancelot gave in reluctantly and saw her seated astride his great war horse in her breeches and shirt, her feet dangling short of the stirrups and her head nodding a little over the horse's neck. A sense of doom came suddenly upon him, and his heart failed, for he feared that their expedition into the forest was fated and the Merlin's misgivings true. He bitterly regretted that he should have any woman beside him, least of all Guinevere, for he could neither help nor abandon her and if the beast came upon him he would be encumbered and weak. As these black thoughts filled his mind he looked up and saw the sun halfway to the horizon. He had left it too long he thought, fear striking his heart of a sudden. They would not reach the fields by nightfall and they would be set upon in the impenetrable darkness of the wood where no stars could reach. With a shudder he stopped abruptly and turned the horses' heads back the way they had come. Guinevere roused herself and looked around her blearily.

"What passes, Lancelot?"

"We turn back, my lady. The sun sinks and I fear lest we have left it too late already."

Guinevere made no reply and they retraced their steps, Lancelot gloomier with every stride. He had entered the woods with high hopes for glory and yet again he would be unsatisfied. He felt resentment in his heart against Guinevere for falling, and yet he knew it was unjust. The dragon had not showed itself, and even had Guinevere been well they would still be returning to the safety of the fields through the mellow afternoon sunshine.

It was warm in the wood now, early butterflies darting ahead of the horses through the wild garlic which lined the path and released its delicious smell on the warm breeze as the horse's hooves crushed it. Bluebell leaves clustered thickly in the clearings, though not yet in flower, while faded violets lay half-concealed amid the shorter grass. Guinevere began to sing wordlessly to herself as she dozed over the horse's neck in the sunshine. The air grew thicker and drowsier in its mid-afternoon repose, and it was hard to believe that there was any menace lurking near. Lancelot himself fell more and more into a reverie as they walked on.

Lower and lower the sun sank and the end of the wood felt still at some distance, but he had fallen into a fatalistic humour and shrugged to himself that fortune would settle the outcome of the day with or without his aid. As the sun's rays struck horizontally through the branches onto their faces Guinevere came to herself and looked about her. Then, wordlessly, she reached down and pulled the boot from her foot where it hung at Lancelot's side. Off came the other and she crossed them before her on the pommel of the saddle and stretched her toes with pleasure as they met the warm air. Lancelot glanced up at her surprised, but she made no explanation, and he courteously turned his eyes from her bare foot and ankle.

"Indeed, it is warm and drowsy here," she said suddenly, in her clear soft voice from above him. "Have we water, Lancelot, in our baggage, or is it all drunk?"

"I fear that the landlord's beer is all we have left to us, my lady," Lancelot said, looking up into her face, suddenly bashful.

"Look, there is the river close at hand," she pointed over his head. "Let us refill our wineskins at the bank before we go further."

"I would rather not tarry longer than is needful, for the sun sinks near to the horizon."

"It will not take long, and who knows where we shall rest tonight? I am feverish, Lancelot, and I cannot wait."

She slipped from the saddle and stumbled a little clumsily in her bare feet towards the margin of the stream. Lancelot hesitated a moment and then followed with the empty water bottle, leaving the horses on the path.

"My lady!" he remonstrated. "Verily, it is foolish to run barefoot among the nettles and brambles of the forest floor lest you suffer more hurt."

"Nay!" she laughed, turning a suddenly wakeful face towards him, "it feels natural to me and I could bear the confinement of those boots upon me no more. Indeed, I feel almost myself in these light clothes after that strange, heavy mail and cumbersome jacket. If I could but taste meat I should feel strong and whole once more."

Lancelot shook his head, puzzled by her mood as he went to the water's edge and filled the wineskin. Her fever had addled her brains a little, he thought, for she seemed bolder and her voice sharper than he had ever known it. Guinevere only smiled and watched him, sitting down on the grass of the river bank and eyeing him speculatively, before looking up into the red rays of the setting sun which bathed her in a fiery light. She stretched elaborately then, like an animal waking from slumber, but with the grace that surrounded her always and had captivated Lancelot from the moment they had first met so many years before. In spite of his fears Lancelot smiled as he watched her, silhouetted by the sunset, arms raised above her head and back arched. The sun drew his attention from her though, for it hovered now only a finger's breadth above the horizon, and he looked instinctively towards the path they had been following hoping for any sign of the forest's end. And then he saw, revealed by this new vantage point by the water, that the wood's edge was nearer even than he had hoped, the open fields a matter of a hundred yards distant. He leapt to his feet and turned back to Guinevere with a look of joy.

"My lady! All is well! If we hurry we can reach the safety of the meadow in a few strides. Let us return to the horses and be gone!" She was not listening. "My lady?"

Guinevere's eye was fixed upon something in the long grass at the edge of the clearing and she was utterly still. Lancelot drew a sharp breath and the pulse that had been quiet for so long during the peaceful afternoon began to hammer again in his head. He drew his sword silently, and edged slowly forwards even as the horses on the path gave a sudden whinny of fright and a moment later he heard the swift thud of their hooves as they galloped away riderless towards the meadow.

"Dragon?" he breathed. Guinevere did not answer. And then, to his perplexity, she began to move stealthily, on hands and knees, not away from but towards whatever had caught her eye. She seemed oblivious of him, as she stopped short of the undergrowth and took up a watching stance again, like a cat hunting in a hedgerow. Lancelot watched, bemused, and opened his mouth to speak but he was too slow. With a sudden bound Guinevere crashed into the bushes and a squeal of pain, that was not human, followed. There was a scuffling and then silence. Lancelot swore an oath and burst after her through the undergrowth. She was not far away. He found her bent over, her back towards him, tearing at something with her hands and teeth.

"My lady?" he asked falteringly. Then Guinevere turned and he cried out with horror, for she held a dead rabbit in her hands and her face was smeared red from the entrails which hung from its belly torn from its warm body by her bloody teeth.

Awakenings

There was no look of shame on Guinevere's face. On the contrary she smiled, showing her blood-stained teeth, and stood up holding out the dead rabbit towards him.

"Meat at last, Lancelot!" she laughed. "And sweet flesh too. Will you take some?"

Lancelot stepped back and passed a hand across his face as though he feared he was dreaming. Towards him she advanced again, still proffering the carcass, and he stepped back in turn towards the glade. Had he looked behind him he might have seen the beast he had sought all day, watching with cold eyes from the trees on the other side of the clearing. But Lancelot's eyes were fixed on Guinevere and he was conscious of naught else. Still on she came, smiling, bearing her bloody gift.

"Take it, my lord," she said again. "Take it, for there is enough for two. It will give you strength for the battle to come, and strength you will need after this trying day."

She was upon him now, and Lancelot caught hold of her by the shoulders. As she raised her eyes to his and then looked from his anxious face to the setting sun, she smiled a smile that struck a chill into Lancelot's heart for it seemed not to belong to the Guinevere he had ever loved.

"Art bewitched?" Lancelot demanded with a sudden dread and with a sudden certainty. "Guinevere what happened when you fell from the mare in the forest? Guinevere!" He shook her shoulders roughly but she only laughed as one intoxicated, her bloody hands reaching for his shirt. Then he pushed her away in distaste, more roughly than he had meant, so that she fell to the floor her hair tumbling around her shoulders and her calico shirt falling open at the neck. She looked up at him, bewildered, and Lancelot groaned.

"My lady, I have hurt you," he cried. "But you are not yourself. Come, let us leave this place and its sorcery! The horses have bolted and whatever frightened them may still be near. Come, my lady, come! All will be well I vow, once we gain the margin of the wood."

Guinevere did not answer for a moment. Behind her shoulder the sun cast its rays upwards in a radiant ark from where it lay on the horizon, the golden light playing on the leaves and branches of the trees across the clearing so that the dragon standing there was utterly hidden from any human eye.

"Help me then, Lancelot," she said in a husky whisper. "Help me to walk. I cannot bear my own weight, for I am undone."

Lancelot stepped forward and bent, torn between loyalty and disgust, to lift her to her feet. As he did so there was a glint of silver from her neck and he saw the fine chain of her crucifix swing out from under her loosened shirt. He set her on her feet, his eyes drawn again to the flash of silver at her breast. This time the chain and its pendant fell in full sight. For a moment he gazed upon it blankly, then he gasped.

Suspended on the chain around Guinevere's slender neck was a tiny key. Of curious workmanship and ancient appearance it was, like to nothing that Lancelot had ever seen before but once. He fell back and passed a hand once more across his face.

"What is that?" he demanded hoarsely. "Where is your crucifix?"

Guinevere looked down at the key and then up at Lancelot's bewildered gaze. A shadow of vexation crossed her face he thought, followed swiftly by a helpless frown. "I know not," she said, and then staggered against him so that he was obliged to catch her and hold her in his arms. She gazed up at him, her nostrils flaring a little as though she laboured for breath, and she ran her tongue across her dry lips as she tried to smile into his dark face. "I know not what has become of me Lancelot."

"Some sorcery has bewildered you," he replied, pressing her face to his breast for comfort, his mind racing to account for the mystery. "But you must help me my lady. Tell me, how did the key come to be about your neck? For God's sake, try to remember what happened when you fell from the mare."

"I have told you all I can my lord." Guinevere's tone was suddenly petulant, and as she spoke she raised her hand to twine her fingers in his hair, pulling hard so that he winced with pain. "You trouble me with these questions and I care not to answer them." Again she tugged, pulling his head back to expose his throat, and a strange humming sound came from her lips as her other hand rose to touch the flesh thus revealed between his mail shirt and his chin. At that Lancelot wrenched himself away, and held her at arm's length to examine her once more.

Unsupported her body swayed but she did not fall, standing there dishevelled and bloody, her hair hanging about her face. Slowly she raised her head to meet his gaze, and with shock Lancelot saw that there was malice and, what was worse, greed in her glance. Now at last his eyes hardened and he drew himself up with a look of sudden loathing, for it was not Guinevere, he thought, that gazed back at him from her dark eyes.

"Thou, thou art the dragon!" he said levelly as he surveyed her. She did not answer. He drew his sword from its sheath with a hand that could not help but tremble, despite his even tone. "All this weary day I have been walking with mine enemy!" He shuddered. "Have I not? Speak to me, and tell me that you are not the beast we sought!"

He recoiled as she held out a hand to him, shaking her head but laughing recklessly, and without cause. Then on she came once more, and her nails seemed like talons as she reached out towards him with a convulsive grasp.

"Speak to me!" Lancelot said, and his composure left him. Suddenly frantic he backed away as she approached him across the grass, her hair loose, her feet bare and her shirt hanging from her shoulder, but grotesque not lovely in her disarray. On she drove him, ever closer to the spot where the dragon waited and watched. "Speak to me, fiend that I may know you for who you are!"

"You know me!" Guinevere said, reaching out her hands as she drew near. "Surely Lancelot you know me. I am your Guinevere, can you not see?"

But she laughed again, even as her fingers clutched his shirt in supplication and he pulled away from her grasp with an oath.

"My lady Guinevere!" His eyes suddenly grew wild. "Where is she? Where is my lady? What hast thou done with her, beast?"

"Done! My lord I have done naught, for here is your Guinevere! Thou ravest like a beast thyself!"

But she had grazed her nails against his neck when he had pulled away so roughly, and as she spoke she saw his blood on her finger. At the sight her eyes flickered, and instinctively she put her finger to her mouth. Across her face passed the same look of relish it had worn above the rabbit's torn flesh and drool started to her lips. Lancelot cried out then in sudden terror, and as her eyes hardened and her fingers groped greedily towards the wound once more he lunged forward, the time for questions ended. His sword flashed in the rays of the setting sun as he raised it high above his head, and even as the dragon watching from the undergrowth started towards him, there was a thud. Guinevere's body lay lifeless, her head swept from her shoulders with one blow of his sword.

Lancelot fell almost senseless as the sword slipped from his hand and his head swam. He lay for a moment, his face pressed into the cool grass, his eyes shut. All that had passed in the last minutes seemed as a dream, and for a moment he was sure that he would wake in the inn at Fowey with no worse prospect before him than a breakfast of beer. But then he listened to the silence and remembered the headless corpse falling to the floor under the bright flash of his sword blade. Guinevere it had been, as it fell; death had not undone the transformation if such it had been. He had believed from his soul that the dragon stood before him in Guinevere's fair frame as he threw himself forward with his blade upraised. Now, lying in the silence unbroken by birdsong, those thoughts seemed as the distemper of a fevered brain. Why had he believed her transformed, not merely enchanted? Could not the beast have placed the key about her neck as she lay dazed after the fall? He had believed it, that was all. The conviction had come upon him with a power he could not fight and he had obeyed. Now he wondered if it had come from without, as a worm to corrupt his heart, or within from some dark rage against her that had overcome his judgement. Reluctantly, he pulled himself to his knees and turned to the body lying on the grass beside him. The chain and its key lay flung aside in the undergrowth and he picked them up absently and thrust them inside his shirt. Then he looked at what he had done and he gave a cry of pain, but not surprise. For the body was still Guinevere's. Her blond hair, caked with blood, half-concealed the features of her face but there was no mistaking it. Her body lay broken beside her smashed skull and her hand, out-thrust towards him, now seemed to beg for mercy.

"Enchanted!" he cried brokenly, and began to sob great racking sobs, laying his face beside hers on the grass. "Enchanted, not transformed! Dead and cold, she is still Guinevere!"

He lay for a moment, lost in grief, until he heard a great rustling in the bushes beside the clearing and the thud of heavy footsteps. He sat up and raised his eyes to meet the cold gaze of the dragon with neither shock nor fear. For what else should the beast do but come now when all deception had ended? And what worst fate could he meet than he had made for himself that day?

The beast looked at him, and Lancelot returned its gaze. Small it was, as the innkeeper had described, no bigger than a man, smooth and green like a two-legged lizard, its sharp teeth showing between its powerful jaws as it watched him. Then Lancelot knelt and bowed his head, a last ray of sunlight glinting off his sword which he held before him, hands folded on its hilt.

"Thou hast triumphed," he said dully, his eyes closed and his voice low. "Thou hast triumphed beast and my life is forfeit. Take it and welcome. Thou hast dishonoured and despoiled it and I have no use for it more."

There was a pause, a sudden cooling in the air, and a dimming of the bright glow against his eyelids. Birds fluttered and called from the thickets around him, as all at once dusk fell across the wood.

Indeed, but I have," a woman's voice spoke, and it was one Lancelot had thought never to hear again. "Indeed, indeed, thou art the victor Lancelot! Open your eyes my lord!"

Lancelot looked up, as if dreaming, to find Guinevere standing before him in the dragon's stead, clad in her shirt and breeches, her feet bare and her hair fallen about her face but no longer bloodstained or vile. At her feet lay the dragon, its bloody head sliced clean from its shoulders, lifeless and cold. Guinevere was crying tears of joy and sorrow all at once. "Look, my lord! The sun is set and all things regain their wonted shapes. I am your Guinevere once more!"

Lancelot rose blindly and clasped her to his shirt, weeping more freely than he had done when he thought her dead. For a moment they clung together, then Guinevere gently disentangled herself from his embrace and tried to laugh through her tears.

"Help me Lancelot! I long to leave this accursed wood, but I have no shoes to my feet! I am no dragon, and I cannot walk through briars!"

~

The road south was bleak at times, running along the high spine of Cornwall. But as the three knights and the dog travelled on, brief glimpses of the sea began to greet them from the far distance, shining blue or brooding grey as the sun shone or disappeared behind thin clouds. For two days they travelled the lonely road, passing through occasional hamlets which straggled alongside the highway for a while and then petered into nothing. The Merlin did not return, and none of the poor folks they met knew anything of dragons. After the charm of the Lord Marc's manor in its enchantment, and the bleak moorland beauty of its real shape, the drear grassy plain they now followed seemed ugly and dull. The folks in the villages were pinched and pale looking as they loitered in the doorways watching the knights pass, or pushed their children indoors as if to protect them from the dangerous strangers. Both nights the companions slept by the roadside, Wolf keeping guard over men and horses as they slumbered.

The third day dawned grey and damp, drizzling rain waking them at first light as it fell on their faces and muddied the grass under their pillows. They rose cursing and dragged their bedrolls across to the poor shelter of a leafless tree, standing beneath its bare branches grey-faced and unshaven, gloomily watching the rain patter on the grass.

"Well, thus ends our independence on this journey," Kay said. "We shall have need of an inn tonight, however flea infested, for the grass will be wet and a fire hard to light after this rain."

"We have been more lucky than we could have hoped, however," Mordred said, shivering slightly, "for the month is but April and we have had many a dry day since we left Camelot."

"Aye, you are right and we could not hope to sleep on the ground every night I daresay," Kay conceded, beginning to smile as he looked at Mordred. "But it is a circumstance made for ill humour to be woken too early and by water. It is only looking at your mournful face that makes me any lighter of heart!"

Mordred opened his mouth to reply but was prevented by Wolf shaking his long coat vigorously beside him, showering him with yet more water. The others laughed, and so the day began.

They bundled their wet blankets onto the horses and left their camp in search of shelter. They had not been riding long when an inn came into view on the road ahead.

"Let us tarry a while," Kay said. "We are all wet and tired, and a wash in hot water and a good breakfast will cheer us up. We need not risk the beds for we should ride on again before long."

As they leapt down from their horses before the door a small child ran past them, out of the field behind the inn and towards a hovel which stood a few yards further down the road. The child was dirty but that was nothing strange. What caught the knights' gaze were the bruises that showed along its small arms. As it reached the door of the hovel a shout rose from within and it lingered in the doorway for a moment before slipping reluctantly inside.

The knights exchanged a troubled glance before entering the dark interior of the inn. Rooms and hot water were soon provided and they assembled by the fire for their breakfast in better spirits and looking more knightly than they had for many days. Bacon and beer made up their breakfast, with bread to dip in the grease. But even as they ate there was a commotion outside the inn and the sound of women's voices raised in anger. As one the knights pushed away their plates and went outside. There they found the innkeeper's wife locked in combat with a dishevelled woman in the middle of the road. The child they had seen before looked on from the doorway of the hovel its thumb in its mouth. Also watching the fray were the innkeeper and the ostler.

"What passes?" Kay asked. The innkeeper shrugged with a shame-faced smile.

"Such as passes each morning, sire. 'Tis bad for business I daresay and I crave your pardon for it. Do not let us disturb your breakfast for all will soon be quiet."

"But what ails them?" Mordred asked. "Do you mean that they fight like this every day?"

"That's about it, sire. Most days there is some such trouble. ''Tis on account of the child there. My wife is vexed to the heart by the state its mother keeps it in, and the way she carries on. My wife is a motherly woman my lords."

"We saw the child's injuries," Kay said. "Does the mother beat the child?"

"She does, but not like other mothers." The innkeeper looked around superstitiously as he spoke. "There be trouble in that house, my lords, and 'tis the child at the root of it. The boy is possessed, that's the long and short of it, and the priest has told her to whip the spirits out of him."

"A priest you say?" Kay looked surprised.

"We are old-fashioned folks ourselves, sire, and would but call on the old seer over the hill if the child was our own. That is what vexes my wife so sorely, for she sees the child mistreated and she has offered to call on the wizard but the mother will not listen. And we hear the child's screams each day, sires. 'Tis enough to make any woman mad."

Gawain was already striding across the road to the hovel. He swept the child up into his arms and brought it back to them, the child beginning to cry lustily in its turn at Gawain's strange face. The boy's cries immediately stopped the fight between the two women and they rounded on Gawain, demanding that he give the child back and pulling roughly at its clothes so that it cried the harder. At last Kay raised his hand and shouted until the women fell silent, panting and red-faced as they glared from knight to knight.

"Peace!" Kay ordered, as soon as his voice could be heard. "Fie on both of you, for you make more noise than two armies in full strife. We have heard what the innkeeper has to tell about this argument and we must intervene, for such is our duty. We wish none harm, least of all this infant, who suffers most at all your hands it seems. Let us go inside and sit quietly, that we might hear your tales and decide what is to be done."

The women were quiet now, and abashed. Neither of them thought to challenge the knights' right to judge them, for the men were tall and stern and lordly. Into the inn they went, Gawain leading the way with the child on his arm and at length they found themselves gathered around the breakfast table once more. As they talked Gawain quietly fed strips of bacon to the child and to Wolf by turns and the two ate what he gave them with equal relish.

It was a sorry tale that the woman had to tell. Her husband and her elder daughter had both died that winter from an illness which had swept through the hamlets along the roadside like a black plague. Illness often came that way, she told them, for strangers were constantly travelling from inn to inn along the road, bringing trade but also disease to the folks that lived alongside it.

The mother had herself recovered, and the small boy had escaped altogether. But soon after the others were buried the child had become difficult and strange. He would wander far from the house, returning only when some neighbour found him huddled in a corner, pale and quiet. He wept constantly and would not be comforted. At length, shortly after the woman had found herself with child again by a husband now dead, the boy had begun to speak in words that seemed to come from the husband's own mouth, some painful and some sad. The mother grew to fear her child, and tired and ill with the pregnancy she had turned to punishment and finally to exorcism. As she spoke of the priest's incantations the knights exchanged rueful looks, for they remembered the long night at Camelot and the fruitlessness of their own priest's labours at Arthur's side.

As his mother spoke the boy watched her, cramming bacon into his mouth in a childish way at odds with the story his mother told. The knights looked from woman to child with stern compassion. They could see that the mother loved the boy, but they could also see weakness and anger that moved their hearts against her. At length her tale was ended and the innkeeper's wife chimed in. She had been longing to speak for many a minute and she now began with vehemence to show the child's bruises and to cry down the local priest who had recommended the beating. In her turn she told of the boy's strange ways.

"And so I tell her my lords," she ended with emphasis. "Call on the old man from Four Lanes and he will heal all. Mayhap all the child needs is a charm around his neck to ward off the spirits, or a potion to send them packing. 'Tis cruel indeed to beat the poor mite and I tell her so each day. Let me call for the old man, my lords, and see what he can do."

Kay held up a hand. "Nay," he said. "Nay, my good woman. This is not our judgement. We come from Camelot, from the court of King Arthur, and I daresay you know well that Arthur has forsworn sorcery of all kinds. For ten years we have banished charms and potions from our lands, and the children there are happier and healthier than any we have seen in these parts. We call ourselves Christians too, but our priests do not beat children if we can help it. Send for this priest and let us examine him. In the meantime let mother and son have food and drink and let us spend some time with the infant to judge of his heart."

Accordingly the mother disappeared into the kitchen with the innkeeper and his wife, all a little chastened and a good deal quieter than before. The knights finished their breakfast with few words, letting the child wander around the room as he willed. He spent some time playing quietly with the fire irons, poking the blaze and chattering to himself. After a time he grew tired of that game and looked around him for another. He spied Wolf lying under the table, his chin on his paw observing the child, and crawled between the men's legs to join him. They heard Wolf grunt and begin to wash the child gently but thoroughly with his long tongue, and they heard the child chuckle and crow as it grasped the dog by the ears and pressed its face into his fur.

"Not a sensible word has the child spoken," Mordred said at last, as they listened. "How can any say that he speaks the words of the dead?"

"As yet we know not," Kay replied. "But let us sit here a little longer. At worst it will give him a little time in a warm room with a gentle playmate, pleasures I fear he lacks in that hovel he calls his home."

The child played on and the knights sat quietly, dozing from the warmth of the fire and their early wakening in the rain. At length the child also grew quiet, and when Gawain peered under the table he saw the boy curled up between the dog's paws, fast asleep.

The peace was broken a little later when the priest arrived. Young and harassed he looked, and poor and hungry too, for he dwelt among heathens and few fed him for his labours. The innkeeper's wife had told him of the judges who awaited him, so he was nervous and his eye twitched as he stammered out a greeting.

"Sit," Kay commanded, and the priest obeyed, folding his hands deferentially on his lap and bowing his head as if in prayer. Kay looked at him with a mixture of pity and contempt.

"We do not persecute your sort in our lands priest," he said, "so do not fear for your safety. Some of my comrades have embraced your faith indeed, and we all swear fealty to our king in a Christian chapel. But the three knights you find yourself among today have little time for doctrine. You find yourself arraigned before a court of common sense and I fear that things will go badly for you."

The priest did not reply but shot a glance in the direction of the kitchen as if in hope that aid would come to him from that quarter. Gawain spoke next.

"Tell us, what do you think ails the child?"

The priest shot him an anxious look. "Well, sire, I know not with any certainty. You have heard the tale I daresay. The woman had beaten the child for his waywardness and strange sayings. She spoke to me and I examined him also. From that I guessed that the spirits of his father and sister might be speaking through his innocent mouth."

"And you hoped to save his innocence by beatings fiercer yet?"

"I tried the remedy of exorcism first, but to no purpose. The child was hardy and resisted all such efforts. Chastisement seemed a way to break down his will and let the Lord enter."

Gawain swore and Kay wrinkled his lip in distaste. But all fell silent, for the child had woken under the table and had heard the priest's voice from above. He was speaking to the dog, in words they could all understand.

"Bad man!" he was saying to Wolf. "Bad man comes and she feeds him! And what else does she give him?" His voice was childish, but the words he spoke were not, and the men shivered for a moment superstitiously. But then Gawain reached under the table and fished the child out, setting him on his knee once more and pointing to the priest. The child turned his face from the young man, hiding his eyes in Gawain's tunic.

"Speak, child!" Gawain commanded. "Dost know this man here?"

The boy peeped at the priest and nodded reluctantly.

"He comes to your house now to see you?"

The boy nodded again.

"And did he come before your father died? Did your father know him?"

"Ess." The child turned his face away from the priest and wound his fingers in Gawain's beard. "He said bad man."

"Your father said so?"

"Ess."

"He said so before he died?"

The child nodded, his eyes large.

"Hast seen your father since he died?"

The child looked blankly at Kay who spoke kindly. "Hast seen your father or your sister these last days?"

"Nay." The child's lip wobbled and tears spilled from his eyes. "They be dead."

"These things your father said to you about the priest, he said them before he died?"

The child only looked blankly at Kay now. Gawain handed him a hunk of bread and his tears stopped at once. The knights looked at one another and sighed.

"How can any know what passes in this small heart?" Kay asked the others. "He cries and sleeps and eats just as a pup would do. How can any know whence this voice comes? A half-remembered phrase, perhaps, for a man he hates. A man who comes to see his mother and makes her beat him. How can he not hate him?"

"Whose is the child in the woman's belly?" Gawain asked suddenly, rounding on the priest. "If the child speaks truth then his father mistrusted you and your visits."

"The man was no Christian," the priest replied guardedly. "He begrudged the mite that the woman gave me to eat and drink in return for teaching."

"So the child is not yours I deem?"

The priest did not answer but set his mouth in a hard line. Kay sighed and looked towards the child, sitting in Gawain's lap eating and watching the men around him with wide eyes.

"Love and warmth and a full belly are what the child needs," Kay said at last. "I will tell the innkeeper to employ the mother about the inn, so that at least the child will eat and have a fire to sit beside. The woman too will benefit from the company, I daresay, for I fear she is lonely as well as weary and such is fertile ground for strange fears and fancies. But you, priest." He turned an unbending eye on the man who quailed before him. "You should have seen all this as clearly as I. What is your calling but to bring comfort to the sorrowful and hope to the lonely? Instead you have filled the woman's head with nonsense and only worsened her plight. Go now, before I turn some of your chastisement back upon your own back."

The priest fled without ceremony and Kay turned back to the others with an angry face.

"I would as lief have the wizard from Four Lanes than such a snivelling priest," Mordred observed from his place by the fire. "Can we not swallow our scruples and flog him after all?"

"If I were Arthur I would banish all such foolishness," Kay replied. "And if we must worship aught I would worship the sun and the clouds for at least they give much and take little. I have no patience with any of it."

~

Galahad's ship was a trim vessel, larger and sturdier than most of the boats and barges that lined the quay at Padstow. It had oars and a single sail to catch what favourable breeze it could. The captain was a foreigner but he spoke to Galahad in tolerable English and Galahad seemed to know something of the sailor's tongue. At last Galahad's luggage was stowed aboard and he returned to where Bedivere and the children stood, pale and silent on the quayside. Ralph mutely offered him Blade's reins, but Galahad shook his head.

"Nay, Ralph. This will be too long and too arduous a journey for him. If land I must cross I needs must find another horse, though I doubt I will ever ride such a noble animal again."

At this Ralph seemed finally to believe that Galahad was really leaving, and he buried his face in the horse's mane and wept. Then he raised his tear stained face to the knight who was watching him with a rueful smile.

"Let me come with you," Ralph begged, twisting his hand in Blade's mane. "You will need one to serve you, sire, and I have sworn fealty to you before."

Galahad shook his head. "Nay, Ralph, you cannot come, however welcome your companionship would be to me in these dark days. This quest is for me alone, both the danger and perhaps the glory. And besides, will you leave your sister to linger all alone at the farm unprotected? Nay – your fealty I accepted gladly, and I have instruction to give you now. First, I grant you free use of all the treasure left at the dragon's cave. Take what you will but use it wisely and you will have a farm to be proud of in a little while. Second, guard your sister for she is precious and gentle, and from this day I pray she will toil a little less and frolic a little more. Indeed, this is my order to you Charity, for when I return I would find you rested and perhaps even a little accomplished as any wealthy farmer's maid might be. Study your needle and the lute that Ralph will buy you, and you shall be a fine young lady I doubt not. And thirdly Ralph, you must take charge of Blade. He is perhaps a trifle high strung for the farm, but with your new-found wealth you may have a little time for the chase and I know you will tend him well."

Both the children were weeping now, for he spoke gravely and they knew at last that he would soon be gone and that in truth he might never return. Bedivere's eyes were bleak and his face drawn, and he too seemed tempted to offer his service to the young knight.

But then Galahad turned to him and embraced him, and tears at last came to Galahad's own eyes.

"Ever a father you have been to me Bedivere," he said, smiling manfully despite his grief. "And never have I faced any danger without knowing that you were somewhere at hand. Indeed, between you and my father I have always considered myself a mere boy. But now comes my test and I must face it alone and grow up at last."

Bedivere returned the young knight's embrace and nodded reassuringly. "You will prevail, Galahad," he said in a voice roughened by sorrow. "Fated you are to succeed, and even if this were not so I have seen you grow to manhood over these last days. Remember to look warily on others, for they may mean you harm beneath their smiles, but trust to your own virtue as you have always done. Remember your knightly oath and follow it, and you cannot err."

Galahad bowed his head for the older man's blessing and then pulled the children close. "I leave these two to your care Bedivere," he said, "for I have loved them well. Promise me you will keep your fatherly eye turned towards them in my stead."

"You have my word," Bedivere replied. "All good that is in my power to do them shall be done."

As he spoke the captain of the vessel approached and touched his forehead respectfully.

"My pardon lord," he said, "but the tide does not wait on men. We must leave immediately or lose many hours."

Galahad turned back to the others and smiled as he picked up his saddlebags and slung them over his shoulder, patted the horse's neck, and stepped back towards the ship.

"Farewell then," he said. "It is fortunate that someone bids me leave, for it is hard to make up one's mind to do it. And still gladder I am to have such friends to grieve for me. Do not fear, we will meet again though many years may pass before that day. And no day will pass, no matter how many years it may be, that I will not think of you and pray for your comfort." With that he turned on his heel, strode onto the deck of the ship and disappeared below, and they did not see his face again.

They watched until the ship had set sail, weighed anchor, pulled slowly away from the jetty and out into the open sea. Indeed, they did not leave until the ship had faded into a tiny speck on the horizon of the ocean. Only then they turned with a sigh towards the village behind them and the weary ride home. As they made their way through the thinning crowd, hardly conscious that the day was almost spent, the Merlin appeared over the heads of the villagers and alighted on Galahad's empty saddle. He looked from one downcast face to the next.

"Well," he said, and his voice was gloomy. "I have failed at last. I admit it. This was all my doing."

Bedivere cast him a churlish look. "As ever Merlin I cannot contradict you, for you always see the truth."

"You are angry with me Bedivere and you have good reason," the bird returned. "And indeed I am angry with myself. I have spent the length of our journey together telling anyone who would listen that your God's magic was as strong as my own, but I did not truly believe it. But now I see that I was right. And for this I believe I deserve the exile that beckons when all is resolved for good or ill."

Appearances

Guinevere was uneasy as she made her way homewards beside Lancelot, along the wooded banks of the river inland from the sea. Their adventure might be over, but trees no longer seemed a peaceful haven to her eyes. She was glad when their road led them up from the river valley, and she breathed more freely when at last they breasted the hill and found themselves looking far over a wide empty landscape.

They talked only a little as they jogged along under the blue sky. At noon they stopped beside a stream and ate the provisions the landlady of The Dragon's Head had given them. Sweet malt loaf with salty butter, the last of the winter's apples, and a flagon of wine made a good meal as they sat in the sunshine and let the horses graze.

"And so we return victorious, my lady," Lancelot said idly, lying back and folding his hands behind his head.

"So we return."

"And will it be a nest or a cage that awaits you now at Camelot? For much has changed since you sat at your window in former days, watching the ocean."

"A nest or a cage!" Guinevere drew a swift breath and shook her head. "Nay, I know not. If we prevail and Arthur wakes, or yet again if we fail, the world will seem so different. How can I tell?"

"And even if we prevail, what then?" Lancelot watched her sidelong. "There will be joys no doubt, but there must be cares too."

"Why do you ask me?"

"Only to know you better, Guinevere. Are we not friends now? True friends at last, after all these years?"

She smiled, and bent her head to pluck at the short heathland turf. "There are always troubles, Lancelot. From the arguments of the maidservants to the feeding of the visitors, there are daily trials at Camelot. And as I am the lady of the household it is my task to resolve them."

"And what of the those nearer to your heart?" Lancelot asked. "Will Arthur be content if all comes right again? And Mordred?"

Guinevere did not answer for a moment and Lancelot looked up, studying her face. "Arthur! Yes, Lancelot, Arthur will always be happy. He has found his life's purpose, and he has lived to see it change the world for the better. Whatever comes in the end, he has lived out his fate as best he could."

"And yet?"

"You asked me of Mordred," she said. "And see how your face darkens when I speak his name! How can I answer your question when you choose to think so ill of him?"

"Not ill, Guinevere. I suspect him of no evil."

"Nor do you look for good!"

"I own I cannot see his virtues as you and Kay and Arthur do. I am old-fashioned, Guinevere, and have an old man's idea of knightliness."

She smiled at that, and since he had closed his eyes again and laid back on the grass she allowed herself to examine his handsome face, and his hair that showed no trace of silver among the black, and his lean strong arms, folded behind his head. "You are not alone in such a feeling," she answered. "Even Arthur forgets Mordred's strengths, and often looks on him as a child. And Mordred himself is his own worst critic. He longs to be valiant. He longs to become a knight like you or Galahad."

"Then he should practise his skills. Naught comes without struggle."

"He does practise them, as far as he is able by constitution or inclination. He is skilled with a bow and rides as well as any. Do you not remember the tournament?" Lancelot only grunted. "But his real talents lie in other fields, and they too have shown their worth. Where should we have been without his map?"

"Lost and blundering, I do not deny it."

"And still his life is shadowed by dissatisfaction, and he suffers when he sees you scorn him. He has never felt the blind partiality of a father's love, Lancelot, and I fear for him."

"Kay will protect him, my lady."

"I do not mean that. Indeed I hope the quest will do him good, for if he triumphs against dragons how can he hold himself cheap? But even now I fear he will fail. He longs for greatness, but his doubts and fears always hold him back and his own intellect is against him. I sometimes think that this is the knight's strength – to think not of what may come, nor question what has been."

Lancelot laughed. "What a poor character for courage or fealty!" He stood up and whistled to the horses. Guinevere followed, frowning as she took hold of the mare's reins and pulled herself up into the saddle.

"Have I offended you, Lancelot?"

He reached over and took her hand as the horses wheeled together and began to jog onwards into the afternoon sun. "I promise you, Guinevere, you never shall. But such sallies hit their mark and shall mend me, if I am not yet past mending."

"I would not change you," she answered. "I would not have you alter from what you have always been."

~

At last the time came for the three knights to part. The road to Helston and the Lizard branched away to their left, while the Land's End lay straight on. The knights lingered at the parting of the ways, and Wolf ran around them in circles excitedly, for he knew that some change was near.

"Well, no dragons have we met together these last days," Gawain said, shifting in his saddle to look back at the way they had come. "May we have better luck apart!"

"No dragons," Kay agreed, smiling wryly at his old friend. "But we have done some good on our way. Our journey has not been wasted."

"Indeed not!" Gawain barked a laugh. "If we still have the thirst for adventure when this quest is ended, we could find much to make and mend in these parts. Let us hope we meet again in peace and may turn our eyes hither once more."

"Let us hope so!"

The three knights circled their horses closely and their hands met briefly. Then Gawain gave a hoarse hunting cry and thundered away down the Lizard road, Wolf at his heels.

"There!" Kay said lightly, to conceal his sorrow. "Hence have we ridden together for many days and the pair of them leave with never a glance behind them! They are souls unto themselves indeed!"

April had passed into May since the company had parted at Bodmin and now bluebells and campion blossomed in the hedgerows, while the primroses and violets lay quietly at the hedge foot eclipsed by their showier cousins. At times woods carpeted with wild garlic lay on either hand, and its pungent scent wafted on the breeze and sent Wolf thrusting his nose into the undergrowth in an ecstasy of sniffing.

When Gawain reached Helston later that same day the streets were thronged with merrymakers and flowers bedecked the earthen walls of the houses. Ale was flowing freely and couples pranced in pairs up and down the streets to the sound of pipes and drums while others crowded around the stalls of fortune tellers, or of old women selling cures and spells for a few pennies. Gawain and Wolf moved slowly through the throng, observing the festivities, Wolf diving off through the legs of the crowd at intervals in pursuit of good smells. Gawain bought a pasty from a baker's stall and ate it thoughtfully as he watched the drunken antics of the young men and the finery of the girls, and scanned the crowd for the dog who had disappeared again. The baker was watching the great knight with curiosity, even as he handed out pasties and took coins hand over fist, and was glad to answer when Gawain asked the cause of the celebration.

"'Tis our special day sire," the man replied as he wrapped up a pasty and handed it to another customer. "We celebrate this way every year, for the deliverance of the town from the spite of the devil many long years since."

"Indeed! And who was it delivered the town from so great a foe?"

"A mighty saint sire. And we drink his good health and eat well in his memory each year!"

Gawain looked around at the witches and wizards who sold their dreams and remedies and potions to such eager customers and thought ruefully that the town's deliverance had been short lived.

"And does your liege lord suffer such revelry unchecked?"

The baker looked at Gawain's fine armour and splendid war-horse and evidently judged him to be of noble birth, for he spoke guardedly as he replied. "Indeed, sire, we celebrate more cheerfully than ever today, for it was but yesterday that our lord was crowned king."

"King!" Gawain exclaimed, looking at the fellow with new attention. "I never before heard of a king in the west!"

"And never has there been such a thing before. But being blessed with wealth beyond measure, I daresay it is only right."

"And where dwells this king?"

"On Mullion Hill, sire." The baker gesticulated up the street. "If you wish to find him, follow the road south until you come to a great heath. Take the track westwards across the waste and you will find his palace hard by the sea."

"A palace is a rare name for a dwelling. Does he live in some splendour then?"

"You will see." The baker smiled and handed over another pasty to a small boy who had fought his way between the legs of the crowd and emerged at their feet closely followed by Wolf who was licking his lips with satisfaction. "Forgive me sire, but I thought from your bearing you must have something to do with the coronation. But you are new to these parts I see?"

Gawain did not reply, but nodded his thanks for the pasty and whistled to Wolf before striking out into the dense crowd and making his way slowly up the main street, and at last southwards out into open country once more.

It was long before the sounds of revelry faded and the shrill pipes were overtaken by birdsong. Gawain ambled along the road, glad to be at peace again, watching the fields and woods with interest as the road bent briefly eastwards and then began to descend steeply into a shady dell where a stream splashed across the road. Wolf had disappeared into the undergrowth in pursuit of some scent and Gawain's horse had stooped its head to drink from the ford when Gawain heard a voice from the woods at his left hand. Gruff it sounded, and seemed to be speaking to itself in an undertone for Gawain could catch no word until it ceased with an abrupt exclamation that carried clearly through the branches. Gawain turned in his saddle to scan the wood and whistled quietly for the dog. A moment later Wolf appeared from the undergrowth, but did not come closer. Instead he lingered at the wood's edge, crouching down on his haunches with his ears back.

"Wolf!" Gawain called softly. "Come here!"

The dog's ears twitched, but he did not move. Gawain lowered his voice still further.

"What ails thee hound? Is't the stranger in the wood there? What hast thou seen?"

Wolf whined and lay down, his chin on his paws. Gawain shifted impatiently and raised his voice. "Come now Wolf!" he ordered. "'Tis no matter what manner of man you have met. 'Twill be but a labourer minding his own business and we should do the same. Here sirrah!"

At last Wolf came reluctantly towards Gawain. He carried his head low and his ears back, the very picture of a dejected dog. Gawain regarded him in puzzlement as they set off up the hill beyond the ford and left the shade of the dell for open fields once more. Either the dog had bitten the stranger or the stranger had struck the dog, Gawain thought, for Wolf looked as though he had done wrong and knew it. On they rode for a good way until Gawain again heard the same grumbling voice he had heard in the wood. This time it came from behind him, and he twisted in the saddle. There was no one in sight, only Wolf trotting dejectedly behind him in the middle of the road. Gawain stopped and leapt down from his horse and stood listening. Wolf lay down and watched him from under his shaggy eyebrows. Silence reigned over the fields apart from a skylark that warbled high above them. Gawain sighed and bent to pat Wolf's head.

"Well," he said. "This is a mystery. Hast seen a man following us? For I heard his voice again just a moment since."

Wolf dropped his head onto his paws and sighed pitifully.

"What ails thee, beast? Come now, this is unseemly in so proud a dog as thee."

Wolf would not be comforted, but turned his head away from his master's hand. Gawain shrugged and swung himself back into the saddle, turning his horse's head once more to the unfamiliar road.

"Woe!" the gruff voice came again, this time at the horse's heels. "Woe and folly!"

This time there was no mistaking it. Gawain and Wolf were alone in the lane, and the voice was coming from Wolf. Gawain stopped and looked down at the dog attentively. Wolf slunk low to the ground his tail tucked tightly between his legs.

"How now, beast!" Gawain said sharply. "What curiosity is this? Hast acquired a talent for human speech of a sudden?"

Wolf groaned and flopped to his belly, looking up at his master with a sidelong glance. Gawain watched him with a pursed mouth.

"Come now!" he commanded. "Speak again, if you are able! How has this wonder come to pass?"

Wolf's ears were flattened against his skull, and his voice when it came was so low Gawain had to strain his ears to catch the words.

"Pastry."

"How now?"

"Pastry, Master!" Wolf glanced up again and then muttered into his paws. "Magic and mischief."

The corners of Gawain's mouth twitched, but his voice remained stern.

"Am I to take it that you have stolen some titbit from the stall of a witch, dog?"

"Only a morsel."

"Hast learned thy lesson, then, to betray the cause of truth. Are you not a dog of Camelot, that should shun sorcery? Well! I wonder how long this miracle will last?"

Wolf shook his head. And then Gawain at last burst out with a hearty laugh, so that it echoed across the fields and startled his horse, who sidled and eyed the dog askance in his turn.

"Well, the Merlin said that thou would bear me company Wolf, in this trial. Now, as ever, I see that his words meant more than they seemed. Let us make the best of it old friend, as long as it lasts – who knows? It may do us some good yet."

Wolf cheered up quickly when he saw that Gawain did not blame him. His tail waved once more above his back and his ears flopped more happily as they resumed their journey. The dog loped along beside the horse easily until they crested a slope and found themselves gazing across the heath that the baker of Helston had described. Flat and bare it spread before them as far as the eye could see, with no tree or bush to break the prospect. Brown and silver sedges covered the ground, and the knight and his dog seemed to step back into winter as they left the lush leaves and wild flowers of the lanes behind them and rode forward onto the grey landscape of the heath.

As the baker had foretold, a well worn track soon branched off to their right heading westwards towards the sea. Gawain turned his horse's head to follow it while Wolf trotted behind looking left and right. He lifted his nose and sniffed, "Mm," he murmured. "Slimy creatures." He trotted across to the edge of the track and stopped, his ears forward and his nose twitching as he looked into the sedges. After a moment he plunged forward, thrusting his nose into the grasses following a sharp waft of amphibian scent. Then he retreated smartly as he came suddenly nose to nose with a wide brown face and bulging eyes. The toad croaked and turned to hobble away into the sedges with a rustle.

"Come Wolf!" Gawain's voice came faintly from some way down the track. Wolf raised his head to see the large figure silhouetted against the pale sky ahead, and he bounded forwards, his tail high.

"Coming master!" he called, arriving at the horse's heel after a moment and running a circle around the beast's hind legs before sniffing at Gawain's boot where it rested in the stirrup. Gawain was looking down at him thoughtfully and he dropped his eyes respectfully. "Master."

"Art able to contain thy speech Wolf?" Gawain asked. "For I have heard you grumbling away to yourself all the time you have been following."

Wolf's tongue lolled out of his mouth as he put his head on one side thoughtfully.

"Have I?" he asked. "I have been thinking but I did not know I was talking too."

"I daresay speech is strange to you," Gawain answered kindly. "But see if you can hide this new power, for a seeming dumb animal would be a useful spy when we reach this king's palace."

"I'll try master," Wolf replied, and trotted along, trying to think without speaking. He did well, but occasionally a grumbled word would escape him and he put his ears back guiltily. After some time he ventured a question.

"Dost think that a spy will be needed, Master?"

Gawain grunted and answered without looking down at his companion. "I know not, Wolf, but I mislike the idea of a self-made king here in the wild west, so lately crowned, for I think it comes too soon on our troubles to be mere chance. And we know too well that power and magic are evil companions. Let us keep our eyes and ears wide open when we arrive there, Wolf, and see what we can discover."

"Ears and noses I should have said, Master," Wolf replied cheerfully. "Your eyes are sharper than mine, but my nose and ears are keen."

Gawain chuckled and leaned down to scratch the dog's head. "So they are, Wolf, and that will be an advantage no enemy could guess we possess so long as you can curb your tongue."

By the time they reached the narrow road that led down to Mullion Hill the sun was setting straight ahead, for the road led due west. The king's palace perched on the coast almost like another Camelot, connected to the shore by a raised stone causeway. At the near end, where it joined the shore, a huge stone statue reared its head as high as the cliffs, its feet in the water beside the roadway. The statue was made of the same rock as the cliffs, mottled green and grey, and it showed a kingly figure bearing a crown, its blind eyes gazing out towards the castle hill and over the sea beyond like a sentinel. Wolf growled at it darkly until they were past and out on the stone cobbles of the causeway. The sun shone low into their faces and a glowing sunset reddened the sky beyond the castle walls as they approached the main gate.

~

A strange smell tickled Wolf's nose as they crossed the inner courtyard of the castle towards the great keep. Earth, fire and water he could smell at once. But there was something strange too, strange and yet familiar, something he had smelt recently for the first time. His tail waved thoughtfully as they followed the king's guard towards the double doors that opened into the throne room. Gawain strode ahead and Wolf kept close to his heel, panting with the effort of keeping silent. The doors swung open and Gawain stopped short in the doorway uttering a curse of surprise. Wolf sat down promptly, certain that nothing should induce him to step over the threshold.

Before their feet stretched a floor that seemed to be made of green ice or glass. And on either side the walls towered up, translucent green too, so that the evening sun shone through the windows onto the reflective surfaces like a flickering fire. At the far end of the room was a raised dais made from the same stuff, and on it they saw two figures seated in great green thrones. They sat alone amid the splendour, watching as Gawain and his dog paused in the doorway.

Gawain cast a bracing glance at Wolf and motioned him to follow as he stepped out across the smooth green floor. Wolf hesitated, for he feared his feet on the slippery surface, but at last his fealty overcame his fear, and he stepped out gingerly onto the strange smooth stuff. His claws rapped on the hard surface as he went and his feet slid away from him a little as he quickened his pace in pursuit of Gawain who was striding out in his great boots with no fear. They arrived at the dais together and Wolf sank thankfully to his haunches at Gawain's side, looking furtively at the king and his companion but keeping his ears and nose keen as he had promised.

The figure on the largest throne seemed that of a very young man, wrapped in a fur robe with a circlet of bronze around his brows, studded with the same green gems that surrounded them on all sides. The youth sat slouched with one leg over the arm of the throne, a disdainful sneer curling his lip as he looked down on Gawain, travel-stained and shabby with his unwashed wolfhound at his side. Beside him sat a young woman, well past girlhood, but not yet old. Her dark hair fell to her shoulders in loose waves that shone almost green in the emerald light, while her clear brown eyes looked attentively down at her guests. She wore a rich red robe edged with gold thread and against it her skin looked warm and glowing. She was not beautiful but she looked full of life and warmth at odds with her icy surroundings.

The young king seemed not to recognise Gawain's might as he eyed him, nor did he cower as the Lord Marc had done under the knight's fierce gaze. Wolf looked from his master to the king and he could see that the young man considered himself the superior. For a moment Wolf lowered his head with instinctive deference, but then his master spoke and his voice reminded Wolf of his true loyalties.

"I am Sir Gawain of Camelot and I come to your realm in peace," Gawain said, removing his helmet and revealing his bushy hair. The king held out a hand, which he evidently expected Gawain to kneel and kiss, but the knight did no such thing. Instead he clasped it warmly as a brother knight would do and Wolf could see the power between the two men shift slightly as the king withdrew his hand in displeasure and shrank back into his furs. Still he did not fear Gawain, but watched him coolly from his high throne.

"What brings you so deep into the west my lord?" he asked, but even as he spoke his lip curled and he answered his own question. "Indeed, let me guess. Your great king as he styles himself has sent you on a mission to redeem us. We hear much of his zeal to bring all Britain under his control."

Gawain studied the king for a moment, then nodded. "You are right enough, sir. I come in Arthur's name and would gladly name these parts his dominion. But I come in peace as I told you and seek no battle here."

"Indeed, I believe not, for you would surely die."

"The west is strange to us," Gawain went on, as if he had not heard, "and I travel here as an ambassador to see and be seen. Will you give me shelter and hospitality in your halls?" As he spoke his eyes moved to the young woman's face. She opened her mouth as if to speak but the king's voice came first.

"In my halls?" The king looked around at the glowing green walls and then back at Gawain. "I think not, Sir Gawain, for as you see they are too beautiful to contain any but the fairest of God's creation." He rose to his feet before Gawain could reply and added, "but tonight I will give you humbler shelter against the cold, and food for your belly if you desire it. There is always room in my stable for vagrants."

Gawain stared for a moment, then swallowed his anger and bowed. "I will accept your hospitality such as it is. And tomorrow, with your leave, I will depart for more civil shelter."

The king waved his hand and the guard who had brought them into the hall led them out again. Wolf glanced back as the king subsided into his furs and he saw that the young woman's hands gripped tightly on the arms of her chair. Then he realised that Gawain was striding out of the hall and he went slithering and sliding after him his ears back.

~

"Impudent youth!" Gawain said as they followed the guard across the courtyard to the stables. "Does he think I have travelled so far to meet such discourtesy?"

Wolf cast a warning look towards the guard who flinched at Gawain's words thinking them addressed to himself. Gawain's face cleared good-naturedly and he slapped the guard's shoulder as they reached the doorway to the barn. "Forgive me, soldier," he said, "The way has been long and my temper is short. Is this to be our chamber?"

The guard nodded and bolted off as soon as he could in evident fear of the knight's rage and his strong arm. Gawain laughed shortly and led the way into the stable ducking his head under the lintel as he entered. Wolf followed behind and looked around at the warm straw and bare floor complacently. There would be many a rat to ferret out and scraps of horse feed to graze upon he fancied. But Gawain was speaking.

"Well Wolf? What do you think? Shall we accept the king's poor hospitality or leave this place and look for other shelter tonight?"

Wolf cocked his head and spoke thoughtfully. "Just as you please, master."

Gawain flung himself down on a bale of straw and groaned wearily. "If we leave we will fare no better than this, I dare say. I saw few cottages along the way and the night grows rainy. Still, it galls me to bow to that runt of a boy."

Wolf gave a grunt of agreement and began to nose about the floor in search of oats or rats, or both. As Gawain sighed and began to unbuckle the bracer from his left wrist Wolf's nose wrinkled with interest and he began to cast about the floor more earnestly in pursuit of a faint but pleasant odour.

"You did well, Wolf," Gawain was saying. "Barely a sound escaped you in the hall despite the strangeness of it. What stuff was it that the walls and floor were made from? If I did not know better I would call it emeralds, but that is scarcely possible."

"Why not, master?" Wolf asked, from where he stood in the corner, nosing at a loose bundle of hay.

"Because the king's life would be worthless, Wolf, and men from all corners of the earth at his doors, ready to tear down his palace in pursuit of the gems."

"It did not look good to eat."

Gawain chuckled. "It is not to eat, Wolf. Men value other things too and will give generously to have what they desire. Men have always loved jewels, just as dragons do, and guard them almost as fiercely." He paused reflectively for a moment. "Though I must confess that I saw no such greed in the queen's face."

"Master?"

"Yes, Wolf?"

"I think I have found something of value in this corner."

"Indeed, what is it?"

"A man child, sire. More than a pup, but not yet full grown."

Wolf backed away from the corner looking ready to play as a small brown hand appeared out of the straw followed by the rest of a boy, about nine years old and very dirty. Straw stuck in his hair and his face was grey with dust. He looked from the dog to the man and then fell to his knees, holding out his hands imploringly, too scared to speak. Gawain gave a grunt of surprise and Wolf bounded forward to give the boy's nose a reassuring lick.

"Do not fear me child," Gawain said gruffly from out of his beard. "What in the world were you doing, hiding in that straw?"

The child looked at Gawain's face and like every other boy in the kingdom he could see at once the kindness behind the knight's bluff manner. Emboldened, he licked his lips and laid a hand on Wolf's fur as if for courage.

"Do not give me up, master! I be too thin and the beast would only spit me out I swear!"

Before Gawain could reply heavy footsteps were heard approaching across the courtyard and the young lad dived back into the hay with a squeak of fear. Gawain followed him to the corner in a leisurely fashion, arranging the hay across the soles of his small feet which still showed between the strands, before turning back unruffled as the guard entered the stable behind him. The man stood awkwardly by the door bearing a bowl and a hunk of bread. Gawain eyed him levelly but did not move.

"What is it?" the knight asked at last. The guard shifted nervously.

"Dinner, sire."

"Dinner?" Gawain moved across and glanced at the contents of the bowl, wrinkling his lip. "Your master sits at a lean board if he calls that stuff by such a name."

"Food, master," the guard corrected himself. "Food from the kitchen by his majesty's orders. He dines alone and he does not share his victuals."

"Indeed? And I'll warrant his food is as fine as his walls." Gawain put out a gentle hand to take the bowl. "My thanks, sirrah. Thou hast borne the rough edge of my tongue before so I will forbear to blame thee again. I shall eat as poor a supper as I have tasted on the road but I will find no fault with you, for you eat as poorly I daresay."

Then Gawain glanced down at Wolf and nodded almost imperceptibly towards the door. "I would take it as a kindness if you would feed my dog," he said. "Perhaps if he comes with you to the kitchen you might find him something."

Wolf trotted after the guard reluctantly, for he wanted to stay and look again at the man child he had found in the straw. The boy smelt sweet and Wolf longed to lick his fingers and toes and listen to his piping voice again. But he was hungry too, and moreover he guessed that the time had come to be a spy for his master. He felt proud and anxious as he loped across the courtyard at the guard's heels.

They soon reached the kitchen and ducked into the steamy gloom where a pot of the thin stew was cooking over a great range. But even before his eyes grew accustomed to the darkness good smells also assailed Wolf's nose and he whimpered in delight, for the king's dinner lay on the table, about to be carried upstairs. There was a large bird of some kind, roasted till its skin glistened gold, a fine ham, and a platter of crusty rolls enough to feed a banquet. Next to all this lay a plate of sweetmeats and Wolf's mouth watered as he sniffed from across the room and smelt honey and nuts and soft poached fruit. Dressed in a robe bearing splendid patterns like waves or rivers in bright blues and greens against an ochre background, a servant was lifting up the platters ready to take them upstairs.

"Who's this?" the robed servant asked. Wolf started at the voice and examined the figure more closely for it seemed familiar, but the robes hid the face and there seemed to be barely any scent.

"Oh – just the dog of that travelling knight out there in the stables," the guard replied. "Been on the road a while I daresay from the looks of him."

"Who? The dog or the man?" the cook asked.

"Both!" the guard replied, and they both laughed as the servant disappeared upstairs with the platters of meat. Wolf cast himself on to his belly and suppressed a growl. Always before human speech had been hazy to him, odd words that he knew breaking through the fog. Now he could understand everything and he did not entirely like it.

"Here, dog!" the guard turned towards him and threw something at his feet. "Get that inside you."

It was the bone from the poor stew given to his master, and Wolf licked it appreciatively before delicately lifting one end in search of the sweet marrow, holding it between his paws. It had been cooking long and much of the goodness had gone, but the long cooking had softened it so that it broke easily between his great teeth and slipped down warm and chalky. As he ate he listened to the talk of the guard and the cook, who stood over the range red in the face from the heat of the fire.

"What did he say to his supper?" the cook asked.

"Not much, but he did not throw it at me, that's one thing. He hazarded a guess that the king did not dine on gruel."

"Any fool knows that," the cook replied. "Well, it will be a change from the fare at Camelot I daresay, and remind him of how his subjects eat."

"They say the people of Arthur's land live on something better than gruel," the guard replied, sitting himself down at the table and stealing a hunk of the fine white bread from the platter while the cook was not looking.

"Fairytales," the cook replied.

"Still, I wonder why his lordship – I should say majesty – dared to keep him so close about the place tonight."

"The devil knows. But he has much to flaunt in the faces of men, and I daresay he could not resist the temptation to insult so great a knight."

"I would not like to insult him," the guard said feelingly. "When I showed him his sleeping quarters I thought he would knock me senseless."

"Well, he did not."

"No." The guard looked thoughtful. "Perhaps the knights of Camelot are chivalrous after all. He wished to strike the king, I could see, but he did not vent his wrath on me."

"You hope for too much, Cedric," the cook said, casting the guard a pitying glance. "There is no rescue for us here, only our lady's grace to protect us as best she may. The knight will travel on and leave us to our fate. And if you tell him how things stand with us I will betray you to the king myself, before he blames me for it. I for one will not go to my doom before my time."

"May we never go to that place," Cedric replied. "But you are right. One man, however great a knight, cannot change anything. Now, if he had an army – ."

195

"If he had an army you should be called on to fight it and be killed by your own rescuers!" the cook said with savage pleasure. "Now hush, for the crone returns, and long may she rot in hell!"

~

The Merlin flew over the battlements of Camelot and swooped down into the courtyard, coming to rest in the branches of a small thorn tree on the lawn. White blossom hung on the branches and drifted to the ground in the light breeze that blew over the castle. Spring was arrived in Arthur's halls, but there was sorrow in the air of the place and the Merlin could feel the weight of the enchantment that bore down on the small island.

A young squire ran through the gateway up from the jetty and the stables where the boys worked and slept. He was carrying a leather harness in his hand and seemed to be on some errand. The bird whistled and the lad stopped, gazing up into the branches of the tree with a puzzled look, until he saw the Merlin perching among the green leaves and white flowers.

"Yes, yes, here I am," the bird said. "And I am a traveller in need of news. Tell me, boy, are there any knights returned to the castle yet?"

"No, sire." The boy's face fell. "Are there none with you?"

"No, child, I have returned alone, although Bedivere will soon be here I think. You may tell go and tell Arthur's men that, if you like. Tell them also that I am returned, and mean to stay with the king. But they are still the masters here, mind, for I will have no more part in men's doings. But I will stay with Arthur until the end, and that may please them, for they have enough to do, I daresay, minding you scallywags."

"Yes sire."

"Run along then boy."

Arthur still slept where they had left him, his hands folded on his chest like a corpse and his fair form enmeshed in frost. He was peaceful, for no nightmares seemed to trouble his slumber. The Merlin flew to his pillow and gently twitched the blanket that covered him, then he sighed and pecked at the king's icy hair a little before preening his own feathers.

"Rest in peace, Arthur," he said. "You at least bear no fault in this matter." He chirruped, and the sound had something of dissatisfaction in it. "Did I not say men must act for themselves in this quest? And yet I have meddled, as I swore I would not, and my meddling has done naught but harm. Well, all that is done now, and I shall rest here and keep you safe. Has that not always been my happiest task?" He tucked his head under his wing and settled comfortably at the king's shoulder, but his voice grumbled on. "And I begin to see that my powers are waning. I cannot thwart what will come. Matters take their course, and I can do little to mend them. To meddle or to be powerless – both are a nuisance, and make a body tired, what with all this flying about from one knight to the next. Well, that is all done with now." And then his voice fell silent, and his small eyes closed, and he slept. Perhaps he dreamed of happier times with Arthur before kingship came, when cares were few, and they had shared their wisdom and thought with one mind, for he sighed in his sleep and nestled closer to the king's neck.

O what can ail thee, knight-at-arms,
So haggard and so woe-begone?
The squirrel's granary is full,
And the harvest's done.

Secrets

The boy's name was Morvan, which meant 'sea' in the strange language of his people he said. His family had lived time out of mind across the peninsula, by the shores of a verdant creek, which filled and emptied twice each day bringing in fish at high tide and leaving the shellfish exposed at low. His people lived well off the bounty of the sea, growing few crops but gathering the wild leaves, mushrooms and fruits of the fertile creek-side woods. They were an ancient people, olive-skinned with black hair and dark brown eyes, and spoke a dialect with a strange lilting accent. They were left to themselves by their neighbours for they took no part in trade nor drank in the village taverns.

But six months ago raiders had come from the palace at Mullion in search of slaves among these simple folk. Morvan's whole family had been taken – father, mother, two older sisters and three younger ones – and brought to the hill at Mullion where they had been set to work mining out the fair green stone that the king displayed in his throne room and wore on his pale brow. Even the youngest children were taken down into the mines to toil beside the adults.

This much Gawain gathered from the boy as they talked quietly in the stable. He also learned that Morvan's three younger sisters were gone. Working in the caves below the castle the slaves heard the roar of fire in the darkness before them and felt the earth shake beneath their feet. At such times the loosened stones would often fall from the roof and crush the people below. Then the king's guards would come and drag away the bodies into the darkness ahead and they would be seen no more. And worst still, the youngest and fairest of the children would be taken away at each full moon, not to return. Morvan's younger sisters had all been taken, one by one. The guards told the slaves that they were gone to serve the god of the mine. But the people had heard the roars in the darkness and feared that the god who dwelt there was of flesh and blood, with sharp teeth and a good appetite.

At last Morvan's turn seemed near for the moon would soon be full once more, and of the children only the oldest and scrawniest remained. But then, the previous morning, as he worked listlessly on a seam of the green glassy ore with his feet in the drifts of grey dust that lay thickly everywhere underfoot, he had found a fault in the ore and daylight beyond it.

Scarcely breathing, Morvan had chipped away at the fault with his small hammer and chisel. Such faults or cracks in the rocks were always the easiest to work, so no one noticed that as he chipped and sweated a band of light began to fatten across his arm and shoulder. After a time he took off his shirt and stuffed it in the gap, trying to hide the light. He worked feverishly at the widest point, making a hole for his body as he worked. By noon he was encased in green glass behind and before him, for as he worked he filled up the gap behind with spoil. When the other slaves stumbled back up to the cave mouth for their noontime meal he stayed silent and still, just a dark smudge in the green wall, not daring to sound his hammer alone in the darkness and wondering if his family would miss him amid the crowd. Then the slaves returned and he worked on through the afternoon, tired and hungry now, but too far encased in the rocks to easily return even if he wished to.

Many times during the day the god in the deep roared and the rock walls trembled. Each time Morvan clutched his hammer and chisel and raised his closed eyes to the daylight, ready to be trapped by the green rocks around him like a fly in amber, and thinking it a better fate than to be crushed by the jaws of a beast. But at last as night fell the other slaves left, and now he cared not who heard him, for the fissure in the hillside was only a hand's breadth away, and he smashed down the remaining barrier and scrambled out onto a bed of thrift growing down the cracked side of the hill.

The fresh air made him shiver and he felt suddenly alone as he remembered that by now his mother would have missed him and be frantic in her grief, fearing him dead beneath a rock fall. Ahead stared the cruel blank face of the sentinel statue by the shore, and beyond that the inland hills which in turn hid his home far away on the opposite coast. He could swim well for he had grown up on the banks of the creek, and the channel between the castle hill and the shore was narrow. But he turned his eyes resolutely away from the beckoning shadows of the mainland. He stuffed the fissure he had made full of grass and leaves, and then he began to creep back through the lengthening shadows towards the main gate. His mother and father were still captives, and his older sisters' fate awaited them two nights hence, when the moon was full. Morvan crept back into danger swift as a shadow under the waxing moon, into the courtyard and the dark warmth of the stable.

He had lain there all the next day while the slaves toiled in the caverns below, waiting for night time to seek them out. But he was feverish, hungry and weak and as he lay amid the straw only wild visions of heroic acts raced across his dreams. Then nightmares came, so that when Wolf found him that evening he was half-crazed and despairing. His body had failed him and he could do no more.

He felt better with food inside him, for he was half-starved. And boy, man and dog fared better than the king had intended, for late at night a lamp approached across the courtyard and a gentle rap at the door heralded the return of the guard. Beside him stood a figure wrapped in the same ornate robes that Wolf had seen in the kitchen, but now the scent was sweeter and he knew that the figure within them was not the same.

"What brings you hither my friend?" Gawain asked mildly, looking up from his couch of hay bales. Morvan lay behind them on the dusty floor, out of sight.

"Dinner sire."

"Again?"

"Nay, real dinner this time, my lord. Meat and drink from my lord's table. Will you take it?"

"Gladly." Gawain stood up and crossed over to the guard, casting the robed figure a glance as he passed. "My thanks to your king for remembering his manners at last."

"Nay," the guard said awkwardly as Gawain sat back down and uncovered the plates, which were piled with all the good things Wolf had already seen. "This is a gift from my lady, sire, who was grieved not to have you at her table tonight."

"My thanks to the queen," Gawain said. "I saw at once that she was a lady of grace and nobility."

"She is all that and more, but she is not the queen," the guard replied, looking a little bashfully towards his companion as he spoke. "She is now a princess, for she is sister to the king, not his wife."

"Indeed! And may I know her name, that I may toast her health while I eat?"

"Rozenn, sire," the guard replied. "Which means 'rose' in the old language."

"Thank your lady for us, if you will," Gawain said. Then he cast the guard a searching look in his turn, for he had already heard from Wolf what had been said in the kitchen that night. "And be of good cheer, my man, for we come in peace, on a mission that with God's grace may bring more good than we aimed at when we entered here."

The guard looked fearful yet glad as he left the stable followed by the figure in the bright robes, darkness swallowing up even the glow of the lantern before they were halfway across the courtyard.

~

Gawain and his companions woke early the next day and gathered their belongings in readiness to leave the castle, for the moon would be full that very night and time was short. Morvan ran from the shadows of the stable when no one was near and leapt onto the horse before Gawain, who wrapped him swiftly in his robe so that only his dark eyes and shock of black hair peeped at the knight's throat, peering at the world beyond. Wolf sat patiently at the horse's feet still puzzling over the strange yet familiar smell that pervaded the castle from gate to kitchen. All at once his face cleared and he stood up on his hind legs, leaning his fore paws on Gawain's leg and speaking low as the knight bent over him, under the pretence of fondling the dog's ears.

"I have been wondering what creature it is whose smell fills the air in this place like a fog," the dog said. "And now I have it. I smelt it yesterday on the heath, but that was not the first time. The first time was at Dozmary pool where we slew the first dragon. Yesterday 'twas the toads and snakes that made it. 'Tis the smell of scaly creatures sire."

Gawain nodded as his eyes met Wolf's. "I do not doubt it," he said. "For what else but a dragon could shake the ground and blow flames through the caves as Morvan described? They have a dragon beneath the hill mark my words, kept for some purpose or other. Providence is kind to those who assay the good, Wolf, and it has led us here."

Wolf dropped back to all fours and wagged his tail thoughtfully as he waited for Gawain's command to depart the castle. He had kept his silence faithfully, spied for his master where Gawain could not go, and used his nose to remember that strange smell. He had done well, and his master was pleased with him. Then his tail slowed a little in its waving as he remembered the robed servant in the kitchen, for that was another mystery and he had not yet solved it. Indeed he thought his master might even fare better with his own eyes and ears when it came to remembering human creatures.

Gawain had settled his belongings and was turning his head towards the gate when a voice hailed him from behind. It was the Princess Rozenn herself, approaching across the courtyard from the great hall her brown hair blowing a little in the breeze. She wore the same red robe as before and it became her even better out in the daylight where she seemed to belong. Her figure was tall and firm, her step easy and elastic, and her cheek was flushed with health and what should be merriment if she had not looked uneasy beneath her smile.

"My lord Gawain!"

The knight halted and turned to greet her. She held out her hand and he courteously raised it to his lips. Then, as they spoke, she bent and stroked Wolf's ears with the same hand. It was strong and yet gentle, and sweet to the nose as Wolf turned his head to bestow a lick.

"You did not think to leave us without a word?"

"Pardon, your highness – I feared we were little welcome to the king. But I should not have left without thanking you for your kindness last night and the good dinner you sent to us."

Princess Rozenn's flush deepened. "I could not see a guest in this house go hungry," she said. "My father was a good and hospitable man, and many a traveller dined at his table. But things are changed now."

"How long is it since your father died?"

"Only six months, my lord."

"Indeed! So the magnificent throne room must have been your father's work?"

"Nay." The princess met Gawain's eyes frankly. "Such riches and the titles that go with them have come upon us suddenly Sir Gawain. And you may blame that change for my brother's rudeness. He has passed from being the carefree child of a country lord to a king, with many beneath him."

"His ill-temper has been well atoned for by your gentleness lady. May God protect you and yours."

"Do not leave us," Rozenn's hand reached out suddenly and grasped at the knight's robe as he took up his reins to depart. "For the sake of the God you speak of, stay a little longer, sire, and we shall show how we can mend our manners!"

As she spoke her fingers tightened on the knight's cloak and, as it fell a little to one side, she found herself gazing into the wide eyes of a small boy, bundled up before the knight in the ragged clothes of a slave and regarding her with terror. Instinctively she stepped back, her own eyes widening in turn. Then she mastered herself and reached out a steady hand once more, carefully replacing the cloak around the boy's slender frame. Her eyes met Gawain's and there was a new understanding on both sides.

"Perhaps after all, you would wish to ride out and explore the country a little," she said, in a voice all at once formal and yet relieved. "But return to supper, my lord, and tell me of your discoveries. I may perhaps be able to help you understand our ways a little better then."

"I shall do so," Gawain said, suddenly resolved to trust her in his turn for she had spared the child. "And in particular I shall be pleased to hear more of the many you spoke of *beneath* the king in this place."

Rozenn's colour deepened a little, but she only stepped back and raised her hand in farewell.

"Until tonight my lord."

Gawain sketched a bow and turned his horse's head towards the causeway, Wolf at his heels.

~

They had to clatter across the causeway and make a long detour before they could come back down to the beach across the channel from the castle out of sight of its many windows. Then Gawain turned his horse loose to graze upon the cliff top before leading Morvan and Wolf down a steep path to the shore. Gawain took off his heavy mail shirt, for he could not swim the channel bearing its weight. He left it behind a rock and tied his boots around his neck before striding out after Morvan who had already leapt into the water and was paddling like a young seal in the waves.

Gawain puffed and blew breathlessly before he got used to the icy water and could strike out clumsily after the boy who swam like a fish even in the slight swell. Wolf paddled manfully behind, his long face suddenly thin as the waves soaked his fluffy snout and his hair hung bedraggled on either side of his nose. Gawain would have laughed but the swim was too serious for that. It was further than he could remember having swum before, for he had never liked the water. There was a moment when he doubted his own strength, but then the thought of the dragon heartened him and he struck out once more and reached the shore of the island, his limbs heavy and his breath short.

Wolf came up out of the water behind him shaking his coat vigorously. They lay for a moment, too breathless to speak, then Morvan sat up and reached out his hand to Wolf who sat down at his feet, and Gawain groaned and shook his own shaggy mane which hung as limp as Wolf's.

"The crevice is there," Morvan said in his strange lilting voice, pointing up the hillside to a clump of gorse bushes where the last golden flowers clung between the faded blooms. "But I fear you will not be able to squeeze through the gap, sire, for it was only big enough for me."

Gawain's great strength was fast returning and he rose to his feet with new energy. "Lead on lad. Once we see the entrance we can make our plan."

The crevice was far too small for Gawain's huge frame. Wolf thrust his nose in the gap and sneezed, for a medley of strong smells assailed him, made up of tired and dirty human flesh and the same foggy smell of dragon he had smelt in the courtyard, but much stronger now. Gawain stuck his head through far enough to see the glassy tunnel ahead. Then he withdrew and sat back on his heels heavily.

"I wonder if there are larger entrances elsewhere on this hillside Morvan?"

The boy shook his head. "There may be sire, if you wish us to search for them."

"No." Gawain regarded the boy thoughtfully. "For there is no time. One thing is certain – we must enter the caves now and find the dragon as soon as we can, for night approaches and with it the full moon. Wolf can speak to us and that is a lucky stroke, for if needs be he can go alone into the mines and search for the beast. But you will have to clear the way through the tunnel for him, Morvan. Then, perhaps, we will have leisure to search for another entrance while he is gone. But we must meet here again, long before nightfall if we are to save the children. Will you do it Wolf?"

"I will," the dog replied, but he could not stop his tail from drooping, for he was a man's dog and he liked not the thought of being alone. Morvan saw his sorrow and though his cheeks paled he laid a hand on the dog's fur.

"I would not be afraid to go back down, with Wolf beside me sire," he said, a little untruthfully. "And I know the ways through the mine more than he. I could go with him if it pleased you."

Gawain regarded him sternly. "Dost really mean it, child? I would not send you into danger again if I could help it, but Wolf would be glad of your company and two might see what one would miss."

"I mean it," Morvan said stoutly, and Gawain could not repress a smile, for the child was like a brave little bird sitting seriously beside the great wolfhound. "Let me go sire."

"So be it. But if you are caught I will be powerless to help you until nightfall, when I may find a way to force an entry to the mines from inside the castle. Go quietly, keep your eyes and noses sharp, and do not try to rescue anyone even if you think you can. What we need now is knowledge. That is all you seek."

Dog and boy nodded. Then Morvan rose to his feet and pushed the hair out of his eyes before scrambling into the crevice, his little hammer and chisel in his hand once more. Now it was easier to move the loose stones and he carried them to the entrance by the handful, passing them to Gawain who sat outside watching for any sign of life on the mainland opposite or the hill below. None came and none watched and little by little Morvan worked himself back through the tunnel. It was barely an hour later when he whistled softly to Wolf and raised his small brown hand to Gawain before disappearing once and for all into the darkness.

~

It was dark in the mine, for the slaves had moved on since Morvan left and the sound of their rhythmic tapping came from further down the passage. As Morvan and Wolf paused, allowing their eyes to adjust to the darkness, warm breezes blew up to them as though they stood on the edge of a volcano. Wolf nosed experimentally at the floor and sneezed again violently, for as Morvan had told them it was carpeted with a thick layer of dust. Wolf's sneeze echoed around the cavern but no one came. The slaves were working hard, and their guards must be deeper down, Morvan thought, out of earshot of where they stood.

At last Morvan tugged at the dog's collar and they began to tread softly down the passage towards the noise. Nearer and nearer they drew until they could hear the slaves' voices and, at length, even their words. Morvan laid a warning hand on Wolf's neck as the tunnel bent sharply to the left and they inched forward to peer around the rocky outcrop.

Just ahead was the group of slaves, the men stripped to the waist and some of the children naked, for the heat was intense. Dim lamps lit their work, while beyond them Morvan could just make out the shadowy figures of the guards. Even as he looked there was a roar and a blast of heat from the passage beyond and there was a momentary lightening as though a flame had flared far off in the deep. Wolf whined and fell to his belly, while the slaves looked instinctively at each other and then nervously at the tunnel roof. The roof trembled, but nothing fell.

"Closer than usual," one slave said tersely to his neighbour as they turned back to their work. "We must be gaining on it."

"Or it's gaining on us," the other man said with grim humour. "We ain't lost no one since that lad two days ago. I reckon it's hungry again."

"Shh," the first man cautioned. "The lad's father's right behind you."

"I didn't say nothing wrong," replied the other sturdily. "Only the truth."

"Quiet there!" one of the guards called out. "Enough talking, get working."

A tremor of rebellion ran through the group, but they fell silent as they were bid. Morvan strained his eyes to where the man had pointed out his father and thought he recognised the dim shape. A group of women worked together nearer at hand and among them he saw his mother. He was glad they had lost no one else since he had left.

Wolf licked at Morvan's hand and drew his gaze away from the slaves. Morvan needed to bend only a little to let Wolf whisper in his ear.

"We must pass these folks unseen," the dog said in a low voice. "I can feel a breeze from the left – there may be a passage behind those rocks where they are working. I will go and see."

Morvan nodded and stepped back as Wolf slunk around the corner low to the ground. Only his claws were likely to attract notice, rapping on the stone floor, so he moved when the men used their hammers and paused when they stopped.

At last he returned, and Morvan was glad to see him for all his brave words.

"There is a way," the dog said quietly. "But we must pass close to some she-cubs who are working on a side passage. Perhaps they are your sisters. Take care and do not let them see you, or we will be lost and so will they."

Morvan bit his lip and nodded, then followed Wolf on all fours into the passage behind the rock face. On they crept, stopping when the noise stopped and crawling forward under the cover of the hammer blows. At last they could see the dim light ahead again, and they knew they were close to the workers. At the mouth of the passage they paused, for ahead of them were the girls Wolf had seen. Morvan knew his sisters at once and suppressed a cry of greeting. He was careless though and in his joy stepped one pace too near, making his own shadow loom out of the darkness before him. He had to jump back into the passageway as the youngest child squealed and pointed.

"Something in the tunnel!" she cried, and the other girls looked around nervously, for of all things they dreaded that the beast would come upon them unawares from the darkness.

"What passes?" The impatient cry came from one of the guards. The eldest of the three girls called back bravely.

"Naught, sir. My sister was frightened by a shadow, that is all. Do not blame her."

"Don't you know better than to scream out like that with the roof in this state? We could all be jelly."

"I know sir. She is just afraid of the dark. She is only young, sir."

The guard's tone softened. "Come back here into the lights then. Work with your parents today."

Morvan's eyes smarted at this kindness, for he saw in it the guard's pity, and pity could only mean that the girls' time was short. He reached out his hand to Wolf and hot tears came to his eyes.

"If I call them, we could take them back to the crevice," he hissed urgently, the words catching in his throat. "Now, before they move away!"

Wolf bit hard on Morvan's arm and pulled him back into the tunnel. "No!" he growled under the cover of the men's hammering. "They will be missed and we shall be caught! My master warned you against this very thing!"

Morvan gazed into Wolf's eyes, an inch from his own, then slumped against the wall his excitement gone. Even as the dog spoke they could hear the girls gathering their tools and moving away to join the others in the main cave. Then Wolf nodded his head towards the darkness ahead and tugged, gently this time, at the boy's sleeve.

It was easy to slip past the guards now that the girls were gone, for the men kept their eyes turned towards the slaves and heeded nothing else. Morvan and Wolf slipped away down the wide tunnel of green glass beyond them, treading through piles of dust and approaching ever nearer to the dragon's roar.

It was lucky that the beast was so close, for the passages would have been utterly dark without the red light that periodically shot up from the deeps below to light their way as the passage wound down and down, deeper and deeper into the hill. Wolf licked occasionally at Morvan's hand for he was glad of the boy's company in a place where no normal dog would venture – if Wolf had been his usual self he might have refused to enter the mine at all.

Now the light and heat were very close. At every corner they paused, expecting to come upon the beast beyond it. But still on and on they went, down and down, the roars becoming louder as they echoed around the passages and shook the walls, and the heat growing ever more intense until the floor burnt Morvan's bare feet.

Then at last they found the beast and understood why the slaves had been gaining on it. At the last corner the passage emerged without warning into a vast cavern. Morvan and Wolf stood on a natural balcony looking down on an astonishing sight.

In the middle of the cavern stood a dragon, bound about and tethered to the floor with stout cords anchored to the floor with iron rings. The beast's scales were a dull brown and its eye yellow. It was big, much bigger than any other dragon the knights had encountered on their quest, and at this moment it was furiously angry. It thrashed in its bonds and belched out torches of flame that shot across the floor and sizzled against the cavern walls.

Pain was the goad that enraged it. Men were standing further along the stone balcony and they were dousing the beast with sea water from above. Even from where they stood the boy and the dog could see a network of sores and open wounds running across the beast's hide where the ropes rubbed against the creature's skin. The salt water aggravated the pain and made the beast roar. Boy and dog exchanged a baffled look.

"Why do they torture it?" Morvan asked. "What good does it do?"

Wolf shook his head. "Men are cruel," he said simply and turned away his head.

A moment later Morvan tugged his collar and Wolf looked at him in surprise, for the boy was laughing bitterly.

"Nay Wolf," he whispered harshly, squatting by the dog and pointing. "They get something by their cruelty after all. Look! Look at the walls!"

Wolf looked back reluctantly. He watched as the beast writhed and roared for a moment, then he cocked his head with new interest as he began to see what Morvan meant.

Beyond the dragon one corner of the cavern was darker than the rest. Where most of the walls glowed green and translucent, the rocks of this corner were the same dull grey streaked with green veins that they had noticed in the cliffs on their arrival at Mullion. The dragon roared, and a tongue of flame shot out and danced on the dull rock wall. The more it suffered the longer the flame licked at the rock face. Then the beast drew breath and Wolf grunted in surprise for the wall was now molten red from the heat. While he watched, showers of grey dust fell to the cavern floor and the wall left behind was turned to emerald. By the alchemy of pain, and the refining power of fire, base rock was turned to green gems.

Morvan was scanning the walls with attention now that he finally understood the nature of the stuff he had been mining these last months, and he remembered how sometimes the green ore had been ribbed as though it had melted and then hardened anew. As he watched, the beast's fire bathed a wall already green, and he could see the seam of ore deepening as little by little the heat from the dragon's fiery breath worked further into the wall.

"What is that moving?" Wolf asked suddenly, gesturing with his nose towards the far wall of the cavern. Morvan screwed up his eyes to look.

"I believe it is the ore melting and running down the wall like water," he replied.

"Nay child." Wolf's eyes were sharper and even through the fog of scents he could smell the sea. "That is not inside the cavern. See, the wall is completely turned to glass. That is the sea."

Morvan gasped as he finally saw what Wolf saw. As high as the ceiling vaulted above them water was washing and moving against the glassy walls, and as he looked he could see strange dark shapes moving past outside the walls.

"Seals!" he cried out. "There are seals looking in at us!"

The cavern was completely submerged, deep under the sea, beneath the hill and the castle above. The dragon had turned almost all of the rocky walls to glass, and as the boy and dog looked around they wondered if its task might at last be done. They could see no passages leading off from the cavern and the walls were unbroken green. In pain and despair the dragon had tunnelled as deep as it could venture and there was no way left for it or its captors to go.

Morvan turned to Wolf and laid his cheek against the dog's fur.

"I see now that we have all been suffering," he said. "And they make one poor prisoner devour another when they bring the children here."

"Come," said Wolf, slinking back into the shadowy tunnel. "I have seen enough. Let us find my master."

Choices

It was just past noon when Wolf and Morvan emerged from the crevice in the hillside to find Gawain lying asleep on the grass beside it. The knight was snoring loudly, a light drizzle falling on his face leaving water droplets in his beard. A cormorant flew past low over the water below and gulls scolded from the rocks. Morvan looked down at the sea and marvelled that the mines had delved beneath its dark surface so far below his feet.

A lick from Wolf woke Gawain, and he sat up ready for news. He frowned as he heard of the beast's suffering at the hands of men, but his hasty words died in his throat as he looked at Morvan who was brushing the dust from his feet gingerly with a look of pain.

"What ails the boy?"

"Nothing!" Morvan tried to look brave but winced even as he spoke.

"Let me see." Gawain took hold of the lad's foot with a gentle hand and spat on his palm to wipe away the dirt. Morvan whimpered and Wolf thrust his nose close to smell the trouble.

"You have burned your feet, child," Gawain said.

"The floor was hot from the beast's breath," Morvan admitted, examining the blisters that were coming with a rueful face.

"You will find it hard to walk back to the castle." Gawain looked up thoughtfully. "I can bear you to the shore and the horse will carry you after, but you will have to swim the channel between. I fear the salt water will sting your wounds."

Morvan's lip trembled a little but he spoke cheerfully. "'Tis not far, sire."

"Well, let us get it over with." Gawain stood up and set the child on his shoulders. "We must speak with the princess Rozenn. It is easy to see she hates her brother's pride and wishes things as they used to be. If she knows of the dragon's plight she will pity it I believe, for I felt kindness in her hand."

"And I," Wolf replied. "She smelt sweet."

Gawain grunted in amusement and strode down the slope towards the water with long strides. "Indeed? And do I, beast?"

Wolf thought for a moment. "Not sweet, master. You smell of home."

"Well, that is good, for I feel far from it now among strange folks and cruel ways. But thou hast done well Wolf and I am pleased with you. Can you swim the channel again?"

Wolf's ears flopped merrily as he loped alongside, happy with his master's praise. "I believe so."

Guards and servants cast them startled looks when they rode back into the castle courtyard, for they had believed that the strangers had left for good that morning. Gawain looked to neither right nor left but returned to the stable where they had slept before and carrying Morvan inside deposited him on the straw unseen.

There was fresh water in the horses' troughs nearby and Gawain sluiced the salt and sand from the boy's feet. Once clean it was easy to see that his feet were badly burned and that he would walk with difficulty if at all. Gawain pursed his lips and said nothing as he produced the remains of the previous night's feast from his saddlebag and shared it with the boy and dog.

"Now, Wolf," Gawain said at last with his mouth full. "Here is another task for thee. Go find the guard that fed us yesterday and tell him that I would wish to speak to the princess alone. Do not fear betrayal for I saw his mind last night and you have heard his words. He will not fail us."

Wolf loped out of the door and loitered around the courtyard for a while, yawning ostentatiously and sloping from one corner to another as though in search of a sleeping place. Little by little he made his way to the kitchen and stood in the doorway, his nose lifted to taste the scents from the darkness within.

"Oh! Here again are you?" the cook came to the doorway not unkindly, taking a crust of bread from the table and throwing it at the dog's feet. "Never forget the way to the kitchen do you, you creatures?"

"Who is it?" came a voice from within. It was the friendly guard and Wolf's ears lifted a little.

"Sir Gawain's dog again," the cook replied, and Wolf snuffled with interest to himself.

"So they know my master's name at last," he thought, "they may feign indifference but I believe they all wish to be saved."

"Here boy," the guard called. Wolf trotted dutifully over to have his ears scratched, standing before the guard his head low. "Is your master back among us after all?"

The cook was in the pantry now, clattering dishes, so Wolf raised his eyes to the guard's face and answered. "Aye. He is in the stable."

The guard's jaw dropped and his eyes were round as he snatched his hand back from the dog's neck. "Witchcraft!" he exclaimed, but even in his fear his voice was low.

"Yes – at Helston I gained the power of speech," Wolf replied calmly. "But will you come now for my master wants thee?"

"What does he want?"

"A word with the princess in private. Will you fetch her to him?"

The guard stared at the dog for a moment and then nodded. "I will. Stay in the stable quietly and I will come."

The cook came back into the kitchen halfway through this speech and laughed.

"Do you think it can understand you, that you talk to it like a man?"

"You never know," the guard replied easily, rising to his feet as he watched Wolf trot back into the daylight and out of sight. "Stranger things have happened."

"You're right there, at that," the cook conceded. "The old Lord would be mad as a bull if he knew all that has passed since he died."

But the guard was already gone in search of his mistress and the cook turned back to his pastry with a sigh.

~

Rozenn was dressed in her riding habit and entered the stable as though she meant only to ride. Her own palfrey whinnied a greeting as she passed by its stall and she stroked it and fed it a titbit before approaching the end of the building where the knight sat waiting, while the guard took up his stance outside. Gawain rose to his feet and bowed over her hand as she reached him. Morvan lay pale-faced on the straw bales watching her face, while Wolf looked on from his corner his nose twitching.

Rozenn greeted Gawain but her eyes were already turning to Morvan as she spoke, and she ended her greeting with a question, "what ails the child?" even as Gawain had done on the hillside. "He looks paler even than before," she added with a frown.

"He is weak from much toil and in sorrow for his family," Gawain said, with a trace of reproof in his voice at which Rozenn coloured. "But now he has injured himself in my cause, exploring the mines in search of the dragon. He found it, sure enough, but finding it he has burnt his feet."

Rozenn stepped over to the bales where Morvan lay. She smiled as she sat down beside him and reached out her hand to his ankle.

"Do not fear me child," she said gently. "What is your name?"

"Morvan, ma'am."

"Well Morvan, will you let me tend your feet? My mother, whom I also loved, left me a precious gift when she died. I have a small power of healing from her and I may be able to help the pain a little."

Morvan nodded, his eyes wide as he looked at her face, and she turned to Gawain to speak softly. "Will you ask Cedric to find my maid and ask her for the balm?"

"I will," Gawain replied promptly and moved to the door where the guard waited. There was something in the girl's eyes that impressed him.

The princess's hands were deft and kind and the balm she spread upon Morvan's wounds was deliciously cool and soothing. The maid had brought soft cloths too, and Rozenn bound up the child's feet and padded his soles so that he could limp a little around the stable in search of Wolf, with whom he curled up in the corner while the knight and lady spoke together. On their voices murmured, rising and falling. Wolf had seldom heard his master's words so gentle or so quiet and he could hear that the two voices blended and wove together as though they should always be speaking. He was tired and the words merged to a fog of peaceful sounds as he dozed.

"Long have we wished for aid," Rozenn was saying to Gawain, sitting close beside him on the bales so that they could speak quietly. "Some of the guards, that is, and the servants and I. We all remember the happy times under my father's rule and we hate this cold splendour and cruelty that has replaced it. Some of the guards like their new powers of course, and relish mastery over the weak, and that is what she relies upon."

"She?"

"The crone, Demelza."

"Ha!" Gawain sat back, and regarded Rozenn with a new understanding. "So this is where she fled! But she has not been here long enough to bring all this about!"

"She has stayed with us these last days," Rozenn said. "But before that she visited the castle often, arriving as a bird before nightfall and assuming her true shape at dusk. Indeed it was she that helped us catch the dragon and it was she that showed us what its breath would do to the stones of the place. She suggested that slaves be brought here to mine the gems out. She tempted my brother and he could not resist."

"And what does she think of you?"

"She knows I am her enemy but she does not fear me yet, for she thinks I am alone and weak."

"Does she know that I am here?"

"She knows that you came last night. She wished my brother to send you away at once but he could not resist the chance to show off his wealth. She will be angry when she knows you are back."

"And the children?" Gawain took the princess's hand as he came to the worst horror. "Tell me about the children Rozenn."

Rozenn dropped her eyes and looked at his strong hand in hers.

"I have wished I was a man so many times since this began!" she said at last. "But how is one to fight magic all alone, man or woman? Still, I have been afraid and weak."

"It is true then? The children have been fed to the beast?"

Rozenn took Gawain's hand between both her own before she answered, and all the time that she spoke she caressed his fingers as if she begged his forgiveness for what she told. Gawain watched her as she spoke. He saw the way her hair fell upon her brown cheek, and the curve of her lashes, and the way that her lips moved, and he found that he loved her even amid the darkness and the evil of which she told.

"The dragon you saw came to live among the rocks of our seashore many, many ages ago. It never harmed us, but dwelt in good fellowship with the people of the place, so that at length we called ourselves the folks of the lizard, and others came to call our lands by the same name. Many among our people thought it a lucky omen, and took their new-born babes to be blessed by it, and indeed the creature seemed to love mankind, and especially our children. All this Demelza knew in her cruel wisdom. After my father died she gained a power over my brother and his followers and they hatched their plan to make jewels out of bare rock. And this is my first shame, for it was in my borrowed form that she first met the dragon and lured it from its den.

"I was ill one evening and took to my bed, and all the next day I lay feverish and half-sleeping. At evening I woke refreshed and soon forgot all about it until I began to hear of things I had done that day about the castle. This puzzled me, but at length I understood it, for I heard it said that it was I who had brought the dragon to the hill and confined it in the caves below the castle. Demelza had gone to the beast in my borrowed form, which the creature well knew as the daughter of his old friend, the Lord of the Lizard. In my form she begged its aid at the castle. Willingly the dragon followed her from the rocks, and only when it reached the palace did the poor creature find it had been betrayed.

"When night fell she showed her true form to the creature. She commanded it to be starved and beaten and tortured to make it work its magic on the rocks. And only at the full moon does she allow it to be fed – just often enough to keep it alive but no more.

"And here we come to the children." Rozenn's grasp on Gawain's fingers tightened and he squeezed her hand in reply as tears started to her eyes. "For Demelza will not let the beast even feed in peace. Knowing its love for our children, whom it knew as babes in arms, she picks the youngest and fairest to send to the beast. Long does it resist, for it weeps to think of eating them, as we would weep to kill a dog like Wolf for our own supper. But after all it is a beast, not a man, and it cannot resist forever. Hunger and weakness dim its eyes and it feeds for self-preservation in the end."

They were both silent for a moment as Rozenn's words lingered between them. Still they clasped each other's fingers like children in the face of darkness. Gawain was not afraid, only grieved, and he was thinking hard of the night to come. But Rozenn was still thinking of the horrors she had heard and seen, and she broke from the knight's side and went to the boy and dog where they lay sleeping in the corner. She knelt beside them and laid a soft hand on the boy's hair and smiled through her tears as he sighed and nestled closer to the dog's side.

"How strange love is!" she said. "A boy for a dog, a dragon for men. How good and wholesome, and how cruel to turn it to evil!"

"And you? Is there any that you love?" Gawain asked, watching her.

"None in this place, now that my father is gone and my brother torn from me." Rozenn returned to sit on the floor beside Gawain, resting her elbow on the bales and her cheek on her firm hand. "Nay, that is not true. I love that child there and the guards and servants who have remained true to the past. I would save them if I could. Can you help me to do it?"

"I believe so," Gawain replied. Then he told her of his quest for the key, and of Arthur's plight. But he also told her of Camelot and Arthur's lands where sorcery was no more, and her eyes cleared and her cheek grew rosy again as hope began to grow in her heart. Long he talked, and wondered at himself, for all knew him as a taciturn man. He told her of his own lands and his castle and his people, and he knew that he was asking her to share them with him if she would.

Rozenn understood, and as she watched his face she saw in him the same things that his squires loved. Here was strength and wisdom. Here was repose and friendship and happiness. Here was kindness and a love for all the things she cared for. Their eyes met and they did not blush, for both knew that there was no need for shame to spoil their happiness. And both knew that things must be mended before that joy could be spoken.

Then they began to make their plans for that night. Rozenn was to enlist Cedric's aid in letting the knight into the mines through the front gate, and finding enough friendly guards to protect him from the slave masters below. Morvan and Wolf were to wait in the stables, the guards were to free the slaves and guard the doors, and Gawain was to go on to free the beast if he could. "Once unchained, it may find its own way back to the daylight through the tunnels it has made," he said. "And if it bears me no ill will I may hope that it will give me the key it doubtless wears around its neck in exchange for its freedom. Then I will return to thee, and we will go to your brother together to show him his folly."

"And what of Demelza?"

Gawain shook his head. "I have no cunning, Rozenn, only strength and good will. I will do what seems right and leave her to other hands."

~

Morvan and Wolf woke in the dead of night. No sounds came from the courtyard and no light shone from the main buildings opposite. The moon had not yet risen but starlight reflected off the wet cobbles and illuminated their faces where it fell through the square window. Morvan sat up and looked around at the silent stable.

"He is gone," he whispered. "Gawain has gone to the beast and left us here!"

"Indeed, he did not mean to take us," Wolf replied, with a consoling lick to the boy's nose. "He never meant to. You are injured and master told me to guard thee until morning. He will return, child. My master will not be defeated!"

"But I wanted to go," Morvan returned. He was silent for a moment and then a sob caught in his throat. "I wanted to find my sisters and my mother and my father. How will Sir Gawain know who to rescue? He will not recognise them."

"My master will save all the slaves never fear," Wolf replied. "Morvan, what are you doing?"

"Getting dressed," the boy replied, pulling his shirt over his head and wincing as he stood up.

"You must not follow!" Wolf growled, standing up in his turn and baring his teeth a little. "You do not know where to go!"

"No," Morvan admitted. He picked up his hammer and chisel and stuck them in the waist of his breeches. "If they had taken me, so much the better. But there is my crevice, Wolf. I can get in that way and search from the bottom to the top."

Wolf growled again softly. "You must not follow."

Morvan ignored the dog, turning to the door and opening it a fraction before peering out into the darkness. All at once he found his shirt grasped by strong jaws and he was lying on the floor with Wolf standing over him, his paw on the boy's chest.

"You must not follow!" Wolf repeated. "That was my master's word and you may not disobey! I am stronger than thee child and I will not let you go!"

Morvan lay still, looking up at the dog's face thoughtfully for a long spell. Almost against his will Wolf's tail began to wave slowly from side to side and at length he could not resist another lick to the boy's nose. Morvan sighed and sat up and Wolf lay down beside him sphinx-like, paws stretched out and alert.

"You wish to please your master don't you Wolf?" the child asked after a pause. Wolf snuffled a little in agreement. "That is your duty is it not Wolf?"

"It is."

"Then listen. If we stay here we can but stay out of trouble. If we follow carefully and go down into the mines we might do real good."

"We might be caught."

"Not if we are careful." Morvan reached out and stroked the dog's ears persuasively. "What if trouble comes to Sir Gawain, Wolf? What if there is some accident with the dragon and your master needs help? Who will help him?"

Wolf shifted uneasily.

"What if your master needs you, Wolf, to protect him from the dragon? What if he does not return from the mines and you might have saved him?"

Wolf's ears twitched and then drooped and a whine escaped him.

"Your master would not blame you for following if you saved his life, Wolf. And if no such help is needed we can creep back here before he returns and he will never know the difference."

Wolf looked sideways at the boy suspiciously. He knew that the boy's words must be wrong for his master had told him to stay, but he could not see where the error lay.

"And you will come back with me before my master returns?" he asked at last.

The boy's hand tightened gladly on the dog's collar. "I promise."

"Come then." Wolf rose to his feet with a grunt. "If my master might need me, I must follow."

~

In the darkness before dawn Gawain and the lady Rozenn made their way to the mines where the guard Cedric waited for them in the shadows of the doorway. As they entered they could feel the flow of air from the tunnel that led down to the mines. A stench rose on the warm breeze, the stink of a dungeon and the acrid smell of burning.

"What luck?" the knight asked as he gripped the guard's arm warmly. "Hast found any allies among the men?"

"Few, lord, for they are fearful, but those we have are good men. I think that more will come over to our side in time."

"Lead on then." Gawain turned to Rozenn and met her eyes frankly. "And here I must leave you, my lady. God willing I will see you again in a little while." He bent his lips to her hand briefly and was gone, leaving her to stare after him into the darkness.

Gawain felt his way into the inky entrance of the tunnel behind the guard before turning a corner to find a small torch flaring feebly in the breezes from the void below. He took it from its bracket and held it high as they went on, the tiny flame flattening and spitting in the draught. After what seemed a long descent down the steep path, more figures emerged from the shadows. Their faces were drawn and their mouths were grim but their eyes brightened at the sight of Gawain, and after a whispered counsel he led them on, down towards the slave pit.

There were few guards in the pit, for the slaves were exhausted and were sleeping soundly, curled together like animals in family groups on the hard floor. The guards dozed over a guttering fire and there was only the briefest of scuffles before Cedric's men had disarmed them and bundled them into a corner, binding their hands like those of the slaves they guarded. Some of the slaves stirred and moaned in their sleep but they did not wake. Gawain looked down on them with compassion.

"Let them sleep a little longer," he said quietly to Cedric, "for they are weary and sad. There is no hurry, for I fear to rouse the castle until we have succeeded below. Wait until I return and we will lead them out together."

Cedric nodded and motioned his men to take the places of the guards around the fire. "We will wait," he said.

Gawain went on alone into the dark tunnel that led further down into the mine. At first all he could hear was the sound of his own breathing, the thud of his heart, and the scuffle of his feet in the dust. But as he went further on into the gloom, he began to hear something else. At first it was so faint that he hardly noticed it. Then he stopped and listened intently. For all the world it sounded like an infant crying, or a cat yowling far away. He thought of Morvan's sisters and his step quickened.

As the noise grew closer it was soon clear that it was no human voice that wailed and keened in the darkness ahead. The hairs stood up on the back of Gawain's neck and he clapped his hands to his ears, for as he went deeper and deeper into the mine the howls grew louder until the walls seemed to shake and the shrill wails set his teeth on edge and hurt his head.

It was still dark though, and it was a surprise when he found himself emerging onto the ledge above the cavern. The dragon was in the pit below, but now its fire was doused and only a dull glow, as of embers, showed where its snout lay propped on a pile of boulders.

Then the creature cried out again, deafeningly this time, and flames belched out from between its teeth. By the sudden light Gawain saw two children huddled together on a rock a little way above the creature's nose, cowering at the noise, their faces contorted by screams. Then Gawain understood. The beast had been given its scanty meal and it was crying for the pity of it.

At the sight of the children Gawain started forward impetuously, and without more thought he raised his flickering torch and shouted to attract the beast's notice. At first he could not make himself seen, for the torch was small and his own voice swamped by the beast's cries, but at last the dragon shook its head, and turning caught sight of the tiny light in Gawain's hand.

It roared so loud that pebbles fell from the roof. Flames shot from between its jaws as it made a rush towards him across the cavern floor. Its bonds brought it up short and it fell clumsily to its knees. Then it was up again, pulling at its fetters and shooting flames towards him in impotent fury.

"It believes me one of its captors," Gawain thought. "It thinks I have come to gloat at its sorrow."

He stepped to the edge of the balcony and waved, holding his arms out wide to show that he held no weapon. He pulled off his helmet and shook out his great hair, and for a moment the dragon paused in its onslaught, for it knew it had never seen this man before. In the brief silence Gawain shouted with all his might.

"Friend!" he yelled. "Be at peace. I come in fellowship!"

But the dragon, too often betrayed, only shook its head and roared again. Gawain stood his ground, arms still outstretched, and waited patiently for the creature to finish. Animals were one thing he understood, and he was in no hurry. Even as it roared and battered against its bonds the dragon was eyeing him, and Gawain held its gaze. Slowly the dragon's roars began to subside. Slowly it fell back onto four feet and at length, with only a hiss and a splutter, its flames died to a dull glow. In the sudden quiet man and beast eyed each other warily.

"Do not fear me," Gawain said, kindness in his tone. "I will not hurt thee."

The dragon growled, its small eye fixed upon his face.

"You have suffered enough I think," the knight went on, stepping forward to the edge of the balcony and squatting on his haunches. The dragon lifted its snout and sniffed and Gawain felt the air move around him. "I am Sir Gawain of Camelot," he went on. "Will you tell me your name? For I know that you too can speak."

The dragon looked as though it meant to answer but all at once it threw up its snout and its eye rolled in fright and rage. It had seen something behind him in the shadow and caught its scent. Gawain turned swiftly to find Rozenn standing at his shoulder.

When the dragon saw her face its eyes lit with the fury of despair. With one convulsive heave of its great body it snapped the fetter which bound its back feet and it came at them fast as a speeding arrow, flapping its wings and lifting from the floor enough to bathe the ledge with fire. Rozenn screamed and Gawain pushed her to the floor as the flames danced and crackled and his mane of hair smouldered and shrivelled in the intense heat. When the noise subsided and the flames died back, Gawain raised his head and saw close to his face that the heat from the dragon's breath had turned the pathway to glass before him.

"What foolishness has brought thee here?" he asked, his voice rough with fright. Rozenn clutched her hair and her face was smudged with soot as she raised it to his like a scolded child. She could not answer. But Gawain knew even as he spoke that it was love, and to atone for his roughness he kissed her where they lay, amid the smoke and dust.

The dragon had fallen back to the ground for its forefeet and wings were still tethered and it could come no nearer. Still, Gawain and Rozenn were trapped. The tunnel entrance lay to their left along the ledge, which now shone a glassy green. If they tried to reach it the dragon could scorch them at its own will. To their right the ledge petered out into the cavern wall and there was a sheer drop to the floor of the cave where the beast waited and watched.

There was nothing for it but to try again. Gawain raised himself painfully to his feet and approached the edge of the gallery once more, now charred and dirty, his cheek black with soot and his hair burnt short in places. But no sooner had he raised his arms in supplication than the beast flew into life again. Again it battered at its fetters and they strained and buckled under its great weight. Again fire raked the ledge. This time Gawain knew the limits of its range and pulled Rozenn to safety in the narrow space between the wall and the flames.

"Let me try!" Rozenn said breathlessly, when the beast's onslaught slackened and it lay drawing breath on its stony bed. "Let me try, for this is my doing!"

Before he could stop her she had stepped to the edge of the path and raised her arms. The dragon's rage surged and boiled anew. Upwards it flew, beating its wings in despair and betrayal, longing to fall upon her and punish her for her sins. And again in its rage another fetter snapped and both Gawain and Rozenn cried out for it seemed their end was near. Wings freed from their bonds the dragon rose level with the ledge, its mighty head only yards from where they cowered against the wall.

But as Gawain clasped Rozenn in his arms and bent his head there was a movement to his left, swift and sudden. The dragon threw up its head to greet this new threat. There stood a shape on the very edge of the stone shelf, looking out at the dragon undaunted. "It cannot be," thought Gawain a little dazed by the light and heat. "It cannot be Wolf!"

Sacrifice

But it was Wolf, standing where no other dog would stand. And then to Gawain's surprise it was Wolf's voice that he heard in the sudden silence, for the dragon had fallen back perplexed by this new arrival.

"Shame on you!" Wolf was yapping, his voice a little shrill from his fright. "Shame on you! Will you kill first and ask questions later like those savages that torment you?"

The dragon sat back on its haunches looking up at the dog, and for a moment the monster looked almost sheepish, like a great mastiff that hears its master scold. Behind them Gawain sat up and crawled forward a little the better to see Wolf's face, for the dog seemed to him now as a fellow knight who held the life of them all in his grasp.

"Will you kill these gentlefolk – this lady and this knight, who are your only hope of escape?" The dragon blew out smoke through its nostrils and eyed Wolf with some perplexity.

"She is a witch!" it said suddenly, its voice rumbling and resounding around the cavern like thunder. "She is no lady! She brought me here and chained me and had me beaten and fed me children! She is no lady!"

"You think this because you have been misused," Wolf returned, his head cocked thoughtfully to one side. "I have seen what the people of this place have done to you. I saw it today, for I crept in here with the brother of those poor children there. How we sorrowed to see you treated so ill!"

The dragon dropped its head and closed its eyes, and at last the great roar from the fires in its belly began to subside.

"At first we could not understand it," Wolf went on. "Not until we saw the jewels you made with your hot breath. Then we understood. We saw it was greed. But not all men are greedy. Many are slaves in the mine like you."

Now the dragon's eyes opened again and it regarded Wolf steadily for a moment.

"Why did you come here?" it asked at last, in a low voice that echoed around the cavern like the purr of a huge lion.

"I came with my master to the castle in search of dragons," Wolf replied. "That is my master there, before you. Our own king lies enchanted and the keys to his prison lie with five dragons in the west. But my master loves all living creatures so well that when he heard of your plight he forgot the keys and wished only to help you. He is here to release you if you will let him."

Now the dragon's eyes turned to Gawain. Gawain pulled himself stiffly to his feet and stumbled across to stand by Wolf, his hand resting warmly on the dog's neck in gratitude and praise. Despite himself, Wolf's tail began to wag.

But then the dragon's eyes turned to Rozenn once more and a small flame belched from its nostrils.

"And this creature?" it asked stiffly. "Why does your master travel with this creature of evil?"

"This is no witch. This is the lady Rozenn, whom you have known since a child, daughter to the lord you loved so well. Can you not see I speak the truth?"

The dragon roared and shook its head and sparks flew into the darkness like fireflies. "So she said to me, when she came to me on the rocks. But then we reached this place and in the darkness she changed her shape and became something vile. How do I know that she is the maid you say?"

Wolf looked at the dragon steadfastly for a moment and then flopped down on his belly on the hot stones.

"Indeed, you cannot know," he said a little dolefully, his ears sagging. "For magic may deceive the wisest. But listen, I am no man, though now I speak with a man's tongue. I can smell a lie for I am a beast and so are you. Come, smell the maid, touch her. If you are a beast as I am you will smell the truth even if you cannot see it."

Wolf rose to his feet and trotted over to where Rozenn still lay in the shadows. Meanwhile the dragon hummed to itself and wove its head to and fro as though thinking over the dog's words. Wolf nuzzled Rozenn's hand and she laid it on his fur.

"You must come," Wolf said simply. "If you love my master you must trust the beast to do you no harm."

Rozenn rose unsteadily and walked forward with the dog to the edge where Gawain stood waiting. There she stood, hand in hand with the man, her other hand resting on the dog's neck. "Come," Wolf said again to the dragon. "Come smell us all. See that we speak the truth and mean you no harm."

Up rose the dragon on its leathery wings, hovering at the height of the ledge like a great moth. It snaked its neck forwards and its huge nostrils approached the waiting group, the long tongue flickering out between its teeth as it tasted the air. As the dragon's head approached them they could not help but flinch, for its teeth were as big as boulders, jagged and sharp, and stained with blood and ashes. They could feel the creature's hot breath skim the air close to their faces. Then it touched them briefly with its tongue, running the tip down the contours of their cheeks, tasting the sweat that stood on their brows, and then flickering experimentally towards their throats. Paralysed by fear they waited, for if the beast smelt anything amiss there would be no escape from its massive jaws.

At last its scrutiny was over and it fell back to the cavern floor where it sat regarding them thoughtfully. Wolf sat down on his haunches and put his head on one side as he watched, and Gawain and Rozenn clung together, weak with relief. "Well," the dragon said. "The dog speaks truth. And you should thank him for your lives, for never more will I trust the word of human kind. But tell me, if you release me from this prison what will you demand in return? For my days are over in this place. I have done my work here and they will not keep me alive much longer. And though I sorrow I am also glad, for life is weary to me now. So tell me the truth. If you wish to take me hence for some other hard duty I would rather die. Do not free me only to enslave me again."

"Poor creature," Rozenn said, and reached out her hand to touch the tip of the dragon's snout, which reached up towards her. "Long have you done the bidding of men! But listen, we seek nothing more from you now. Sir Gawain will break your bonds and you can go upwards through the tunnels to the cool night air. Stretch your wings, and you can fly away from this place into the night and find peace and solitude where you will."

"Only one request have I," Gawain added. "Beast, I seek a key, as the dog told you. I do not see it around your neck but you are a dragon and dragons I was bid to find. Do you have it?"

"I do not have it now." The dragon sighed and a small flame escaped through its teeth as it growled. "It came as a mystery to me some weeks ago, and I thought it a promise of hope to come. But the witch took it from me again as I slept, and laughed when I missed it, saying that all hopes had ended." The dragon's face brightened and for the first time it looked on Gawain with a kindly eye. "But she was wrong!" it said. "Release me now and I will do you this service before I flee. I will find the witch and kill her and give you the key. Release me, and I swear to do this or remain in torment."

Before he could reply Gawain's attention was caught by a growl behind him in the darkness. It was Wolf and he was staring into the shadows at the other end of the ledge. There was movement there, and Wolf caught a scent on the breeze that blew through the cavern.

"'Tis the witch herself!" he yapped, turning to Gawain with his hackles raised. "Fear not master, I shall have her yet!"

Fast as a greyhound Wolf flew along the ledge and within a few strides he had found the witch. He grasped her robe but it tore away in his teeth and she turned back into the shadowy tunnel as elusive as a fly. Wolf sprang after her again and this time laid hold of her ankle, growling and tugging her back towards the cavern. Demelza howled in pain and flapped against him but she was carrying something heavy and she could not escape. Whatever she was carrying was alive, for Wolf could feel it struggling. As they stumbled back into the light Gawain and Rozenn cried out and Wolf let go of the witch's leg in surprise for she had Morvan in her arms.

He had crept into the cavern behind Wolf and listened to the debate between dragon and dog. But then he had seen his sisters down on the rocks below and he had crawled away on hands and knees unmissed in the excitement, searching for a way down. In the mouth of another cold dark tunnel he had run straight into the arms of Demelza.

She looked as old and wicked as ever as she held the boy in the vice of her bony arms. Wolf crouched back on his haunches, forepaws extended before him, ready to pounce at the first opportunity. Gawain was coming at a run with Rozenn at his heels, but as she saw him coming the witch cackled and stepped closer to the edge, holding the child out over the sheer drop to the rocks of the cavern floor below. At once Gawain stopped and held up his hands in a gesture of peace.

"Ha!" the crone shrieked. "Do you think I am a fool? Do you expect me to believe you will not harm me if I let the boy go?"

"Do not harm the boy!" Gawain called in return. Out of the corner of his eye he could see Morvan's sisters watching pale-faced as their brother clutched at the witch's robe. "He has done thee no harm!"

"Do you think that I care for that? I shall certainly drop him when I have dealt with you. There is no bargain to be struck here, Gawain. There is no dunce like Lord Marc for you to treat with, only I, and I do not make treaties."

"What do you want?" Gawain asked. "Why come here if you will not treat? For I will release the dragon with or without your leave, and then you had better be far away!"

"You do not frighten me, Sir Gawain," the hag returned. "For I have magic and thou hast not. See how easily I can fell you!"

Even as she spoke there was a shimmer in the air about her, and her body writhed and then ran suddenly liquid as her shape changed. Where she had stood there was now an eagle of tremendous size, still clutching Morvan in its talons as she flapped her wings and launched herself from the ledge, flying over the abyss towards them and gaining speed as she found the warm draught rising from the pit. They could see the key now, hanging between the feathers of her neck as she hurtled towards them, Morvan screaming in fear at her feet. She flew straight at Gawain, neck outstretched to gouge him with her great beak. But once more Wolf came to his master's aid. As fast as the eagle came, so came Wolf, and as the eagle bent towards Gawain Wolf leapt with all his might. His teeth clamped on to the bird's wing and the eagle banked, thrown off balance. Gawain reached out his arms as Morvan thumped against him, and clasped the child tight as the eagle released its grip and dog and bird fell towards the cavern floor. They smashed into the rocks beside Morvan's sisters and Wolf lay stunned for a moment even as the bird took off again and circled the abyss safely above the dragon's snapping jaws.

A cackle of laughter came from the eagle's great beak.

"Still I have you!" she crowed, while the dragon strained at its fetters beneath her. "Now your faithful companion is below you, Sir Gawain, out of reach! If you wish to see the creature live then leave now, take the maiden as your prize from this quest, and go back to your king. You will not get the key Sir Gawain for I am wiser than a dragon and you cannot wrest it from me."

"I can try!" Gawain replied, squaring his shoulders as the bird swooped around his head cackling. "You are not invincible."

"You think yourself so high and mighty, Sir Gawain, serving your great king Arthur! But men are so weak. See how I have ruled them while they think themselves so strong! Easily I broke Rozenn's brother with dreams of riches and easily will I break you. Greed and love – bad and good – I turn them all to my own purpose!" Again she cackled, full of her own cunning. "See, then, I will bargain with you after all. Leave me the dragon and the key and I shall spare these weak creatures you love so dearly. You are defeated Sir Gawain and you must own it!"

So busy circling above Gawain's head was the eagle, and so proud of her cunning, that Demelza did not see that Wolf had recovered from his fall. He sat up dizzily, shook his head, and then looked around. At his side was the one remaining bolt and tether that fettered the dragon's forefeet to the stone floor. The tether was made of hide, stretched and twisted and very strong, but Wolf's teeth were stronger. He grunted cheerfully to himself and lay down to apply his large white teeth to the tasty rope even as the eagle circled above, calling taunts to the knight and his lady on the ledge, while the dragon strained and battered against its last bond, snapping uselessly at the bird as it passed.

When the end came it came suddenly. Wolf's teeth gnawed rapidly through the rope and the weakened fetter snapped as the dragon lunged again. Into the eagle's flight it crashed, sending the bird spinning across the abyss, a helpless blur of feather and claw. The dragon followed, roaring and blazing in its fury. They crashed into the glassy wall where the blackness of the sea stared in. For a moment afterwards there was only the sound of their bodies falling senseless to the cavern floor beside the children and the dog. Then came a cracking report, so loud that Rozenn clapped her hands to her ears. Across the cavern on the opposite wall they could see a change. Cracks were spreading out in a web across the face of the glass wall from the shock of the impact and a groaning shudder echoed through the cavern.

"Wolf!" Gawain cried, falling to his knees on the edge of the abyss. "Are you alright?"

"Yes master!" Wolf's voice came weakly from the inky darkness below.

"You must lead the children up here, out of the pit. Can you see a way?"

"There is no way master. But I saw the key fly from the crone's neck as she fell. It is only a little way below you, hanging from a rock."

"Never mind that now. Look for a way out of the pit."

Another groan echoed around the cavern from the glass wall. Wolf's voice came back calmly.

"There is no way out master. You must get the key and go."

"Wait there and I shall come to you. I love you too well to leave you Wolf."

Gawain could almost hear Wolf's tail wagging and see the grin on his faithful face. "Then I am content, master, except that I did not think to find my end so far from thee. But there is no remedy, for there is no way up or down." As he spoke the glass wall trembled and Wolf's voice grew urgent. "Master! Get the key now, or it will all have been in vain!"

Gawain threw himself onto his belly and felt down into the void. For a moment there was nothing, then his fingers closed on a cold chain and the key was in his palm.

Below him Wolf was speaking cheerfully to Morvan's sisters, whose sobs echoed around the cavern pitifully.

"Come now!" Gawain heard him saying kindly. "All may yet be well. Grasp my neck there – that's right. See how safe we feel together! My master will save us yet, fear not, for he is the bravest and best knight in Christendom."

Tears spilled down Gawain's cheeks into his beard as he listened to the dog's brave lies amid the groaning of the walls and the sobs of the children. He scrambled to his feet and at that moment the glass wall shattered. There was a roar as the sea gushed into the pit below and the children's cries were silenced. Then rocks were falling about his head as the whole hill shook. Gawain found Rozenn's hand in the darkness, swept Morvan into his arms, and turning raced into the tunnel hearing the sea at his back filling the void. Morvan was screaming for his sisters and Gawain's own heart was breaking, for if he were the bravest and best knight in Christendom he still could not save his best friend.

~

It was almost dawn when a tapping came at the chamber window where the Merlin kept guard over his king. A herring gull was perching precariously on the sill, its huge yellow feet slipping on the stones. It flapped its wings clumsily as the Merlin hopped out of the window, clicking his beak in irritation at the commotion.

"Pardon, my lord," the gull said. Its voice was harsh, but its eye was humble as it regarded the small hawk beside him. "I come in haste as you bid me do when there was news from the west."

"Well?"

The big bird gulped foolishly as he told his tale of Gawain and the flood at Mullion Hill. The Merlin listened quietly, with a bright eye and said nothing until the bird's tale was told. Then he ruffled his feathers and turned his beady eye on the gull. "Do something for me, dear gull. Fly west once more and seek out Sir Gawain. Take him my greeting and comfort him, for I feel his sorrow and I would not have it so."

The gull was regarding him with its great foolish eye. "And will you not go to him, master?"

"I will not. I have sworn to meddle no more, and I do not trust myself beyond this chamber. I will see his dear face soon enough, when all return to Camelot."

Merlin's gull found Gawain later that day, still lingering among the ruins of the castle at Mullion Hill. The hill was fast becoming an island, for it had collapsed from within and the sea was rising around it. The causeway would soon be gone. Only the sentinel statue would remain, waist deep in water, still gazing out to sea.

The ruin of the people was worse. None of the slaves had got out of the mines alive, for the guards had awaited Gawain's orders, as he had bid them, and when the deluge came there was no time to unchain the prisoners. Some few guards had escaped. Most of the castle servants had survived by running from the trembling buildings. But the king was dead, crushed by the weakened walls of his great throne room, which had crashed about him.

The key dangled from its chain in Gawain's great fist, but his face was grey and weary as he surveyed the wreckage and watched Rozenn tending to the wounded. Morvan followed at her heels, his face pale and his eyes red from weeping, for he had no family now.

The gull settled on the broken wall where the knight was leaning.

"It is a heavy price to pay!" the gull said soberly. "A heavy price indeed!"

Gawain turned his eyes towards the gull with little surprise. "What phantom or demon art thou?" he asked.

"I am come from the Merlin." The gull fixed its earnest yellow eye upon Gawain's face. "I am come with greetings and counsel from him, if you will have it."

"I would have both with a hearty good will if I thought them true," Gawain said, "but I have lost all hope of comfort on this quest."

"The Merlin bid me give thee this token," the gull answered. "He told me to remind you of your talk together, some long days since, when you asked him what fate awaited you on this journey. Do you remember it?"

"I do," Gawain replied, remembering that first day of hope on the quest and looking upon the gull a little more kindly.

"He told you then that he could not see your future. Now he commands me to say that he knows you bear two keys, and he bids me tell you that your work is done. He calls you back to Camelot, and he swears that no more harm will come to you on this quest."

"And am I to go alone?" The knight's eyes turned to Rozenn, but she was busy tending to her people and she did not hear.

"I think you must, Sir Gawain, for the time is not yet for peace and happiness. But the Merlin also bid me tell you that happier times may come." The bird ruffled its feathers and its voice changed. "And you shall have my company, should you desire it, for a little way."

Gawain looked at the gull and smiled, for he could see its kindly diffidence. "I will have it and welcome, if you will go with me," he answered. "And indeed, I am ready to go at once, for I cannot look upon this ruin without shame."

"It was not your doing," the gull told him. "It was Demelza's cruelty and contempt for living things that brought this about. Still, I think we must leave now or risk being trapped here for many days, for the sea is rising."

Rozenn turned as Gawain laid his hand on her shoulder and led her aside from her work.

"You are leaving," she said, as she wiped a hand across her grimy forehead and looked into his face.

"I must go, Rozenn, for Arthur needs me, and the water is rising."

"And shall we ever meet again?"

Gawain shook his head, looking around him at the ruins. "Indeed, I know not, for you must be lady of the manor now, and bring some order to this confusion."

She nodded, following his gaze, and her lip trembled a little. "Do not blame yourself, Gawain. It was not you that trapped the beast in the cave, nor smashed the walls." She reached up to touch his cheek, and tried to smile. "I will miss you, and your kindness."

Gawain took her hand and pressed it to his face. "If Arthur is restored, and the kingdom won, I shall return," he said. "For you are the fairest lady I ever saw."

Then Rozenn kissed him, and after that Morvan came forward shyly to squeeze his hand despite his tears. Gawain could hardly bear to see the lad's pain. The big knight's shoulders sagged and his face was dismal as he splashed across the flooded causeway and bent the horse's steps eastwards across the heath, the gull flying in front of him with slow easy beats of its wings. Without Wolf at his heels the journey back to Camelot seemed long and the way cheerless.

I saw their starved lips in the gloam,
With horrid warning gapèd wide,
And I awoke and found me here,
           On the cold hill's side.

Friend and Foe

The bleak grassy plain of the high road grew higher and bleaker still as Kay and Mordred ventured further westwards towards the Land's End. At length they found themselves on a hilltop looking down on a grand prospect. A wide vale lay before them and beyond that the sea opened blue and vast, close to view for the first time in many a mile. Farmsteads and pastures bounded by stone walls lay scattered across the plain below, while the grass of the opposite hilltop petered into brown bracken and heather at its peak, growing over strange tumbled rocks and cairns.

"Well! This is a sight to make the heart swell," Mordred said. "Drear have I felt these last days, and drear seemed the folks we met, but this is grand and free!"

"Ancient too, I guess," Kay replied, pointing towards the stone cairns ahead. "Those are barrows, are they not, from long ago? People have lived on these plains for many a long age I should think, long before Christ was born or even the ten commandments cast in stone on the mountainsides of Judea. I wonder what kind of folks they were and if their lives too were dogged by magic?"

Mordred shook his head. "By magic and by men," he replied. "For the last days have shown us how men may torment each other even without wizards to teach them."

Kay smiled a wry smile of agreement, and then urged his horse forward to start the descent down the heathy hillside towards the richer pasture below.

"Here are many small farms and cottages," Mordred said from behind him. "I believe we are in the estate of some lord or other. I wonder where he keeps his manor?"

They soon found out, without the need to ask for directions, for the house lay to their left as they descended the slope, in a sheltered spot on the side of the vale looking westwards towards the hilltop barrow. The grand house dominated the landscape, its large windows looking out towards the hill and the sea beyond it like a watchtower.

"Let us hope that this fair prospect is real," Kay said. "For we have no Merlin with us this time, to forewarn us of danger. But we must hazard a visit to the manor come what may, for we cannot ride through his lands without some courtesy."

"Here too we must soon be seen, even as we were at Bodmin," Mordred said, cowering slightly under the manor's gaze. "I wonder if we shall receive so warm a welcome?"

But they saw no sign of life as they came closer to the house. There were no labourers or stable lads to be seen and the front door was shut. Closer to view the windows were grimy and blind.

"Perhaps the lord is from home," Kay hazarded. "For which I would not be sorry, for I would pass through this landscape as soon as I might. You called it free, but I am not so sure. I feel enchantment crackling against my skin like the threat of a thunderstorm."

"It is a fine spot for a dragon however," Mordred observed. "Perhaps it watches us even now from the barrow on the hilltop."

"That is somehow not a cheering thought," Kay smiled grimly. "But I cannot wish away a dragon, for find another we must."

They dismounted on the gravelled courtyard before the door to the manor and ran up the steps, hammering at its old wood until Mordred noticed an ancient bell suspended from an iron bracket at the corner and used his sword to strike it into a clamour. The racket died away slowly and the knights stood quietly while the horses pulled at the grass which grew between the cobbles of the yard. Kay began to hope that the manor was deserted as the minutes lengthened. But then a scrabbling sound of bolts being drawn came from within, and the door creaked slowly open, sticking against the stone step as though it had not stirred for many a long day.

A man of great age stood there. His hair was long, and scant, while a matted beard grew from his chin. He looked like a wizard from a storybook, and Mordred flinched under his gaze.

"Is the lord of the manor within?" Kay asked, eyeing the old man with curiosity. "For we pass through his lands and thought to pay him a courtesy."

The old man regarded them rather balefully. His eyes were watery and pale, and he looked as though he had eaten seldom and slept less for many a long day.

"Who calls upon him?" he asked at last with a voice that seemed as rusty from long disuse as the hinges of his door.

"I am Sir Kay, and with me rides Sir Mordred," Kay replied. "We come from Camelot, high seat of King Arthur, in search of dragons to undo a mighty spell and conquer the magic of the west."

"And what would you have of the lord of this manor?"

"Permission to cross his lands, good will and perhaps even counsel if he will give it."

"The first you have." The old man eyed them guardedly. "The second you may have, and the third is this. Evil spirits dwell in the cairn up yonder, which blight this land and have blighted its lord still more. Wife and child did they take long since, and the lord has neither slept nor rested for many years. Vanquish the barrow wights and you shall have my blessing. Return me my family and you shall have reward. I know of no dragons in this land but if you wish to conquer sorcery there you may begin."

With that he shut the door in their faces.

~

The knights took counsel together under a gnarled thorn tree close to the old man's house. As they talked a soft but persistent drizzle began to patter onto the young green leaves above them. The sky was a leaden grey but the air was bright and warm and small birds fluted from the branches above their heads. Spring had reached the valley and the soft rain promised more than it threatened.

"Well?" asked Mordred. "What in the Lord's name are we to do now? Are we to humour the old madman or ride on our way?"

"Not a madman, I think, but in deep sorrow. He said he had not slept or rested and that was indeed how he looked. I wonder how long ago he lost his wife and child?"

"Many years, he said." Mordred sighed and lay flat on his back watching the raindrops fall onto the grass around him. "Are we to believe his tale?"

"Why not? Many a barrow wight have we sent back to slumber these last ten years. They are always troublesome and the people fear them, and many tell tales of men passing within their cairns and not returning for long ages, if at all." Kay cast a glance at Mordred. "So to answer your question my son, I believe we must help the old man whether we will or no. First because that is our cause. Arthur charged us long ago to banish sorcery and bring peace wherever we find it. And secondly we rode to the man's door and sought his words. We cannot shirk them just because today we look for dragons instead of ghosts."

Mordred shrugged and rose to his feet. "Be it so then, I bow to your wisdom and will not fight it. But it will be a weary climb to the hilltop."

Dusk had fallen before they reached the stone cairn on the summit of the hill. Daisies glimmered in the fading light amid the short grass and looking back they could see for many a mile around. The sea lay grey and vast in the twilight behind them and it made Kay shiver as he climbed to feel its quiet power at his back.

At length they found themselves on the hilltop at the entrance to the domed stone barrow. Grass had grown up between the rocks at its base and moss and lichen sprouted from the worn grey surfaces of its stones, running like veins over its ancient lines. The barrow itself was huge, like a prostrate giant brooding over the everyday life of the lands below.

"Many a soul must lie within these peaceful rocks," Kay said, breaking the silence in which they had made the ascent. "And many a warrior too, I should think, for this is the grave of no common mortals and we may meet our match. But we are living men, and they are only spirits. As ever before, a stout heart will turn them to dust and air. Remember Mordred that our strength will lie not in arms but in belief. So long as you believe them but figments they cannot hurt you. As you have noticed before, magic strikes at the mind not the body."

Mordred nodded grimly, but he clasped his sword hilt nonetheless. "It would be an easier prospect in the broad sunlight," he said, a trifle shamefaced. Kay grinned encouragingly through the gathering darkness.

"So it would," he agreed. "But had we come in the noonday we should have come in vain for this is their time and we must bide by so much of their rules at least."

The knights drew their weapons and stood before the door to the barrow, which was blocked by a stone larger than the rest and of beautiful smoothness and regularity of shape. Still, it looked as though it had never moved for many a century as grass grew up before it and brambles scrambled across its face. Just as this thought crossed their minds a soft voice spoke out of the darkness behind them.

"Being as you observed of spirit, we have no need of doors and windows."

The knights spun about, holding out their weapons and straining their eyes into the darkness. A trace of amusement rippled through the voice.

"Nor of iron neither."

No form was visible but the voice spoke again, this time almost from above their heads.

"But you are welcome, knights, welcome as all visitors to our resting place. Will you enter?"

"Nay!" Mordred responded hoarsely, a note of anxiety in his young voice. "Never! What, enter and never return to the daylight?"

"How can that be, Sir Mordred, when you say that we are but figments to be banished into dust and air?" This time the voice came from behind them once more and the knights circled again cautiously, scanning the shadows.

"'Twas I said those words," Kay spoke up then in a firmer tone that gave Mordred courage. "And I for one have no fear to enter your barrow for it is but the resting place of bones long mouldered."

"Indeed! Then what am I?"

"Oh, you are the spirit of one such poor soul, I grant it," Kay replied. "But your place is not here, whoever you are. You belong in another place and we are come to send you thither."

Then all at once the speaker stood before them visible to the eye, bathed in a misty light as though he carried his own world with him and was no part of the soft dark landscape where they stood. He was indeed a warrior from an ancient time as Kay had guessed. Leather armour laced across his bare shoulders and a sword of intricate and beautiful design hung at his side. His hair was long and dark and faint blue lines patterned his face and body, drawn or tattooed in woad. He was young and tall and fair to look upon, and Kay felt admiration despite himself, for this was a man even as they were, judged by the same standard and thirsty for the same glory when he had lived.

"Whence come you?" the warrior asked then. "And why do you feel a duty to see after my spirit? What harm have I done to thee?"

"We come from the strongest fortress of our age," Kay said. "And we have sworn an oath to send all sorcery out of our land. We find that our people live more happily in a world of flesh and blood and we are bound to protect them."

The warrior regarded Kay earnestly for a moment and then gestured towards the barrow beside them.

"If you are truly not afraid," he said, "enter my halls and sit with me and tell me of your fortress and your battles and your oaths. It will pass away this long night and perhaps we may learn of each other. I can offer you the dream of wine and ale and good food, if you dare take it, and the hours will be pleasant to you."

"We will enter," Kay replied. "But we will take no food or drink and we will resist your dreams for there lies enchantment. If you will have such obstinate, ungrateful guests, take us within."

He laid his hand on the stone of the doorway and at once it moved aside. With a last backward glance at the stars the knights stepped forward, stooping as they entered the dark low walls of the barrow. The door swung shut behind them and then the gloom was impenetrable and the silence complete, for no breath of wind found its way through the overgrown walls into the crypt. Kay could feel Mordred at his side and could sense the young man's fear. He spoke cheerfully, but his own voice sounded faint and muffled to his ears.

"We will suffer an illusion of light at least, that we may see our hands before our faces and read your own visage as we talk."

Immediately a soft glow suffused the cavern and the two knights looked about them. They were standing in a low chamber at the centre of the barrow. On both sides they could see doorways to smaller chambers with low stone plinths within them. From these plinths glimmered whitened bones, even as the daisies had shone in the dusk on the hill outside.

Then their host stood before them again, gesturing to small stone benches for them to take their ease. The knights sat down warily while the warrior flung himself onto a bed of dull coloured blankets that had materialised out of the darkness behind him, lit by the same warm glow as before. A goblet appeared in his hand, and he drank slowly, watching his guests over the rim with dark eyes.

"And now what?" Mordred asked, settling his legs more comfortably as he watched the warrior wipe his mouth with the back of his hand and throw down the cup which vanished before it could hit the floor. "Were we your usual victims, what would you show us within these walls?"

The warrior frowned. "Call none victims! None stay with us unless they desire to do so. But we make our visitors comfortable with a cheering light and a good feast. Fine wine and merry company. Will you not have these things too?"

Even as he spoke ghostly images of the things he named flickered before their eyes. Fair maidens and strong men smiled from the shadows and they half thought they could hear snatches of music hovering at the threshold of sound.

"We will not!" Mordred spoke boldly. "We will suffer no trickery!"

"It is not trickery my lord," the warrior answered. "Not in the way you mean. All the faces you see and music you hear existed once and inhabit the dreams of those who lie here. Would you deny us our memories of pleasure?"

"I would deny you naught," Kay spoke up firmly, "if you kept your memories to yourselves. But like all conjurers you would meddle in the real world and make mortal men sad."

There was a silence for a moment. The warrior turned his eyes from Mordred's young face to Kay's lined one and then spoke softly.

"So. That brings us perhaps to your real purpose in climbing so high in order to be meddled with. Remember, I did not come down to the valley to whisk you hither."

The two knights exchanged a glance and Kay spoke up once more.

"You are right, lord. Did you but sleep peacefully within these walls we would have left you be, for we seek no quarrel with the dead. But someone in the valley below sought our aid to recall those dear to him from your world. You see, you have indeed meddled in the real world and we must protect our own."

The warrior shifted in his seat and then drew his sword from its sheath, regarding it thoughtfully for a moment before tracing its intricate patterns with a ghostly finger. Then he looked up at the knights and his voice was sad.

"Do you know how old this sword is?" he asked at last. "If you knew, you would also know how long I have lain here under the earth. My sword is not made of iron but bronze, and soft bronze at that. It mattered not against the enemies I faced for there was no iron in the world at that time. Yes, long have I lain here.

"And see my face, lords. See how young and fair I am. I was laid in this tomb in the twentieth year of my life. Young and strong and skilled with my bronze blade I was not ready to die. The companions that lay around me were my followers, for I was a lord high in renown in my lifetime, and the battle that brought our deaths brought much sorrow to our lands for the best and noblest were borne away into the darkness. Here we lay for many ages and the world outside these walls changed but little, so that we loved to look upon it in the dark night when none would fear us. So we did not depart for that other place you spoke of. Why should we? This was our world still and we knew no other. Indeed, our people built this barrow on the hill that we dead might survey our kingdom from the hilltop and that the people might remember us, and keep us with them in their landscape. We did not call that magic."

"But at last the world did change, though slowly," Kay replied. "And now the people at your gates fear you and do not remember. This is no longer your world after all."

"Perhaps." The warrior inclined his head. "And for a time we almost lost heart. But yet those people down in the valley do still believe in us even while they fear, and some sorrowful souls seek us out if their lives are sad and a burden to them. Here they enter and here they stay, if they wish it. Those outside our walls think that we hold them by force but it is not really so."

There was a pause and then Kay spoke. "We seek a woman and her child," he said. "The lady was wife once to the lord who dwells in the valley below. They entered here long ago, he told us, and he has found no rest without them."

A look of pain crossed the warrior's fair young face and he was silent for a moment. Then he turned and called out into the darkness in a tongue that none of the knights recognised. His voice seemed to echo into the void, as though the barrow were in truth a vast hall with many winding passages. From far away a woman's voice answered. The knights' hands went to their sword hilts as a thrill of fear prickled through their bodies. Then a new light glimmered in the gloom of the corner and a woman stepped forth from the shadows, leading a small child by the hand. Young and beautiful, she seemed a fit companion for the warrior as she reached his side. Like him she was tall and slender, with dark hair that fell like a curtain around her oval face, and on her arms and ankles she bore dull bronze torques that gleamed like armour. The young warrior reached out and took her hand and the three fair souls, man woman and child, looked out of their world of light into the gloom where the knights sat watching.

Kay looked at the young woman's face and then at Mordred. "Long has she been here, I deem," he said quietly, "unless the lord in the valley wedded this maid in his dotage."

"Of an age we were on our wedding day," the woman answered. "Both young, both foolish. I have no knowledge of the time I have passed in these halls for it seems but days to my mind. Is he much aged then, my lord below?"

"Aged beyond your imagination," Kay said gently. The girl closed her eyes.

"Poor Godred! He has been alone for many a long year."

"He has, and he says that he cannot rest without you. Will you not return to him?"

The young woman turned and looked at the warrior beside her. "Nay," she said softly. "Nay, I cannot help him now. Here I would stay for better or worst."

"Why sayest that?" Kay urged kindly. "Will you not have flesh and blood after all, instead of phantoms?"

The girl laughed bitterly, and Kay's skin crawled as the sound echoed in and out of the many chambers around them.

"Flesh and blood!" she exclaimed. "Aye! You would give me that indeed! For when I crawled up this hill so long ago, I was cruelly aware of my flesh, which burned, and of blood which caked my face! Godred loved me indeed, but that did not stop him from beating me and my child! Why do you think I ran to this desperate place as it seemed to me then, if not in search of release from my flesh?"

"And have you found it?"

"Aye!" the girl's voice softened and she lifted the warrior's hand to her lips. "Love and peace and joy have I found under the earth and I will not renounce them!"

Kay regarded the lovers soberly and hesitated before he broke the silence that followed.

"Your husband is old and frail in these days," he said, in a gentler tone than before. "He cannot hurt you now. There is no need to fear returning."

"Perhaps." The girl turned her dark eyes on the knights and looked at them with a puzzled look. "But why should I wish to return? Here the days pass in joy and good fellowship and I have found my heart's companion."

"Do you not crave the daylight in this dark place?" Mordred asked then. Knight as he was, he was bashful as he gazed upon the girl's great beauty. "Would you not wish to feel the sunlight on your face and the breeze in your hair?"

The girl laughed incredulously and turned to the warrior. "Seek the daylight my lord? What do they mean? How can aught compare to this?" She waved her hand around her appealingly and the warrior caught it between his own.

"These lords will not enter our world," he explained, watching her face with love in his glance. "They choose to sit in the darkness of the grave for fear of enchantment."

"Then you cannot see what surrounds us?" she asked, turning to the knights. "Cannot you see the light which shafts from the roof in great pools of golden sunlight?" The knights shook their heads. "Nor the flowers which grow in the walls, more beautiful and fragrant than any without? Nor the warm fire and the rich tapestries, nor taste the wine like nectar and the earthy ale?"

"None of it!" Kay smiled at her wonder.

"Then indeed you might tell me to return! But to what? To old age and infirmity and death in another world than this where dwells the lord of my heart? Would you part us thus?" Her lip trembled and a tear fell on to their transparent hands, still twined together.

"But what of your child?" Kay asked then. "Would you keep her here forever? In the world above she could find love and marry and bear children of her own. Will you deny her that?"

The girl looked down at the child who stood at her side, clutching her mother's gown with babyish fingers and watching the knights with round eyes.

"Marry and be beaten in her turn!" she said energetically. "Never!"

"Not all husbands are cruel." Kay replied. "You have found one here who is not. But even he has stolen you and enchanted you and kept you from the world. Is that not a different kind of cruelty?"

The girl turned to the warrior distress on her fair face. "Let them not say such things my lord! Willingly I came and willingly I stay!"

Kay turned his eyes reluctantly from the girl's face to Mordred's, and then his face grew grave, for Mordred had started to his feet, admiration dawning on his young face as he gazed upon the maid and the warrior before them. "My lord, let us go!" he exclaimed as he turned impulsively to the older man. "Let us leave this place where we have no quarrel! Never did evil show so fair a face!"

Kay frowned, for in his heart he felt the same wish, but disliked that the wraith should witness his doubt. "Peace Mordred!" he returned, more harshly than he meant, and the young knight fell back onto his seat, silenced and suddenly pale. Kay turned to the wraith and his maid and spoke more gently. Still doubt could not help but show in his eyes.

"The lad at my side speaks truth when he says that we have no quarrel with you," he said. "Winding are the ways that lead us to where we stand, and it seems that the maid has good reason to shun her earthly life. But we cannot pass by and turn a blind eye to your ways, even if we wished to, for it is against all we have fought for. Many may seek death in our world when life seems too hard but we cannot let them seek a life of enchantment instead. It is all or nothing for us. If we permit one act of sorcery to stand then our quest will never be fulfilled."

Kay turned to Mordred then, and took his hand. He tried to speak kindly, but Mordred was watching him with an angry face. "Mordred," he said. "Here is a hard lesson for you, my son, but it cannot come too soon. Perhaps you had thought our oaths to Arthur a simple matter until now, and why should you not? For you are yet young and unlearned in the ways of the world." Even as he spoke he could see that his words only made Mordred angry. "Why! Even the Merlin knows that if we prevail, as he himself wishes, he himself must leave our lands. We have made a hard choice, for not all magic is cruel and ugly. On this journey we have witnessed malice and stupidity in both wizards and men. Are we to be surprised then, that we are to find some beauty and goodness in magic too? And indeed these creatures that stand before us are not sorcerers themselves but only men and women who have passed into another realm."

Mordred did not answer, but dropped his eyes, and Kay turned back to the warrior. When he spoke it was with respect, as for a fellow knight. "What are we to do then, friend? If we cannot leave the maid here, and we wish not to return her to her lord, is there a third way?"

It was the girl that answered. Her face was as pale as Mordred's and tears sounded in her voice, but now she was calm. "If you gave me my wish I would go with my heart's companion into the long dark," she said, "if that is where you wish to send him. And after all, I am old in the years of the world. I have had my lifetime. Take my body back to Godred that he might bury me, and mourn, and be at peace. But let my spirit go with my lord's whither we know not.

"And yet I would have you take the child after all, for I cannot give her death and her father cannot beat her now. Take her back to him and let her know the joys and sorrows of a mortal life." The woman knelt to embrace the child tightly, and tears ran down her face as she added, "perhaps I will meet her again one day, if there is any meeting to be had in the place we go to." She pushed the child's hair away from her small face and kissed her, while the child stared back and began to cry, frightened by her mother's tone.

"Be it so," Kay replied gently, looking from the weeping woman to the young warrior's face. Grief and anger he saw there, but resignation too.

"I was not ready to die at twenty," the warrior said, watching the child and woman as they clung together and the woman whispered tender words of comfort into the child's ear. "For I had yet to know the joys of love and of peaceful days. But since then I have known both, and if you must send me to that other place thither will I go without complaint. But I am sorry to quit the world at last, for it is still sweet to look upon and the way forward is dark to my eyes."

"God forgive me if harm should come to thee," Kay replied, as the woman rose and came towards him, putting the child's hand into his own. "For your souls are pure and your hearts warm. But come what may it is full time for you to go. Leave this world to the living and find your own place among the dead. Your bones will remain here friend, be assured, for I will suffer no desecration to come to this mound so long as Arthur rules the land. But come now, it is time to part."

Tremulously the woman turned to her ghostly lover and twined her arms around his neck. Cheek to cheek they stood, and breast to breast, as the warm light that surrounded them slowly dimmed, and then went out.

~

Mordred wept freely as they rode from the manor where they had left the woman's body and the child to the old man's care. Kay stroked his horse's neck thoughtfully, as though for comfort in its warm living flesh. He thought back over the day and found himself wishing that they had never gone to the manor, but ridden on through the bleak landscape as he himself had half desired. Now as the sun began to sink over the hill and valley the air was still and peaceful. The air of mystery and magic had departed, though the barrow still dominated the skyline and would long bring solemn thoughts to passers by. Kay glanced back at the mound on the summit as they rode away from the broad vale and its cairn, and he wondered what new world the warrior and his lady had found when they left this one reluctantly behind.

Faith

Rain came sweeping in from the sea at nightfall, and Kay and Mordred found shelter in a barn by the roadside. Mordred fell into a deep sleep of weariness and sorrow as soon as he rested his head on his saddle blanket, but Kay could not sleep. Their good fellowship seemed somehow to have faded since they had parted from Gawain, and now, more than anything, he yearned for Arthur. Arthur would have known what to do with the poor souls they had met in the barrow that day. As he thought back over the adventure he feared he had torn the mother from the child with too much cruelty. And yet he also feared his own pity, for it seemed to betray the oaths he had made to his king long before.

But in this dark hour before dawn Kay found himself doubting even his own oaths, and he feared lest his king lay at the mercy of knights who might fail him. He himself pitied the creatures of magic. Mordred worshipped anything that was beautiful. Galahad sought glory through a prophecy made by a wizard. Lancelot had fallen prey to magic in the past, when cloaked by his desires. Despite their vows to forgo sorcery and stand as men alone, they were all perplexed and weak. He stared out at the rain gloomily for a moment, then his shoulders straightened and his face cleared. The dawn was nearing and so was the Land's End. Come what might, they could travel no further westwards, and in his heart he felt that the end was very near. He glanced at Mordred, now peaceful in slumber, and at last he closed his own eyes and sought the same comfort.

As both knights slept Morgan le Fay came to Mordred once more. This time it was certainly no dream. Mordred felt a hand shaking his shoulder and he grumbled sleepily before opening his eyes to see her anxious face bent to his own. She was drenched from the rain, her hair dripping around her face, and she shivered as she clutched a thin cloak around her shoulders. He sat up with a cry, but she hushed him, turning her eyes fearfully towards the other sleeping knight. "Do not wake Sir Kay, Mordred," she whispered. "If he finds me here he will slit my throat."

"Nay, cousin," Mordred returned, but he too spoke in a low voice as he threw aside his cover and stood up. "You wrong him to fear it."

"Nevertheless, let him sleep. It is you I need." She pulled at his arm, and they went to the doorway, standing in its shelter as the rain blew past in the wind.

Mordred stared at the figure beside him, still uncertain if he woke or slept. "How did you find us?"

Morgan cast him a sideways look and smiled. "Can you so easily forget that I am a witch?"

Mordred shook his head and gazed on her, still half bewildered. She was not the fair vision she had seemed in his dreams, but he knew he loved her nonetheless. "What do you want with me?"

"Oh – something and yet nothing." Morgan stared out into the storm, and her face grew solemn. "A warm embrace and a kindly face in a harsh world perhaps."

"You may always have that!" Mordred moved closer and wrapped his arms around her against the wind and rain. He could feel her shivering, and her hair lying wet against his shirt. "Where have you been?"

"Wandering like a lost soul, cousin!" She tried to laugh, but her teeth chattered. "There is little kindliness between witches I find. And each day your cause grows stronger, so that the end seems near. What will become of me when Arthur wakes?"

"Whatever you choose, Morgan. I know my uncle will bear no lasting grudge, for the Merlin told us that this enchantment was not really of your making. For my own part, if we prevail and magic is banished from the land, I would have you stay a mortal woman and be my wife."

Morgan leaned back to look in his face. "And will you really be so kind, after all that has passed?" There was a look in her green eyes he could not read, but he thought that she marvelled to find him still her own.

"It is not kindness, but love, Morgan." Mordred smoothed the hair from her face and bent down to kiss her cold lips. "I have always been alone. You, my uncle, and Guinevere have been my only real friends. Where else should I look for a wife?"

Morgan did not answer, but turned her gaze back to the rain. "Yes, I should like to marry you," she said. "And with Galahad gone in search of the grail perhaps your uncle will make the wise choice and name you his heir. If magic is to be no more I could be content with earthly power."

"I do not know Arthur's mind," Mordred replied. "And if Galahad returns with the grail his claim will be more than mine. But I can think of no higher honour than to follow my uncle to the throne."

Morgan only smiled. For a moment she rubbed her face against his shirt where it lay damp against his skin, then she spoke more briskly. "Now listen to me, Mordred," she said. "For in truth I came to aid you, if I can. There is no longer any hope of a victory for magic. All the other keys are found, and Arthur's knights have prevailed as I might have guessed." She shook her head. "For all he abjures magic, there is a powerful charge of it about your king which protects his knights even when he sleeps!"

"Do not speak thus, Morgan. I cannot wish for the king's defeat."

"And yet I think you have found much good in the old ways, on this quest."

"I have. And much of beauty and grace too, so that if I had my wish I would keep something of magic back when all is done. But that is not to be."

"No, and so I will help you Mordred, and show my good will to the round table, so that they may judge me kindly in days to come. You will find the last dragon at the Land's End, lying at the foot of an old tower that stands above the headland and shows a beacon to warn passing ships of danger. Three beautiful maidens lie imprisoned in the tower, and around the neck of one is the key you seek. The beast that guards them is young and strong, and three times fiercer than any of the other dragons, for it has not one but three mighty heads on its shoulders."

Mordred swallowed. "Is it a beast of great size?"

"Passing great, Mordred. Three heads to face two knights!" She shuddered and hid her face in his breast. "I could wish the odds were more even!"

Mordred held her against him, but his eyes were dark. "And so this is the beast we must fight," he said, as if to himself. "And now the time comes, again I feel my weakness! Would that I were as the others are, full of thoughtless valour!"

Morgan pulled away again, and took his hands, looking into his face earnestly. "Do not fear, Mordred. Tomorrow may yet hold surprises, and perhaps your sword may stay in its sheath and your wits may win the day. When you look on the monster keep your head and your heart cool, and use your strengths. Remember all the things you have read, and all that I have taught you." She glanced towards the dark barn behind him. "Do not let Sir Kay turn you from your own knowledge. This is your test, Mordred, not his."

"And will you be there to help me?"

"Perhaps. And now I must go, before Sir Kay stirs and lops off my head."

"You speak in jest, cousin."

"Of course I do, Mordred. I am wise enough to see into men's hearts I hope, and to know that goodness dwells within Sir Kay."

"I wish you would stay." There was a sudden glamour about her as she turned to leave that reminded him of his dream and made his pulse quicken. He caught her hand, watching her mouth as she smiled.

"Prevail tomorrow and you shall have your reward!" And then she slipped away, back into the rain.

~

"Was it wise, Mordred, to meet the wench alone?" Kay shook his head. "You should have woken me."

"I feared you a little," Mordred answered. First light was dawning outside and they were collecting their belongings together. "You know I love my cousin, Kay, despite all that she has done. I feared you might hurt her if she came upon you so suddenly in the dark."

"I am grieved that you should think so."

"Indeed I do not really think so now, Kay, with my waking reason. Perhaps I myself was confused by the darkness."

"Or else fallen under her spell. But we will say no more of that now. At any rate you look no better for her visit – you are pale, Mordred."

"I slept badly. And I believe I am ready to bid this quest farewell."

"And I!" Kay stretched and rubbed his grimy face. "Well, my son, let us ride on to find this hydra-headed beast, if it really exists. Is your sword sharp?"

"I hope so."

Kay looked at the young knight's wan face and then clasped his arm kindly. "Do not be afraid, Mordred. We have been spared to face this last battle together, as we always planned."

The rain had stopped and a sea mist hung about them as they stepped outside. Birds were beginning to stir, and their calls drifted across the fields from a small copse on the hilltop. Unshaven and dishevelled from many nights on the road they swung into their saddles and set off at a canter along the soft dirt track towards the sea, spraying mud and pebbles behind them from the horses' hooves. The rain had left the hedgerows damp and starred with dew and the horses' hooves made a muffled thud on the muddy track. Soon steam rose from their sides into the moist air, and at the top of the hill the knights drew them back to a walk and began the steep descent down to the coast.

Isolated farmhouses and ramshackle cottages dotted the track that led down to the sea. Herds of cows grazed in the meadows on either hand, fresh from their morning milking, and raised their heads to watch the knights ride by. Some soon put their heads back down to the lush grass, others rolled their large eyes and shied away as they passed. A dog ran out of a farmyard barking insistently, while a donkey tethered alone in another field lifted its head and brayed loudly into the morning air. Far off a cockerel crowed his greeting to the day.

The sun was lingering just beneath the horizon when they breasted the last hill and looked down to the sea. Below them, at the foot of tall grassy cliffs, curved a beach of white sand lapped by blue water. A village huddled further along the bay, and a few boats bobbed at anchor close to the houses where the water was deep. Then the sun rose and the mist began to clear away, and for a moment the knights paused, struck by the loveliness of the prospect.

Mordred was the first to recover. "See, we have reached our destination at last," he said, pulling the map from his saddlebag. "That dark cliff rising behind the village must be the Land's End, for I can see the great rocks close in to the shore that they call the Longships."

"And that must be the beacon the witch spoke of, atop the headland," Kay returned. "And so it seems we may not visit this small paradise below us, but must keep to the high cliffs. What say you, Mordred? When the beast is defeated shall we return to dip our feet in the blue water?"

Mordred nodded, but all at once his throat was dry and he could not speak.

The beacon tower loomed on the hilltop in plain sight as they rode on, but it took an hour or more to reach it. The rain held off, and sunlight bathed the village below, but the sky was purple over the sea as though a storm approached. Mordred could feel a tingling in his scalp, and he wondered if it were fear or only approaching thunder. All seemed dismal to his eyes as they turned their backs on the pretty village below and ventured on towards the bleak headland.

When they came to the beacon they thought that Morgan le Fay had been playing a joke upon them, for it stood half ruined and deserted amid tangled undergrowth. At the tower's foot they halted, and Kay gave a hoarse shout. A sudden gust of wind blew from the sea, but below it they thought they heard a faint cry from the window above. Then, in an instant, the world around them changed. They threw up their hands to shield their eyes from a sudden radiance that blinded them, and then, blinking a little, they gazed around in wonder.

They stood no longer in the real world of bleak grassland and a stormy sea, but rather in a painted landscape, which depicted the tower and the cliff and the sea behind them with all the patient art of a monkish scribe. The brilliant light came from a golden frame which enclosed them, arching up over their heads where the sky should have been, and ending in elegant flourishes far above. A sliver of sky showed beneath, but it was made of blue enamel, as vivid as a sapphire. The grass was emerald green, soft under foot like silk, and silk-petalled roses clambered over the mossy walls of the tower, which stood ruined no longer. As they looked up trumpets sounded silvery and sweet and, as though summoned, the dragon appeared before them. It was pearly white, dazzling in the brilliant light, with scarlet scales beneath its wings that glowed like fire. Three beautiful heads on three swan-like necks swooped down to eye the knights, and they saw that its eyes were rubies, hard and cold, yet gleaming with a fiery glow. Having turned its six eyes upon them it settled at the tower foot like a huge cat, wrapped its tail around its body and leaned its three chins on its foreleg. They hardly felt afraid, for they thought they were dreaming – until they eyed each other and saw that they had themselves become paintings in their own turn. Skilful indeed was the artist, for their armour shone with silver and gold leaf and the hair hanging about their faces was as fine as strands of silk, but they were no longer men but boys, smooth-skinned and fair. Mordred looked down at his hands and saw they were as slim and soft as a maid's. Afraid, he clutched at his sword, only to find it was now paper instead of iron. Before he could cry out in fear, a clear voice called from above, and the two knights looked up to see a lovely maiden with long golden hair leaning from the window of the tower above their heads.

"Are you come to release us?" she asked eagerly.

"Oh – sirs! What joy to see a new face beneath us!"

"Where are we?" Kay asked. He meant his voice to be rough, but in this painted place all was smooth, and to his own ears his voice was musical and sweet. "What enchanted realm is this?"

"They say it is Avalon, Sir knight.

But how we came here we cannot tell aright."

"Avalon!" Mordred turned to Kay. "Are we dead then?"

"No, my son." Kay looked about him, and his hand felt for his paper sword. "Remember the Merlin told us that the magic would deepen as we went further on. And did not Morgan le Fay say that victory was near? Depend upon it, this is but the last desperate trick of our enemies."

"Avalon!" Mordred was already marvelling to himself and looking about him. "Never did I think that I should see this place with living eyes! And yet somehow it seems familiar to me, as though I have seen it but lately in a dream."

Kay spared their surroundings no more study, but turned back to the maiden at the window. "How many maidens are you?"

"Three, sire, fair and true," she answered.

"Three maids to be guarded by three heads of a beast.

We have sojourned here long, in quiet and peace.

But the waiting is wearisome, and the days are long,

And ever more dearly we wish to be gone."

"Whence came you, and what is your name?" Kay asked. The maiden shook her head and looked mournful.

"I cannot tell thee, lord, and that is my shame.

All memory has fallen from us, of days gone by.

The air itself sighs in our ears like a lullaby.

Art come to free us from this cursed sorcery?"

"Let me see your companions," Kay answered At once two more fair faces appeared at the window, one surrounded by red curls which fell from the casement like a shining rope. The third lady was dark, and her face was pensive as though with sorrow or deep reflection. Mordred looked on her and his memory stirred, for something about her reminded him of Morgan le Fay, now robbed of all earthly imperfections. Her face was ivory and her eyes were emeralds, and when they met his own he blinked, dazzled by their brilliance. Then he remembered where he had seen the tower and the dragon before, and he cursed softly with surprise.

"What manner of world is this!" Kay was marvelling.

"There is no mystery," Mordred answered, looking back at the maid's eyes with new understanding. "We stand but in the page of a book. And now I remember it Kay, for I read it in my uncle's library last winter."

The knights eyed the dragon, which seemed to mean them no harm so long as they stayed far from the doorway to the tower. Kay took a step closer and it lifted its head warningly, its red eyes gleaming. Mordred shook his head.

"Do not fight it, Kay. I remember now how it was defeated in the story."

"Tell on," Kay answered, dropping his hand gladly from his sword hilt. "And see how providence guides us, that you should know the very tale!"

Mordred shook his head. "I only know that in the story I read there was only one princess, not three. But to gain her the knight had to answer a riddle."

"And then?"

Mordred grimaced. "The knight was a fool, and could not answer it, though the answer was as plain as the crest on your helmet."

"And you knew the answer?"

"I did, Kay."

"Come knights of wisdom and renown!" The dark-haired maiden spoke from above their heads and they looked up again into her strange jewelled eyes.

"Come and lay your weapons down!
We ourselves can give you the keys to the keep –

Three rhymes for three heads – answer aright, and the dragon will sleep."

The knights exchanged a look. Kay's was suddenly troubled. "Do you think it wise, Mordred, to do as she says? We are knee-deep in magic, and I can hardly feel my feet."

Mordred shook his head, but his face was clearing. "I can see no other way, Kay. And you were right – it is a happy fate that makes us fall into a book, of all enchantments! What could be fitter for my talents? Let us hope Morgan le Fay spoke the truth when she said my wits might serve our turn. The maids must ask us three riddles. For each right answer we give one of the dragon's heads will fall into slumber. If we answer them all we may enter the tower at will, and free the maidens. One wears the key we seek about her neck, and our task will be done."

Kay still looked doubtful, but Mordred was already turning back to the three women with a wry smile. "Ask on, then, maidens, I am ready! Riddles have ever been my pleasure."

It was the golden-haired maid who spoke first. She leaned on the windowsill, her chin cupped in her hand, and the knights gazed up, a little mesmerised by her loveliness.

"Gentle as the green sward, good as gold,
Utterance ever sweet, ne'er harsh nor bold," she began.
"In gowns of white I vowed to serve my people,
Now the queen of all, from ditch to steeple.
Each I look on loves me, lord or knave,
Vanquished alike the craven or the brave.
Ever steadfast to my lord I stay,
Resolute and pure, bright as the day.
Ends now my rhyme – who am I? – can you say?"

Mordred was already smiling with relief, and he turned to clasp Kay's hand in a warm grasp. "'Tis my lady!" he exclaimed, "'tis Guinevere for certain! How should we not know her, from such a rhyme? For every line is true and sweet, just as she is!"

"You are right Mordred," Kay answered, pointing to the dragon, "look how your answer serves!"

One of the three heads had laid itself gracefully down upon the silken turf, and its fiery red eyes were closed. Still the other two heads watched and waited, and the dragon shook out its wings a little, with a flash of sudden scarlet. Now the red-haired maiden was speaking, and the knights stepped closer to hear, for her voice was soft and low. This time the riddle was shorter and Mordred's smile faded as he listened. His ivory face flushed red and was pouting like a girl's as she finished.

"Motherless child, maimed by pride,
Only loved by few, and loving fewer,
Ready with my wits, my only guide,
Disdainful of the faithful and the pure.
Rue and anger follow at my side,
Ever longing for a world gone by,
Doom lies on me – who am I?"

"I am Mordred!" he answered hotly. "But your words are poison, maid, for all your sweet red lips and honeyed voice! I love all my brethren, and I love the world I live in! Still I will not deny I must be the answer to your riddle."

Kay pointed as another of the dragon's heads fell into slumber beside the first. Still the last head watched them balefully, its ruby eyes hard and cold. Mordred shivered suddenly, and his scalp crawled, as though the storm approaching in the real world had broken for a moment into the painted landscape where they stood.

"These maids are seeming fair," he said. "But their words cut like a knife!"

"The riddles are not of their choosing," Kay answered. "How can they be, when they desire to be rescued? Be strong, Mordred. This is your test and no other's."

There was a pause before the last maid spoke. She looked down upon the knights with her emerald eyes, and her hair swung across her small dark face. Then she spoke and the knights' hearts grew cold, for her words seemed more like a curse than a riddle.

"Graced by the master's hand, gift of a king,
Restless to be found, to wreak my doom.
At my accomplishment the bells shall ring
In Camelot, first for joy, then for a tomb.
Lovers shall flee; friends shall fall; lost shall be everything."

The dragon watched the two knights with its one fierce head while the others slept. The maidens leant from the window eagerly, their lustrous hair falling down among the roses while a golden curtain stirred behind them in the window. Mordred closed his eyes and pondered, and Kay waited patiently. But even as he waited his hand moved to his painted sword and the dragon eyed him and bared its teeth a little. Kay knew that Mordred had no answer even before the young knight looked up at him, his face pale.

"It is a prophecy, not a riddle, Kay," he said. "How can we know the future? Not all the learning in the world may find that out."

"Should we try to guess?" Kay asked. The dark-haired maiden who had spoken last spoke again.

"Beware, Sir knights, to lose what you have gained!

Answer falsely, and all the dragon's heads will wake again."

Kay muttered a curse and clutched fretfully at his paper sword. Mordred frowned as he gazed on the maiden whose riddle had defeated him, and this time he thought he saw her smile, teasingly, in a way that was all too familiar.

"Let not success escape thee, child, despair thee not!" she said, a little mockingly.

"Use only the little learning thou hast got!"

Kay was not listening, for he was eyeing the dragon thoughtfully. "Two heads still sleep, Mordred. Perhaps even our painted swords may defeat one head of a painted foe!"

Mordred shook his head. "Nay Kay, what force of arms could help us here with swords that are but paper and gilt? No, we must follow the tale if we wish to win the maids."

"And what did the knight in the tale do, Mordred, when he failed as we have done?"

"He spoke words of power, words from the old language. The dragon fell dead and the princess was in his arms. That was the end of the tale, Kay."

"But we cannot do that!" Kay was shocked. "What of our oaths, Mordred? What of the Merlin's command to us to abjure sorcery?"

"The Merlin did not foresee this, Kay," Mordred answered. "Do you not see that this is the answer? You said that this was my test – well then, the test is to remember what I have read and use it wisely. And by some stroke of fortune, I was dreaming of this tale just the other night, and the words which summoned the princess from the tower."

"And will we follow slavishly a book of sorcery?" Kay asked. "Is it not for us to rewrite the ending of the story in Arthur's way? Let us fall upon the dragon even with our bare hands if we must, and let men's might triumph over magic!"

But Mordred would not listen. He had shut his eyes and was already speaking, and his voice sounded strange and harsh to Kay's ears. "*Dos omma!*" he cried. He held his arms out to the maidens at the window and spoke aloud the old speech Morgan le Fay had taught him as if he relished it. "Come to me, maidens! Fear not the beast that binds you! *Dos omma!*"

Endings

Sir Kay was stern and silent as he crossed the channel to Camelot, and the ferryman watched him sidelong and wondered at Sir Mordred's absence. Guinevere, watching him approach from the battlements, wondered too.

"Sir Kay returns alone," she said, turning to Lancelot who leaned beside her. "Do you realise, Lancelot, that you and I are the only pair to have returned together? Bedivere came back without Galahad, and even Gawain has lost his dog. How close I feel your sword blade now against my neck! I believe I am blessed to have seen Camelot's walls again as a living woman." She turned back to watch the approaching boat and her face grew grave. "But I hardly dare to hear that Mordred is dead, for he has been as a son to me."

"No knight of Camelot has yet perished on this quest."

"I pray he will not be the first."

They went down to the courtyard to greet Kay, the last traveller to return to the castle. He was thin and his face was grey, and he would say little of his adventures. "Let us wake Arthur," was all he said, holding out his key to their view. "Then there will be time enough for tales."

The knights who gathered at the king's bedside that day were changed from those who had set out on the quest weeks earlier. Then ten years of ease had sat easily upon them, now they were gaunt and weary. Then they had been six, now there were only four. Guinevere still wore her boy's clothes and a bow at her back. "Until Arthur wakes I am no queen," she had said to her servants. "Let me stay a knight in his service a little longer."

The Merlin looked sombre as he watched them enter the chamber and stand awkwardly, two knights too few, in Arthur's peaceful presence. Arthur alone among them was unchanged, still bound about with frost, his eyelashes lying white as goose feathers on his pale cheeks. He lay still and calm, as though far beyond the troubles of this world. The Merlin turned his eyes to the knights, looking from one worn face to the next, and his sharp eyes softened.

"Well met, knights of the round table."

As before, many weeks ago in this same chamber, they knelt at the bird's words and bowed their heads for his blessing. "Much has passed to trouble you and your hearts are sore, but still the quest has not broken you." The bird's voice was kind, and they looked up at him hungry for comfort. "Whatever yet may come, you have brought the keys to Camelot, and Arthur will awaken. Then at last you may ease your burdens a little, for he will guide you as he always has. Be of cheer, my friends."

"Cheered I will be," Bedivere answered, rising stiffly to his feet, "when I feel the warm grasp of his hand in mine. Lead us on, Merlin, to wake him aright. Here is my key."

"And mine," Lancelot added, rising and pulling his key from his shirt.

"And mine." Kay stepped quietly forward to stand at Arthur's feet and study the face he loved so well.

"And here are two more," Gawain said, his two keys dangling from his fist. The Merlin looked kindly from the burly knight to the queen, who stood by the bed her hand on Arthur's cold forehead.

"Let Guinevere take the first key, Gawain," he said. "For it was by her wisdom that it was won."

The knights gathered around the bed, keys in hand. Together they bent and placed the keys in the tiny locks. Together they turned the keys. And together they watched as the fine silver filigree of frost turned easily to mist and vanished from Arthur's form. In a moment more the pallor left his face and darkness shot through his hair like a thawing stream. His eyelids fluttered, and with a sigh he opened his eyes and looked about him from one grave face to another. Such a heavy enchantment, Kay marvelled, and yet so easily dispelled! Perhaps the trials they had suffered had after all been only a dream.

For a moment all was silent, and then Arthur's face creased into a smile, and he struggled to sit up. "What long faces!" he said. "Am I dead or dying?"

Then Guinevere was on her knees beside him, weeping, and he lifted his hand to her hair in wonder as he saw her knightly clothes. The others sighed, and exchanged glances, and smiled for the first time in many days. Lancelot walked away to the window to hide his tears, and Kay sat at the bed foot his sword across his knees and his head bent. Gawain looked down on Arthur benevolently, his face shining red, and even the Merlin seemed to smile, hopping to the bedpost and preening his feathers.

It was then that Arthur saw the bird, and a great shout of joy burst from him. In a moment the Merlin was on his wrist, and all were talking at once, telling the king of his own enchantment, and the Merlin's return, and the nature of the quest they had undergone to save him.

As always it was the Merlin who silenced them.

"Peace!" he cried, raising his little foot from Arthur's wrist. "Peace I say! The quest is fulfilled and the king is restored, but the story is not ended yet. Let Arthur rouse himself and eat, for he has fasted too long, then let us meet at the round table as of old, for it is there that your tales should be told. Begone, all of you, and let the king find his feet in peace!"

~

So they gathered at the round table once more as the sun sank low across the courtyard and slanted in through the windows. Every eye was drawn to the two empty seats where Galahad's golden hair and Mordred's clever face should have been. Arthur sat in his chair and studied the gaunt faces of his knights, and marvelled to have missed such an adventure. He turned his eyes to Guinevere and saw a new quiet strength in her gaze as she exchanged glances with the other knights. Last he looked on the Merlin, and his eyes filled with tears, for the bird had been his father, his teacher and his friend for many a long year.

"And so we gather again at this table," the bird began. "We parted many days ago, with a quest before us to restore the king. Now the quest is done and the king is restored. But as I told you then, more hung by this quest than the waking of Arthur, for the old powers in the world had laid him low and this gave you the chance to meet them in battle. Courage and sacrifice were needed, and both have been given. In one last struggle against sorcery you have proved your worth, and the last efforts of magic have been overturned. Now the land is yours to the sea on all sides. The west is won, and the king will find himself new duties in ruling it and bringing it the comfort of his peace. All this you have done, and I honour you."

The knights did not answer, for at that moment the memory of their losses weighed heavily upon them and the Merlin seemed to feel it.

"But now is the time to tell our tales," he said, "and for Arthur to share your glory and your sorrows. More than one face is missing that should be here, and for once even I do not know all that has happened to make it so. Tell on, my friends, and let us share our wisdom."

And so they told their tales, of Bodmin, of Fowey, of Padstow, and of the Lizard, and they were long in the telling, so that afternoon had passed into evening and evening into night before it came to Kay's turn to speak. At last, by the light of candles, he told his tale of the Land's End. First he told of the shades in the barrow, and the others shivered as the shadows danced on the ceiling above them and caught in the hollows in Kay's thin face. Then he told of the last adventure within the pages of a book, and the mystery of the riddle that Mordred could not answer.

"He would not listen to me, Arthur," Kay said, and even in the candlelight his face was grey at the memory. "Because the book he had read used the old magic, he could see no other way to defeat the dragon. In his heart I think he was glad to speak the words of power he had read so often but never used. After that it all ended very quickly. Just as he had promised, the dragon fell dead and the maidens were with us. For a moment he was joyful. But then a storm seemed to break over us from nowhere, and all at once there was darkness, and forked lightning, and rain. We fell to the ground, and when we opened our eyes we were back in the real world by the old tower with thunder raging above us. Next to us on the grass sat Morgan le Fay with the key in her hand, and I realised then that she had been the dark-haired maiden in the tower, whose riddle we could not answer.

"So much for her love for Mordred! 'You alone have failed in your quest,' she said to him with a cruel smile. 'Now Arthur's quest shall fail too. Had you fought the dragon Camelot would have prevailed, and every shred of magic in the world would have vanished from this hour. Instead something will now remain, and I am glad of it!'

"Mordred looked on her with a look of pain in his face that haunts me still. Then he sprang to his feet and fled as though demons pursued him. I tried to catch my horse and follow, but he was gone too quickly. Morgan le Fay handed me the key and bade me return here to wake the king. 'You have won, Sir Kay,' she said to me. 'All but one scrap of magic will be gone from the day you wake Arthur. But something will remain, and for that I take the credit. I have saved something of my world.'"

It was Lancelot who broke the silence that followed. He threw his sword across the room so that it shattered the peace of the chamber, and he jumped to his feet to follow it.

"Damned brat!" he said. "Between them he and that woman have brought all our sorrows! I would snap his neck like a rabbit's if I had him here."

"Peace, Lancelot," the Merlin answered. He had been sitting in the shadows, listening to their tales with his eyes shut and his face in a frown. "This hatred for Mordred will lead you to sorrow if you will not curb it." He sighed. "And yet I too grieve sorely that Mordred has failed."

"What did the witch mean, by what she said to Kay?" Arthur asked him. The bird ruffled his feathers and pecked at his breast for a moment and did not answer.

"Speak, Merlin!" Arthur said. "What makes you so silent? I never before heard you lost for words."

"Not lost, but puzzled," the Merlin answered, and the knights stared, for they had never heard the bird admit to doubt before. "I have spent the span of your life, Arthur, trying to protect you from your fate, and now at last I do not know what to say."

"Protect me!" Arthur laughed. "Indeed, Merlin, that is hard to credit! Have you not made me a king, and sent me to war, and made me fight all the terrible powers of magic? That was a strange mercy!"

"All this I have done," the Merlin answered. "And all the time your own minds opposed me, though you never knew it. Magic I bade you fight, but as fast as you banished dragons and giants from the land you welcomed in your new God, with his grail and his promise of life after death. I should have seen then that I was defeated. But I kept on, foolishly, in the hope you would triumph despite yourselves."

The knights exchanged glances, but did not speak. "Now Mordred has failed, as I should have known he would, and it will be as the witch said. When the sun rises all of magic will disappear from the world, all except for the one thing saved by Morgan le Fay. She is a clever witch, to turn my own works against me! But she will be disappointed, for it will not be her own powers that will remain. Like me she has always underestimated the power of the new magic, yet all unwittingly I fear it will be Galahad's God and his grail that she will have saved."

"You fear it!" Arthur exclaimed. "And yet it would be an empty world without them, I think, and I do not know how to sorrow that they should remain! Think of Galahad – would he forget the grail if it were gone? All his life he would sigh for it, and the same would be true for all men in their different ways. The people's prayers would go unanswered, but they would not cease to pray, for men will not forget all the strange beauty of magic."

The Merlin flapped his wings irritably. "Well, there you are then, you with your human hearts! Now I see I have wasted my time over all these years. What! Arthur himself rejoice that his quest to banish all this foolishness has failed!"

"And what would you have us keep, instead of the grail?" Guinevere asked from her place at Arthur's side. "For you spoke strangely, as if God and the grail were the very last things you would have endure."

The Merlin hopped across and pecked at her sleeve peaceably. "I am an old, bad-tempered creature," he answered. "That is all, Guinevere. So do not heed me. Only at sunrise will you begin to see what has gone. It may take much longer to find out what has remained."

"I would it were you," Arthur said, holding out his hand to the bird. "Do you think you might stay with me, Merlin?"

"I would it were Excalibur!" Lancelot said, his fists clenched. "Then Arthur would remain invincible in the world, and Camelot secure!"

Gawain grunted and cast Kay a sidelong glance. "Do you think it could be the dragons?" he asked, a little shame-faced. "It grieves me to think I shall never see their like again."

Guinevere was thinking, and her brow was furrowed. Arthur looked at her and smiled, taking her hand.

"You are pensive, my lady. What would you keep from the world of magic?"

She did not answer him, but looked at the Merlin. "Those riddles, Merlin."

"Yes?"

"Mordred should have guessed the third, had he been as clever as he thinks himself."

"He should."

"Why do you say that?" Kay looked up with interest. "How can we guess something that is yet to come?"

"There was no need to guess, for the answer was in the riddle," she replied. "Though perhaps I should not have seen it, had one of them not concerned me. The first riddle, Kay – that was about me, was it not?"

"Aye." Kay frowned. "Did I not tell it to you?
Gentle as the green sward, good as gold,
Utterance ever sweet, ne'er harsh nor bold.
In gowns of white I vowed to serve my people,
Now the queen of all, from ditch to steeple.
Each I look on loves me, lord or knave,
Vanquished alike the craven or the brave.
Ever steadfast to my lord I stay,
Resolute and pure, bright as the day.
Ends now my rhyme – who am I? – can you say?"

No one spoke for a moment, then Guinevere laughed, looking around at the rest. "Do you not see, my lords?" she asked. "Do you not see my name in the rhyme? And what was the second riddle? I cannot remember the words exactly, but I know the first line began with an M."

"The first letter of each line spelled out the answer!" Kay dropped his head into his hands with a groan. "What a fool I have been! I was so sure it was Mordred's test that I did not use what brains I have."

"So what was the third riddle?" Arthur asked quietly, turning to the Merlin. The bird shook his feathers and did not speak.

"He fears to burden us with too much knowledge," Guinevere said. "But it is too late now, for I at least shall not forget Morgan le Fay's words.
Graced by the master's hand, gift of a king,
Restless to be found, to wreak my doom.

At my accomplishment the bells shall ring
In Camelot, first for joy, then for a tomb.
Lovers shall flee; friends shall fall; lost shall be everything."

There was silence for a moment. Some of the knights hardly knew what she was saying nor grasped the purpose of her words. But Arthur did, and so, after a moment, did Kay.

"The grail!" Arthur said. "This third riddle speaks of the grail. And how can this be? Can this really be what the grail shall bring?"

"Wait a moment!" Lancelot held up his hand. "What are you saying?"

"The meaning of the riddles," Kay answered. "The first told of the queen's virtues. The second told of Mordred's folly. The third spoke of what is to come when the grail is found. Joy at first, then death. Something about lovers. Something of battle. The end of Camelot."

Again there was silence, and in the sudden quiet a bird could be heard singing outside the casement. Dawn was nearing and the sky was grey. Arthur glanced at the window and then held his hand out to the Merlin.

"Quickly, Merlin, tell us what this means before day comes, for I have a cold feeling that you and your wisdom will soon be gone."

Again the Merlin ruffled his feathers, and he answered with a question of his own. "Did you never wonder, Arthur, that I set you against the magic that had made me what I am, and made you a king?"

"I am not so wise, Merlin. I believed you when you said the kingdom would be happier without it."

"And so it has been, Arthur, and you have done well." The bird hopped to him and nuzzled his ear for a moment. "Your lands are peaceful and your people are happy. Whatever comes, you will be remembered for that."

"And yet?"

"From before your birth you have been the subject of a prophecy, just like Galahad. Ordained was our first meeting so many years ago, and fated the moment when you pulled the sword from the stone. But your fate did not end there, it stretches out before you still. Galahad's fate was only ever a part of your own. He is ordained to find the grail, but the finding of it will also accomplish your fate."

"What fate, Merlin? Why did you never tell me of it before?" Arthur shook his head impatiently. "Speak plainly now! For the sky is brightening and the sun will soon be rising."

"I never told you the full prophecy of the grail, for I always hoped that your valour would banish all such folly in good time," the Merlin answered. "But Mordred's weakness has prevented that, and now I believe it was your fate that made him weak. It was your fate that made him fail, so that the grail might endure even if all the rest of magic was gone. For just as he could not change the story he found himself in, nor can I. The grail must be found if your story is to follow its fated path. Then two from Camelot shall betray you, and another shall bring your death. I am grieved that by the witch's riddle this should be known. But after all, we all must die."

"But what of Camelot? Who shall rule Camelot after me? Will it be Galahad?"

"Galahad shall die at the moment his hand touches the grail," the bird answered. "And Camelot shall fall. There shall be no king after Arthur."

The day was brightening outside and the birds were now in full chorus. As they watched the Merlin's form began to waver, and they had to screw up their eyes to keep him in their sight. Guinevere was frowning.

"You said just now that Morgan le Fay had turned your own works against you," she said. She held out her hand and the bird came to her. She could hardly feel his talons on her wrist as she looked into his small indomitable face. "Merlin, who was it set the enchantment on Arthur? Who was it made all of Morgan le Fay's wishes come true? Who sent us on this quest to banish magic once and for all?"

"I," the bird answered, puffing out his chest boldly. "It was I that did it! For I began to see that Arthur would never banish God and the grail of his own accord. The only hope for Camelot was to make you act, and to bring about one last battle between men and magic that would drive out your God with it, whether you willed or no." Even now, the bird could not help looking a little pleased with himself, even as he spoke of failure. "Yes, I used Morgan le Fay and her anger, to set the quest in motion, but in the end her cunning outwitted my own, for she is a woman as well as a witch. I never learned enough of your human hearts to lead you where I wished. Galahad would not heed me, and nor did Mordred."

Gawain's had face flushed red as he listened, and now he advanced on the Merlin angrily. "And was it your doing, then, wizard, that I lost my best companion?"

The bird did not quail. "I have done worse than that, Gawain, for there is other innocent blood on my beak and I grieve for it. But none of it was really my doing. It was Arthur's fate that governed all, and only now I begin to see its true power, for I could not defeat it. I have only succeeded in banishing myself, while this evil will linger on."

"What nonsense is this!" Gawain cried roughly. "Did you not tell me once that there was no such thing as fate?"

The Merlin looked back at Gawain, and the last look they saw on the bird's face was its characteristic mix of exasperation and pity. "And would it have comforted you then, Sir Gawain, to have known what was to come?"

The sun rose, and in the flicker of an eye the bird faded and was gone. Guinevere began to weep. Kay and Lancelot exchanged troubled glances, and Bedivere bent his head in prayer.

"Look!" Lancelot spoke suddenly, pointing up to where Excalibur hung above them. The others followed his gaze and their heads swam a little, for they could see straightaway that its curious glow had faded. It hung there all at once an ordinary sword. But Kay was still pondering the bird's words and he spared the sword no more than a glance. Instead he was remembering his eldest squire. The boy had died, he now saw, more or less at the Merlin's bidding.

"I will not miss him!" His words fell harshly into the silence of the rest. "We are better alone!"

His words woke Arthur from his reverie and he glanced towards him. "Yes Kay, it is done," he said, and there was a new strength in his voice as he looked away from Excalibur and rose to his feet, his face clearing. "And you are right – it is better so." He held out his hands to them, and warmed their hearts with his smile. "Come, do not despair, my friends, for the world is changed, I can feel it already! Magic is really gone, and we stand here alone, natural creatures in a natural world for the first time. Who knows what new powers will govern it? Let us put this prophecy into the past, along with all the rest. For myself, I will choose to believe us free at last, and our fates for the first time undecided!"

"Except for death," Kay answered quietly. "For as the bird said, that fate awaits us all."

~

Galahad was weary. He had left the ship two days before, and now he was riding across desolate countryside under a sun that was already fierce just an hour after daybreak. The plants that grew by the roadside were wilting, and dirt rose under the horse's hooves. Ahead on the horizon was the dust cloud that Galahad had been following day and night, made by the dragon as it sped across the baking landscape. There was little hope of overtaking the creature on this level plain, for its great feet went swiftly over the rough stones which forced the horse to tread carefully, and the hot sun only warmed its blood and lent it speed.

There the dragon went, ahead of him, in plain sight. And along he plodded in a pursuit that seemed endless. Then, without warning, the dust cloud seemed to dissolve before his eyes. He shook his head, and wiped the sweat from his eyes, and stared again. The plain was empty. Nothing moved. The beast had vanished without trace.

At first he thought that it must be sleeping. Then he began to wonder if it was dead, killed by its exertions under the hot sun. On he rode towards the spot where it had vanished. As he grew closer he strained his eyes to see the shape of its body lying on the ground, but there was nothing, only a boulder and a stunted olive tree to break the flat plane of the horizon.

"Arthur has prevailed!" he exclaimed under his breath, through lips cracked by the sun. "The king wakes, and dragons are no more!" A wild joy rose in his throat as he thought of Camelot and the knights gathered in triumph at the king's bedside. But then a shadow crossed his face. "And will it remain?" he asked himself hoarsely. "Will the book be there, lying in the dust? Or has it vanished along with all other wonders?"

He rode on towards the spot, uncertain of what he would find. And then he found his thoughts turning back to Camelot, and the taste of wine and the savour of good food, and he stopped to drink a little precious water from his meagre wineskin. The cool clear stream revived him. A girl's face flashed before his eyes and he smiled.

"Charity! Art a fine young lady yet?"

Then as he rode on, a little dreamy from heat and thirst, pleasant pictures formed in his mind. Suppose that the book were gone! Suppose that the grail too had vanished along with the dragons! When he had searched and failed to find it, could he not turn his steps back towards the coast? Would there not be a boat waiting for him, that would bear him back to Padstow, and a pony to hire at the port? Then he would ride along the cliffs once more, to the farm nestling in the valley. The birds would be singing, and the cow would look up from the grass of her meadow as the sun set. A boy would be whistling somewhere far off, and a maiden would be standing in the farmyard, her hand shading her eyes from the sun's rays to watch him approach. Then – and then – .

Here was the spot where the dragon had vanished. He could see its tracks in the dirt one moment and the next they were gone. He pulled the horse to a halt and slid down from the saddle, his legs a little weak under him. There was no book to be seen, and his heart lurched. There was no book! No wait – what was that, lying in the shadow of a boulder by the roadside? His hand closed on the leather binding, and the loose page that told of its history caught the breeze and was gone as he opened the book at the page of the maps.

A sob caught in his throat. He stuffed the old book in his shirt, and mounted his horse once more. The dragon had been going east, and Galahad turned the horse's head the same way. He supposed that was as good a direction as any.

> And this is why I sojourn here,
> Alone and palely loitering,
> Though the sedge is withered from the lake
> > And no birds sing.